BLACK PARROT, GREEN CROW

A Collection of Short Fiction

BY

HOUSHANG GOLSHIRI

EDITED BY

HESHMAT MOAYYAD

MAGE PUBLISHERS
WASHINGTON, D.C.
2003

LIBRARY OF CONGRESS CATALOGING-IN-PUBLICATION DATA

Gulshîrî, Hushang.
[Short stories. English. Selections]
Black parrot, green crow : a collection of short fiction / by Houshang
Golshiri ; edited by Heshmat Moayyad.-- 1st ed.
p. cm.
ISBN 0-934211-74-4
1. Short stories, Persian--Translations into English. I. Moayyad,
Heshmat. II. Title.
PK6561.G775A6 2003
891'.5533--dc21
2003010048

PAPERBACK
ISBN 0-934211-74-4

Manufactured in U.S.A

AVAILABLE AT BOOKSTORES OR DIRECTLY FROM THE PUBLISHER
VISIT MAGE ON THE WEB AT WWW.MAGE.COM OR CALL
1 800 962 0922 ❖ OR E-MAIL ❖ INFO@MAGE.COM

Contents

Introduction 7
Heshmat Moayyad

Behind the Thin Stalks of the Bamboo Screen 17
Translated by Jahan Moslehi

A Good Social Story 21
Translated by Farkhondeh Shayesteh

The Man with the Red Tie 29
Translated by Heshmat Moayyad

My Little Prayer Room 43
Translated by Farkhondeh Shayesteh & Mark Luce

Both Sides of the Coin 53
Translated by Franklin Lewis

The Wolf 71
Translated by Paul Losensky

My China Doll 79
Translated by Fatma Sinem Eryilmaz

Portrait of an Innocent I 89
Translated by Franklin Lewis

Portrait of an Innocent II 99
Translated by Sunil Sharma

Portrait of an Innocent III 115
Translated by Franklin Lewis

Portrait of an Innocent IV 131
Translated by Alyssa Gabbay & Heshmat Moayyad

What Has Happened to Us, Barbad 149
Translated by M.A. Pomerantz

My Nirvana 167
Translated by Judith M. Wilks

Nightmare 189
Translated by Naeem Nabili

Green as a Parrot, Black as a Crow 197
Translated by Heshmat Moayyad

Big Bang 201
Translated by Stephen Meyer

Banoo'i, Anne and I 211
Translated by Heshmat Moayyad

A Storyteller's Story 219
Translated by Heshmat Moayyad

Three Poems 233
Translated by Franklin Lewis

Acknowledgments

I would like to express my sincere gratitude to my friends, former and present scholars and students of Persian literature, who participated in this project. Translating Golshiri's stories was an arduous but rewarding challenge. Without their support, knowledge, and talent this task could not have been achieved. Judith Wilks deserves my warmest thanks for reading the manuscript and for the many improvements she offered. To my wife Ruth, I feel enormously grateful. She meticulously corrected, edited, and typed the text, and also prepared the glossary and notes with her typical exactness. Last, but not least, I most sincerely thank my dear friends Mohammad and Najmieh Batmanglij who, once again, unhesitatingly welcomed this project at Mage Publishers.

Introduction

As the reader may have noticed, the title of the present collection is deceptively similar to the name of the shortest and least elaborate of the stories included here, namely "Green as a Parrot, Black as a Crow." This story is, or perhaps appears to be, as simple as any children's story. Compared to Houshang Golshiri's other stories, both its plot and its style of narration seem surprisingly plain, if not feeble and even dull.

However, anyone familiar with the political atmosphere of Iran—and the ongoing confrontations between the clerical authorities of the regime and the modernist writers and intellectuals—would be likely to assume that the usually quick-witted author must have intended to make an encoded statement in this seemingly harmless parable. After all, the story was first published in 1983, only four years into the reign of the new regime, a time when the battle to crush any resistance to the dictates of the theocratic state was still in full flare. This new regime did not satisfy the expectations of the liberal poets and writers who, once again, felt cheated by the leaders of a state that had benefited from their full support during the revolution. Now, instead of the promised freedom and justice, the "green parrot" was delivering the "black crow" of the ominous days to come.

Golshiri's life and, in a way, his achievements as one of Iran's leading writers of the second half of the twentieth century, mirror, at least partly, the history and fate of his fellow Iranians. Endowed with talent and intelligence, and possessed by the firm resolve to overcome the extreme poverty and hardships that fate had imposed on his parents and siblings, Golshiri, to a great extent, succeeded in shaping his own life, becoming a model of astute intellectual leadership, in turn animating a generation of aspiring writers. He struggled to improve his personal life, as the nation had struggled many times for freedom and reform since the middle of the nineteenth century.

Golshiri was born in 1937 in Isfahan. His difficult childhood years were first spent there, and later on in Abadan where his father had found a blue-collar job in the oil industry. In 1954 the family returned to Isfahan where Golshiri finished high school. Already in those early years as a teenager and high school student he felt a responsibility to help his family overcome their humble circumstances, even as he sought to improve and shape his own future. During the next twenty years, while earning a Master of Arts degree in Persian Literature, he held various menial jobs and taught at elementary and high schools in Isfahan and the surrounding villages.

Decisive in the start of his career as a writer was his association with several like-minded young intellectuals, including the promising—but too early deceased—novelist Bahram Sadeqi (1936–86) and Abu'l-Hassan Najafi, who later became well known as a lexicographer. Together they started a biannual magazine called *Jong-e Isfahan* (*Isfahan Anthology*), which served as a platform for expressing their ideas and displaying their talents. Prior to the start of this magazine, Golshiri had already published several articles, poems, and a short story in *Payam-e Novin* (*The New Message*), which was one of Tehran's progressive magazines. However, it was in the eight issues of *Jong-e Isfahan* where several of his poems and short stories, among them *The Man with the Red Tie*, appeared and that the birth of a remarkable literary talent was announced. From then on, his activity as a writer proceeded with amazing speed. His works started to appear in the capital city's literary periodicals as well. The following is only a partial list—a complete list of his writings still needs to be prepared.[1]

Methl-e Hamisheh (*As Ever*), written in Isfahan in 1968, was his first collection and included seven short stories. Only a year later, his best-known short novel, *Shazdeh Ehtejab* (*Prince Ehtejab*), followed. In 1971, still in Isfahan, his third book

---

1. Meanwhile, there exist quite a number of articles and books on Golshiri and his works in different languages. I owe a great deal of factual information to Hossein Sanapur's *Hamkhwani-ye Kateban: Zendegi va Athar-e Hushang Golshiri* (Nashr-e Digar, Tehran 1380/2001).

Kristin va Kid (*Christine and the Kid*) was published. It consists of seven interrelated stories, allegedly portraying his love affair with a British woman, who at the time lived in Isfahan with her husband and child. Four years later, in 1975, *Namazkhaneh-ye Kuchek-e man* (*My Small Prayer Room*) came out, offering nine stories. These volumes were followed in rapid succession by fourteen other books, some short story collections and novels, others essays and literary studies.

Nobody seems to know exactly how many papers and stories Golshiri left unpublished at the time of his death in June 2000. There exists, for example, a large novel called *Barreh-ye Gomshodeh-ye Ra'i* (*The Shepherd's Lost Lamb*), the first volume of which was published in 1977. The remainder, an unknown number of volumes, has been censored and never released. Some other works follow: *Jennameh* (*The Book of the Jinnis*), published by an Iranian publisher in exile (Baran Publishers, Stockholm 1998).

Ma'sum-e Panjom, ya Hadith-e Zendeh bar Dar kardan-e an Savari keh khwahad amad (*Innocent Five or the Story of the Hanging of the Knight Who Shall Come*), a novel (Tehran 1979).

Jobbeh-Khaneh (*Arsenal*), four short stories (Tehran 1983).

Panj Ganj (Five Treasures), five short stories (Stockholm 1989).

Tafannoni dar Tanz (*An Attempt at Satirical Writing*), a novel (Stockholm 1991)

A'ineh-ha-ye Dardar (*Mirrors in Doors*), a novel (Tehran 1992).

Dast-e Tarik, Dast-e Rowshan (*Dark Hand, Bright Hand*), five short stories (Tehran 1995).

King of the Benighted, the English translation of *Shah-e siyah pushan*, published by Mage Publishers in 1990 under the pseudonym Manuchehr Irani. The original Persian was published by Baran Publishers in 2001 in Sweden. This novella resounds with the voices of two political prisoners narrating the savage treatment to which the opponents of the regime, amongst them innocent women and girls, are subjected. The narration is introduced by a short version of one of the seven stories of Nezami's epic poem *Haft Peykar* (*The Seven Beauties*), composed in 1197. I know of no commentary ever written about Nezami's poem which is more penetrating than Golshiri's application of its symbolic relevance to the political reality of the period during which he wrote.

Golshiri also wrote a few plays and film scripts. Shortly before he died, his essays and critical articles appeared in a two-volume set called *Bagh dar Bagh* (*Gardens Within Gardens*).

Prince Ehtejab was his most acclaimed piece of fiction. Written thirty-two years after Sadegh Hedayat's[2] *Buf-e Kur* (*The Blind Owl*), it was received as the second-most innovative novel in Persian literature. A few of his later short stories were written in the same modernistic form, though slightly different devices were used. *Prince Ehtejab* is, in the words of Michael Hillmann, "the stream of consciousness tale of the contemporary descendant of a landed aristocracy left with hereditary tuberculosis and the photographs of deceased relatives on the walls of his living room, neither of which he can cope with or control."[3]

Golshiri was familiar with modern trends of thought and techniques developed in the twentieth century. William Faulkner, whose work Golshiri had read in Persian translations, is mentioned by his students and friends as his most important source of inspiration. As for content, however, *Prince Ehtejab* must be considered entirely a creation of Golshiri's mind and experience. Unlike Hedayat's *Buf-e Kur*, which in its surrealistic, psychic, and almost ethereal world of bitterness and despair, that offers only distant allusions to Iranian art and social experience, *Prince Ehtejab* by contrast depicts with nearly realistic details the decaying figure of a typical member of the ruling Qajar dynasty in the early years of the twentieth century. Golshiri, unlike Hedayat, did not come from a privileged aristocratic background. Whereas Hedayat, a rather lonely, pessimistic individual who at the age of forty-eight committed suicide, never actively participated in any political movement, Golshiri was deeply committed to the fight against social injustice and political despotism in his homeland. His sincerity and devotion to this task was matched by his restless and energetic activity that never slowed in spite of dangers and threats all around him.

Golshiri was one of a handful of Iranian novelists who developed a style of his own. It consists, for the greater part, of a patching together of events, which take place under a variety of circumstances, and conversations between different individuals at different times. The reader has to follow

---

2. Sadeq Hedayat: b.1903 in Tehran, d. 1951 in Paris by committing suicide; one of Iran's first and most renowned writers of short stories in the 20th century.
3. Michael Hillmann, ed. *Literature East and West*, vol. 20, *Major Voices in Contemporary Persian Literature*. Texas: University of Texas Press, 1976. The volume offers a brief autobiography of Golshiri, pp. 245-50, and the full translation of *Prince Ehtejab* by Minoo Ramyar Buffington, pp. 250-303.

the gradual emergence of a fascinating story by putting these scattered pieces together like a puzzle. Golshiri crafted this cryptic style skillfully, aiming, perhaps, at the intelligence and seriousness of his readers. He certainly discouraged simple-minded individuals and, more importantly, meant to fool or mislead police and security agents whose disposition towards any criticism leveled against state policies was not exactly benevolent. However, instead of the code words then current among intellectual opponents of the regime (like "night," for example, to mean the dark ongoing period of the monarchy soon to be followed by the daylight of freedom), Golshiri chose to devise methods—allegories and ambiguity in characters, shifting times and places, and disguising real intentions or directions—in order to divert the attention of the ever-suspicious authorities.

The gender-blindness of the Persian language served him well as a useful tool to fool impatient or superficial readers and exhaust their willingness to continue reading an exasperating text, being unable to untangle its complex structure and dig deeper into the layers of the intended messages. Sometimes he begins a story, or a paragraph, in its middle with a verb. For example with "*goft*," without announcing the subject Golshiri leaves it to the reader to discover whether it was "he" or "she" who "said" or "spoke" or "answered" or only "thought to himself," with all of the possibilities conveying a meaning, each one in a given context. The reader must read attentively and carefully look for clues to untie the complicated connections. This clever, mischievous use of a linguistic trick increases the tense expectation of the reader and, like a detective story, raises the level of suspense and uncertainty in the story.

Golshiri had the nature of a political fighter. His participation in the anti-establishment struggles of the 1970s was not limited to the use of the power of his pen. He also took part in the early stages of political activities that were organized by teachers, students, and other dissident groups. His involvement landed him in jail twice for several months in 1962 and 1974 on charges of "wrong" political affiliations and extremist views.

He was one of the prominent members of the Writers Association of Iran that was formed in 1968 but soon fell apart under the unacceptable demands and conditions set by the government to hold tight control over their activities. In 1977, on the eve of the Islamic Revolution of 1978–79, the Writers Association of Iran was revived, this time more vigorous in its aspirations and enjoying greater support from academic and professional anti-regime circles. The so-called "Ten Nights" of reading poems and delivering provocative speeches against the system of suppression and censorship by fifty-nine poets and speakers, sponsored by the Writers Association of Iran and was hosted by the German Goethe Institute in Tehran from October 10 to 19, 1977, an unprecedented occasion for the Iranian intelligentsia to air their grievances and celebrate their victory. According to all accounts, Golshiri played a significant role at different stages of this successful event.[4]

The joyous mood of freedom following the revolution did not last more than a few months, if not only a few weeks, at least for the young anti-reactionary and modernist segments of the population. The anticipated freedom failed to materialize. The enthusiasm of the masses was dashed all too soon. Persecutions and the mechanism of censorship reappeared more fiercely and less compromising than ever before, only this time blasphemously, in the name of religion and God.

Golshiri, like his fellow writers and other progressive segments of society, was completely disillusioned yet remained determined to continue his efforts for the achievement of the cherished goal of freedom and justice. He did not join the stream of Iranians who, like never before in the recorded history of Iran, left their homes and started a new existence on other continents. Instead, Golshiri decided to stay, to write, to fight, and to train a new generation of younger talents. His courage as a writer who would not be tempted by any compromise that offered less than the complete and perfect freedom of speech, exposed him to serious and life-threatening dangers. As reported, even leaving his house to run a simple errand became a risky undertaking. It was very hard on his wife, who often feared she might not see him again. As for the quality of his writings, mounting threats forced him to pull the camouflage cover of his style tighter and use even less understandable allegories.

Energetic participation in all sorts of literary events, repeated trips to Europe, the even faster pace of creative writing and publishing inside and outside of Iran, the steady contributions to journals, the training of younger talents in the art of novelistic writing, and even more daring and risky attempts to revive the above mentioned Writers Association of Iran in the post-revolutionary period could not stop a growing sense of disillusionment from penetrating his mind and soul. Without withdrawing from any one of the activities that were still permitted, he grew more philosophical and less jovial and exuberant. This does not suggest that his earlier works

---

4. Ahmad Karimi Hakkak: "Protest and Perish. A History of the Writers Association of Iran." *Iranian Studies, Journal of the Society for Iranian Studies,* 1985/ vol. 18, no. 2–4, pp. 189–229.

are overflowing with happiness and hope. It simply indicates that earlier on he was more of an optimist, that he still had faith in the ability and sincerity of his fellow Iranians, and that he could not believe that they would once again succumb to the promises of an outmoded regime that theoretically had outlived the validity of its claim.

The four stories titled "Portrait of an Innocent" belong to an earlier period. They depict a rather spooky environment, especially the third one, with the masterfully woven warp and woof of its texture of classical romanticism and modern realism. The second one, however, ridicules the old practice of some Iranian Shiah villagers who, for reasons of prestige and economic prosperity, would create a place of reverence that then would develop into a center for religious ceremonies for the surrounding areas. In one such village the inhabitants plan to erect a respectable grave, an *Imamzadeh*, claiming it to be the resting place of a martyred *seyyed*, a distant descendant of the prophet Mohammad through his daughter Fatima. Golshiri turns this practice into a farce by having the villagers plan the decapitation of a simple seyyed, proclaiming him as a martyred saint of Islam. The most amusing device in this process is the utter stupidity of the victim. During ceremonies and feasting, down to the last moment, it does not occur to the seyyed to wonder or ask why the villagers honor him in such undue fashion and feed him so lavishly.

A glance at another story of this period, "My China Doll," illustrates how effectively Golshiri applies the internal monologue technique to the feelings of a little girl. Talking to her broken china doll and a dwarf while arranging and rearranging them in a room, the girl imitates her mother's and grandmother's speech patterns and behavior, thus subconsciously mirroring what we know to be the plight of her father in jail. The story in its three levels of the imprisoned father, the broken doll, and the disrupted life of the family is a sad and touching comment on the insecure political conditions of the times.

The story "The Man with the Red Tie" demonstrates Golshiri's sarcasm and humor in a refreshingly obvious manner. It is the mocking description of a SAVAK (National Organization for Intelligence and Security)[5] agent who is charged with the job of watching an innocent person and collecting information about him. The man's red tie—taken as a sign of political affiliation—arouses the agency's suspicion. What starts out sounding like a serious detective story turns into a brilliant farce with many hilarious details.

---

5. Iranian secret police from 1957 to 1979

In the serious story titled "Both Sides of a Coin," the narrator sounds like a historian debating with himself—in the style of an internal monologue—searching for an answer to the reality of Iran's history and its never-stabilizing political turmoil during the last two centuries. It seems that the narrator, who is identical to the prisoner in the story, is holding a mirror in front of the eyes of the recent generation of Iranians to show them the recurring process of their repeated rises and falls, and the faces of their kings, leaders, heroes, political victims, and honest martyrs who all reappear without the present generation having learned a lesson from them. In this as in a few other stories (like in "Portrait of an Innocent IV"), Golshiri engages his characters in a debate about the never-ending failures of the political systems, repressive regimes, police brutality, ignorance of the masses, and lack of liberty and safety—particularly for intellectuals and dissidents.

However, the stories written immediately after the Islamic Revolution are hopelessly bitter, shocking, and dispirited. *Panj Ganj* (*Five Treasures*), the volume demonstrating this depressing reaction to the events following the change of regime, could not appear in Iran and was only published years later in 1989 in Sweden. "What Has Happened to Us, Barbad" and "My Nirvana," two stories from this particular volume included here, are eloquent testimonies to the mood of that period.

"What Has Happened to Us, Barbad" expresses even in the rhetorical question of its title, the plight of a family that instead of celebrating victory is plunged into disappointments and physical and psychological troubles, including their young son's loss of speech.

In the second story, "My Nirvana," the sense of defeat leads to a religio-philosophical emptiness of life. The woman, who loves living in freedom and luxury, takes her husband's money and leaves for London, while the increasingly ill and helpless husband, an accomplished and respected judge, continues his miserable existence with the help of a maidservant. The Buddhist concept of Nirvana appears as the final solution, a closing circle for this unhappy and hopeless life on earth.

Golshiri was one of the few Iranian writers whose writings reached Europe and beyond in his own lifetime. The presence of a large contingent of Iranian immigrants in European countries and the United States increased awareness about writers such as Golshiri, and at the same time facilitated the process of inviting them for speaking events and organizing academic and ethnic Iranian audiences.

Golshiri's first trip to the United States in 1978 was made possible through an invitation from the International Writing Program. He visited Iowa City, where he spent several months. In the following years he repeatedly traveled to Europe and participated in conferences and gatherings with Iranians, gave talks, and read from his works at numerous universities. Bern in Switzerland; Berlin, Bonn, Aachen, Heidelberg, Hanover, Köln, Düsseldorf, Bremen, and Frankfurt in Germany; Rotterdam and Amsterdam in Holland; and London and Paris are places he visited. He was a welcome guest at the Heinrich Böll Haus in Germany, once even with a stipend for nine months.[6] Germany honored him by awarding him the Erich Maria Remarque Peace Prize.[7] Golshiri's thank-you speech, given at the award ceremony in Osnabrück, Germany, in July 1999, was printed in the prestigious German daily paper *Die Frankfurter Allgemeine Zeitung* on July 29, 1999.

In 1992 he came to the United States for the second time and visited Iranian communities in Boston, New York, New Jersey, Houston, Los Angeles, and Chicago (where in addition to giving a public talk he spent one evening at our home where a number of friends, colleagues, and students had gathered to celebrate the publication of *A Chicago Anthology. Stories from Iran, 1921—1991*).

I had never met Golshiri before. Due to orthopedic surgery I was homebound for a number of months and thus was not aware that Golshiri was in town. The day before the celebration party for *Stories from Iran* the phone rang. A voice on the other end of the line said in casual Persian and in a mockingly reproachful tone: "*Aqa*, tomorrow evening you have a party at your house and you have not invited me! How come?" It was Golshiri. Needless to say, my wife and I were delighted. The next evening, April 25, 1992, the first guest to arrive for the party was Golshiri. I wel-

6. Originally the family residence of the German novelist Heinrich Böll (1917–1985), the house, located in Langenbroich in the Eifel Mountains. Böll received the Nobel Prize for Literature in 1972. He established a foundation and the Heinrich Böll Haus, a retreat for writers and artists. Preference is given to men and women from countries where political and economic conditions severely curtail creative output.

7. The novelist Erich Maria Remarque (1898-1970), known best for his war novel *All Quiet on the Western Front*, was born in Osnabrück. In 1933 the Nazis banned his novels. He left Germany and in 1939 immigrated to the United States. In 1943 his younger sister Elfriede Scholz was executed in Berlin.

comed him. We embraced. And it felt like seeing an old and familiar
friend. His cordiality, the lack of pretentiousness, the absence of vanity,
and the expression of genuine sincerity in his face and words were enough
to win the affection of those who did not know much about him. The
other guests arrived. Dinner was served. And several hours passed in enjoyable conversation. Each guest received two copies of *Stories from Iran: A
Chicago Anthology* and everyone present signed all copies. After a while,
noticing that nobody smoked and no alcohol was served, he asked laugh-
ingly: "What is this, man? No smoke? No drink? How then do you live?"
"Well, that is why they kill us [my Baha'i coreligionists] in Iran." The
answer was, of course, sarcastic and Golshiri burst out into boisterous
laughter. I took him to the next room and opened the window. He smoked
some cigarettes and we talked. But his throat remained "dry," as he put
it. Later that evening, before the guests started to leave, he read part of a
story he had written about a trip—real or imaginary—of the poet Mehdi
Akhavan Saless from Tehran to Mashhad. He gave me the copy before he
left. Shortly after his death I was able to publish that story in the magazine *Kaveh* (in Munich), not knowing that it had been published that
same year, shortly before he died, in *Bagh dar Bagh,* a collection of his
essays and articles.[8] The translation of this story, "The Story of a Storyteller,"
is included in the present collection.

Golshiri's untimely death on June 5, 2000—he was only sixty-three
years old—shocked Iranians everywhere. Thousands of people accom-
panied the casket through the city streets of Tehran to the cemetery to
bid farewell to this much admired advocate of freedom and human rights.
The New York Times remembered him in an obituary on June 12, 2000.

I cherish his memory—as perhaps everyone who knew him does—as
a powerful and creative writer who fought for freedom, and as a person
who was honest, unassuming, intelligent, and restlessly active. He will be
remembered as one of the best writers of Iran in the twentieth century—
one who made Persian literature richer and more enjoyable.

HESHMAT MOAYYAD

---

8. Vol.2, pp.573–83

Behind the Thin Stalks of the Bamboo Screen

TRANSLATED BY
JAHAN MOSLEHI

When I came up the stairs, I saw him lying next to the washbasin, all stretched out.

"Where is she?" I asked.

And then I saw the woman, who had wrapped herself in her thin home-veil and was crouching in the corner of the room.

He lifted his legs behind him and brought his hand up to his face. I went closer. I set down the half-bottle of vodka next to him. The sandwiches were still in my hand.

"What the hell is wrong with you, huh?" I asked.

He had opened up the magazine and was holding his hand in front of his mouth. The picture was of a blond, naked woman who was standing behind a bamboo screen. Of the woman's body, only her head, one breast, and one arm and thigh could be seen. The rest of her body was a vague but graceful sketch behind the thin stalks of the screen.

"Won't you leave it alone?" I yelled. "Who was it, in the first place, who put it into your head to go find this picture when there is a live one standing there?...."

When suddenly he got up and reached the basin and vomited. I looked at the woman and her black staring eyes and at the lock of hair that was lying on her pale white forehead, and then back at him, who was still vomiting.

I clasped his shoulders. "How much vodka did you drink, huh?"

He only had the chance to say, "No, man...."

And he started again. Only he didn't throw anything up. He stiffened his hand against the wall. He was bending his head over the basin. His straight hair was covering his forehead.

"Then what is it, huh?"

With his hand he motioned towards the woman, who was still sitting in the same corner and staring, and he bent down further over the basin. The woman's clothes were sprawled on the bed, and only her eyes were visible.

"Her mouth...."

"It smells, huh? You should have given her a piece of gum," I said.

"No!" he yelled. "It's not just that. Her mouth is crooked. It's really something. Even when she doesn't laugh, three of her teeth are visible."

I did not look at the woman. I knew that she was still looking at us, with those same black and staring eyes. She looked at me. Her small and boyish face had turned red. Her hair even covered her eyes. Her red lips were shaking.

"But it was you who found her. You were the one who said that you liked her eyes."

"How was I supposed to know that underneath that veil?..."

"You shouldn't have looked at her mouth."

He leaned over the basin and started vomiting, such that his entire body shook. I held his head under the faucet and poured water on his hair. While his head was under the faucet, he slowly said, "I took off her clothes."

"Like in the photo, huh?"

He lifted his head up. His face had become more flushed. His lips were still quivering.

"So what did you want me to do? If you can't look at her face, then what are you supposed to look at, huh?"

"So?"

He motioned to the woman. "Go and see. Behind that damn veil, she is still naked."

I looked at the woman. She was still sitting there motionless, and just like the time when she was standing under the shade of the trees on the street, only her black eyes were visible.

I held his hand. It was ice cold. He was still shaking.

"Until you've had one glass, you can't."

"No, I'm not one to do that."

"You're not one to do that, you alcoholic?"

"I wasn't talking about alcohol," he said.

I pulled him by his hand and sat him down in the middle of the room. I opened the bottle with a knife. I filled three glasses.

"Will you drink?" I asked the woman.

"She is dumb," he said.

And he gulped down the glass of alcohol. The woman's hand emerged out of her veil up to her elbow. It was white. She grabbed the glass and took it under her veil and drank, and right there she wiped her mouth, and once again she extended the glass. Only her wrist was visible.

"Should I pour some more?" I asked the woman.

"Didn't I say she is dumb?" he said.

I filled all three glasses and took out the sandwiches. Each of us took one. The woman was eating her sandwich behind her veil and was looking at us with her black eyes.

Again, he got up, went to the basin, and started.

"Your stomach was empty," I said.

"Please…," he said. "Please, tell her to go."

"You don't need to want her! No one is forcing you," I said, and I threw the magazine toward him.

"Please give her money so she leaves; take it from my side pocket," he said.

And he turned on the water. The woman got up and went towards the bed. She picked up her clothes. I only saw up to her wrist. She turned her back to us. Beneath her veil, which was now pulled up a little, two bony and white legs were visible. They were amazingly white.

"You don't have to go. If he doesn't want it, to hell with him," I said.

"Please, give her the money. Let her go," he said.

The woman turned around. Only her eyes were visible.

"Her entire body is spotted and stained. Her entire body! There is not a healthy spot on her body. Believe me," he said again.

And he went to his pocket and took out several ten toman bills and held them in front of the woman. The woman grabbed two bills and went towards the door. We had only seen her wrist. She picked up her shoes and started walking. As she was going down the stairs, I could not hear the sound of her feet. When the door shut, he flipped through the magazine and found the picture. The woman's necklace was of ear shells.

"Pour," he said.

I filled two glasses and I looked again at the chiaroscuro of the woman's body that was visible from behind the thin stalks of the screen.

"She's pretty, isn't she?" he said.

"To our health!" we both said.

A Good Social Story

TRANSLATED BY

FARKHONDEH SHAYESTEH

The Writer has decided to write a social story. For this reason, after eating his food, which was a plate of meatballs, a piece of bread, and a green pepper, plus half an onion, he returned to his room. The Writer likes to crush the onion with his fist.

The Writer, hiding from the eyes of his mother, who is religious and who is on the alert for the smallest indecent movement of her bread-winner son which she can use as ammunition to push him to get married and settle down, poured some drops of lime juice and a piece of ice in a glass, and slowly climbed up the stairs. Then he picked up the bottle of arrack, which was on the shelf behind his published works. Although these works could be regarded as solid evidence of the Writer's anti-social tendencies, they were clipped from the country's "important" magazines.

The Writer spread out his mattress and put a bunch of paper and a pen in front of him and lay down. Of course, he didn't forget the arrack, and he didn't forget that his story should be short either, because he had only one pen that was half-used. Also, there was only enough arrack in the bottle for one night.

How should the story begin? The Writer took a gulp:

A paralyzed old man is sitting on the stairs of the porch. His crutches are lying on the stones of the porch, and his wife, who wears a white scarf and has a few gray hairs…. The Writer thinks that black is better and the scarf becomes black and he lets a few gray hairs show on the forehead of the old woman. The house is old. It is the kind of house that has colored glass windows, a pool and a copper ewer and definitely a well.[1]

---

1. This type of ewer has a long spout, and typically is used for washing oneself in the lavatory.

The Writer knows where all of this will lead. Again, they will say, "The end of your story is so hopeless." Others will say again, "You always...." Even if only for these complaints the Writer takes a sip.

Mustache? Well, it is obvious that the main character of a story, a social story, must have a mustache, a black mustache, a thick mustache, a mustache that lends a person dignity, a mustache whose bottom edge reaches down across the lips, and sometimes one could chew the tip of it, and maybe.... The Writer chooses, and the main character is standing at the door with his hand on the frame of the door, in a sleeveless undershirt and striped pajamas, and he is talking about something. With whom? It is not important. But, even people with mustaches need to have parents. The Writer chooses. The old woman is knitting and the paralyzed old man knows that his son is standing at the door and he can even hear his voice. So the existence of the well is not dangerous anymore. That black opening cannot make the Writer drag the paralyzed man toward it, make the paralyzed old man go by the well and look down, look down into that darkness, and perhaps listen to the echo of a sound, the sound of falling crutches hitting against the walls of the well and then...then?

Mr. Monazzah is discussing something. What is important for the Writer is his strong and decisive voice, which passes through the humid vestibule, down the dark and long hallway, out into the sunshine, and to the ears of the paralyzed old man. The old man is smoking or not smoking. But he is looking at the kitchen door. The kitchen door is closed. On each leaf of the door a design in the shape of an orange has been carved for decoration. The old man looks at the dent on the right leaf of the door. Above the door there is a latticed window with panes of colored glass. There is a lock on the door. Behind the door there is a well, with that dark opening and its water at the bottom that ripples if a small pebble falls into it, and if crutches or a person, makes a splashing sound.

The old woman is knitting a sweater, a black sweater for her son who is standing at the threshold of the house in his undershirt and striped pajamas and talking to someone. The old woman wraps the yarn around the knitting needle. When the ball of yarn moves she is amazed and looks at the pool and at the waveless green water on its bottom. The pool does not have any fish. The dirty dishes from lunch and even the cups and saucers from morning sit unwashed on the edge of the pool.

The house is old. It has three rooms. In front of the threshold of one of the rooms, which definitely has sliding doors, hangs an unbleached calico curtain with two pulleys and a rope with which one can pull the curtain up. The Writer does not know yet whether he should spread a rug or a kilim in the room. But he puts a clock on the mantelpiece. And he nails a picture of Dostoyevski on the wall over the mantel. The existence or non-existence of books on the room's shelf does not provide any help in recognizing the characters of the Writer's story. But the Writer decides to fill up a few shelves. With what kind of books? This is not important either. He has spread two rugs on the floor of the room behind the porch. At the far end of the room to the left side is the bedding, over which a blanket has been spread. There is nothing on the shelves. But on the overhead shelves…. The Writer thinks there is nothing wrong with placing a china bowl, with floral designs of red roses and green leaves, on the opposite overhead shelf and perhaps a….

Mr. Monazzah is still discussing something. But he has lowered his voice so that the Writer or the paralyzed old man cannot hear him. The vestibule is dark and on its far side there is a stairway leading up to a fenceless terrace and to a room whose doors and curtains are closed. The whispering of a woman and a girl can be heard from behind the doors and the curtains. The woman is old and gray haired. The Writer decides that the woman is to be the sister of the paralyzed old man, and that the girl is not to be beautiful; meaning that her hair is to be short and unbrushed and she is to be bleary-eyed, and the comforter will be drawn up to her chest. The Aunt says, "Get up, dear, go walk a little on the terrace, you have no idea how sunny it has become."

The girl says…or does not say any words and pulls the comforter over her face and begins sobbing. The voice of Mr. Monazzah can be heard in their room and even on the porch, saying, "Love is ridiculous. As long as our society is in misery we must give up paying attention to sensuality. Don't think that I am against sleeping with women and such things. No, sleeping with a woman is a piece of cake. But we are responsible too. We must get busy with fundamental matters. We must, for the sake of…."

The Writer wants to explain the continuation of their conversation, he goes and tears down Dostoyevski's picture and instead nails Maxim Gorky's picture on the wall above the shelf, and he takes another gulp. Mr. Monazzah says, "For example, look, my cousin is in love with me. Believe me. Even last night she said it when she had a fever. Don't say that she is definitely playing sick, or these are my parents' plans or even my aunt's. She had a fever of exactly forty degrees. Her forehead was so hot that I pulled my hand away. But what did I do? I just laughed. Yes, I laughed. Love is ridiculous, especially when…."

Whoever the partner is, he says, "But what do we do with this damn thing?" And he points down and laughs.

"Why, that is easy. We must find a way for it. In my view masturbation is not a good thing. It makes you idealistic. With married women? Well, we have to be role models, because people count on us. (Mr. Monazzah rubs his mustache.) The only thing that remains is a prostitute. The best way is having relations with a prostitute...a prostitute. Once a week and that's it. Overdoing it is not good; it makes you addicted to women and luxuries. From now on we have to get used to hardship."

Mr. Monazzah and his cousin are five years apart in age. They have been playmates; even when they were small they used to swim naked in the pool. (How many times? It is not important, either.) Although now her breasts have grown and her neck is white, and she has a mole on her cheek, there has never been a time that they have hugged each other in the hallway or near the well. Mr. Monazzah gives books to Miss Monireh and then occasionally they both sit on the same terrace and discuss them. They have even read *What Is To Be Done?* page by page together.[2] Now the poor girl has put *What Is To Be Done?* under her pillow and moans and she does not know what she is to do. When they were reading the book, the girl was against the idea of a husband and wife living separately in two rooms. But Mr. Monazzah gave her reasons and he even read a few pages of the book until he could convince Miss Monireh. But all of a sudden Miss Monireh said, "But we do not have two rooms, we have only this one. Besides, the roof of your room is leaking and has become damp."

Mr. Monazzah said, "We must pay attention to the realities. As long as a person has no security he must not give in to marriage and such things....If tomorrow, or the day after tomorrow I...."

Miss Monireh cried and said, "I can't stand you being far away from me"

Mr. Monazzah rubbed his mustache and from there he looked at his profile in a mirror that was hung on the wall. His mustache was thick. It was black, and it had covered his lower lip.

The Writer is acquainted with a prostitute. He even has read some of his works to her. But Delbar[3] only sits and watches with her eyes open wide from surprise. Then she laughs, loudly. She lets her dark disheveled hair fall on her shoulders. Sometimes she stands up and dances. Of course, the Writer taps a tune with his fingers on the back of a tea tray and Delbar dances in black lingerie which has white lace sewn to the hem of its skirt,

---

2. The title of several Russian books, one of which was written by Vladimir Ilich Lenin. Tolstoy also wrote similarly titled books, *What Must Be Done?* and *What Then Must We Do?*

3. *Delbar* literally means heart-ravisher, or sweetheart, but here it is the prostitute's name.

and on her nipples are affixed two red roses made of cloth. She dances a kind of Arabic dance, one that sometimes resembles belly dancing. But the Writer only looks at her shaking breasts and at the lines of her groin, and sometimes at her thin, white hands and keeps tapping. But if Mr. Monazzah could not tap, if he wanted to sit and review *What Is To Be Done?* with Delbar?... The Writer runs a risk. At the present time, as Mr. Monazzah is discussing something, it has been three whole years that he has been going to Delbar's house once every week and clumsily tapping a tune and Delbar has been dancing ineptly and laughing loudly.

The Writer knows that Delbar is not interested in conversation. Only when she gets drunk does she become talkative and talks about the neighbors, and about the Engineer who once, when he drank a half-bottle to the bottom, talked about marrying her, and about her child, who is with the nurse, or about the misery she suffered today by taking her child to the doctor, and the doctor's instruction about the medicine she would have to give her child, morning, noon, and night, spoon by spoon, in order for the child's bowels to move again.

Delbar is not an official prostitute. She has only a few acquaintances who pay for her expenses. If someone would appear who would guarantee her expenses, she definitely would get rid of the rest. For this reason she tries to cook quince stew better, and tries to ensure that the trays under her cups and samovar are shiny, and possibly that her sheets are clean. Sometimes she even warms up some water and washes Mr. Monazzah's feet and dries them with a towel. Delbar does not get pregnant anymore. The Writer and Mr. Monazzah are sure of this by now.

As the sound rises, Mr. Monazzah shakes hands with the person with whom he is talking. Mr. Monazzah knows that the sound must come from the hitting of the old man's crutches. But the lock is strong. It is a Russian lock, a combination lock that cost him twenty-two tomans. That is why Mr. Monazzah even makes a precise appointment with his companion, with whom he was discussing things, to return the book he borrowed and perhaps have a drink and continue the discussion again. Mr. Monazzah very slowly reaches the hallway from the vestibule and then sees his father, who is leaning against one of his crutches. He is holding on to the wall with his left hand and hitting the lock with the other crutch. The old woman is standing on the porch. The black ball of yarn has rolled from the porch into the garden near the pool. The water of the pool is green. It does not have any fish. In the garden there is a crooked short fig tree whose figs are still unripe. The old man is still beating on the lock.

Mr. Monazzah passes by the pool. He passes through the shadow of the fig tree. The old man is still beating and now he is leaning his left shoulder against the wall and beating harder. The lock moves about in the hasp. The Aunt is bending over the side of the terrace. The Aunt says, "Dear brother, you've started again!"

The old man is still beating and Mr. Monazzah tries to catch the crutch in the air and he does.

The lock is still moving. The dent on the carved orange decoration of the right leaf of the door has become deeper. The door is antique; it is valuable. Mr. Monazzah says, "With this behavior you can't convince me to marry her. You can't!"

The old man tries hard to take the crutch out of Mr. Monazzah's hand. The lock is not moving. The old woman is standing. The Aunt is bending over the side of the terrace. The distance between the terrace and the cobblestone of the yard is four meters and three centimeters. "*What Is to Be Done?*" is under her pillow. Miss Monireh looks out from the corner of the room's window shade. The corners of her eyes are not bleary. She has fixed her hair with her right hand.

Miss Monireh is not pretty. But she is decent. She is not a domestic kind of girl. Her mother washes the dishes and also cleans the house. Instead, Miss Monireh has read all of the books in Mr. Monazzah's room. Several times she even has asked Mr. Monazzah to find her a picture of Maxim Gorky to put above her shelf on the wall. She is interested in discussion. She believes that a woman must have economic independence. She goes to evening adult education classes. She even took the eleventh grade exams this year. She only has to retake religion and composition. She says, "One must not be superficial. A woman is not a doll." She has a family album too. She has placed her pictures next to Mr. Monazzah's pictures everywhere. She even has her deceased father's picture. The Aunt would not agree for her picture to be taken by a stranger.

Mr. Monazzah is still holding on to the crutch, and the old man, who is leaning against the pillar, tries to take the crutch out of Mr. Monazzah's hand, but he can't. His mouth remains open. Sweat is beading on his forehead. Sometimes his lips tremble, and the few decayed teeth that remain here and there on his gums appear. Mr. Monazzah's father cannot speak as a result of a partial stroke. He only opens his mouth and moves his lips, and from time to time grunts, rasping from the bottom of his throat, too.

The Aunt says…or does not say anything. Because the Writer does not know yet what she should say. He only knows that the Aunt should bend over more and shake her hands and say something that would show sympathy with her brother, and at the same time would not offend Mr. Monazzah and perhaps would not make her daughter complain later.

Mr. Monazzah releases the crutch. The old man leans more closely against the pillar and his crutch. Mr. Monazzah bends over. He holds the lock in his hand. He turns the dial of the lock a few times and stops on some numbers. When the lock opens, he removes it from the door and throws it in the pool. Then he opens the doors and tells his father, "Go ahead, nobody is holding you back. I am not interested in getting married."

The pool's water becomes wavy. Mr. Monazzah's mother sits on the edge of the porch and moves the knitting needles. The ball of yarn rolls into the fig tree's shadow. The Aunt straightens her back. She passes by the edge of the terrace whose bricks are loose and looks at the old man and at the waves in the pool, and then at their own room's curtain that is still moving.

The old man places the crutches under his arms. Mr. Monazzah opens the pair of doors more and says, "Here you are!"

The sound of Aunt's footsteps echoes in the stairway. Miss Monireh opens the door and stands on the door's threshold. The sunshine bothers her eyes. She is short and thin. Her complexion is white, her hair is black, and her breasts are small. She is wearing a cotton floral dress. The old man walks and goes toward the door. Mr. Monazzah is standing and watching while resting his hands on his hips. The Aunt is still in the stairway. The old man passes through the entrance of the kitchen and reaches the mouth of the well. He holds his hand on one of the pillars. His right crutch falls. He bends down and picks up the crutch and leans it against the pillar. He holds his hand to the stone on the edge of the well, and bends over the well and looks down watching the darkness of the mouth and smelling the water. He even sees some small waves in the bottom of the well, and the slow movement of the water at the bottom of the well. The water is cold, and twice as deep as a person.

Just when the Aunt and the old woman, who has let the sweater fall and has pulled herself down from the porch, reach the pillar by the well and Miss Monireh gets to the shadow of the fig tree and Mr. Monazzah lifts his hands from his waist, the old man bends over. He bends over into the well. He bends more and cries, quietly and silently.

The Writer, whose pen has run out of ink and who has no arrack left, falls asleep, even though he knows his story once again is not a social story.

The Man with the Red Tie

TRANSLATED BY
HESHMAT MOAYYAD

Mr. S.M., File No. 12356/9, is a man with short hair. That was all I knew about him, and that he probably wears glasses. His photo shows a thin line across his nose. No other special marks are visible on the picture. His address as recorded in the files is:

Hakim Qa'ani

10 Doulat Lane

I left home early in the morning. I knew the shopkeepers in the neighborhood would not even open their mouths if I showed them my ID card or revealed my position. I had combed my hair and attempted to carefully cover the bald spot on top of my head with some strands of hair. I had also combed my mustache several times. Even after I had shut the door behind me, I went back in again to examine my appearance and to check the knot of my tie one more time.

I was supposed to get there early in the morning. I took a taxi. I have listed the fee for the taxi on my monthly expense report that I submitted to the accounting office.

I started with the grocer at the head of the alley. I bought a package of cigarettes and a box of matches. I have listed the cost of these items on the monthly report as well. After all, as you know, I did not smoke then.

When I handed the grocer a one hundred-toman bill he got confused and asked, "Anything else?"

" No, thank you. But...I would like to know what kind of person Mr. S.M. is. It's really a family matter."

He was busy searching in his cash box, gathering the crumpled ten and five- toman notes together.

"Oh, that man, Mr. S.M., is not worthy of your consideration," he said.

"It has to do with my niece though," I answered. "You know, girls have to get hitched, the earlier, the better."

"I know that. But after all, that Mr. S. M...."

"What about him?"

"Oh, nothing. I mean...he doesn't seem to have a job. That is...he stays home all the time. Only around noon he comes in here and buys some cheese, worth about a toman or so, a couple of onions, two packs of cigarettes, and perhaps a box of matches. And in the late afternoon...."

He handed me the change. I did not count it.

"Count them," he said.

"What for? I beg your pardon, Haji Aqa."

"And he eats eggs for dinner."

"That's all?" I asked.

"Yes," he said. "It seems that some evenings he goes out for dinner and then the next morning he comes in later and buys his cheese and sometimes a package of tea as well."

Well, what can one make out of those bits and pieces of information? Perhaps someone else might conclude that Mr. S.M. eats out someplace else and that only occasionally, in order to mislead.... Or that he, perhaps, spends his money altogether on other things. Well, it was just these points....

But when I talked with the baker and the owner of the grill shop on the other side of the street I learned the following: Mr. S.M. buys two pieces of bread in the morning and another one either at noon or in the afternoon. Most of the time he eats half the bread while walking home. Occasionally he comes again later in the day and buys some stale bread for the evening. He does not go anywhere else and has no other way of wasting his money. In the evening he has a drink while standing at the counter—but just enough to get his throat wet— some Pepsi, and occasionally he eats some beans. Even before finishing his first glass he lights a cigarette. Really, he smokes a lot. But I am not supposed to jump ahead of myself. Indeed, I'd better leave this for later.

The next day I went there again and knocked at the neighbor's door. A woman opened. She was chubby. Her eyes and brows were black. Her complexion did not lack color either! Nor was she quite right, but I being so old....Well, after all, I am not a piece of wood either.

"Hello Ma'am. Does Mr. S.M. live here?" I asked.

"No, Sir, he lives next door. This is Mr...'s home."

I knew this already. I also knew that he is not an obtrusive person. His file contained no information other than his first and second name, his title, his job, and his special features, namely his hat and thin mustache.

"Excuse me, please. Do you think he is home right now?" I asked her.

"I don't know," she answered. "Only when the clumsy guy appears on the terrace can one be sure that he is home. Or when—"

"I am a relative of his," I interrupted.

She did not seem to have understood and went on

"How should I know? He doesn't turn on his record player in the morning."

"Does he listen to foreign music?"

"Yes, he does."

"He doesn't bother you, does he?"

"No, he doesn't," she said, "but when he walks on the terrace…. By God, please, ask Mr. S.M. not to walk so often on that terrace."

We talked for some time. As I have said already, the woman was not unattractive.

"May I leave a message or?…"

"Yes, of course," she responded.

But now I didn't know what to say. I only had the urge to find out whether he has an affair with this woman. I didn't find out, though. But then later on I learned that…. Well, let's put it off for later.

Here is what I gleaned from my conversation with the woman.

1 – Mr. S.M. walks on the terrace. When? There is no fixed time. He also smokes.

2 – In the evening he listens to foreign music. Occasionally he sings. His voice is husky. This can be considered a reliably distinct feature.

3 –He keeps his light on till late at night. Every night? The woman seems to have seen it only now and then.

4 – Every time he returns home, he has a few books under his arm and a cigarette in his mouth.

5 – He is not married. (The woman giggled.) He must be good-looking, Mr. S.M., I mean. You cannot tell from the photo, though. See to it that the picture in the file is replaced by a new one!

I said good-bye to the woman. I don't know whether you might want to start a special file on her as well. It's up to you to decide. If you do open a file for her, make a record of the following characteristics: a mole close to the dimple of her chin, black eyes, deep red lips. She appeared to be rather coquettish. Her thin veil slipped again and again and I could see her neck and throat, at moments even the swelling of her breast.

Mr. S.M. is a lucky chap.

My own neighbor is a terribly virtuous woman; her husband is constantly mumbling and grumbling. He thinks I am an important person. Every single day I have to help him out with one thing or another. His wife is rather pious. Except for one eye, only her husband has seen the rest of her, and the bath attendant at the public bath, and occasionally.... Yes, believe me, I did not manage more than once! After all, the woman is ugly. Her neck is crooked. On top of her head she has a bald spot with a radius of three centimeters. Her lower parts, though, are not bad. Her special marks are the round bald spot on her head mentioned above and a mole close to her navel.

Several days later I saw him. It was at sunset. People can be divided in two groups: those who spend their evenings at home and busy themselves with wife and children, occasionally also with a book or a flowerbed, and those who go out. Members of the latter group you can find standing on street corners, hanging out in cafes or going to the movies. Mr. S.M. belongs to the second group. At first I did not recognize him. That is to say, I was not sure. He sported a van Dyke beard, dark glasses, and a broad red necktie. He wore a black suit. His shoes were not polished. I am sure he presses his pants by way of putting them under his mattress, and even that not carefully enough. At first glance I spotted two creases in his trousers at the level of his knees. The creases of course cannot be considered distinguishing characteristics for him. His glasses, the van Dyke beard, and the necktie, however, can be, since they have not changed during a long period of time. He wears the dark glasses even at night. The mysterious appearance and the eyes hidden behind smoke colored glasses are alluring. But I did not rush. I tried hard to control myself. I even mumbled the office instructions a few times to convince myself not to rush. I'd like to recommend having these instructions and regulations printed in a small pamphlet and hand a copy to each of the associates so they may go over them every morning. This will give them more courage as well as reduce the possibility of their committing errors.

Mr. S.M., File No. 12356/9, was walking along on the sidewalk. He had a leather-bound book under his arm. I was not able to see what book it was or when it had been published. I came face to face with him. I tried hard, even looked at his picture I had taken from his file and carried with me until I recognized him. I crossed the street, walked back on the opposite side and waited for him at the intersection.

In my opinion, individuals who wear dark glasses, or even normal glasses, are the most dangerous, or at least suspect, people since we don't know what is going on behind those glasses, whether he or she has seen you, has looked carefully, and has recognized you or not.

It was for these reasons that I felt compelled to take off my hat, loosen my tie and put it in my pocket in order to be able to look closely at his beard and glasses and even at his red tie.

I wonder, of course, why Mr. S.M. wears a red tie since it does not match his suit. It would look smart if he wore a purple or even a navy blue tie. You should ask him this question at the proper occasion. Perhaps this is the only tie he owns. I do not know. Do not forget to ask him about it.

When I came close to him I saw he was holding a cigarette between his lips and was searching for a match. He found one, tried to strike it, dropped it, and searched for another one. Just as I was about to pass him, while in my mind I was going over the rules again, he said, "Sir, do you happen to have a match?"

I didn't have any. You certainly remember that I did not smoke in those days. At that moment I realized a person in my position needs to carry matches, or a lighter, even a shoehorn, a pen, and a nail-clipper, simply to be ready to start a conversation at any given opportunity. I got annoyed at myself and after I left the place I went and bought a lighter. It was rather expensive but I did not list it on my monthly expense account. I thought it should be considered a personal item. However, I added the hat I just bought.

I was standing there on the sidewalk. The place was crowded. I squinted and then I saw Mr. S.M. coming. The lighter was in my pocket. I was fiddling with it. Mr. S.M. finished his cigarette, threw the butt away and took another one out of his pocket. I believe he empties the cigarette pack into his pocket. Which pocket, you ask? I do not know. Or perhaps he takes them from the package in his pocket one by one with his fingers. I have not yet confirmed that. Then he began searching in his pockets. He searched through all of them. When he was about to start all over again with his search I reached for my lighter, turned around and strode in front of him. But he had already found a match and was lighting his cigarette.

Mr. S.M. is not friends with anyone in particular. Or if he is, I have not been able to find out with whom. Sometimes he exchanges formal greetings with some individuals.

When a respectable-looking man is walking along on the sidewalk every evening and he encounters the same people at the same time coming towards him from the opposite direction, they, seeing him so often, surely must develop a sense of recognition and eventually take him for an old friend or acquaintance who now wears glasses, has grown a beard, or has gotten married—hence the fat stomach. They say hello, they sometimes even stop and exchange some words of formality without knowing each other's names, talk about the high price of liquor, about the bad weather, or recent earthquakes, always addressing each other with "Sir" or constantly trying to remember the name of the other guy.

Here is the result of my experience. I also know many such street acquaintances with whom I have been exchanging greetings for years.

The difference between Mr. S.M. and myself is that I know the names of all these street acquaintances, but Mr. S.M. does not know them, nor does he remember them. One evening I carefully observed him and noticed that those street acquaintances pass by him, look at him, are startled by his respectable appearance, and greet him. But Mr. S.M. pays no attention and continues on his way. The other fellow turns around, frowns, steps haltingly forward, perhaps fixes his tie and then walks away. The next evening, when they happen to run into each other again, it is likely Mr. S.M. who says hello, the other fellow is again perplexed and reaches for his hand. Then they stop and for a few minutes they exchange some pleasantries.

Several evenings later I passed in front of him again. He showed no reaction. He was either smoking, reaching for a match, or lighting a cigarette. This went on until one evening I got up courage and followed him to the Sa'di Restaurant, right at the beginning of Jami Street. This restaurant must not be ignored. Without doubt there is good reason that Mr. S.M. frequently goes there. I went in. Mr. S.M. was standing at the counter. I sat down at a table close to the wall and ordered a glass of beer. I know there is no provision in the office rules for a person like me to have a drink during working hours. But I had no choice. That is why I ordered a beer instead of liquor. Once a person consumes alcohol he is apt to speak out freely what is on his mind, or at least you can smell out certain things from what he says. If one drinks and drinks a lot, well, you know, loneliness and the inability of making friends or associating with other people may make one too talkative.

Mr. S.M. was gulping down his drinks, glass after glass followed by a Pepsi and two spoonfuls of beans. He put his book down on the counter. It was Rumi's *Mathnavi*,[1] the second volume of the Boroukhim[2] edition. You could see the tip of a bookmark between the pages. He finished the

---

1. A mystical poem of 26,000 rhymed distiches, written by the great poet Jalal al-Din Rumi (d. 672/1273).
2. A well-known publisher in Tehran

first cigarette, pushed the next one between his lips and started fumbling for matches. I don't know why he first searches in his breast pocket and then in the back pockets of his pants. Ask him that question as well. I got up and turned on my lighter.

My lighter works with gas. There is this nude blonde on the side. It is a good thing to have. I had practiced a lot so I was able to hold it under Mr. S.M.'s cigarette with the first flick of my finger. However, he rejected it by waving his right hand, and while the cigarette dangled between his lips, he said, "No thanks. Cigarettes must be lit by a match."

And with the other hand he searched in his pockets and found one. He then filled his glass and proposed a toast, "To your health!"

I quickly filled my glass and gulped down my beer. Foam was pouring onto the table. Mr. S.M. left the restaurant, took a taxi and was gone. I tried hard to find a cab as well but was not able to.

Mr. S.M. so far as I can tell has not had an affair with a woman. He may, of course, have had some with a prostitute. He earns some income from some inherited real state. Only a person like Mr. S.M. can live on a yearly income of 4520 tomans. He is not very talkative. It is due to his mustache and the short beard more than anything else that one forgets about his mouth. If he did not smoke and occasionally pour down a glass of alcohol I would certainly note in the beginning of my report that the man has no mouth.

Now that I have obtained all those valuable pieces of information after all my running about, I do not feel ashamed of myself and can be proud of having been able to prove once more the accuracy of my respected superior's opinion.

Mr. S.M. is forty years old. He does not have any venereal disease. His file must contain this information. He never combs his hair. I may add that Mr. S.M. strokes his head and smoothes out his hair with the same hand. His glasses are dusty. He doesn't carry Kleenex or other items like that.

One evening I observed him when he stopped and faced the wall. I had walked behind him all the way. I went on, passed him and stopped under the trees opposite the Jamali Miniature Shop and squinted at him. He had a book under his arm. Street acquaintances were passing by him. Mr. S.M. took off his glasses, cleaned them with his red tie, which does not even have one white or black dot, and continued walking again. When he saw me, he greeted me. I greeted him back and said, "I haven't had the pleasure of seeing you for quite some time."

He answered, "The pleasure is mine."

I went on, "Mr. S.M., a new book?"

He seemed ill at ease, took the book in his hand, showed it to me and said, "It is not new. This is Dostoevski's novel *Crime and Punishment*. You know this, of course."

"Oh, yes, it is interesting."

Now I got confused. We most certainly must read this book, even if it is by official office order. Or we should memorize a list of the world's great books along with the names of their authors, and possibly some of the interesting parts of the books—Said list should state which books are useful and which ones are harmful.

I say, nobody should remain unemployed. Everyone must be kept busy, somehow, somewhere. Unemployed persons cannot be watched. We do not know where to find them, where to make inquiries about them, how to understand their thoughts. Actually, all of their time must be filled up. They should be occupied mornings, afternoons, and evenings with tasks such as reading files and checking bank accounts, correcting papers, even studying and taking exams, checking refrigerator and baby walker payments. Magazines, movies and cafés are, of course, all right.

But when a person is unemployed, stays home all day and goes out only in the late afternoon to meet some twenty or thirty fellows, chats with each of them for about two minutes about the weather, constipation, addiction to cigarettes, and maybe also about the Vietnam War, how in the world is it possible for anyone to find out where he stands?

And when he says, "the weather has turned cold," does he really mean the weather and does he really mean cold? A person who works in an office or teaches a class or studies cannot avoid exposing himself or giving himself away. But a jobless person?...

Mr. S.M. has no steady employment. An unemployed fellow who only walks up and down the sidewalk heading for, let's say, the Sa'di Restaurant at the beginning of Jami Street, you can only meet and talk to him in that restaurant. And if we happen to be there at that very moment when he is searching for matches and we help him to light his cigarette (I have billed the office only for the two matches and several cigarette packages that I offered him during the first weeks) we surely will succeed standing close to him and ask, "Mr. S.M., how can you shut yourself in at home from sunrise to sunset?"

If at that very moment when he has run out of cigarettes we offer him one from our imported cigarette package then, and only then, we may be able to get him to talk.

Mr. S.M. does not smoke imported cigarettes. He says, "No, thank you. I smoke only 'Zar' cigarettes."

Or we could ask him, "What is a good book and which one describes best Hitler's crimes?" or "Who helped Hitler to power?"

Mr. S.M. said, "Hitler was a nobody, believe me….To your health!…He was only one link in a chain. He started to believe little by little that he came to power through his own astuteness and God knows what, or that he alone could decide which country to fight or not to fight."

The recording tape ran out just at the point where our conversation began to be interesting. I drank some, in fact two glasses—one after the other.

What Mr. S.M. said at the beginning of our conversation was unimportant and not worth keeping in his file. He insisted I should grow a beard. He said, "It suits your face. It would cover your hollow cheeks."

He was trying to light my cigarettes. Lately I have gotten into the habit of smoking a couple of cigarettes after having gotten my throat wet. They taste delicious.

He didn't let me pay. He said, "No way! Everyone pays for himself."

He even took five rials from me and added them to five of his own for the tip. I consider the payment for the drinks my personal expense.

After we left the restaurant I tried to invite him over to my place. But he refused and said, "I can't possibly bother you. Impossible…."

He took my hand into his sweaty one and squeezed it. His eyeglasses had slipped down his nose. I said, "You certainly want to go home and finish your book."

"Who knows which one of them one ought to continue reading," he answered.

"I would very much like to see your library," I said.

"Library? It isn't a library, just a few books scattered here and there."

He then laughed and said, "It was kind of you to keep me company. Very kind of you."

He said goodbye and again took a taxi. This time I managed to find a cab as well but the driver was not able to make out Mr. S.M.'s taxi.

I wrote all of these notes that very same evening.

Mr. S.M. keeps his promises. He owns the house he lives in. Please, have everything in his file that contradicts the above statements corrected. He does not loan out his books. He sleeps little at night.

What if all the above patterns of appearances and behavior only serve to disguise or mislead, what if they are masks to cover up what is going on inside this dangerous person? Take the eyeglasses, the beard, the red tie? These suspicions forced me to follow Mr. S.M. step by step and surprise him now and then when he was in conversation with a street acquaintance.

I would say, "Hello, Mr. S.M."

He would look at me from behind his dark glasses, and I was aware how helpless he felt since he couldn't introduce his two street acquaintances to each other. With a low voice he would return my greeting, shake my hand and squeeze it the whole time while we were exchanging pleasantries. And I would stay around waiting for them to continue their conversation. His street acquaintance would at times light a cigarette, or search in his pocket for his rosary, and then abruptly say, "Goodbye Mr. S.M." Mr. S.M. would let go of my hand, shake the other person's hand, and then start walking with me.

He would keep silent just only squinting at me now and then from behind his glasses. It is gratifying to think that I was able to tear at that false veil of dignity for at least a few minutes.

I would ask, "Well, Mr. S.M., any new books you have read lately?" or "Won't you travel to Arak this year, Mr. S.M.?" and many other subjects, all recorded in file no.12356/9.

This method does not produce the desired results in the case of every person under observation. The fellow may suspect you and wonder how this stranger, only a street acquaintance, has gathered so much information about himself.

The case of Mr. S.M., however, is quite the opposite. The more information you offer about him, the more he tries to compensate for his own forgetfulness and occasionally for his lack of knowledge about yourself by smiling at you, squeezing your hand, offering you a cigarette, and addressing you over and over again with "Dear Sir, oh dear Sir...."

Mr. S.M. is one of those people you would call a "bookworm." He loves to keep his books clean, spotless, leather-bound. When he gets home one evening and finds out that, for example, the bolt of his door has been pulled open and his papers are messed up, or finger prints, possibly wet ones, are left on the pages of many of his books, he becomes dejected and does not go out at sunset for a whole week.

With regard to these times the neighbor woman says, "He may be ill. He doesn't listen to his records. As soon as it gets dark, he starts smoking and paces back and forth on the terrace."

She did not display her neck and breast any longer. Only those black eyes were visible. She had opened the door just a little and said, "I believe he is home now."

I pretended to have other things to do and said, "All right, I will call on him later."

I thought to myself, if I entered his house now, he would surely become suspicious. Therefore I paced up and down the sidewalk of Chahar-Bagh

Boulevard, six full evenings from 6 o'clock onward until he finally showed up. I greeted him. He did not answer or didn't hear me. Loudly I repeated, "Hello, Mr. S.M."

He did not even nod his head. His hands were buried in the pockets of his overcoat. He walked fast. I started to follow him. Street acquaintances passed by, greeting him eagerly and even loudly, but he answered none of them. He continued to walk briskly, his cigarette stuck between his lips. There was no book tucked under his arm. He may have stuffed it in his wide coat pocket.

Do ask him about this point.

After Mr. S.M. entered the restaurant, I bought a pack of cigarettes, and went in. To endure six full evenings of drinking alcohol and smoking without having company to talk to is very a difficult proposition. I can't understand how Mr. S.M. is able to do so for so long....

When I entered, I saw Mr. S.M. sitting at a table, the same table next to the wall. One half bottle of Vodka, two Pepsis and a plate full of kababs were on the table, and some cheese, bread, and greens as well as some yogurt.

I went to the counter and ordered a one-quarter bottle of Vodka and a Pepsi. I don't like beans. I had ordered with a loud voice. Mr. S.M. looked up. He had laid his glasses on the table. His eyes are hazel colored. He has a slight squint in one eye. It is not unlikely that the photographer has retouched the picture in Mr. S.M.'s file. Official photos to be kept in files should always be taken by the office photographer.

"Hello, Mr. S.M. I hardly see you any more."

"Hello, dear Sir," he answered.

We shook hands. His hands were sweaty. He pulled a chair and offered, "Sit down, please."

That evening I got seriously drunk. But I remember well that Mr. S.M. paid the bill. He pulled a bunch of bank notes out of his pocket and gave a two-toman tip.

When he left the restaurant, he asked, "Would you care to walk some?"

It was rainy but we started to walk nevertheless. Mr. S.M. talked all the time about the merits of beards, especially the short ones. He remarked, "Shaving one's chin is a chore. A man whose hands shake and therefore is likely to cut himself in several spots every day should instead grow a beard."

The rain had become heavier by the time we reached the Si-o-Seh-Pol Bridge "thirty-three arch bridge." Mr. S.M. insisted that we take shelter in one of the niches. I could not stand on my feet any longer. I believe Mr. S.M. held my arm to support me. I said, "I have to take leave now."

Or perhaps I intended to say it but didn't really. Nevertheless, we did go into one of the niches. There was no policeman in sight to watch the area. Of course, I was not afraid. Or perhaps I was but do not remember. We must have said things that I have forgotten by now. But I do recall that Mr. S.M. pressed my hand several times and once he even kissed my face. He was constantly saying, "My friend, my friend!"

By now the rain was pouring down heavily, so heavily in fact that we, that is Mr. S.M. and I, could only hear the rushing noise of the river below the bridge dashing over the piers underneath the pillars. Now and then the reflection of some distant lights would blink in the water.

As we got up, I said, "Mr. S.M., how about jumping down and being free forever!"

He answered, "All right, I agree. But allow me at least this one cigarette...."

He had just lit his cigarette. I remember exactly, we walked on along all the niches. I hit my head against the arches four times. As we reached the end of the bridge, Mr. S.M. said, "Let's walk on the sidewalk."

The rain had gotten heavier still. Mr. S.M. had surely finished smoking his cigarette as we reached the end of the bridge. He offered me one and pushed another between his lips. He struck a match but it went out right away. He took off his overcoat and threw it over both of our heads and lit the match. I pulled out my ID card and held it up to Mr. S.M.'s face and said—or perhaps I did not say anything—but right under the streetlight on the other side of the bridge I held it in front of Mr. S.M.'s face. Mr. S.M. looked at it, read it aloud while I listened. It was my name, all right, and a complete list of data and the 3-by-4-inch photo with the thin mustache. The photo on my ID is ten years old. I have no doubt that Mr. S.M. did not even smirk. I don't recall, however, whether he had taken off his glasses while reading, or not. He shook my hand. He fumbled first with the collar of his jacket, then with the collar of my jacket and then even with the collar of the overcoat that covered us both and was now soaked wet from the rain. He finally found a pin and with it attached my ID card to the collar on his side. And then we walked on together in the rain along the river, covered by the overcoat, and we sang. Mr. S.M.'s voice is not bad. At first he sang alone, then we sang together. We repeated these words: "Come, let us go and drink wine, and keep drinking, keep drinking." And we walked on in the rain. Mr. S.M.'s arm lay around my shoulder and mine around his. A night watchman, with his hand on the handlebar of a bicycle, walked towards us and said, "But...gentlemen, this time of night?..."

"Please come closer," said Mr. S.M. and started walking.

The watchman leaned his bike against a tree and came over. The street lamp was not far off. When he caught up with us, Mr. S.M. motioned towards my ID card. He just pointed without saying a word, without even hinting at me. The watchman bent over. Rain was pouring down the tip of his helmet when he saluted at once and said, "Pardon me, I apologize."

The he retreated backwards towards his bike, jumped on it and pedaled away.

Mr. S. M., while holding on to the collar of his overcoat with one hand, was still presenting my ID card with the other to the watchman, who by now had put some distance between himself and us.

Afterwards we took a taxi. Mr. S. M. draped the overcoat over his arm. I don't know whether we did or did not go to the place where Mr. S. M. usually went every evening after his drink. When we got out of the taxi, Mr. S. M. put his glasses on my eyes and said, "They will serve you well. You might be held liable, but nobody knows me."

However, I have no doubt that he was well known there since the door opened as soon as he had knocked and shouted, "Master."

There was a long entrance hall, then a room where a charcoal brazier.... No further explanation is necessary. That evening I smoked several portions. Mr. S. M. naturally assisted me and kept telling me, "Hold your nose, my dear. It's a pity to waste a wonderful puff."

He smoked as well, maybe he did, maybe he didn't. I can't remember. I wanted the taxi to drop him off first. But he refused and said, "No, no, my dear. Impossible!"

The taxi drove me home. That night I didn't fall asleep until near dawn. I was dizzy and out of it. Colorful pictures and thoughts crossed my mind. It was morning, I believe, when I finally dozed off. I didn't wake up until noon. Only later in the afternoon when I was ready to go out did I realize that I had left my ID card with Mr. S. M. I put on his eyeglasses. Shaving is a real headache. That afternoon my hand was so shaky I cut my chin twice. I took a taxi and drove to the alley where he lives. I knocked at his door. The neighbor woman said, "I think he's gone out."

Yet I was convinced that he had not gone out but was at home and did not want to answer, or he was asleep. Not sure what to do, I waited. But then it occurred to me to look in the Sa'di restaurant. It was after sunset. I believe about 9:00 pm or so.

"He just left," the "Baron" told me.

He wasn't down at the river either. Despite being quite dizzy, I managed to find that certain house. Of course, I was wearing Mr. S. M.'s glasses

"Master!" I shouted.

They opened the door and again I smoked a few portions. These are my personal expenses. The owner of the place assisted me. He said nothing about smoke and holding one's nose.

"Mr. S. M. left just before you arrived," he said.

I know that you, despite your kindness towards me, will undoubtedly not condone my offences reported in this account. I am aware of my mistakes. But, believe me, I do not recall now why I suggested to Mr. S. M. that we kill ourselves and be free. Perhaps our actions that evening were provoked by the rain, the rushing sound of the river, the distance between us and the stone piers beneath the bridge, or the loneliness we both felt in that niche. Or, perhaps the actual motive was the smoke colored glasses behind which Mr. S. M. was hiding. When a person's eyes are concealed, when he realizes or imagines that he cannot be seen, particularly a person like Mr. S. M. who reappears after not having shown up for a whole week, he certainly fancies doing something he has never done before, acting quite different from the regular hectic race of running like a dog. As for the ID card, I really do not forgive myself. However, it was exactly like showing one's ID card to oneself in the mirror, or looking at oneself and simply combing or not combing one's hair. Don't worry about the ID card. I ran into Mr. S. M. the following evening at 6 o'clock on the sidewalk of Chahar Bagh Boulevard. He was walking in his usual style, smoking a cigarette and wearing dark glasses. His tie was red. His shoes were not polished, and another crease had been added in his trousers to the two previous ones. He carried his overcoat on his arm. I greeted him. He recognized me despite the dark glasses. He even addressed me with my name several times. He then put his hand in his pocket and started to fumble around. I took off the glasses.

"Please, here."

Mr. S. M. had put the ID card in a plastic cover so it would not get wet in the rain again. The number of my ID card is completely wiped out.

"Please, keep the glasses. It is a gift, albeit a humble one."

Together we went to the same Sa'di Restaurant and standing, at the counter, we had some drinks and then went to that certain place.

"None of your ties go with your suit," said Mr. S. M.

And I retorted that his tie didn't match his black suit either. I said it, and even yelled it.

And here I promise your Exalted Honor that I am never, never willing to wear Mr. S. M.'s tie that is red, completely red without any white or black dot or even a stripe.

My Little Prayer Room

TRANSLATED BY

FARKHONDEH SHAYESTEH & MARK DAVID LUCE

When I was small, I didn't think about it at all. I knew it was there. But it wasn't important, because it didn't bother me. When I pulled my socks off, I just had to bend my left foot a little, just like this, in order to see that it's still there. You couldn't say that I am six-toed. It's just a red piece of flesh with no nail, next to my left little toe. That's all. Well, it was there before, and always. My mother used to say, "Don't take your socks off, never take your socks off."

She meant, not in front of strangers. For me, except for her and maybe my father, everybody was a stranger. When we went to the bathhouse with my father, we never used the public bath. Mother wouldn't allow it. In this neighborhood no one else knew; that is probably why she used to say, "Don't go swimming with the children."

I still don't know whether this was out of fear of the small and large whirlpools in the river or because of my foot—my little toe, if you can call it a toe. I went anyway and would jump into the water half-dressed. When I finally had to get out, it was enough to stick my foot in the sand or in the gravel so it would not be seen. And besides, if no one knew that it was there, no one would see it. And maybe no one would have even thought anything of it because it is so small. But that's why Mother said, "We must move out of this neighborhood."

So, we moved here. None of the kids knew. If they had known, or if, for example, just one of them might have seen it, they probably would have come to our door yelling, "Six-toed Hassan!" like in the old neighborhood.

Here no one ever taunted me like that. The truth is that it was my fault. I'm not talking about that last time. Because he was so small and thin, how should I say, with a curl of black hair that fell over his pale forehead, or because his eyes were so bright, I thought he wasn't a stranger. Strangers —for me—were always those people to whom my head reached up only to their waists, or those who could hold my head in one hand, and then if they wanted to, they could use their index fingers to play with my forelocks. If I could see their eyes without raising my head, their cheeks certainly would be dusty or red, but not pale, small and hollow. He had leaned his crutches against a bench that stood in the entrance of the house. He was just sitting in the corner of the doorway. I asked him, "What happened to your foot?"

He said, "Can't you see?"

He looked the other way. There was nothing, just the continuation of the alley. The shadow cast by the wall shaded half of the alley.

I said, "You've got a cast on?"

It wasn't visible, but I assumed that his ankle was broken. He just nodded. He was looking at the same place at the end of the alley, I suppose. There was no one down there. Even if there were a tree, or a dog, I certainly would follow the line of the shadow and continue.

I said, "It'll get well. It'll get well soon."

He said, "No, this is the second time that they put it in a cast."

His left ankle was thin; it was so white and thin as if it were a reed, or the smaller twin of his right ankle, just like my smaller twin of my own little toe.

I said, "Do you want me to show you something?"

He didn't look, and just said, "What?"

I said, "My foot?"

He looked and said, "What about it?"

I said, "I don't know, you need to look."

While I was untying my shoe, he asked, "Is it broken?"

I said, "No. But promise not to tell anyone."

He didn't say anything. He just looked, I suppose at my left sock while I was taking it off. I thought it wasn't necessary to make him promise. Surely, he wouldn't tell. His lips were small and red.

He said, "It's nothing."

I said, "Look, I...."

And I showed him. I put two fingers under it and raised it up. It was a piece of red flesh without a nail– smaller than all of the little toes in the world, like some twin potato or cucumber. You have seen such things, haven't you? Sometimes a baby potato or cucumber has grown next to a bigger one. But, the only difference is, those cucumbers and potatoes are cucumbers and potatoes. Except some small cucumbers have a little white flower on the top. But mine was just a little piece of flesh with no nail. So, I didn't think there was any reason to call me Hassan the six-toed.

From the look in that little boy's eyes though, I realized it was a toe, or because later on everybody said so. At night when I wanted to sleep, I pulled off my sock and looked at it—the same way that little boy did. I even tried to snicker like him. I still do this, even though I'm thirty-five. I put my hand under it and show it to myself, but I don't snicker anymore. I said that it was like a piece of red flesh. Don't you think that I haven't thought about it—even once—about getting rid of it?

But now, every time I remember it, my right hand starts really shaking. It was in that neighborhood. To tell the truth, if my mother hadn't arrived, I would have definitely chopped it off. When she saw the kitchen knife in my hand she said, "What are you going to do?"

"Nothing," I said.

She said, "Tell me the truth, what were you going to do?"

My sock was on my foot. But she knew, probably from my eyes, the same way that I knew from that little boy's eyes that he was a stranger, like everybody else in the world. That's why we moved to this neighborhood. My father said, "Everybody has something, anybody you see has something extra or something missing."

My father didn't. When he was lathering up his face with soap and therefore had to close his eyes, I bent down and looked. I think my mother didn't and many other people didn't either. But my father was certain, as if he had seen everybody's feet. He probably said it for my sake. But it was indisputable, that I had something that no one else could see, even if I had my sock off. Whenever—I'm not talking about now—whenever I would talk to someone, I was thinking about telling them, suddenly, just in the middle of the conversation, I wanted to say, "Look, I have six toes—the sixth one isn't really a toe. Let me show you."

Now, it's different. Now for me it's something private, something that only I know about. Mother and Father died ten or twelve years ago. And certainly all of those neighborhood kids have forgotten all about it, perhaps they have even forgotten me. Only I know that it's there, it's something that separates me from the others. I sit in front of a mirror. I also place a mirror on the left side of my left foot. Then, with two fingers, I slowly raise it up, in such a way that I can see underneath it, and even can see the space between that toe-like red piece of flesh and my foot. After the water has boiled, I pour it into a basin. Not because my feet smell, no—I put my feet into the water. First, I wait until the heat of the water reddens both of my feet. Then I start massaging all of my toes. I start with the bigger one, for example from the big toe of my right foot. But in the middle of doing it, I get bored before getting to the left foot and go directly to it. Slowly, I rub it and I only wash it with soap. After I have dried my feet, I look at it again in the mirror, in both the mirrors. It's there, always there.

I'm not an absent-minded fellow. It's never happened that I lost my umbrella, or even my fountain pen. Some people are this way; they are worried that perhaps their hats are not on their heads, that maybe they forgot them in a taxi or somewhere else. But I'm always worried. I always have been. It's happened that I wake up and think that I've lost something, or in the middle of the night I awake suddenly and think that it's not there, the thing that I don't know what it is. But it's enough for me, even without turning on the light, just to stretch out my hand and know that it is there, still little, still red, and nail-less. Now, even if the stove had gone out, or if Mother, with her bony face and eyes that seem to be crying forever, would be dead, it still would feel the same. It is as if no one else in this world were as lonely, so lonely that even the room feels smaller, with the windows closed and the curtains drawn. And even if you pushed aside the curtains and opened the window, the cloudy sky would still be clouded and all the lamps of every house in the world would seem to be turned off.

Well, there are these kinds of things, and also…oh, I don't know. But to tell the truth, I think I'm a moody person. That is to say, sometimes I'm happy, I joke with others. I drink, I come and go, but suddenly—not that I remember it—I sit down in a corner, or come home to my room, lock the door, sit on my bed, and stare at it until my eyes become teary and blurry, and I make myself believe it doesn't exist, and my little piece of flesh becomes so small as if it's disappeared, and then it looks just like everyone else's small toe. It's not from tight shoes, or from their shape, narrow-pointed shoes that only have room for four toes and not five. Maybe it is. Because of this I think I am going to certainly lose it someday. Isn't it true that everybody's little toes are getting so small that possibly one day they will disappear?

It's because of these things that for no reason at all, I get depressed. In summer I feel better, especially with sandals and no socks. Perhaps it doesn't make any difference. Because any shoes I wear, I know it's there. Whenever I am walking with someone, or even when quarreling with someone, or when I am in school and get upset—I am a teacher—it's enough for me just to look at my feet, at the spot where I know it is, with its delicate curve and its red tip. And then I don't need to smoke anymore like other people or maybe search for a cozy little tavern, which has only one table with one chair.

But...well, the problem is just this. When a man is with a prostitute (or someone of that sort), she doesn't have to take off her socks. I remember one of them who only took one sock off. She had pulled down the other one, the black sock on her left leg, down to her ankle.

I asked, "What's the matter with your other foot?"

She said, "What do you mean?"

I said, "Nothing"

She said, "No, tell me."

I said, "Believe me, I didn't mean anything."

She said, "No, tell me, what you are thinking? It's blotchy, isn't it? It's burnt, isn't it? There is a burn the size of my palm. Red flesh, no?"

I said, "Why don't you stop. I told you, I didn't mean anything bad."

When she started to cry, I thought about showing her. My hand even went to my sock. But, it was her mascara and long false eyelashes, and especially the few tears, which made her powder and rouge and I don't know what else run, all shouted to me that she was a stranger. I pulled up my socks, first the sock on my left foot. Then I felt compelled to put the rest of my clothes back on. That's why I told you I am vacillating or maybe I am a skeptic for no reason. When people wrap scarves around their necks, for example, or wear gloves—even though it's cold—I believe there is something fishy. And how about underclothes, everyone's clothes? Well, they are right, I also have a right not to let anyone know or see. Not that I'm afraid. Those days are over. Now, no one would ever call an adult, "six-toed"— well...they might though—just like that little stranger with the pale forehead and the small red lips called me that without saying a word.

Then...it was just a few months ago, when I thought once again that this one might not be a stranger. And at first she wasn't. And now...to tell the truth, sometimes you think you have seen her, in fact many times, but each time you wake up you can't remember how she was. And when you close your eyes again, and again you try to remember her, you see she is not one of them. And all of them, among them this brunette, with their skin hidden under a layer of cream and powder and who knows what else, are strangers. When I saw her, I knew she looked familiar. Her hair was black. I thought her eyes were black. They weren't. They were hazel; a black spot reflected my image, which was shaded by her long eyelashes just like those rays around the circle of the sun. And now she appears in my deepest dreams with those hollow cheeks, with her small chin and lips, and you worry that she may break into tears at any moment. Her name…no, no need to mention it. Just like this piece of flesh next to my little toe on my left foot that I won't allow any stranger to see.

I think you begin to fall in love when you get attracted to a certain voice distinct from all the others, when you can walk down unknown alleys with your eyes closed without the need to hold her cold little hand in yours.

She said, "I'm sure that you haven't told me everything."

I said, "Believe me, there is nothing more to tell."

"A girlfriend?"

"No."

She said, "It's impossible. You're not ugly and…I don't know…you don't look so bad."

"I was bashful," I said.

She said, "I know that. But how about when you drink, like that night?"

She was talking about the night when we were walking. It was on a path between two gardens. Maybe it was because the weather was so chilly, or there were so many leaves under our feet…I don't know, there was a kind of pleasant sadness in the air, and at that moment you couldn't help telling that you liked all the light filled windows even though they were closed.

"Tell me that you love me," she said.

I said, "Do I have to say it, can't you see."

I don't understand why they don't believe it until you say so, just like that thin little kid with the broken foot.

I said, "Look."

She said, "This is nothing."

I placed my two fingers under it. She saw it, I'm sure.

But she said, "Well?"

I said, "Come on, look, I'm six-toed."

This one wasn't a stranger anymore. But maybe I was afraid to tell her, tell her and finish it.

So she said, "You haven't told me everything about yourself."

She was right. The problem wasn't just my left little toe. There is always, I think, something hidden somewhere, behind the trees for example— even when it's not night-time—well, there is something, or just now behind the drawn curtains of my closed windows. How about inside a closed cupboard? It's probably for these reasons that I couldn't say, "I love you."

When you have time to sit down and think about all these things, all of the things left in the dark and in the shadow, or you think about all of the closed doors and the dark corners of old vestibules with their dank smell, you can't say to anyone anymore "I love you," even to the best girl in the world. Even if there is a small black mole behind her earlobe, it does not change anything.

She asked, "Why didn't you telephone me?"

I answered, "I had work to do."

She said, "What work? You always go to your room and I don't know.... Do you call that work? Aren't you afraid of being lonely?"

No, not everything was this way. It was enough for me to have a drink and then start walking. Don't think that, when I'm drunk, I would go and search in that dark corner to convince myself that it's not there, since after all only something as worthless as a little pebble would escape the alley lights.

I only look for and wish for things that I really want. Besides, I think that everything has something extra or something missing that is more important and more interesting than the thing itself, that if it is seen, if everyone can see it, you wouldn't say that it is extra. When it becomes part of that thing, part of its structure, then it is laid bare, is in the sunlight, like a room that has only four walls, a ceiling and no shelves, yes, that is the loneliest and most pitiful room that you can imagine. If I were a religious man, I would certainly build myself a little prayer room, a little prayer room like a nobleman's little prayer room, "An inlaid designed door with printed curtains for a little room with a little dome and a molded prayer niche." It was because of all of these things that she drove me crazy. But, I knew that if she'd find out, and if she'd see it, it would be over.

Of course, it wasn't all her fault, either. All of us are this way. When we become aware of something, when we see it in broad daylight, it's finished. Even if we love her, it's out of pity. I wanted that prostitute who had pulled the black sock on her left leg down to her ankle more than any other woman in the world, and I'm talking about that time. And there were things about her—I am talking about that young girl—that I didn't know before and couldn't grasp, but I knew it was there. That's why I suggested marriage.

She said, "Don't rush. We need to get to know each other better."

Well, I thought about "it" and knew it wouldn't work. Of course I didn't want to lie to her or hide anything from her. But there are things that only belong to you, that are connected only to yourself. Suppose the most beautiful, the nicest girl in the world were to sit next to you and you could wrap a lock of her dark hair around your finger or kiss her thin white arms, who could guarantee that there wouldn't be a moment when you didn't know what to do with your hands? Besides, every year has four seasons and in autumn the leaves are sure to fall and sometimes you get so cold, and the sky is so gloomy that…you understand what I mean, it's enough to stretch out your hand even if it's dark, and with the tip of your left or right thumb and index finger you feel that it's there, this thing that belongs to you and nobody else knows about it. And if you want to and do not act like a fool it will always remain for you and with you. Therefore, when someone says, "I'm very lonely." or "I'm sad," I think about my room with its four walls and ceiling.

Well, what can one do? If it weren't there, so little and so red, I certainly would play with her curls. The girl wouldn't say that I was lonely, or…I told you that I had suggested marriage to her and she had said that we shouldn't rush.

The next morning she woke up before I did. She was sitting by the bed, on the floor, looking at my feet. I suppose that I woke up from the touch of her two cold fingers.

She asked, "What's this?"

I said, "What?"

I pulled together the toes on my left foot, in such a way that she would forget she had seen them. But I didn't even try to bend my left foot a bit, or hide my foot in the softness of the mattress. She had seen "it." So it was over and she was finished with me. Even though I had seen that look in all of my dreams, I shivered and I knew I loved her.

She didn't understand and didn't want to understand. People to her are like those usual pictures, which you see inside dictionaries next to the entry for "human" labeled—head, neck, chest and foot—two feet. The left foot has five toes.

I asked, "Look, my dear, can you tell me why you like the clouds?"

She answered, "Well, because they are beautiful, they change their shape constantly."

I said, "Not really, not precisely."

And I wish I could have said, "Because they have six toes!"

She asked, "Why are you so quiet?"

I answered, "Because they have something extra, and even if you think their form is stable, you will see that their shape will change instantly."

She said, "That's what I said."

I said, "I know. But I told you it wasn't precise. Look, for example, if you had told me everything about yourself that first night, you wouldn't have been so interesting."

She said, "You mean, this thing…."

She spoke about it in a demeaning manner. She didn't understand. I think that it's in a painting, in stories, in everything and people, some of them, might have things under their skin, they must have.

We broke up. She got scared. She was probably right.

She said, "What about our babies? You must definitely have surgery. It's nothing."

Kids, kids, all about kids. What about me? What about my sunsets, all of my sad sunsets, when darkness grabs not only all the earth but all of human existence? In the light, everything is itself, distinct from everything else. But when darkness falls or shadows are cast, nothing is itself any longer; forms turn blurry and loose their identity.

She held it with her thumb and index finger, just like when you take a dead mouse by the tail to throw it away.

Now I'm happy. But my uneasiness is that only one person knows, the one who knows that I have one extra toe, someone who has seen me truly naked. And this is very sad.

Both Sides of the Coin

TRANSLATED BY

FRANKLIN LEWIS

If you really want to know the truth, I killed him. Believe me. Or maybe you could say we killed him, though not, of course, with a knife or by pushing him, or anything. You can be sure of that. So, how then? That's just what I want to make clear for you. That's why I said, "If we could be alone, it'd be better." If I offended them, so be it. I mean, I could see it wouldn't get anywhere, with your brother, or even your wife, it wouldn't be possible to talk about it so openly. Or maybe it's that I can't be completely candid in front of a group of people. In the second place, I wasn't sure they'd understand. As for you? I don't know. Maybe I've no choice. Maybe because I just had to tell someone. You know what I mean? By the way, don't think I'm trying to clear myself by confessing, or my buddies, for that matter. I don't expect forgiveness from you. Not that it doesn't bother me, 'cause it does. It was bothering me from the very beginning. But when I explained it all to one of those same buddies, he told me, "Go on, you're nuts. They found his hat and cane. There was foul play involved." When I told him what I think, he said, "Okay, so you can go to the prosecutor with it." He was kidding, of course. I didn't mean to tell you all this. But see, that guy—my buddy, I mean—didn't want to think of himself as having had a hand in it. Or perhaps he suspected that they had shoved the guy. So did all the others. So after that, I didn't tell anyone else. I said to myself, let them go ahead and think that the old man, too, got…you know what I mean? I didn't want to mention anything about it to you, either. That's why last week, when you came to see me and introduced yourself, I blew you off. I thought perhaps you had come to get an affidavit from me. Or, for instance…well, you are his son, after all. Maybe you doubted the story of how it happened, that is to say the things that were printed in the newspapers, and so you came. But let's be clear about it from the beginning, just so that your mind will be at ease: it happened just like everyone says it did, and—as it so happens—just the way it was written up in the papers. I believe it was on the 26th of March, 1955.[1] But aside from all this, there is something else that has really been bugging me. Because whenever I recall everything in detail, I see there is still something missing, it doesn't add up. What? I don't know. Maybe that's why I said at first that I killed him, or that we did—so I wouldn't be forced to hide certain things. Once you're in over your head, it doesn't matter how deep you go. Or maybe it does, I mean, at least in this case. I don't know. If I didn't say anything last week, it was more on account of the others. You remember I said, "There's a lot to tell. I don't think this is the place. We will see each other again"? Maybe I needed to clear things up for myself. I guess I told you.

Remember, of course, that I was never one of your father's buddies. Far from it. I never knew him before, hadn't even heard of him. Later, of course, I asked around to find out about his past, what he was like, who he was. Your father was no greenhorn. He had seen much worse than this. Like, later on I heard…from whom? I don't remember. As I was saying, I heard that your father was one of the riflemen in the Sepahsalar Mosque the day that the artillery fired on the Parliament. Or was he one of the Azerbaijan Committee?[2]

The following month, when they caught him, he had a bunch of illegal pamphlets on him, stuffed in his pockets and under his arms. I suppose you know all this better than I do, but I didn't know about it, not in those days, I didn't. As I said, I never knew him at all, not until that morning

---

1. The date given by the Iranian calendar is 5 Farvardin 1334, just 4 days after *Nowruz*, the Iranian New Year, and during the traditional days of celebration, which include visits to family members.

2. Mohammad-Ali Shah acceded to the Qajar throne in January 1907, just months after the new Constitution had been accepted by his father and predecessor, and the first Parliament convened. A new period of press freedom and open criticism of the government began. By the end of the year, the Shah had been compelled to dismiss some of his corrupt ministers, but not before threatening the constitutional partisans with force of arms. An attempt was made on the Shah's life in February 1908, after which he moved to curtail press freedoms and expel some of the leading constitutionalists. When his demands were not met, the Shah ordered the Sepahsalar Mosque and the Parliament building be bombarded with six canons, a command carried out with the assistance of Russian officers on 23 June 1908. The Azerbaijan committee was a civilian militia formed by the constitutionalists which acted in defense of the Parliament on this occasion.

he came to see me. It was before the morning routine started. Some of them used to get up early in the morning and hang around by the garden pool, or out there under the trees—the ones who got up at the crack of dawn. He had a cane in his hand. He was wearing a suit. He had on one of those fedora hats, and a vest and tie, and a gold watch chain…well, it was like he had come to say hello. As soon as I laid eyes on him, I thought, "Why, he's even waxed his shoes." And he had! And that suit! Let me tell you, it was like it had come freshly pressed from the cleaners, and we were behind bars! You know what I mean? Not that no one else ever dressed up, they did, but only on visitation days, if they had a visitor. From the cellblock he came walking straight at me. A few of the guys were still asleep here and there. Do you know, he came right up to me! He stood there and said hello. Then he pulled up the stool that was standing next to the wall and sat down, right next to me. It was a bit surprising. At first I thought he was a detective or someone like that. But so early in the morning? So then, who was he? I hadn't seen him before. They had only recently moved me there. Two days, it had been. It was crowded. I didn't feel like going out or walking at all. I didn't move. He introduced himself. He held his hand out. I was by now practically standing. I didn't shake his hand, I remember that. I just couldn't. It wasn't so much that I hadn't shaved or washed my face, but the short underwear and sleeveless undershirt I was wearing. Dressed like that? In front of your father, who didn't have a single speck on his uniformly dark clothes? I think I just pulled the blanket up to my chest.

Your father asked, "Sir, are you Mr. Sayfollahi?"

"Yes," I said.

"I'm not disturbing you, am I?" he asked.

And that's how our acquaintance began. So, why did he come directly up to me and how had he found me? It doesn't matter. No, why say that? Of course it matters. Somebody must have told him. The day before I had spoken with one of my acquaintances, I had complained. Not a lot, though, because I knew you shouldn't whine. It's enough for you to say one thing, and next your buddy will start in, and before the day is out, everyone is whining. Maybe it just slipped out of my mouth, or maybe deep down I hoped to find someone to commiserate with me, or someone who knew what's what. Something like that…you know what I mean? After all, a person cannot all of a sudden accept that everything is all over. Of course, it wasn't all over. But as for me, at the time I'm talking about, I had no hope, especially after five months stuck in those things—the two-and-a-half by one-and-a-half meter ones that…you must have heard about them. And then, how much can a person take? I bet you are about to say, "Then what about the great heroes, how can they?..." True. But being a great hero depends, for example, on one's physical stamina, on one's muscles and physique, that is to say on how many days one can take it. Or maybe it depends on having an idea or something, something you can stand behind or take strength from. Then, of course, there are the times when a person puts everything on the line and only wants to defend himself. Why, for instance? Because maybe he doesn't like the way his adversary looks, or maybe he senses that it isn't just anybody's problem, or path, or vision, but it's a question of not giving in to the guy standing in front of him, imperiously puffing on his cigarette.

Your father had come to tell me these things. For example, he wanted to know why I had said, "Let it go, man. It's all over now." Or why I had complained, "This is no way to live." Of course, he first apologized for butting in. He even mentioned that it wasn't because of his white hair or the many times he'd been around the block that he considered himself entitled to speak to me or advise me. No, he only wanted to clarify the matter. He would say, "In places like this, a person has to be careful what he says, careful what he does." He took out his cigarette box and offered me one. I wasn't in the habit of smoking before breakfast, but I didn't push his hand away. Well, I was a bit angry, too. I didn't know why he was saying these things, and why to me. I wasn't suspicious. Because there was nothing left for me to play cat-and-mouse about. The skin on my chest had healed up, the week before. There was only a small brown spot left. My wrists were still hurting.

When he was sure that I hadn't been kidding, or that I hadn't spoken from, let's say loneliness or listlessness—I mean, when I said, "My words were not so superficial"– he began, just like somebody reading out of a book, with the typical calm of an old man of sixty or sixty-five years of age. He spoke of life, of sunrise. I guess that, a month or two before, he had been able to go up on the roof on some pretext or other. I don't remember why. Anyway, it's not important. It was as if he was seeing the sunrise for the very first time. He talked about the play of the colors and such things, and of the people walking on the other side of the barbed wire. He had seen a child playing. With a ball, he thought, though he hadn't seen the ball. He talked a lot, talked with emotion. But all in all, the things he said were like the editorial of some local weekly paper. At first, the man himself and his mannerisms were of more interest to me than, for example, that he had seen that life goes on as usual beyond the barbed wire, plodding as ever drearily along. But then I got my dander up not to give in to him. I don't know why, exactly, maybe it just happened. Or maybe that teacher's tone of his made me dig my heels in, or it really could just have happened because he was suffocating me. He spoke nonstop, exactly as if he were reading a speech, or delivering something he had memorized ahead of time word-for-word. What histrionics! He was so sure of himself when he spoke that you would have thought nothing was amiss. Now, of course, I know why. Now I know why he spoke so carefully, so calmly. He didn't concern himself with my reaction, maybe it wasn't even me he was talking to. What he said seemed just like a long-winded interior monologue that gives no clue when it might end. That's why I was forced to cut him off. I don't remember now what I said, but I'm quite sure that it was mostly because I wanted to conceal the thread-bare state of my army blanket.

I guess anyone else in my situation would have done just the same. They would surely have felt the same—that his white shirt, or the smell of his cologne, or even the crease in his trousers gave the old man the right to be hopeful, to give advice, or maybe to ask a person to answer a series of questions—and given all that, you just couldn't just shrug him off. And those are the very reasons why I stood my ground. Maybe because he had forced me to play the role of a man in despair, I told myself better to play the part well than poorly. At first I spoke ambiguously, just as he had when speaking in generalities. He wouldn't buy it. He rejected my reasons one by one. At first, on that day, he didn't speak of his own experiences—he didn't want to get into matters in detail and, let's say, question the evidence or examples I submitted, or find inconsistencies in what I said. He continued on with, I suppose, the rest of that same sermon. He spoke about the beauty of nature and, oh I don't know, about honeybees and the rustling of leaves. He spoke of his canary, too, and how he would ask his kids to take care of it whenever they came to see him. And about how early he would get up in the morning, out of long years of habit. And then, like someone who had just discharged his duties, or completed a formal oration, or like a person with some life-and-death matter to attend to somewhere, he took his watch out of his vest pocket, pressed the release, and said, "My, my, it's already seven fifteen!" Then he excused himself, got up and walked off, cane in hand, all prim and proper.

To tell the truth, I was angry. As he was walking off like that with his head held high and his deliberate stride, I thought he must be feeling quite proud of himself for having been able to save one despairing person today. Believe me, I didn't mean to insult him. And I don't mean to belittle or, I don't know, speak ill of your father now, either. I'm just trying to explain to you how I felt that day. I remember I was so angry that if one of the other fellows who had just woken up had not asked, "What was that all about?" I certainly would have called him back and told him that...then I saw...I don't know. I only remember telling this fellow, "Forget it, the guy is...." Forgive me. You can probably guess for yourself what I said. You see, you find a lot of that sort of people in there. Sometimes they even gang up together to humiliate a guy, to turn him into a flunky. If a fellow lets himself fall into their clutches for even a moment, he's done for. And in that restricted environment, where people can constantly rub it in by a word or a gesture, they'll make you writhe in it. Only in there do you realize how cruel people can be, even people who...you know what I mean?

What I am trying to say is, I thought at the time that your father was one of those flunkies, and that the matter had ended that day and would go no further. But the next day he turned up again, at the same time as the first day, before morning prayers. After sitting down on the stool, he leaned forward on his cane and asked me how I was. Well, he had caught me unawares again, in that same condition, with unkempt hair. If I had at least had an opportunity to splash some water on my face, that would have been one thing. Your late father had shaved, with a double-blade, I bet. He had combed his gray mustache. And there I was, shamefaced, especially at not yet having rinsed my mouth out. "How are you feeling today?" he asked.

Well, if you had been in my place, wouldn't you have thought, "Here he comes to mess with me again!" or at any rate, suspected him of looking in to see how much fruit his guidance of the previous day had borne? At first I thought I'd lay into the old man, to say for instance, "What business did you have doing anything to wind up in here? At your age you should have grandchildren hanging about your neck and shoulders, playing with your mustache!" Then I said, fine, since he wants to play, very well, hallelujah! Then I thought, the hell with washing my face and hands or shaving. In fact, looking like this will help reinforce what I'm going to say.

So I said, as matter-of-fact as could be, "It's horrible. I didn't sleep at all last night. My head hurts, too. On top of that, if you really want to know, I'm fed up. And all for what, for whom?"

"It isn't for anyone's sake," he said. "With two or three pills you can solve sleeplessness and that sort of thing. That's no excuse. Secondly, if a person decides to follow a path, he should see if he can do it. I mean, for example, can he put up with the consequences? It's true that someone who sets his hands to a task, even if he fails, is worth more than someone who sits around twiddling his thumbs, but...." Of course, I cannot now recall if he said these things that same day, or on some other day. But I remember that he spoke with such self-confidence that a person would suppose his confidence and faith were an integral part of his clothes, like the white of his shirt, or the shine of his tiepin or his cufflinks. His cufflinks were silver, it seems like. I don't exactly remember.

Yes, well.... He had started in again and I didn't want to lose the upper hand this time around. I think I told you. It seemed at first like some kind of game to me—either by necessity or by chance, this half of the dialogue had been dealt to me. I don't mean to say that I didn't at all believe in what I said, but at the very least I can assure you that, for my part, not all of the dimensions of the role I was compelled to play were clear to me. I couldn't begin logically. I jumped around from one subject to another. But your father knew what he wanted. He wouldn't let us lose track of the point. I don't recall what we said. If you want to know the truth, I usually don't remember the things that are said, not all of them, but I do remember how I felt that day, or on some other day. For example, your father's expression. Or the logic of his premises. It seems like he was talking about the future, of possibilities we had not tried, and paths that could still be taken, and so forth.

Aside from the difference in the way we looked, the difference in our ages kept us from being completely candid with one another. Anyway, it kept me from being completely candid. Sometimes, maybe, sometimes when I would get hot under the collar and I saw that I really did have the right, I'd get angry. I'd shout, come up with reasons from here, there and everywhere. But the old man would soon figure out when I was, you know, putting on an act, or was speaking out of anger. He'd wave his hand, or his head, as though he were trying to shoo those reasons or that artificial passion out of the way, like a pedestrian blocking the sidewalk, and with a "please be logical" or, I don't know, a "I would have expected more of you," he would force me to be candid. But I wasn't completely candid. I told you. Then I saw that if I thought about it carefully, I could come up with reasons, reasons that at times were even logical. And you know why? Because when you believe in something with your whole being, you no longer see any need for conjuring up reasons. You think that one movement, one sentence—on account of the faith that is behind it—is enough to convince the one you're talking to. But when you don't believe in what you're saying, that's when you set forth premises, flail around looking for evidence, even trying to be dispassionate, stay impartial, and then you finally realize—realize with horror—that you've managed to convince not the one you're talking to, but rather yourself. You even believe in it. That's when you really get going. You rejoice in a new discovery you make, in—oh, I don't know—an approach you take that had never been attempted before. Little by little I got to the point where I could with a single sentence—a single movement and the faith that backed it up—stand up to the old man and sometimes with enthusiasm and intensity, not only defend the beliefs that had formed and taken root during our discussions, but sometimes even, I would realize how much self-control was required to retreat in front of your father. But your father would never blow up. In order not to disturb the others, he would ask that we speak softly, since a number of them were still asleep.

I remember that the second day he went away unsatisfied. I thought he wouldn't show up anymore. Of course, the next day I saw him and we nodded at one another. If I were to compare it to something, his smile was like the design on a coin, or an integral part of the coin, but separate from it at the same time. This, of course, is how I think of it now. That day I thought the old man was happy. And maybe he was. He had a knitted garment draped over his arm, one of the things that they knit in such places. His hair was white, combed and white. His embossed cigarette box was at his side. He didn't offer a cigarette. That's why I thought he wouldn't come by anymore. But I was ready for him—I had shaved at night. And when I heard his footsteps and the sound of his cane, I put my shirt on. I had washed it the day before. When he sat down next to me, I was already sitting, almost crouching, and the blanket was folded in two at my feet. This time I think I said hello first. The old man was in good spirits. But he didn't smile, he was serious, even sour-faced. I remember thinking that he looked just like a child who has been forced to swallow some bitter medicine.

He asked me how I was doing again. Naturally, by that he meant my mental state. Well, it wasn't bad. That is to say, it wasn't so bad on that particular day. I had gotten used to the general quarters. It was hard, but I had seen worse, when about fifty or sixty people are crammed into a single room. There was a tin drum in a corner of the room. You know what that was for. The room had a window-thingy for food and what not. Sometimes we had no choice but to sleep sitting up. They would empty the tin drum at the beginning of the week. You can't imagine it, especially when they would carry someone away and then bring him back and release him among us. Well, it was mostly the waiting that wore us down. Or the noises of the others. In such places a person comes to realize how it is possible to hate people and love them at one and the same time. It was enough for you to feel that the existence of some person or other, some annoying piece of flesh, was the reason that you couldn't stretch your feet out, even if only for a moment.

Yeah, at a time like that you start to hate all people on account of this one person's existence. Of course it would also sometimes happen that the same person whose snoring was driving everyone crazy would suddenly wake up terrified, and apologize for, I don't know, for disturbing anyone. Sitting next to a person like that for an hour and listening to his suffering is enough to make him indebted to your kindness for life. It's funny, but I remember—this last time, of course—there was one fellow who would set the guys' joints, if they were exercising or something, for example, and an arm or leg got dislocated. But even though he had set one of the guys' fingers crooked—such that no one was willing for him to even touch them anymore—as soon as somebody fell down, he'd show up nevertheless with his bowl of warm water and an egg yolk and a patch of cloth. Well, as I was saying, at this time conditions were better. From the point of view of food and clothes and other things. But the difference was that a person had been all alone before. Now, see, there was the smell of body sweat and, I don't know, the hand that shared your bowl, or that held the lighted match to your cigarette, and lots of other things. For example, sitting around together at night, commiserating, and sometimes the sound of sobbing out loud. But then there were times when the same guy you had shared your bowl with would, a half hour later...do you see what I mean? Not everybody is Jesus, after all.

Well, I explained these things—the situation—for your father. Naturally in greater detail than I said here. For example, I would say who had done what, or what so-and-so had said the day before. All that sort of stuff. At first, your father said he agreed. He said, these things happen. He didn't mention the morning view or the sound of the leaves underfoot or—I don't know—the pillar or the coin-like disc of light anymore, just generalities instead. Now I think that during the days, while he was knitting or, let's say, walking, he would weigh his answers in the balance. And that's why the next morning he would reject my arguments of the previous day with specific reasons. He'd say, "We always want to lay the blame on someone else's head, and we think that if this fellow hadn't, let's say, done such and such, it would have worked out. Well, this is true, that is, it wouldn't have worked out as badly. But when it comes to the big picture, if we think about it, all of us are victims of our way of looking at things." You get what I mean?

Your father, it seems to me, wanted to say that in the past forty or fifty years we were always looking to someone else. For example, he would say that when we were going to codify the law, we just translated the laws of Belgium, or I don't know what European country, verbatim. He would say, "When we put our faith in them and rely unquestioningly upon them, they suppose we are just an extension of themselves, an integral part of their own being, as if there were no one outside of them. Because it is just an imitative entity, if it asserts itself once in a while, it's not worthy of attention. Well, don't you think that such people have the right to think: whatever we do, this imitative extension will accept, bow its head, even look high and low with its own eyes for reasons to affirm our actions?" He was saying, "What right have we to complain, then? So they'll sit down at the table with a full hand and, if they lose the hand, well, they lose. Because the wager they hold in hand is nothing but air, a worthless thing. And then the game begins. It's happened several times so far."

He gave example after example, explaining where something happened and why. His reasoning was good. He didn't talk about himself, at least, not at first. Later on I found out that he had apparently had a hand in it himself. I said apparently. For instance, he gave the example of Mirza.[3] He explained why this happened and why that. He would say, "You see, they always leave us hanging just at the crucial moment." Even so, he believed that they were afraid of an ancient nation, especially one with a magnificent culture. His evidence was that, not only did they plunder it and, for example, cut the country into pieces, but in particular, they appropriated its poets and writers for their own, which fact couldn't be denied. What about the plunder of antiquities? He would say, "They are afraid, believe you me, my friend, that such a land might...."

I don't know. You understand what I mean? What he was driving at was this: "It was we who started it all in this part of Asia. I remember it all." Now he was no longer giving an oration, I mean, sometimes something

---

3. Mirza was a common title, and there are several patriotic figures to whom it may allude here. Perhaps Mirza Aqa Khan Kermani, who is specifically mentioned later in the story, may be intended. Other important national patriots who opposed the Qajars include: Mirza-ye Shirazi, a high-ranking cleric who led the 1891 revolt against the Qajar monarch's Tobacco Regie, a debilitating concession to a British interest, granting it a 50-year monopoly over the production and sale of all tobacco in Iran; Mirza Kuchek Khan Jangali (1881-1921), a nationalist who defended Iran against Russian and British incursions during World War I and tried to establish an independent communist state in the Caspian province of Gilan. Since the gentleman in our story is about 60 or 70 years old in 1955, perhaps the latter incident is chronologically more likely.

would occur to him, during the conversation, and I—I admit it—would stubbornly resist, even though I could see the old man was right. Sometimes I would, as they say, truss him up, by repeating the words he himself had used. Like him, I would bring the history of the past to my aid, saying, for example, that we have been like this, always. Like it or not. And so forth. If you really want to know the truth, most of my arguments were in the nature of a debate or confrontation, with victory as its goal.

By the seventh or eighth day, I was accustomed to your father's visits. I'd shave, get dressed and sit there prepared for an hour's debate and whispered disputation, and sometimes for shouting and yelling, and even clenched fists and so on. Sometimes I saw myself as if putting the past on trial, you know what I mean? The entire past, top to bottom! But it was if all the past, the past forty or fifty years, its defeats, its distorted understandings and its shallowness, for me all of it was crystallized in your father. Most of my information about it I got from your father, from his examples, his experiences. I knew that he had wound up in there for absolutely no reason, I believe he had written something in his newspaper, some time back, and now, as they fell to settling old scores, they stuck it to him. But, at the same time, I realized he was being beaten with the cudgel of his own past. Actually, I didn't see much of anything in his past, or I didn't want to see it, because of the forced circumstances of my long debate with him. And since I saw the old man supporting himself with this history—you will forgive me, I was going to say, with that stinking heritage—that he still wouldn't give up, well it made me livid.

At times I thought, what use is it beating my head against a brick wall. In the first few days, I never once caught your father trying to trick me in our discussions. You know how I mean. For example, when I got bogged down in a particular point, I would make use of my knowledge of Kafka, let's say, or string together a list of foreign writers and then….The old man wouldn't fall for such shenanigans. He'd appeal to events themselves, things that had happened, that he had felt, or that I had told him. And also, sometimes he would cite some authoritative book. But towards the end, that was quite unusual. And if he alluded to someone else's beliefs, it was mostly to emphasize what he was saying himself, not as evidence in support of the thinker's ideas.

By the twelfth or thirteenth day, I was making the discussion personal, that is, I talked about my personal life. Not, of course, with the intent to complain. Things just came to mind. No, I just had to tell someone. And who better than your father? I told him everything, by which I mean how I came to meet my wife. But what could the old man understand, especially when I was speaking jealously about the woman? I left it to him to put the pieces of the puzzle together. Now it's different, I can recall everything from beginning to end. I mean, when a person is involved in something, he only sees bits and pieces, and is unable to tie it all together and make sense of it. The duration of a given event can be perceived only when a person is distant from the event. Of course, I don't want to go into all that now. Maybe I've just gotten used to things. The passage of time makes us addicted to everything. I even said so to your father; it was in those last days, it seems like. I said, "You have become addicted to being, and also to being hopeful. When you get up in the morning, you put on your hopefulness just like a hat and coat and tiepin."

You know, by that time things had descended to the point of insulting him about pressing his trousers or, for example, shaving, or to your father's prim and proper walking. Well, that's how it was. I told you my goal was to win. Of course, at that time, I didn't know, I mean your father had not alluded to it at all. But then I realized that he was in more or less the same situation as me. You do know what I am talking about? That is, his wife, I mean your mother....I told you that it's no longer important to me now.

He came on the last day, he laughed, he talked, he made his points, he heard mine, and he went and didn't come back again. Two or three months went by and he didn't come. I thought, maybe I have no visitation hours, maybe he is sick, maybe such and such....A month or two later I found out, that is, suddenly I opened my eyes and I saw that everyone but me knew. All that I'm saying has nothing to do with your father's situation, but, well, in general there is some resemblance. When a person's concentration is entirely focused on inking a ditto machine,[4] or on knocking heads with mullahs or their retainers, or satisfying this Seyyed or that broker, and all this just to introduce them all to one another, and then to see all of a sudden that others—which is to say the very ones that your father had set in motion—were now ahead of the game and beating their own breasts, as if...well, my situation was more or less the same. I mean, all at once I opened my eyes and saw that the person who had been my last refuge, who I one day might have been able to lay my head down on the ground next to without any reservations, and stroke her hair, her neck,

---

4 *"Havâs-ash jam`-e zhelâtin,"* a reference to the grease or gelatin used in the process of lithography or jellography to cause the stone or metal platen to retain ink in the desired places. Although this process was also used for books and newspapers, it seems here to suggest the surreptitious printing of dangerous or illegal political pamphlets or manifestoes.

or I don't know, her chin....You know, once in a while a person needs to touch, I mean with his own skin—for instance, with his finger tips—to think through them, maybe to lay his hand on another person's forehead one night and say, "So, what are you thinking about?" and have that person tell you, free of any inhibitions.

I said all this to your father, and much more besides. I guess I've told you. Maybe, if I hadn't been afraid that others would see or hear, I would have started crying. Well, what if they had set me free, what then? Your father listened. Then he walked out. He excused himself and went. I got really livid. Now, why'd he have to do that? I couldn't figure it out. The next day, I pretended to be asleep. One of my friends who shared the same cell called me when he got there. He even shook me. That's the day your father started. I don't exactly remember what he said. But I do remember he said these words, "For the wife, your beliefs are an integral part of you. However strange, or fresh, or—I don't know—complex they may be, they are not all of you. Do you suppose that any woman, or at least that woman, could have put up with such ideas?" He said, "Only men think in abstractions and absolutes or, at least, that's how Iranian men are." And then I had to explain to him again what had happened, even the details.

Actually, it didn't bother me so much that my wife had, for instance, done this or that, or slept with this or that guy. What bothered me was that everything I had done could be made up for with one night of sex. Stripped of all honor, one can't just carry on. You know what I mean? Not that I didn't love my wife. But I was willing to stay in that little one-and-a half by two-and-a-half room forever to keep it from happening. I know she had done it for my sake. But there was nothing left of me. I don't remember anymore what I said. And I still can't figure how your father could keep his dignity and composure. Of course, his arguments were useless. He knew it, too. He knew it, but he kept pounding away. For example, what good did it do me that your father talked of the satisfaction that comes with forgiving? Or, for example, about my wife's sacrifices; or even to detail for me precisely how it's possible for a woman to sleep with someone and not give in. In spirit not to give in, he meant. Now I can grant that, to some extent, he was right. But in those days, no...how can I put it? Not even now. I was going to say that in our era, at least, it wasn't a question of spirit. Because they could extract the spirit through the pores of your skin with tweezers. These are the things I said to your father. I said that people see my body, not my spirit. I said that's why...in reality, I don't remember. The other things I do remember because later on I said them to that woman, too. I mean, in reality, even before that, she knew that everything was over. She asked for a divorce. I heard she has a kid now, from her second husband.

I talked with your father about other things, too. For instance, I told him about how my friends betrayed me, because they were scum, or because they were afraid. You know, some of them came with complexes, complexes about not having a car or a house, or not having the opportunity to mix with women. See, it was enough to set these in front of them to keep them from turning their faces away. A desk, a telephone, and a chair or two was enough. One of them, of course, had to be a swivel chair, had to be sure of that. But your father had lots of tricks like this up his sleeves. He had seen a lot. But he would say, "Look at the long haul. There have been some real giants and you only know the ones who have been talked or written about. There were others, too, who…." He would give examples, instances of sacrifice. I don't know, he talked about Sur-e Esrafil[5] and Mirza Aqa Khan Kermani. He told me how they lopped off the heads of Khabir al-Molk and Shaykh Ahmad Ruhi under a sweetbrier tree, right in front of Mirza, and he didn't even bat an eyelash.[6] On their last night, Mohammad-Ali Mirza[7] takes a notion into his head to see them. Maybe he wanted to understand their beliefs. I don't know. He forces one of the Constitutionalists to go see them, and he himself stands listening at the door. That same guy, I guess, related the story like this,

5. Probably Mirza Jahangir Khan "Sur-e Esrafil," one of the leaders of the Constitutionalists, a great orator, and publisher/editor of the journal *Sur-e Esrafil* ("*Trumpet of the Resurrection Day*"). This journal, founded in 1907, was especially hated by the reactionary monarchists opposed to the establishment of a parliament. On 12 June 1908 Mohammad-Ali Shah demanded that Mirza Jahangir and seven other Constitutionalist figures be expelled from Tehran and press freedoms curtailed. When the Parliament was bombarded on 23 June, Mirza Jahangir Khan was captured, and the next day the Shah had him strangled and his journal closed down.

6. Mirza Aqa Khan of Kerman was a constitutional activist and poet who wrote for the reformist Persian-language newspaper, *Akhtar* (published outside Iran, in Istanbul). His brother-in-law, Shaykh Ahmad Ruhi, helped translate James Morier's *Haji Baba of Ispahan* to Persian. They were both followers of the Babi figure, Subh-i-Azal, but later made common cause with Jamal al-Din al-Afghani, encouraging the Shiite religious leaders to join with the Sunni Turks in opposing the colonial European powers. Following the assassination of Naser al-Din Shah in May 1896, they were arrested in Istanbul along with Mirza Hassan Khan Khabir al-Molk, and extradited to Iran (Persia), where the Crown Prince, Mohammad-Ali Mirza, had them imprisoned in heavy chains for two months before executing them in Tabriz on 17 July 1896.

7. Mohammad-`Ali Mirza, the Crown Prince at the time of this event, became Shah in January 1907 shortly after the first Iranian parliament had been convened. Eighteen months later, he opened fire on the Constitutionalists and the Parliament.

"I had a tallow-burning lamp in my hand. When I opened the door of the room where they were jailed, they were lined up, standing and in chains, under the false archways in the basement. Their necks were bent. The chains were fixed to manacles at the back of their necks. You couldn't recognize them anymore, the way they looked, or maybe because it was dark, I didn't recognize them. I guess Mirza Aqa Khan recognized me. He called me by name. He told me why they were there. He gave me courage. He was fearless." In the end one of them, I think it was Mirza Aqa Khan Kermani, told that guy, "If you knew why we're here, you would kiss our chains."

He spoke of Sattar Khan,[8] too. About his being barefoot and the incident with the Russian flag. How proud he was as he talked about this. It was like he was Sattar Khan, himself. "Me, come under the Russian flag?! I want the seven climes to fly my country's flag!"

When I would say, "So what good did it do? Where did it get us? Who won in the end? What do you say of Seqat al-Islam?[9] Or, for example...," he didn't miss a beat. He was an experienced man. Not that he had argued a lot with others, but he had a ready answer for everything. Now I know why. I mean, I think he had given himself the third degree about the matter many times. He never once missed a beat. It was as if he had guessed what I would say ahead of time. He'd say, "Well, what did you think would happen?! It's always been like that. You have to fight every second." He'd say, "Who sets the table and who sits down to eat, huh? The cooks, the servants? No. The ones who are already sitting all around the table slide themselves right up to the food, nice and easy, as though they had always been sitting there at the meal. And the way they sit there, it looks like they have no intention of ever getting up." By that he meant the Constitutional Revolution, of course.

I'm boring you. But, well, that's exactly the things we would talk about together. I was used to it. Maybe it was a kind of pastime for me and the others. But for your father? No. To tell the truth, he was fighting, fighting

---

8. Sattar Khan (1867-1914), a patriotic figure in Iranian Azerbaijan, led the Constitutional forces defending Tabriz in 1908-1909 first against the Royalists, and later against Russian troops. When the pro-constitutionalists had lost hope and raised the Russian flag, Sattar Khan refused to give up and rallied the constitutional supporters. Hailed as a hero, he later refused to comply with the national Parliament's directive that insurrectionary forces disarm.

9. Seqat al-Islam was a leading cleric and pro-constitutionalist in Tabriz. The Russians took the city in December 1911, at which point the second Iranian Parliament was dissolved by the Shah and the Constitutional Revolution defeated. The Russians then had Seqat al-Islam executed with several other Iranian patriots in January 1912.

with all of us. Don't think that he might have said something about you, let's say, or heirs and inheritance. Up to the very last day, it was the same old things. He'd come, we'd talk, and he'd go. I believe I'd seen him on one of those last days, in the afternoon, walking around the yard. He was shaking his cane. He would stop every now and then, and it was like he was talking to someone under his breath. I thought he was sick or something. But then, the next day, he showed up again, just as he had been on the first day, as if it were the very first day we had seen one another. Dry and formal, ready for a fight. Just like two sword fighters.

I told you that he was a real fighter. Towards the end he even tried tricks. He'd use Islam and Sufism and even the poets to back him up. One day, he recited Bahar's entire poem, "The Early Morning Bird," and the poem about Mt. Damavand, too, with fantastic pride. He had a good voice. He'd recite the poems of Farrokhi, as well.[10] I even remember he cited one of the stories of the *Golestan* as an example, or rather as an authority, proving the correctness of his beliefs.[11] He'd say, "Now just suppose we had given in? Then what?" He was yelling. Believe me, sometimes he'd even resort to counterfactual sophistry. He'd say, "Supposing that we stripped one of them of their weapon, and an opportunity had come up to empty the chamber. How do you know we would aim straight, huh? What if our hands were to shake and we were left with one side of our body paralyzed? Then what?!"

He'd consider every single one of the problems, one by one. Of course, there was no mention of the specific opportunities we did have, we were speaking only in general. He'd give lots of examples. About, I don't know, Haj Sayyah,[12] and how he threw himself out of the second story of a

---

10. Mirza Mohammad Taqi Bahar (1880-1951), the greatest classical poet of Iran in the 20th century. He supported the Constitutional Revolution, later became a member of Parliament, and was counted among the greatest scholars of literature and history. He edited a democratic newspaper, *New Spring,* beginning in 1910. Farrokhi of Yazd (1889-1939), a leftist democrat and poet who published in the pro-Constitution papers in 1910, he later published a Marxist paper in Berlin, before returning to Iran during the reign of Reza Shah Pahlavi, who put him in jail, where he died.

11. The *Golestan* of Sa'di, written in 1258, the most famous book of Persian prose, containing anecdotes, often humorous, illustrating ideas of statecraft, practical ethics and social mores.

12. Hajj Mohammad-Ali Sayyah (1836-1924), author of an extensive travel diary to Europe during 1877-ca. 1910, which led him to compare and critique Iranian government and society. An early supporter of constitutional limitations on the monarchy, he ran afoul of Naser al-Din Shah and was banished from Tehran and later imprisoned in Qazvin.

building when they were trying to get him once, during the time of Naser al-Din Shah. Supposedly he just breaks his back. One of the guys, I don't remember which one, said to the old man, "We're talking about making a decision, the rest of it is easy. If a person decides to do it, he can even use the light switch here, or I don't know, toss himself off a rooftop or throw himself into a pit or a ditch." He was saying, "If we accept that all roads are blocked, if we think that wherever we may step they have already set a trap for us...."

The old man couldn't take it anymore. As I said, he was shouting, he didn't want to accept that you had to give up. He was saying, "Well, if that's what you believe, why are you sitting here just talking?" It seems to me he even said, "If you are all such scum, if you've screwed everything hopelessly up—I'm talking about all of you!—why don't you just do your miserable selves in?" Now this was really not like him at all. I swear, he was pointing to each of us, one by one. When someone said with a laugh, "Why, we're such scum!" your father nearly grabbed him by the collar. I could see that I couldn't take this anymore, I wanted to let the matter go, to give him a filial kiss on the forehead and ask his forgiveness. But it wasn't possible, we had fallen into a rut by this time. The ones who would come up and gather around us would now and then interject a humorous crack. When the old man saw that it wasn't just one person he had to talk to, it would make him more obstinate. Sometimes he'd call out to them for support, asking if they hadn't seen a certain thing with their own eyes, rebuke them. And then, he'd look at his watch and, whatever time it was, he'd excuse himself and go. I guess that was enough for today. Even if it was a bit repetitive, still, you see, these comings and goings, and the discussions, were a kind of hobby for me. Not just for me, for all of us.

That morning, when the commotion started, we knew. They were saying that your father had been taking his usual daily stroll, when he gets to the edge of the sewage ditch that was on the other edge of the yard, near the trees. I guess they had emptied the toilets into it a long while before...as I said, when he gets to the sewage ditch, he sets his cane and hat on the ground, and without looking at anyone or saying anything, he throws himself into it headfirst. The guards were saying, "He acted so fast that there was no time to do anything." One of my cellmates had seen him, too, headfirst...I don't know. Maybe the old man was afraid he'd change his mind, or that he'd miss the chance and they'd stop him. The sewage ditch wasn't very deep, but he threw himself in headfirst. Headfirst! And into a...you know what I mean?

The Wolf

TRANSLATED BY
PAUL LOSENSKY

Thursday noon I was informed that the doctor had returned and that he was sick now too. There was nothing the matter with him. The doorman at the clinic had said that he had slept straight through from last night until now, and when he awoke, he just wept, choking on his sobs. Usually on Wednesday or Thursday afternoons he set out and went to the city with his wife. This time too he had gone with his wife. But when the truck driver had brought the doctor, he had said, "Only the doctor was inside the car." It seems he was numb from the cold. He had left the doctor at the door of the coffeeshop and gone on. They found the doctor's car in the middle of the pass. At first they had thought that they would have to hitch it to a car or something and tow it to the village. They had gone with the clinic's jeep to do this. But when the driver got behind the wheel, and several others pushed, the car moved. The driver said, "It's because of last night's cold—otherwise, there's nothing the matter with the car." Since there wasn't even anything wrong with its windshield wipers, no one thought of his wife until the very moment the doctor said, "Akhtar, so where is Akhtar?"

The doctor's wife was short and thin, so thin and pale that it seemed as if she'd collapse any minute. They had two rooms in the clinic. The clinic is on the far side of the cemetery, that is, exactly one block away from the settlement. His wife was no more than nineteen years old. At times she would appear in the passageway by the clinic door or behind the windowpanes. Only when it was sunny would she leave the side of the cemetery and walk about the village. She usually had a book in her

---

This story was first published in *Stories from Iran: A Chicago Anthology 1921-1991*, edited by Heshmat Moayyad (Mage Publishers, 1991).

hand and sometimes a packet of sugar candy or even chocolate in the pocket of her white blouse or in her handbag. She loved the children very much. For this reason, she usually came out along the path to the school. One day I suggested to her that if she wished, we would be able to assign a class to her; she said that she didn't have the patience to deal with the children. The truth of the matter is that the doctor had suggested it to keep his wife occupied. At times, too, she would go to the canal bank together with the women.

After the first snow fell, she disappeared. The women would see her sitting beside the heater reading something or pouring tea for herself. When the doctor would go to pay calls in other villages, the driver's wife or the doorman would stay with the lady. It seems Sediqeh, the driver's wife, understood first. She had told the women, "At first I thought she was worried about her husband because she'd start suddenly, go up to the window and pull back the curtains." She would stand next to the window and gaze into the white, bright desert. Sediqeh said, "When the wolves start howling, she goes up to the window."

Anyway, in the winter, if the snow falls, the wolves come closer to the settlement. It's the same way every year. Sometimes a dog, a sheep, or even a child would disappear, so that afterwards the villagers would have to go out in a group to find, maybe a collar or a shoe, or some other trace. But Sediqeh had seen the wolf's glistening eyes and had seen how the doctor's wife stared at the wolf's eyes. One time she didn't even hear Sediqeh call out to her.

After the second and third snows fell, the doctor was unable to visit the outlying area. When he saw that he would have to stay in his house four or five nights a week, he was ready to join in our social rounds. Our get-togethers were not for the women, but, well, if the doctor's wife came, she'd be able to join the women. But his wife had said, "I'll stay home." Even on the nights when it was the doctor's turn to host the get-together at his house, his wife would sit next to the heater and read a book, or would go up to the window and look at the desert or, from the window on this side of the house, look at the cemetery and, I think, the bright lights of the village. It was at our house, I believe, when the doctor said, "I must go home early tonight." Apparently he'd seen a big wolf in the road.

Mortazavi said, "Perhaps it was a dog."

But I myself told the doctor, "Wolves are often seen around here. You have to be careful. You should never get out of the car."

My wife, I think it was, said, "Doctor, where is your wife? In that house next to the cemetery?"

The doctor said, "That's why I must go early."

And then he said his wife was fearless. And he admitted that one night, at midnight, he had wakened with a start to see her seated next to the window on a chair. When the doctor called out to her, his wife said, "I don't know why this wolf always comes up, facing this window."

The doctor had seen the wolf sitting right on the other side of the fence in the dim light of the moon and howling occasionally at the moon.

Anyway, who would have thought that a wolf, large and solitary, I believe, sitting opposite the window and staring, would little by little become a problem for the doctor and for all of us besides. One night he did not come to our get-together. At first, we thought his wife had fallen sick, or the doctor at least, but the next day his wife came herself to the school in the office car and said that, if we would give her the children's drawing class, she was ready to help.

The truth of the matter was, there were so few students that there was no longer any need for her. When we gathered all of them in one class-room, Mr. Mortazavi alone was sufficient to handle them. But, anyway, neither Mortazavi nor I could draw well. We settled on Wednesday morning. Later I brought up the matter of the wolf and said that she shouldn't be afraid, that if they didn't leave the door open or go outside, for instance, there was no danger. I even said that if they wished they could come to the village and take a house.

She said, "No, thank you. It's not important."

Then she admitted that at first she was frightened, that is, that one night when she heard the sound of it howling, she felt that it must have jumped over the fence and was just then sitting behind the window, per-haps, or the door. When she lit the lantern, she saw its black form leap over the fence and then saw its two glistening eyes. She said, "They were exactly like two burning coals." Then she said, "I myself don't know why, when I see it, see its eyes or that stance...you know, it's exactly like a German shepherd, sitting upright on its front legs and staring for hours at the window of our room."

I asked, "So, why do you?"

She grasped my meaning and said, "I told you, I don't know. Believe me, when I see it, especially its eyes, I can no longer budge from the window."

We talked of wolves in general, I believe, and I described for her how, when wolves get very hungry, they sit in a circle and stare at one another for hours, that is, until one of them rolls over out of exhaustion; then the others pounce on it and eat it. I also talked about the dogs that get lost occasionally, and only their collars are found. The doctor's wife talked about them too; it seems she had read Jack London's books. "I now know wolves well," she said.

The next week when she came she drew a flower or a leaf for the children, I believe. I didn't see it, just heard about it.

It was a Saturday when I heard from the children that they had set a trap in the cemetery. At the third bell, I went myself with one of the children and looked. It was a big trap. The doctor had bought it in the city and put a side of beef in it. Later that same afternoon, my wife informed me that she had gone to look for the doctor's wife. She said, "She's not doing well." She said, I believe, that the doctor's wife had told her that she was afraid she would not have children.

My wife had consoled her. They had been married for a year. Then my wife brought up the subject of the trap and said, "They're usually skinned here and the skins taken into town." My wife said, "Believe me, all at once her eyes opened wide, and she began to tremble and said, 'Do you hear? That's its very call.' I said, 'Really, madam, now, at this time of day?'"

It seems the doctor's wife ran to the window. It was snowing outside. My wife said, "She pulled back the curtains and stood next to the window. She completely forgot that she had a guest."

The next morning the driver and a few farmers went to inspect the trap. It hadn't been touched. Safar said to the doctor, "It certainly didn't come last night."

The doctor said, "No, it came. I heard its call myself."

To me he said, "This woman is going crazy. Last night she didn't sleep a wink. She sat next to the window all night long and looked at the desert. At midnight, when I was wakened by the wolf's call, I saw my wife fiddling with the door latch. I screamed, 'What are you doing, woman?'"

Then he told me she had a flashlight, switched on, in her hand. The doctor turned pale, and his hands were trembling. We went together to inspect the trap. The trap was intact. The side of beef was still in place. From the footprints, we realized that the wolf had come up to the side of the trap and sat right next to it. Then the trail of footprints went straight up to the fence around the clinic. I saw the woman's face at the window. She was looking at us. The doctor said, "I don't understand. You at least say something to this woman."

The woman's eyes were wide open, staring. Her pale skin had become paler still. She had gathered her black hair together, and it spilled down over her chest. She seemed to have no makeup other than eyeshadow. If only she had at least put lipstick or something on her lips so that they wouldn't be so white! I said, "I've never before heard of a hungry wolf passing up all this meat."

I also described the footprints for her. She said, "The driver said it wasn't hungry. I don't know. Perhaps it's just very intelligent."

The next day they brought news that the trap had been pulled up. They had followed the trap line. They had found the wolf; it was half alive. They killed it with a couple of shovel blades. It was not all that big. When the doctor saw it, he said, "Praise God." But the doctor's wife said to Sediqeh, "I saw it myself this morning at the crack of dawn sitting on the other side of the fence. This one that they caught was surely a dog or a badger or something."

Perhaps. It's not unlikely that she said these very words to the doctor, for the doctor was forced to get the police. One or two nights afterward, policemen stayed in the doctor's house. It was the third night when we heard the sound of shots. The next day, when the police and several farmers, together with the clinic driver, followed the trail of blood as far as the hill on the far side of the settlement, they saw wolf tracks and a disturbed patch of snow in a ravine behind the hill. But they had been unable to find even a single piece of white bone. The driver said, "The godless bastards, they even ate the bones."

I didn't believe it myself. I said so to Safar. Safar said, "When the lady heard about it, she only smiled. The truth of the matter is that the doctor himself told me to go and inform her. The lady was sitting next to the heater and seemed to be drawing something. She didn't hear the knock on the door. When she saw me, the first thing she did was turn her paper over."

There's nothing special about the woman's drawings. She'd drawn only that wolf. The shining red eyes on a black page, a black ink sketch of the wolf sitting, and one too of the wolf howling at the moon. The wolf's shadow was greatly exaggerated, in such a way that it covered the entire clinic and cemetery. One or two as well are sketches of the wolf's muzzle, greatly resembling a dog's muzzle, especially the teeth.

On Wednesday evening the doctor went to the city. Sediqeh said his wife was ill. The doctor had told her so. I didn't believe it. I myself had seen her Wednesday morning. She came on time and taught the children drawing. She drew one of those same sketches of hers on the blackboard. She told me so herself.

When I asked her, "But why a wolf?" she said, "However much I wanted to draw something else, it wouldn't come to me. I mean, when I put the chalk to the board, I drew it automatically."

It's a pity that the children erased it when the bell rang for recess. In the afternoon, when I saw one or two of their drawings, I had expected the children wouldn't be able to draw it properly. But in the event, the children's sketches, all of them, turned out to be just like German shepherds, with ears drawn back and tails that wrapped around their haunches.

Thursday noon when I found out the doctor had returned, I thought surely he had left his wife overnight in the city and gone back to work. Still, he had no patients, that is to say, none had come from the other villages. But, anyway, the doctor is a responsible man. Later, when he went to look for Akhtar, everyone went to the pass in the doctor's car and the clinic jeep. The police went too. They found nothing.

The doctor, though, didn't say a word. When he woke up, if he wasn't weeping, he just stared at us, one by one and with his wife's wide open, staring eyes. I had to give him a couple of tumblers of arrack so he would start talking. Perhaps he didn't want to talk in front of the others. I don't think they'd had a quarrel or anything. But I don't know why the doctor kept saying, "Believe me, it's wasn't my fault."

When I asked my wife, and even Sediqeh and Safar, none of them remembered the wife and husband ever having raised their voices to one another. But I had told the doctor not to go. I even told him that there would surely be more snow in the pass. Perhaps the doctor was right, I don't know. Finally he said, "She's not well. I don't think she can stand it here. But after all this, why these pictures?"

Later I saw them. She had drawn several sketches of wolf paws, one or two of their drooping ears. I said, "I believe...."

The doctor was not able to speak properly. But I gathered that snow was falling heavily in the middle of the pass, so that it covered all the windows. Then the doctor noticed that the windshield wipers were not working. He had had to stop. He said, "Believe me, I saw it, I saw it with my own eyes, standing in the middle of the road."

Akhtar had said, "Do something. We'll freeze to death here."

The doctor said, "Don't you see it?"

The doctor even put his hand out through the window, thinking he might wipe the snow off with his hand, but he saw there was nothing he could do about it. He said, "You know yourself that it isn't possible to turn around there."

He was right. Then, the motor shut off, I believe. When Akhtar shone the flashlight beam about, she saw that the wolf was sitting right at the side of the road. She said, "It's the same one. Believe me, it's completely harmless. Perhaps it's not a wolf at all, maybe it's a German shepherd or some other dog. Get out and see if you can fix it."

The doctor said, "Get out? Don't you see it?"

Even as he said this, his teeth were chattering. He turned pale, exactly the same sickly color of his wife's face when she stood behind the window and looked at the desert or at the dog. Akhtar said, "Should I throw my purse out for it?"

The doctor said, "What good would that do?"

She said, "Well, it's made of leather. Besides, while it's eating the purse, you can do something about it."

Before she threw her purse, she said to the doctor, "If only I had brought my fur coat."

The doctor said to me, "Wasn't it you who said that you shouldn't go out or open the door, for instance?"

When Akhtar threw her purse, the doctor did not get out. He said, "By God, I saw its black form, standing there at the side of the road. It wasn't moving or howling."

Then when Akhtar turned the flashlight to follow her purse, she couldn't find it. Akhtar said, "Well then, I'll go myself."

The doctor said, "Why, you don't know anything about it," or perhaps he said, "You can't fix it." But he remembered that before he knew it, Akhtar had gotten out. The doctor did not see her, that is to say, the snow prevented him. He did not even hear the sound of her scream. And then, I believe, out of fear, he shut the door, or Akhtar shut it. He didn't say.

Friday morning we started off again in a group from the village. The doctor did not come. He couldn't. It was still snowing. No one expected us to find anything. It was white everywhere. We dug everywhere we could think of. We found only the leather purse. On the road, when I asked Safar, he said, "There's nothing wrong with the windshield wipers."

Me, I don't understand. After all this, when Sediqeh brought the pictures for me, I was still more confused. A hastily written note was pinned to them, saying something like "As an offering to our school." When she was about to go, she entrusted them to Sediqeh, saying that if she didn't get better or if she couldn't come on Wednesday, she was to give the drawings to me so that we could use them as a model. I couldn't tell Sediqeh, or even the doctor, but after all, what appeal could sketches of dogs, such ordinary mutts, have for the village children?

My China Doll

TRANSLATED BY

FATMA SINEM ERYILMAZ

Mommy says he's coming back. I know that he's not coming back. If he were coming back, Mommy wouldn't be crying, would she? I wish you'd seen him. No. I wish I hadn't seen him either. Now, you be Mommy. What am I supposed to do if your hair's blond? Look, Mommy was seated this way! Place your feet together! Put your hands on your forehead! No, not like that. Her shoulders were trembling, like this. The newspaper was in front of her on the floor. I can't cry like Mommy. Daddy could. If Uncle Naser wants, he can, too. That's why grown-ups are grown-ups. They can say, "Don't cry, Maryam." Or say, "Why are you picking up the matches, child?"

OK, I picked them up to pick them up. I don't really want to light them, do I? Daddy is nice, he never said, "Don't do that!" But then why did he say, "I don't want to see my Maryam cry!"? I want to cry, but I know I can't. I mean, if I could cry like Mommy for Daddy, I would. I just can't. Do dolls also cry? I know that you can't, like Mommy, like Grandma, like Uncle Naser. If you can, then why didn't you cry when that little devil Mehri broke my doll? I'm talking about my china doll. You were sitting just like now and watched her do it. Did you see how much I cried? Grandma said, "Don't cry, Maryam, I will take it myself to the china shop to have it repaired."

I said, "Then what's going to happen?"

She said, "It's going to be like it was before."

I said, "I don't want it, I don't want it. It'll be like our big tea-pot."

Daddy said, "If my daughter doesn't cry, Daddy's going to buy another one for her, a bigger one."

He didn't buy it. Daddy's nice. If he came back, I'm not gonna say, "Buy me one." I'm not gonna cry, either. Do you remember how much Grandma cried? I told you already. In her black dress she fell on Grandpa's grave and cried. I also cried. Daddy didn't cry. Maybe he cried, like dolls do; like you do, when nobody sees your tears and no one hears a sound. I can't cry like that. You can't even believe how much I cried. Later, I realized Grandpa won't stretch out his cane any more. He used to say, "My dear Maryam can you tell me, how long is my cane?"

I said, "Seven spans, Grandpa."

He said, "No, five."

I said, "Seven."

He said, "Ten and a half and the size of your little finger."

I said, "No, seven."

He said, "Measure it, measure it yourself."

So I did. He didn't think I could do it until my hand reached the handle of his cane, then he grabbed me by the wrist and sat me on his knee. It was just what I wanted. I put my hand in the pocket of his vest and took off his watch. Grandpa opened its lid and held it up to my ear. I said, " Your hands are so old, Grandpa."

He said, "Well, just old."

His hands, the back of his hands were funny, like his face. He used to say, "It's all their fault, my dear."

He was talking about the hands of his watch; he was talking about the red one that always ran faster than the other. Where's his watch now? Is it buried with Grandpa in the ground? You wouldn't know. And you, Dwarf? You be that same little guy. Always coming and going! Slowly, go over there, now come back over here; don't move so fast back and forth, you'll make me dizzy, all right. Daddy was over there. I didn't recognize him. Dwarf, you stay here, I mean keep going there and coming back. Mommy had taken me by the hand. She said, "What are you going to do with the matches, dear?"

"I don't know," I said.

But now, I know. I put them side by side. One here, one there…like this. Mommy and I'll be on this side of the matches. And Daddy on that side, on the other side of the matches. Dwarf, you go in the middle. Now, we, here on this side, have to keep screaming. The people on the other side of the matches have to scream, too. Daddy shouted, "How is my little Maryam? Let me see you blow a kiss to Daddy."

Now you, Dwarf, come here, by my side, over here. So Daddy can't see I'm blowing a kiss to him. Daddy said…I don't remember what he said. Mommy had taken me by the hand, like this. Daddy said, "My little daughter shouldn't cry, OK? Daddy is doing well."

Daddy didn't look like Daddy. Like the dwarf, who also doesn't look like Daddy at all. If that little devil Mehri hadn't broken the china doll, I would have put her there now, in Daddy's place, next to those others on that side, next to my Daddy. Mommy said, "Now, don't say 'where is my china puppet?' OK."

I said, "Mommy, then where is Daddy?"

She said, " He is over there, darling. Behind that man. He is coming over. Don't you forget now."

It wasn't Daddy; he looked funny. From his smile, though, I recognized that Daddy was Daddy. Then Daddy said, "Let me see Maryam blow me a kiss."

I've already said that. After that he didn't say anything more to me. He talked to Mommy. Now the china doll is supposed to say, "Esmat, I will not see you disgrace yourself before them."

The china doll is supposed to shout and talk and keep pointing at the dwarf. Now you say, "Then what's going to happen; what's going to happen to you?"

Then Daddy said, "What? What's going to happen? It's all clear from now on. There is no charity distribution in here. But whatever happens, you mustn't let the child grieve."

He was talking about me. After that I don't know what Mommy said. He screamed. Everybody screamed. There was such a clamor; they all let out such cries that…it was like when that little devil Hassan blows his trumpet.

No matter how much Grandma shouts no one can hear what she says, either.

Now you say, "Esmat, dry your tears. I don't want them to see you cry." You must point at the dwarf again. I didn't see Mommy crying. I said, "Mommy, I want you to hold me in your arms."

Mommy said…I don't know what she said. I don't remember. It wasn't that I was tired. I just wanted to see if she was crying so that I could start crying myself. Mommy dried her eyes, like this. Now you, Dwarf, stand in front of us, in front of me and my mother, and all of these people, who are over here. Stretch out your hands, like this. Now say in a loud voice, "Ladies, the time is up, please leave."

Now turn around to Daddy and to the others and speak. Say something, say something so that they all go away, that Daddy too goes away. Daddy had grown thin. But he was smiling, like when he hugged me or when he tickled me under my arms, exactly like that. But now I can't laugh. Uncle Naser pulled that brat Mehri's ear and said, "Child, what do you want from Maryam's dolls?"

Well done. If the china doll still existed, if Mehri hadn't broken her, right now she would turn around and wave. I must also wave, like this. After that I must also cry. Daddy wanted to come. He couldn't. You, Dwarf, go over there, and stop Daddy. Mommy said, "Didn't Daddy tell you not to cry?"

I wanted not to cry. I always listen to Daddy's words. If he comes back, even if he pulls my ear, like Uncle Naser, I won't cry. I'll never hit Daddy, either. He used to say, "Hit me!"

I slapped him on the side of his face. He laughed. He said, "Hit me harder!"

I hit him, once on this side, once on that side, just like this. Dwarf, but you fall down. Daddy didn't fall down. Get up now. I'll hit softly, with only a finger, I'll hit Daddy like that, if he comes. Maybe I hurt him. Grandma said all the time, "Dear God, now what's going to happen to my son, if what they say is true?"

I said, "What are they saying?"

Mommy said, "Grandmother, please, in front of Maryam!?"

Mommy is bad, not all the time; only when she doesn't let Grandma speak, about Daddy that is. She is bad when she says loudly, "Grandmother, please!"

She also says the same thing when Grandma cries. But once she herself broke down and cried; she cried in front of me. When Uncle Naser came...Dwarf, you be Uncle Naser. Come here. When you come in the house, you're supposed to stay right here. Come in, take this paper in your hand, it's the newspaper. Mommy said, "Now that you want to, open the door yourself."

Dwarf, now when you see Mommy, you have to bend down your head like this.

Hit yourself, too, hit yourself hard. But you can't do it. You have to hit your head hard, with both hands, and squat on the floor, like me, no, like Mommy. Squat and say, "Brother, what a grave misfortune has befallen us!"

Dwarf, give her the newspaper.

Mommy turned the newspaper upside down. Mommy's hands were shaking. She said, "Where is it, then?"

Uncle Naser hurried to Grandma's room. Now you read. I don't know what. Say something, like when they talk on the radio, or on Uncle Naser's television, they just sit there and talk. Mommy said, "They are reading something; look how they always lower their eyes."

You can't see it. Maybe. Mommy doesn't lie. Or she does; didn't she say, "Your Daddy went to Abadan to buy you a doll; as you know, here there aren't any"?

Uncle Naser said, "I'll buy her one myself."

I said, "I don't want one."

Of course I want one. If Daddy buys it…if he comes back. He isn't coming back. If he was, why did Mommy cry? She read and cried. They sometimes smile, too, when they read the newspaper. Like this. But now, I can't smile like them. Mommy can't, either. Uncle Naser came by my side, he patted me on the head and tousled my hair. You, Dwarf…no, I don't want you to touch my head. Uncle Naser tousled my hair in a funny way. I didn't like it. It's not that he messed up my hair, like that lady. The one who…all right, don't be mad at me, Dwarf, you're going to be the man now. Your desk is also here, a great big desk. On your desk there is, I don't know…all kinds of things. Mommy, Grandma, and I went in. Uncle Naser didn't come with us. He said, "You go ahead, I'll be right over there, waiting for you at the ice cream stand."

I said, "I'll also go with Uncle Naser."

It's not that I wanted any ice cream.

Then Daddy said, "Don't say that, don't ever say that."

Mommy said, "You should come with us; do you understand? Remember to say to the man: I want my Daddy."

Uncle Naser said, "Yes dear; when you return, I'll buy you two ice creams."

I said, "I want it now!"

Mommy said, "Maryam!"

You too say loudly "Maryam!" Grab my wrist and pull it. Then knock on the door, a big door. Now there is a head…. Come, Dwarf, look through the hole I made with my hand, at my Mommy, and also look at me. Now like Mommy you have to say some things so that I understand that you, Grandma, and I have come to see Daddy. Say it now. When the door opened, we went in. That same man said…I don't know what. He was big. He was taller than Mommy. He was also fat. Grandma said, "May God take me instead of my son."

She said it softly. Now Dwarf, you are that man; you are big and very very round, and you even have a mustache. Smile and say, "Please stay in that room."

After that a woman came. She was pretty, like my china doll. No, the china doll is Daddy; it's not here, so it's Daddy. That woman is really here. She was just like those women who speak on TV, no, who read from the newspaper and keep smiling. Mommy cried. That day when…that same day, I mean that day, you know. I already told you. The woman came and said, "Ladies, you have to excuse me."

Afterwards she also said some other things. First she put her hand on Grandma's chest. Grandma said, "Madam, but I…."

Mommy said, "Grandma, please!"

She said it softly. But her face was like when she said it loudly, just like when she wants to scold me. Now she doesn't scold me anymore. If she'd only scold me! Even if she grabs my hands and hits me on my knuckles a couple of times, I won't cry. Even when I took one of Daddy's books, she didn't scold me. She only took it from me and put it in its place. Now you say, "Maryam, my dear, you shouldn't take Daddy's things."

I wanted to say, "Daddy isn't gonna come back anyway." I didn't say that. I thought if I didn't say it, he'd come back for sure. If I touch his books, if I just tear one of them a bit, he would appear. He'd grab both of my ears. He wouldn't pull them hard. Only a bit. He'd say, "One day Daddy will cut his daughter's two ears and place them in her hands."

If I had been bad or wanted to go out with him, he'd say, "Now Daddy is going to come and pull both her ears and look his Maryam in the eye."

One day, however much he wanted to give me an angry look, he couldn't. Uncle Naser could. Not anymore. He grabbed Mehri's ear and pulled it. Daddy wouldn't. Then both of us started laughing. We laughed a lot. Then I also pulled Daddy's ears. Daddy's ears were small. When he was sitting down, I could grab them and look in his eyes. The woman sat down next to me, like this. She said, "May I, little lady?"

Grandma said, "Now, why her?"

Mommy said again, "Grandma, haven't you heard what the lady just said?"

Then the woman put her fingers in my hair. Mommy had braided my hair. She'd gathered and tied it at the top of my head. You can't even imagine how pretty I looked. Because of that the woman kissed me. Then she put her hand…look, now I am that woman. Good, if I put my hand under your skirt, will you like that? She also did it to Mommy…. Grandma, too. Grandma said, "God help me!"

Mommy didn't say, "Grandma, please." She should have said it. The woman said, "Little lady, you are very pretty. Do you go to school?"

Mommy said, "No, she's going next year."

What's it to her? I'll put my books in my bag. I'll make a bow with a red ribbon like the ribbon of Uncle Naser's Mehri and place it on my head, Mommy will do that. I can count to fifty. Daddy taught me. One, two, three, four…I can't do it now. Daddy said, "My daughter is going to be a painter. My daughter is going to sit right there, at her own desk and paint so that Daddy can do his work."

Then he sat at his desk and read. No matter how many times I said "Daddy!" he didn't hear me. Then when I cried "Daddy, Daddy!" he put down his glasses. He said, "What is it my dear?"

I said, "Look at what I've drawn, Daddy."

He said, "Let Daddy see."

Grandma said, "If you ever draw a picture of me, your Daddy is going to burn in hell."

She thought he would! Daddy laughed. He looked and laughed. He showed it to Uncle Naser. It was no big deal! See, like this, this is Grandma's belly. Well then, now this is her head, and these are her eyes. Her mouth has to be very big because she scolds me all the time. Daddy said, "Where is her nose then?"

I said, "Her mouth is so big that you can't see it."

Just like it is now, she doesn't have one. OK now, Dwarf, you sit down at your desk…and this is Mommy. Wait till I draw Grandma's hand. My hand was in my Grandma's hand. Now you, Dwarf, get up from behind your desk, come here, and smile. Say "hello" to Grandma and Mommy. Then bend down and pinch me on the cheek. Just like this. All right, it didn't hurt; but, well, I didn't like it, either. Dwarf, speak to me, say, "What's your name?"

With that huge mouth of hers Grandma is supposed to say, "This is Maryam, she kisses your hand."

Then a man brought tea. He didn't bring one for me. I don't like it anyway. Now Grandma is supposed to say something that I don't understand. Talk, but talk about Daddy. Say, "After all, Sir, whatever they may be, they are young. They've read some things…."

She was talking about Daddy. Mommy's face looked strange. Dwarf, you aren't supposed to see that. You are turned towards Grandma, and you have to hold your tea. Say, "Well, the rest is in their own hands. Whenever they come and…."

I don't know. He talked like the newspapers. I think he wanted Daddy to come, sit down like this, and look at his newspaper from the corner of his eye and talk like him.

Now you talk, like Mommy, talk about Daddy, say something that Grandma doesn't understand, either. Now Dwarf, say, "All right. Please come tomorrow. If you'd like, bring the child, as well. Perhaps he'll agree."

Grandma hit me with this part of her hand. I understood why she hit me. I lowered my head. Grandma hit me, she hit me hard. I looked at her. She made a strange face. You could only see her nose. Now I have to say to the Dwarf, "Sir, I want my Daddy."

The Dwarf is supposed to say, "You'll go and see him, my dear. But remember to say, 'Daddy, when are you coming home?'"

Mommy said, "If that doesn't work, then what?"

Dwarf, you are not supposed to understand that Mommy was talking about Daddy. Now say, "Well, make her do it, repeat it many times until she remembers it."

Mommy didn't say anything else. Grandma said, "She's talking about my son."

Dwarf, say…no, first put your hands behind your back and go towards your desk. Then say, "All right, all right, I don't know what else."

Now, Dwarf, we are going, Mommy, Grandma, and I. Come here. Bend down and say softly, "You haven't told me your name, pretty little girl."

Then you also say, "You come tomorrow to see your Daddy for sure."

Daddy wasn't there. Daddy didn't come. Now, I am supposed to say, "Mommy, why doesn't he come then?"

She said, "I don't know. It must be that Daddy doesn't like Mommy."

"Why not Mommy?"

You say, "Daddy is nice, my dear."

"No, he is bad, he doesn't like Mommy."

That's what I told Mommy. She didn't say anything else. She only wiped her eyes. Grandma didn't come. She couldn't. She was lying on her bed all the time and moaning. Grandma's legs hurt. Uncle Naser comes and sits down by her side and talks to her. He doesn't bring that little devil Mehri. When I come by Grandma's side, they stop talking. Now, Dwarf, you have to say…no, don't say anything. I'll be Uncle Naser and say, "It's tomorrow, Mother."

Grandma said, "If I could only see him! I am afraid to die and not see my son again."

Mommy said, "Don't say such things, Grandma."

She said, "I just know that I won't see him."

When Mommy saw me she stopped crying. She wasn't crying for Grandma. She was crying for Daddy.

Uncle Naser said, "They won't let anyone in. But still, one might be able to see him. My sister-in-law and I are going."

Mommy said, "Brother, please!"

She didn't say it loudly. Uncle Naser said, "You little devil, were you here?"

I said, "I'm also coming."

Now Mommy is supposed to say, "Maryam!"

If she hadn't said that they would have taken me with them. They didn't. Uncle Naser said, "If you're a good girl, I'll buy you a big doll."

Daddy wouldn't say, "If you're a good girl." He said, "What kind do you want?"

I said, "Exactly like the old one, actually I want the old one."

Daddy said, "If they put it back together, it'll look ugly."

Grandma is supposed to say, "Have you seen him?"

Uncle Naser said, "Only for a minute. He was doing fine."

I said, "Did he have hair on his head?"

He said, "Yes, my dear." He also said to me, "Uncle Naser must cut off Maryam's ears and place them in her hands."

I said, "He wouldn't say that. Now Daddy wouldn't say that."

Whenever Daddy said that, I'd put my hands on my ears and run away. Daddy would laugh and come running after me. Now Grandma must say, "Why didn't they let you in?"

Uncle Naser said, "It was surrounded; they weren't allowing anyone in."

I said, "What does 'surrounded' mean?"

Uncle Naser didn't say anything. It's OK, I don't care. I already know that there were twenty, no, at least fifty men like dwarfs. You stand there, Dwarf…and one also here…many others. The china doll was supposed to stand in the middle, if she were still here. Mehri threw her on the floor in anger. I know that she did it because she is mean. Uncle Naser said, "Tomorrow they'll write it in the newspapers, for sure."

Mommy said, "I don't think so."

Grandma said, "If my feet would allow me; if I only could!"

Grandma can't stand up anymore. If only she could! Uncle Naser and Mommy carry her by the arms. Like the china doll when both of her legs fell off. Her head was also broken. She was in three pieces. Daddy said, "Throw it in the garbage can."

I said, "But, is she dead, Daddy?"

He said, "Dolls don't die, my dear, they break."

I said, "No. They die. Dolls also die, like Grandpa."

I buried her myself. In the garden, I dug a small hole for her. I wrapped the remains in my white handkerchief, then I buried her. I even poured

water on the grave. Then I also cut a few roses and fluttered their petals
on the grave. If Grandpa were alive, he wouldn't have let me cut them.
The man sat next to Grandpa's tomb. He read some things from a book
that I didn't understand. He read quickly and moved his head from side
to side. But now, we don't have any red roses. We had some when Grandpa
was alive. Grandma said, "Then his sister came. She gathered his bones,
washed them in rose water, and buried them underneath the red rose tree.
He then turned into a nightingale, flip, flip, flip…." The nightingale went
and perched…I don't have the patience to explain it to you anymore.
Grandma doesn't have the patience, either. Uncle Naser said, "Don't cry,
Mother! He will stay there a few years; then he'll come back."

Mommy said, "How many years?"

You say, "How many years?" and then hurry into that room. I also
wanted to cry. I didn't. Then Daddy said, "Don't cry!" Daddy said, "No,
my Maryam must not ask for Daddy, not from them." He said it on that
day when Daddy didn't look like Daddy. He was like the china doll, like
when that little devil Mehri broke her. His face had become so strange.
Mommy was lying on the bed. Uncle Naser said something that made
Mommy speak. You say it. No, don't. Mommy said something bad.
Mommy is very bad; sometimes she's bad, when she talks to Uncle Naser
to spite him, when she talks about Daddy. Daddy was very big. He'd lift
me up and put me on his shoulders. He said, "My Maryam has to come
and stand on Daddy's hand."

Like this. He'd say, "Close your eyes!"

I'd close them. Then I'd go up, that high. He'd say, "Now open your eyes."

I was up, close to the lamp. Mommy told me. Haven't I told you already?
Uncle Naser saw me. If he hadn't seen me, he'd say, "What're you looking for here, child?"

After that they didn't say a word. If they'd said anything, if they'd talked
about Daddy in front of me, Daddy would have come for sure. The Dwarf
didn't let him. You hit him with these hands, eh? Daddy was like my china
doll. He was broken to pieces. You're bad. I'm also going to tear off your
legs. I'm going to break your hands. I'm even going to rip off your head.
I'm not going to bury you, either, like my china doll that I buried, underneath the red rosebush. I won't cry for you, either. But it's just that I can't
stop crying.

Portrait of an Innocent: I

TRANSLATED BY
FRANKLIN LEWIS

My Dear Brother,

I got your letter. It made me very happy. As for us, we have our health and no complaints, except that you are far away, and as for that, I hope we'll soon see each other again.

Well, everyone is just fine, and they all remember you in their prayers. The daughter of Kal Hassan's been betrothed to Asghar Fath Allah. Their wedding will probably take place before the month of Moharram.[1] Uncle's wife gave birth once again, this time to twins. She has seven girls now, not counting those two—may your life be as long as theirs were short. Mirza Amu is doing well. He supposes he's going to get to go to Mecca this year. Asghar's mother sends her greetings. I sent a package of quince to you, but you didn't mention it in your letter. If it hasn't arrived, write to me, so I can check into what wonders Abdollah may have managed to work this time! He said he had sent it for you through one of his acquaintances, but I can't believe it!

Two weeks ago, I wanted to send you a sack of rice, but I had a bad feeling about entrusting it to Abdollah. By the way, Abdollah couldn't even get up. Nothing had happened to him, but, well, his leg was swollen. It wasn't serious. When the Doctor saw him, he said it would get better. He wrote a prescription and we gave him the medicine, but it didn't get better. Hour by hour the swelling got worse until it looked as puffy as a cushion. He couldn't walk, not even with a cane.

None of this is important, but in order to make it clear for you—not because I want to go into it—but since here you write down that you've heard some things from here and there, and it's got you worried, I don't want you to be in the dark. Abdollah was not exactly on the straight and

---

1. Moharram is the first of the Islamic lunar calendar.

narrow, but even so, he was useful in the village. With that old broken
down vehicle, he'd haul folks' junk or taxi passengers about. And now,
well…how shall I explain it? One day he went into the fields. Now, whether
he was drunk or not, nobody knows. Maybe he was—maybe he had a
bottle of arrack and he went to the qanat[2] to down a couple of shot glasses.
And on the eve of Friday congregational prayers, to boot. Nothing wrong
with it—you know me, I'm no zealot –but well, after getting drunk, while
he was zooming along toward the village, on the road by the edge of the
cemetery, whether premeditated or not (that's on his own head!), he drew
eyes and eyebrows on Hassani with a piece of coal. He then put his own
hat on Hassani's head. He made a mustache for him with a handful of
wool, and what a huge mustache! If for no other reason than the mustache, I can't believe he was drunk. And what's with the wool? Surely he
had to have thought about it ahead of time. Let's say he found a piece of
coal somewhere—in an old hearth, maybe—but what is all that wool
doing in a body's pocket?

The next day people had found out about it. A few of them had actually seen him standing next to Hassani, fiddling with him. Surely you
remember Hassani? That old tattered overcoat's been hanging on him for
quite some time. The coat belonged to the village lord. With those two
arms and that tall, lanky frame, no crow, no bird dared to come within
shooting distance of the grounds around the ruins of the fort. To top it
off, someone, nobody knows who, killed two crows with some of the rub-
ble stones, smeared their blood on the collar and front of Hassani's coat,
and then hung the crows from his hands. So what need was there for
Abdollah to go and draw such big eyes for Hassani and make him a mustache that could be seen a hundred meters away? Of course, no one objected.
Everybody who saw it probably laughed and said, "Great job, Abdollah!"

But what about the children? You know what I mean? The kids, even
Asghar, not that he was afraid, but, well, if I didn't take him by the wrist,
even he would surely not have been willing to go all by himself within
ten feet of Hassani and see the masterpiece that Abdollah had made of
him. And that's my own kid's reaction. What of the other folks' kids, of
my students? Let's say in their case that we've always talked a lot about
monsters and demons and genies and fairies and all that in front of them.
Anyway, it's how they've been brought up. So when the wind blows through
Hassani's coattails, and those two crows open up like hands, well, you
can just imagine.

---

2. Qanats are man-made underground water channels. For thousands of years they
    have been used in Iran to bring water from the foothills to the edge of the desert.

But then what's Naneh Soghra's excuse? Naneh Soghra's no child anymore. It was at sunset on the next day, or maybe it was late afternoon on
Monday, when the rumor spread. She was passing by that direction, a
full-grown woman. She had picked some grass and was carrying a bundle of it on her head when she caught a glimpse of Hassani. Was it dark
or not? They didn't say. But just between you and me, it was getting dark.
And the woman was alone. It was too far from the houses for anyone to
hear her. They found her in the morning. Ali, the field watchman, found
her, next to the stream. No one figured out who had done it. Somebody
must have done it. You couldn't accuse Hassani of doing it. Whoever it
was had hung a wide belt—really wide—from the top of Hassani and had
put a skull in the wide pocket of his coat. Maybe the wind was blowing
and billowing his sleeves. Maybe it was making the wings and feathers of
those crows flutter. Even the hairs of that big mustache were moving. It
happened something like that, I'm sure. Otherwise, why would a grown
woman, after they revived her with vinegar and loam, start screaming and
swooning all over again as soon as her eyes fell on Hassani?

About now you'll be saying, "Why couldn't they just knock Hassani
over with a good kick and be done with it?" But don't you remember how
in many places they would set up a gourd, or a donkey skull, or something on the top of a stick? Or if they had recently scattered wheat or
barley seed, or when the black cherries began to ripen, they would send
a few kids into the field to shout and throw stones? Otherwise, the birds
wouldn't ever let the seeds take root and sprout and flower and bear fruit.
And as for the children? Well, their mothers don't mind to have something whose name they can invoke when the kids talk back or act bratty,
to win a spate of peace for themselves.

If only the snowball had stopped rolling right there. It goes without
saying that all the women stopped walking that route. Who'd have believed
it? The women had frightened the kids so much, they were themselves
seized with fear. They'd all go through the black poplar thicket and behind
the ford to get to the field. Then, and I know you won't believe it, but I
swear upon the setting sun in front of me, and this not in the dusky twilight of the dawn, but in the full light of morning, Taqi the Waterer—who
for a span of thirty years, by God, had been in the fields every night—
had come running toward the village. He was acting mad and ran straight
into someone else's home—this at a time when the wife of Mirza Yadollah,
with head uncovered, was standing by the oven. The poor woman was
pregnant, and all alone. Taqi ran into the middle of the courtyard and
said...or, maybe he didn't say anything. His tongue wouldn't budge. He

only said, "Oh, no!" That's all. Then he fell to the ground. Mirza Yadollah's wife miscarried that very night. Think about it—Taqi the Waterer, in the morning's light. I think the sun was already well up in the sky! After they huddled over Taqi and brought him to again, his eyes were like two bowls of blood. He was foaming at the mouth. When I saw him, there was hardly anything left of him. Just skin and bones.

I told him, "Come, Taqi, what the hell's happened to you? Be reasonable, man, what's wrong with you? You know you've caused the death of a child—and a boy at that."

He said, "Well, sir, I couldn't help it. I saw it with my own two eyes!"

"So?" I asked, "What about it?"

He said, "Oh dear, how can I explain it? It looked just like a ghoul, a desert phantom. It was running right after me along the highway. With a gun. I swear to God it had a double-barreled gun slung over its shoulder."

You see? He was completely irrational. When a few of us went out to the field, we saw Hassani right there in his place. And there was no gun, either. Even the crows had fallen to his feet. Believe it or not, we stood there, all of us, stood at a distance, watching. Do you get the picture? From a distance. His hands were moving. Just the hands. Taqi is a full grown man. It was daylight. Now listen to what happened to me. It's not something I heard from this or that person. That same night, I had already nodded off to sleep when the mother of my Asghar[3] woke me and said: "Listen, man! Listen!"

"To what?" I asked.

"Just listen," she said.

I knew what she meant. It was a godsend that our mother was sleeping in the storage closet. It's true that her sleep is light, but I didn't hear any sound coming from the storage closet. Maybe she was already awake, or perhaps had heard something before the mother of Asghar did. I sat up and listened. I heard nothing more than what you could have heard! But she had hold of me by both wrists and was shaking so hard that it made my hands shake, too. "Do you hear it?" she kept asking.

With all that, I could barely strike a match and light the lamp. I heard her teeth chattering. The chattering of my wife's teeth was the only sound I did hear. There was no sound, not even the sound of the dogs barking which you would hear all the way until morning on other nights. The roosters weren't crowing either. I picked up the lamp and headed for the

---

3. A polite circumlocution by which traditional Iranian men avoided saying the more suggestive word, "wife."

door. The door was shut—we had bolted both latches. The weather was warm, but even so, we had shut the door.

My wife pleaded, "For God's sake, don't open the door!" You know how women are—I wasn't afraid at all, but I thought the poor woman might faint on the spot. I went to the window and pulled back the curtains. There didn't seem to be anything there. I couldn't get the window latch open. It wasn't cloudy. No, it was clear. The stars were huge.

I said, "You see, there's nothing there."

But there was. I mean I thought that there must be something that was keeping the dogs from barking. And what about the roosters?

My wife said, "It's gone now. Since you turned the light on, I don't hear anything anymore."

"Then go back to sleep. Let's at least not give the kids a fright," I said.

My heart was pounding anxiously. I was thinking, God, God, at least let my own dog bark. He was sitting under the fig tree, half crouching, but standing on his forelegs. His ears were laid back, listening. His tail was still resting on the ground. A dog's sense of smell is strong. I knew it must not be a wolf. If there were snow, maybe, but...I called out, "Piri, Piri!" I said it softly, and that's why he didn't hear. Or maybe he heard, but didn't turn around or wag his tail. He was like a piece of solid stone, half crouching, facing the door of the house.

"Do you hear?" my wife asked.

"What?" I asked. "There is nothing there."

It was a godsend that my wife was sitting in the bedclothes. If she had seen, if she had come to the window and seen Piri, how he was half crouching and listening, she would certainly have made me do something. I closed the window. This time I fastened both latches. For my wife's sake I didn't close the curtains.

I said, "You see how superstitious you've become!" I turned the light low and set the lamp within arm's reach and lay down. Now I was just waiting, ears cocked to hear when Piri would bark. How long was it? God, I don't know. Thank God my wife fell asleep again. But I was awake the whole time. And then I heard. No, I wasn't imagining it. I hadn't gone all superstitious. It was just like a footstep. Not at all like someone was walking, though. It was more like the sound of someone hopping along on one foot. It was like the sound of a stump hitting the ground. Like the sound of a stump which had been covered in felt. The sound was not coming through the air, but from the ground, through the pillow. But through the air? Nope, it wasn't. When I lifted my head up from the pillow, I didn't hear it anymore. But as soon as I put my ear to the carpet, or even the felt under the carpet, I could hear it. There was a noise. It wasn't constant; sometimes I even thought it had stopped or faded in the distance, but after a few moments, no, a few hours, I could once again hear the sound of a felt-wrapped stump thudding on the ground. When I put my ear to the wall I heard it, too. I don't know when it was that the dogs all at once started. First the dogs of the next neighborhood up started barking, and then Piri. Piri was howling, howling as dogs do in bad omen, at a certain house or at the moon, and it makes a person shiver with the fear that the dog might have wind of something and that tomorrow or the day after, someone in that house will die. The sound didn't stop, but it was much softer, almost like it was gone. That is, I had sat up in the bed in order not to hear it. I wrapped the covers around me and sat there. But I was still cold. I wasn't leaning on the wall; I knew the sound was traveling through the wall. The dogs stopped making noise only at sunrise when the windows had turned bright with light.

At noon I got news, that is to say, the school custodian informed me that they found the village lord's daughter in the field. I don't think you'll remember her—when you left I guess she was not yet twelve years old. Now she is a full seventeen, no eighteen, years old. Nasrollah was saying that they found her at the feet of Hassani. She was lying there, that is to say she was asleep, with a bandana on her head, in the wheat that had just started to sprout. Her dress was not muddy. Of course, the ground was not muddy, but still, she wasn't even dusty. She had no shoes on her feet. When the men reached her, the village lord gave her a kick in the side. First she rolled over and then got up. She gathered herself together, looked at Hassani and then at the men. She didn't laugh, but Nasrollah was saying that she wanted to laugh, or something about her eyes made the men think she was laughing. Then she set out in the direction of the village. Narges was going in front and the men behind her. She wasn't running. But the men were walking quickly, especially the village lord, who was walking very quickly in front of everyone else. Maybe he wanted to catch up with his daughter, but he didn't.

After that, the next day, I mean, well, you know how people talk, I myself heard that, and I don't now remember from who, that the village lord sent for Naneh Kobra, the women's bath attendant. My wife said that Naneh Kobra said that Narges has nothing to worry about. I likewise thought that there ought not to be anything to worry about. I mean, looking at it rationally, it doesn't seem that anything could have happened to her. I suppose…. I don't know. As I said, I heard its footsteps. A few others heard them, too. Master Qorban heard them, but he said that he heard them in a dream, or maybe he was asleep when he heard them.

When he woke up he didn't hear them anymore. Even when he put his head back down on the pillow and tried to sleep, he didn't hear them. Maybe it was Naneh Kobra's fault that my wife said those things a week later. She swears that the neighbor's wife was finally able to unlock the sealed lips of Naneh Kobra. I didn't believe it and I still don't. It's true that for a couple months no one saw hide or hair of Narges in the streets or even in the public bath. I thought, so maybe she doesn't feel like looking people in the eye.

It was a month ago, I believe, that my wife said they had seen Naneh Kobra going into the field with the copper bath basin on her head. When? At sunset. She turned into the fort and went to the field along the cemetery. So who saw her? She said that she had sworn not to tell anyone. A week later she said she had seen the village lord's daughter in the bathhouse. She was as pale as yogurt. Her nipples were turning black. And then talk of this eighteen year-old girl was on absolutely everyone's lips. How could anyone believe it?

I myself saw her. Let's see, it was on the second or third day of school in the end of September. I lined up the pupils and gave the class monitor a ball and had him lead the class to the fields, on the other side of the *qanat*. A half-hour later, I set out to look after the kids. I was going along the highway not paying attention when I suddenly caught sight of Hassani. I saw there was a little mound or something in front of him, the size of two shovel-fulls of dirt. But it was, well, like the grave of a child. How much room does a two or three month-old embryo take? I was dumbfounded. And at sunset, a woman all alone. What guts Naneh Kobra has! You know I'm not as stout and sturdy as I used to be. Forty-three years is no small span of time. I knew that Hassani couldn't walk, to say nothing of following or chasing after me. I never even imagined he could be behind me. But, believe me, I wasn't sure of what was right in front of my face. This time I felt it wasn't in the ground, not vibrating in the ground, it was in the air, or coming through the air. I heard the sound of his footsteps vibrating in the air. To tell the truth, I felt I was hearing the sound of that felt-wrapped wooden foot beating in time with my heartbeat. The sound of my heartbeat was keeping time with the sound of the wooden footsteps. In such circumstances, even if you were still as stout and sturdy as in your youth, what good would walking faster or running do? Especially for me, since after running four or five steps, my heart starts beating hard. When I got to the other side of the qanat, none of the children were there. I was about to go back, but where? It didn't seem as though my heart would calm down even after stopping. When I sat down, they turned up, not in line, but singly or in small groups, here and there. Two of them were missing, too. The class monitor said that they had run back home. The class monitor was crying, his clothes were all wet. When he was about to jump over the stream, he had fallen in the water. What could I do, and with that damn sound of my heart? I lined the kids up. I lined them up in two rows this time and marched them back. We did not return by way of the cemetery. We went behind the thicket and headed for the school.

If you were here, you would believe how the wife of Haj Taqi, even after all the medicine and herbs she took in order to become pregnant, would go up to Hassani. How she would circle five times around Hassani and then pour three jugs of water in performance of the ritual ablutions, first over the head and on the right side of Hassani and then on his left side, and from there go to the baths.

And then, what about Abdollah? The day before yesterday, as he was coming from town with a few passengers, he makes a bet with them in the car, with one or two of them, or maybe they managed to get Abdollah's goat. And this is at night! They say that there was a bet for him to go and dig up that mound at Hassani's feet and get to the bottom of the business. He had a flashlight, too. Those two or three passengers stand by the cemetery, in the road. Abdollah sets out. They could see his silhouette. Hassani was visible, too. The wind had been blowing. Abdollah shined the flashlight right on Hassani. Hassani's mustache couldn't be made out from that distance, but the men could see both of Hassani's hands were moving. Abdollah was walking with the shovel over his shoulder. He went up to Hassani, right up to Hassani. Where does he put the flashlight? It's not clear. But everyone could see that Abdollah was in the light. Not Hassani. They see Abdollah bending over and standing up a few times, then no one can see what he's doing. It goes dark and suddenly they hear him shouting. He wasn't shouting, no, he was screaming just like women do. What could they have done about it? It's obvious that no one dares to go forward. Meanwhile, Abdollah is screaming, by this time he's actually just moaning. When they told us about it and we went off to the fields with lanterns, we saw Abdollah lying on one of the graves, not far from the village. He still had the shovel in his hand. Two toes of his right foot were chopped off and he had no shoes on. Why? We never found out. His shoes were on Hassani. That is to say, they were there, under Hassani's overcoat. You could only see the toes of the shoes sticking out. The flashlight was in Hassani's pocket. It was turned off. Hassani was standing there. He had two feet. The little pile of dirt hadn't been touched. I think that they had piled it back up and smoothed it out, like a grave, like a little grave. Abdollah is a country boy. You can't say that he didn't know how to use a shovel. So, why was he pushing off on the shovel with his left foot? What about his shoes? You can dig better with shoes on your feet. Why had he taken his shoes off? That mound of two shovels full of dirt wasn't anything that would take such a long time to dig up. But it is mostly the shoes, the problem of the shoes, that stumps a person. Maybe he took the shoes off after he sliced through his toes? Or maybe they had to chop his toes off and that's when they took the shoes off. When? No one even bothered to look if there was a problem with the shoes or not.

The two toes of Abdollah were hanging on by the skin, barely. We could only staunch the bleeding in his foot. When the doctor came, he looked at the wound and bound it. But it was too late. His right foot swelled up like a cushion. Then his face swelled up so much so that you couldn't even recognize him. The doctor said, "We have to take him into town so they can amputate his right foot." Abdollah was shaking his head. No one wants to walk around on one foot. He just shook his head. Why don't any of them talk?! I just don't get it. Yesterday his time ran out. This morning they took him out into the field and right near Hassani, exactly next to that grave—not grave, but that mound of two shovels full of dirt—they buried him.

Now, you can think what you want. Make up your own mind on the basis of the stories you hear from here and there. But as for me, I'm no child, nor am I like Naneh Soghra or like Taqi, who turned all superstitious. You know your own brother better than that! But as God is my witness, if I hear at this moment that I don't know who or when or where…. No matter who says it now, I would believe it.

It's true that Master Qorban and the village lord, as they were inscribing his gravestone and reading the Fatiha[4] and the funeral rites for him, they saw the wind blow off Hassani's hat and carry it away. But you know, it's not a question of his hat, or of that mustache which Abdollah, God rest his soul, made for him with the wool. Because if a hard wind blows this very night, in the morning people will certainly see that nothing is left of the mustache, or if it rains, even just a light sprinkle, his eyes will surely be washed off. No, I realize these things, but it's a question of the damn beating of my heart and the air, the vibration of the air, because whatever it is, it is in the air. Now I, right this very minute, hear those two patent leather shoes of Abdollah and I know that you, even you, hear it too, the sound of two large stumps of wood hitting the ground. Piri surely hears it, too, the way he doesn't make a sound and half-crouches on two feet, with his ears laid back, and makes out that strange but familiar scent with his sharp sense of smell.

I'll write more for you. My wife and children say hello.

---

4. Fatiha is the first chapter of the Koran.

Portrait of an Innocent: II

SUNIL SHARMA

O *Imamzadeh* Hossein,[1] by the blood of your ancestor's throat, the time
and hour when Shemr[2] severed his neck from his body, I don't need anything. No, I don't want anything from you, just intercede for me with my
shameful face before your ancestor that he may forgive my sins. You know
well that it wasn't my fault. It wasn't for money, no, I swear on your head,
it wasn't. Actually, how can I say it, it was, it was for money. They were
offering me three sheep plus a hundred tomans.[3] They had made a collection. Five tomans and three rials[4] of it was my contribution. I sold a
chicken in order to come up with the five tomans and three rials. I gave
more than everybody. The headman Ali only gave three tomans. Do you
understand? I gave two tomans more. May it be sacrificed for your head;
money is nothing. Let me tell you from the beginning so that you know
what I went through, up to now, even last night. Yesterday I wanted to
come inside, before you. I had put my shoes under my arm, I entered the
door of the shrine with them under my arm and came inside. I came up
by the stairs. I had grown a beard. I had a felt hat on my head. I don't
have it now. I had pulled down the felt hat. Mash[5] Taqi was seated on the

---

1. *Imamzadeh:* A shrine dedicated to and named for a descendant of an Imam.
   Imam Hossein: Grandson of the Prophet Mohammad, younger son of Ali and
   Fatemeh (q.v.), and the third Imam of the Shiah. Hossein and his family and followers were massacred in 680 C.E. at Karbala, in Iraq, by an army of the
   Umayyad caliph Yazid (q.v.). This tragedy is commemorated annually in Iran during the month of Moharram.
2. Shemr-e Zeljawshan: The general who killed Imam Hossein (q.v.) in the Battle at
   Karbala; thus, a cruel and merciless person.
3. The principal unit of Iranian currency, comprised of ten rials.
4. The smallest unit of Iranian currency, ten rials comprising one toman (q.v.).
5. Mash/Mashhadi: Title of respect for one who has made the pilgrimage to Mashhad, the burial place of Imam Reza (q.v.)

bench by the entrance and was reading the Koran. He got up, his finger in the closed Koran. I don't want to trouble you with what I am saying, I know that right now you are sitting with your ancestors, in paradise, under trees next to flowing water clear like tears. They are all there, all the seventy-two persons [6] to whom may I be sacrificed, are there. I know that you are speaking of me, of your own alienation and dejection. What was I saying? I am telling you so that you know what I am going through. When I greeted him at first Mash Taqi did not recognize me and replied, "*Salam* to you." His voice was changed; it was quizzical. He had hennaed his beard. He said, "Salam to you. Are you a stranger?" After all, all strangers come here. From the time that you cured that blind man, and restored the health of the son of Gholam Hossein of Afjeh, everyone comes to kiss your feet. Some say, "No, it's not a miracle." Mostly the ones from Deh-e Bala, "upper village." But I know it is, I know that you can perform miracles. Many came from Deh-e Bala to kiss your feet. A month before that I understood that the people from Deh-e Bala also gradually became convinced that you perform miracles. When I sat down to have dinner, there was my wife Fatemeh and the two little children too. Suddenly I saw that there were rocks being thrown at the house. One struck the windowpane that shattered all over the room, another fell right next to Asghar. It nearly hit my child's head. I cried out, "You non-Muslims, unbelievers, I did not commit any crime. Why are you doing this?" It became more and not less. One stone hit Hossein right on his back. I have named him after you. I had vowed that if I had a boy I would name him after you. Now he is ten years old. I went on the rooftop. I was in such a hurry that my head struck the lintel above the door. May I be sacrificed for you. I was happy. I deserve everything that I go through. I saw several dark figures; they were moving down. They went down over Sayfollah's roof. They weren't kids. I figured it out from their dark forms. And all that in an unfamiliar place! After all, what did I have to do with Deh-e Bala? May my eyes be struck blind. I myself did it. I saw that if I went after them, if I made a hue and cry, it would make things worse. You know what happens when villagers bear a grudge against someone, particularly against me, an outsider…you know that. You know it very well. You too were in exile. You know what a bunch of villagers can bring upon a stranger's head. I didn't say anything. I came down. The next night nothing happened. On Friday many people from Deh-e Bala came to welcome you.

---

6. When the fighting began at Karbala, Hossein, it is said, had only seventy-two companions, eighteen of the family of Ali and fifty-four supporters.

In the middle of the night, we were sleeping in the yard when suddenly I saw rocks coming from all sides. They weren't small pebbles. They even threw some pieces of bricks. I realized that Deh-e Bala was not the place for me either. The next morning I took my wife and children by the hand and left for Khosrow Shirin. I sent a message to the headman Ali that I would sell my home and property in Deh-e Bala at half price, if he would like to buy it, by God. Do you know what he said in reply? I was in the coffeehouse in Khosrow Shirin. My children had fallen asleep on the benches in the coffeehouse. Fatemeh sat there weeping. Ali, the headman's son, came in. He didn't greet me. You know that villagers always say salam. But he didn't. He stood at the doorstep. I said, "So, what did your father say?" He said, "My father says that even if it were free it would be expensive. Nobody wants to be tied to your land." I deserve it. I deserve it, but, by your ancestors, what fault is it of the innocent kids? What crime have Hossein and Asghar committed? Asghar just turned three. At least they should feel sorry for them. I wanted to bring them to kiss your feet but was afraid I would be recognized. In the end Mash Taqi did recognize me. Khosrow Shirin was not the place for me either; they didn't accept me. Wherever I wanted to work, it didn't work out. In the morning, the coffee shop owner said, "Look Shemr, people aren't happy with your staying here. It's better if you gather your things and leave." Do you see? He called me Shemr, not even Mostafa Shemr. He didn't take any money from me, saying, "It brings bad luck. Spend it on your wife and kids." I didn't want to talk about these matters. Why not, I will tell you, I will tell you everything. If I don't tell you, if you don't know, who else should know? Forget about today, but what will I do on the day of resurrection tomorrow? On the very day that we wanted to put up an arch over the shrine, an arch for you, I had a hunch that I was in trouble. I carried mud for you. Ten men had come from Deh-e Pa'in, "lower village." It was fixed that each day ten people would come. But I went there myself. We had informed Ostad Faraj of Deh-e Bala. He is a capable man. It is said that his father's father built the dome of Baba Qassem. The tile work is the work of Ostad Faraj. When you performed the miracle we had moved to the village of Afjeh. We were there for four years. Then we went to Deh-e Bala. I told you that. But I didn't tell you why they kicked me out of Deh-e Pa'in. I was carrying mud for Ostad Faraj; two men were trampling it. I had vowed that I would be there everyday. It had been a week that I had been toiling for you. From morning to afternoon in the heat I carried mud. I also had two beasts of burden. The headman Ali came and stood over me. From his shadow I knew that he was standing over me. I was pouring the mud in a heap when suddenly he reached out and grabbing my wrist said, "Never mind, don't bother." I said, "I have made a vow." How could I have known what he meant? He said, "I know. You have earned a reward for yourself, now let the rest of the people earn it." I said, "What's it to them?" He said, "If you want to know the truth, people are not pleased that your hands touch the shrine." Do you see? This too from the headman Ali. Headman Ali said this. People are not pleased! The handle of the spade was in my hand. But I realized that it wouldn't be right. If I could answer one of them, if God would remove one of my sins, it would be a lot. Khaleq, Mash Taqi and Faraj were all standing behind headman Ali. There was nothing I could do. I dropped the spade, looked at the shrine and sighed. The first layer of the dome had not been finished yet. We had brought in a stonemason; I myself had gone to the city to get him. I went on foot to Deh-e Bala. Then I went to Khosrow Shirin. You know well what a distance that is. I waited two days till a car appeared. The stonemason was not willing to come. I convinced him. I told him that it was a meritorious deed. I told him that you were a *seyyed*[7] of the proper lineage. Then he agreed. When the headman said this—do you understand?—I went towards the village. The headman yelled, "Take these two animals also." Do you understand? After all, what wrong did the animals do? I came home. My wife was baking bread. She was wearing the red scarf on her head that I had bought for her in the city. With that same hundred tomans. I had also bought her a printed blouse. I ran to take the red scarf off her head. She had tied it with a knot and it didn't come off. As I pulled at it my wife fell down. I told her, "Give it to me, woman." She was looking at me. Like you, she was looking at me the way you looked at me. I held on to the scarf and my wife kept moving back. I pulled on the scarf to tear it up. It was new. How I had wandered around the city to find it! Her eyes were turning white and I realized what a wrong thing I was doing. I started thinking of you, of your alienation. All of me is thinking of you, those eyes of yours, in my dreams. No, I cannot say it. You yourself know better since every night you come to me. Sitting down, I undid the knot of the scarf and said, "Woman, who told you to wear this?" It wasn't her fault. She had no idea where the money for it had come from. I threw the scarf into the oven. Then when I looked at her I saw that she had retreated into a corner. She was wearing the blouse with the flowery print. I don't know what came over me. My wife screamed

---

7. Seyyed, one descended from the Prophet Mohammad, and thereby entitled to
   special respect and privileges.

and I ripped her blouse to shreds and threw it into the oven. She was screaming and screaming. The neighbors came up over the walls. When they yelled, "Hey, Mostafa Shemr, what's going on? What are you doing to your wife?" I saw that she was naked. She was only wearing a slip, and in front of all those strangers. I stood in front of my wife and shouted, "You infidels, what do you want from me after all?" I picked up a log and advanced menacingly towards them. They all fled. My wife was not crying, she only clutched her throat with her hands and kept looking at me. I said, "Get up and put something on." She said, "By God, have pity on me." But I hadn't done anything...no, I had. I had and now I have come before you. It is true that I am to blame; it is true that I am here shameful before you, before your ancestor, the noblest of the martyrs. But so are they, they who got the money together, made collections, bought sheep, and collected a hundred tomans. I also gave money; I gave five tomans and three rials. After all, I had not the least notion of what was going on. It was they themselves who stood here and watched, watched and wept. I, too, wept. You saw, yourself, how much I wept. Now they are blaming me for everything. They gathered together, saying, "You must leave here. We will buy your house and property. Go to Afjeh. Go to Deh-e Bala. Go to Khosrow Shirin. Go wherever you want but there is no place for you here. Aqa does not want you to remain here." Headman Ali went to Afjeh and bought land for me. He bought a house, from my own money. He bought it with the money from my own property. They didn't contribute a single *shahi*, "cent." The mud of your arch had not dried yet when we packed up and left for Afjeh. They postponed building the terrace. When I was in Deh-e Bala I had heard that they were building a terrace for you. They even built a pool of water. I had not heard that. Now nobody tells me anything anymore. I am sure they built it when you cured that cripple. It has fish. What big fish! They are fish from the canal. I had told them to build Aqa's tomb next to the canal. But you weren't there, you don't know it. Perhaps you will find out now. Now you know everything. You know how Mash Taqi looked at me when he recognized me. He got up and said, "It's you, Mostafa Shemr. Didn't we tell you not to come here?" I said, "I came to complain about all of you to Aqa." He grabbed my wrist. I tried to force my way in. I pushed him with my shoulder. I had four packets of candles in my hand. I didn't want them to fall out. I know they are dear to you, but I didn't do it purposely. Just as he grabbed my wrist they fell on the ground. He didn't let go of my wrist, no, he didn't. At that moment he began to shout. He kept shouting, "Hey, Faraj! Faraj, go out to the fields and inform headman Ali." He gripped the waistband of my pants. I said, "O God, by God, I must get in before you in supplication, whatever happens I must get in. If I had gotten in they wouldn't have been able to throw me out. I came towards the door. I saw your tomb. They had put in a lot of nice bars for you. This colored glass is nice too. How wonderful! The mirror-work on the pillars is great too. It is the work of a city craftsman. Now I can't see it. You can't see it with the light of only one candle. I must light another candle for you. Let me light it, let Mash Taqi find out. I made a vow. There are forty votive candles for you. I can light them four at a time, for the four corners of your grave. If you want to know the truth…well, you know the unseen. You can read the heart of this shameful one. I am afraid. I am afraid of the dark. But you know what Mash Taqi will do if he sees that the tomb is lighted. I hadn't even reached the tomb. My hand was about to reach it, when Mash Taqi also reached out for me on the floor. He reached out and shouted until a group of people rushed in. I didn't know who they were. They came inside with spades. They didn't even take their shoes off. You see that my head is bandaged. I didn't see who it was. He hit me on the head from behind. I was getting close to the tomb, Mash Taqi was holding on to my legs. I couldn't hit him. I swear to you that it was for you that I didn't hit him. I realized that they were inside. They yelled, "Hey Shemr, where do you think you are going? Didn't we tell you?…" I hadn't yet reached it, my hand hadn't yet reached it when something hit my head. In this very spot that is bandaged; it was hit by the back of a spade. I was still conscious. I saw the tomb. I saw the bars. I saw the mirror-work around the tomb. As I stretched out my hand I could only touch the mirrors with my fingers. I only saw blood in them. Mash Taqi was still holding on to my legs. I could still drag myself on the ground but he wouldn't let me. I was stretching my fingers over the mirrors that had become red when I was hit again. I was hit on my waist with the handle of the spade. Then they all began to hit me. They kept shouting and cursing and hitting me, and that too before the grave of the holy one. I had come to you for refuge, but the villagers don't forget. Then I don't know what happened. But I remember that my hand reached the tomb, even my face reached it. I rubbed my face against the mirrors around the tomb. I extended my hand to touch the stone, this very stone slab, so that I could grip one of the bars. I couldn't. My hands didn't reach it. Mash Taqi didn't let me. They kept hitting me. If my hand had reached, I wouldn't have let it go even if they had cut my five fingers. I don't know what happened next. After my hand reached the tomb, I don't know. You know better what happened next. You saw it all yourself. I had left my kids in Habibabad. I paid them thirty tomans to take us there. I have told you already that the people at Khosrow Shirin also didn't want to see us. They knew that too. They must have realized that you had performed a miracle. The news hasn't reached Habibabad yet, but I know it will reach there. I, who had land, a house, a life, a reputation, have now gone there, with wages of only three tomans a day. You know, with wages of only three tomans a day. Now I don't know what will happen. God help me if they find out. First they will say, "Mostafa." Then, the peddlers will remind them to say, "Mostafa Shemr." Then they will forget to say, "Mostafa." They will only say, "Shemr." Even if they don't tell them, even if the peddlers don't remind them, everyone will find out. My fate is written on my forehead. You have written it so that everyone knows it. When I regained consciousness I saw that they had thrown me next to the ruins of the fort. There was only a dog there; it was night. The dog was barking when I woke up. He had smelled blood. They had bandaged my head. There was also a lamp next to me with a bundle of bread and these candles. The candles were bloody. They are still bloody. I saw their dark shadows on the other side of the fort. I couldn't count how many there were; my head was muddled. You know yourself how many there were. I got up. One of them yelled, "Hey Mostafa, get going. You shouldn't be seen in this village." It was Khaleq's voice. Do you recognize him? The one who found you? The same one who informed people that there was a seyyed in Khan-e Mirza, a seyyed of proper lineage. He had seen you. He came to the villagers and said he could only be found there but it would cost a bit. They made a collection. I didn't have anything to give. I had no idea what they wanted it for. If I had known I would have blinded myself and given something. But no, I wouldn't give anything. If I had known, I wouldn't have given anything. I picked up the candles, just the candles. What did I want the bread for! The dog was barking. I opened the bundle and threw it in front of it. Your dome was visible from there. I didn't want to leave but I had no choice. They were standing there. If I had gone towards the village you know what they would have done to me. I picked up the lamp and set off. On the road I realized that the blood hadn't stopped flowing. It had soaked my whole body. I am sure the wound on my head started bleeding again when I jumped down the wall of the shrine. But let it flow. Is my blood redder than your blood, than the blood of your great ancestor, than the blood of those seventy-two people? When I reached the top of the hill I could no longer see their shadows. I had no strength left in my legs. I sat there on top of the hill. Again, Khaleq's voice was loud as he said, "Mostafa, hey Mostafa." The dogs kept on barking. There were a lot of them; all the village dogs were there. They hadn't reached the hill yet, but from their barks I guessed they would be getting to me soon. At that moment, I was alone, a solitary man with a lamp! I knew the stream had no water but I was thirsty. However much I searched I couldn't find any water. At one place, there were piles of hay and the ground was muddy. I don't need to describe this. Whatever I suffered I deserved. I am telling you this so that you may know. I am telling you so that you may know what I too suffered in exile. I am telling you so you can intercede for me before your ancestor. I soaked the waistband of my pants in the mud and put it in my mouth. My mouth was still dry when I heard the sound of the dogs on the hill. There were also two men there. They had come with a spirit lamp and were urging the dogs on. I took off. I passed the stream and realized that I would not be able to go over the hill up to the other side; I proceeded on the bank of the stream. They called out from behind the trees, "Mostafa, hey Mostafa." I threw the lamp on a stone. You know why. Then I made my way around the hill, and around the crops. I could still hear the barking of the dogs. Right there in the open, I lay flat on my back, weeping for my abjectness, and then for your abjectness, for the thirsty lips of your ancestor. I kept weeping like I am now. I again heard Khaleq's voice. It was his voice. But I knew they could no longer find me. I just wept. I wept for my children who were strangers in Habibabad. I wept for my wife Fatemeh. She too suffered a lot; she too had to listen to reproaches, in Deh-e Bala, in Afjeh, in Khosrow Shirin, in Habibabad. In Deh-e Pa'in when she had gone to the bathhouse, the women hadn't let her open her bundle close to them. They had turned their backs to my wife, to a woman who was in the last stage of her pregnancy. No one spoke to her anymore. When my Hossein was born no one came to her assistance. I myself helped deliver the newborn child and cut his umbilical cord. That same night I gave him his name. I called him Hossein in memory of your abjectness. Khaleq's voice did not stop. He kept on yelling. I saw their lamps. I said if my legs have the strength I will go. I will go farther, to a place by the canal of Deh-e Bala. Then I no longer heard their voices. I had lost consciousness. When I got up in the morning the sun was up. My fellow villagers were on the other side of the trees with their harvest. I went to the stacks of wheat. I took some grains from the ears of wheat and ate them. I knew it was unlawful. You yourself said this, you said this during the days of Ashura[8] that it is unlawful. You said that one

---

8. Ashura, the tenth day of the Moslem lunar month Moharram, when Imam Hossein and his followers were martyred at Karbala.

should not eat what belongs to others, one must not look at a strange woman, if you see a stranger help him in memory of Imam Reza.[9] I couldn't help not eating. For two days I hadn't even eaten a piece of bread. For your obeisance, I came on foot where there was no path for two days. I didn't even sleep at night. You had summoned me; if you hadn't I wouldn't have had the will. I lay there in the wheat until nightfall. The sun was hot, like noon on the day of Ashura. What can I say? You know better. I had made a vow. Don't grieve for me, may I be sacrificed for you. Just forgive me. I know you will forgive me. I climbed your wall and came up. But you will forgive me, you will forgive all my sins. Didn't you say that the prophet had forgiven the Jew who threw ashes on him, the messenger of God, everyday, and when he was sick the prophet had gone to visit him? Didn't you say that he forgave all the people of Mecca? Didn't he forgive the liver-eating Hend[10] who ate Hamzeh's liver?[11] His Holiness Ali[12] was also forgiving. I came towards the village. Next to the village, I lay low in the harvest until the lamps in the village were extinguished. Then I went along the cemetery. When the dogs barked my heart fell. I returned to the field and when their barking died down I set off again. I had no life left in me. I clutched the walls of the houses and went on. At one point, I saw Khaleq's dog above me on the wall of his house. It barked and jumped down. Then it stopped. I saw its shadow. It wagged its tail. Do you see? Khaleq's dog remembered me. Tears welled up in my eyes. I petted its head and wept for you, for my loneliness. I leaned back on Khaleq's wall. You know better that he was responsible for whatever happened. A dog has a character but a human doesn't. Now I ask you, by your ancestor Fatemeh Zahra,[13] tell me whose idea was it that the village needed an Imamzadeh? It was Mash Khaleq, wasn't it? So what had happened? They didn't want to be less than Deh-e Bala. They didn't want to all go there for Ashura. It all happened over the fight for the canal. When there was no water in the canal of Deh-Pa'in they said it was due to the canal of Deh-e Bala. When there was a fight, those two youngsters—Khaleq's son and Yadollah's boy—died in the skirmish. No one found out who

9. Imam Reza (d. 818), the eighth Shiah imam, is buried in Mashhad.

10. Hend, female cousin and supporter of the Prophet Mohammad

11. At the battle of Ohod (near Medina) Hend, as tradition reports, was so enraged that she cut open the body of the Prophet's uncle Hamzeh, a non-believer, and bit into his liver.

12. Ali (d. 661), the Prophet's cousin and son-in-law, his fourth successor and the first Imam of the Shiites.

13. Fatemeh Zahra, the daughter of the Prophet, wife of Imam Ali, and mother of Imam Hassan and Imam Hossein.

killed them. But when the headman, Mash Taqi, Khaleq, and the headman's son are present, they look and weep, of course, they know who the
killer is. A villager doesn't forget. They committed no crime. They wanted
their village to be prosperous and the canal to be full of water. They said
the land of Deh-e Pa'in was cursed, God punished it. Khaleq came and
found you. He came back and said, "In Khan-e Mirza there is a seyyed
who is an old *rowzeh khan*,[14] every breath of his is truth, he is a seyyed
of proper lineage." The villagers pooled their money together. I didn't
have any. They also gave money for your trip. They also gave you the
money in advance for your reciting the *rowzeh*[15] during the ten days, saying, "If we don't do this one month before Ashura, another village will
hire him." They planned ahead. Do you remember the pomp with which
they brought you to the village and carried you to the house of the headman? We men-folk had come to pay our respects to you. Do you remember
how I kissed your hand? I kissed it three times. You were seated up there,
puffing on a hookah. The headman was seated on one side of you, Khaleq
on the other. People kept coming and going. Each one was drinking tea
and then left. I had come too. Do you remember when I kissed your hand
you asked, "What is your name, Mashhadi?" I replied, "Your slave Mostafa."
You said, "What is this mustache that you have grown, Mostafa? You look
like Shemr-e Zeljawshan." Do you remember? Then they got Faraj's daughter for you. I remember your wedding night. You stroked your beard
which was dyed with henna. It looked beautiful. When they wanted you
to wear the bridegroom's clothes, you said, "Come on, I'm too old for
that!" Nobody listened to that. But they didn't play music. They didn't
play music for the sake of your ancestor. The women ululated. There was
also a game of sticks. I only came in once quietly and then left. I couldn't
bear to see it. If my eyes would meet your eyes...do you understand?
Khaleq was saying to me, "It is meritorious. Anybody who gets what he
wants will pray for you. Anyone who is healed, you too will earn merit.
Now think of our village as well!" My wife didn't know, she didn't get the
news. In the morning she brought some cream for you. When she returned
from seeing you she said, "Aqa, right at the beginning of the night...."
and then laughed. I laughed too. We didn't have bad intentions. I knew
that you had the ability. Faraj's daughter wasn't bad, she was pretty. You
must know with what fanfare the headman got her for his own son. I

---

14. A professional reciter of the stories of the early Shiah martyrs, especially those
    of Karbala.
15. Rowzeh, the recitation of the story of a Moslem martyr at a memorial gathering.

heard this when I was in Deh-e Bala. It was Faraj who went to the city and bought a helmet and armor of chain mail. The helmet was too small. But the chain mail was the right size. He also bought boots and a pair of red pants. We plucked some chicken feathers and put them on top of the hat. These are the same ones they hung on the standard of the *ta'ziyeh*s.[16] Do you see? There it is. The headman tied the straps of the armor. I was shaking. Khaleq said, "Mostafa, Mostafa!" My feet wouldn't fit into the boots. Hossein, the barber, shaved my face and my head, right to the roots. When he shaved the hair of my head the hat fit. But it was still a bit tight on my forehead. He greased the tips of my mustache and twisted them. When I looked at the tips I was afraid of myself. How could I have known? When I kissed your hand that day, three times, when I wanted to leave the yard the headman came behind me and said, "Don't shave your mustache. Let it remain this way. Aqa prefers them like this. I will send you some boiled rice tomorrow, eat it with your kids." The boots were tight, I told you already. The headman and Khaleq had to use such force to get my feet into them. They pressed the tips of my toes and the back of my feet. The headman said, "These are not feet, they are spades." He did not laugh. Nobody laughed. I was happy. Now that I have told you I was happy I feel embarrassed. I don't know, perhaps it was meritorious. They put a sword in my hand too. It wasn't really a sword. It had no hilt. It was only a blade. They had sharpened it and it was shining. Hassan, the barber, had sharpened it. When I had arrived at the headman's house I saw that he was seated in the hayloft and was sharpening it. I started shaking. Hassan, the barber, looked at me and said, "May God's power be with you." I wanted to turn back but Khaleq stood at the doorstop blocking my way, he said, "Where are you going, Mostafa? Are a hundred tomans plus three sheep too little? You can buy a piece of land. Right from my property, anywhere you like, with the right of access to water so that you will be free from serving this person and that. And think of the merit." I entered the room. You saw me, didn't you? Khaleq said, "First go and kiss Aqa's hand." I didn't want to come. The headman's son came after me. I was in the crowd. We were in the square beating our chests; I was beating mine harder than the others. Until then no one in our village had beaten his chest. We used to go to Deh-e Bala to beat our chests. I was beating my chest for you when suddenly I heard the headman's son calling, "Mostafa, Mostafa!" He was standing in front of Faraj's

---

16. ta'ziyeh, a dramatic enactment of the martyrdom of Imam Hossein and his 72 companions in 680 at Karbala; one of the Shiah rituals of mourning during the month of Moharram.

shop and calling out. He didn't see me, I went to him. He said, "Father says enough of the chest-beating. It is noon already." The people didn't know. How would they know? Everyone stepped back—from the time when the headman kept sending for me or had me sit next to him in the rowzeh, they were all respectful towards me. The people stepped back and I went up to the headman's house. I told you that I saw Hassan, the barber, who was sharpening the rusty sword. Then I put on the clothes. I feared the red pants the most. The helmet had chain mail on two sides. It was an iron helmet and was heavy. You know the rest well. Why should I repeat it? When I came inside, in the doorway, do you remember? You were seated up high with a glass of tea in your hand. It was tea sweetened with rock candy. There was a hookah in front of you. Khaleq was behind me. Tapping my back he said, "Greet him, Mostafa." You laughed. The tea was still in your hand. I was clenching my teeth. I held the sword behind the curtain of the room. I did not greet you. I have said this already. But you said, "Peace be upon you, Mostafa. It looks good on you." Then you glanced at the headman who was standing on your other side with his arms folded on his chest. Then you looked at Mash Taqi who was standing with his back to you, in front of the niche, bent over with his shoulders shaking. I was also weeping. But you didn't see it. You didn't see that like now I was shedding tears. I looked at the tips of my mustache, at my boots, and I wept. I couldn't clean them off, as much as I'd shined them, until at last they sent for wax from Mohammad Ali's shop in Deh-e Bala and polished my boots with it. When I looked at my red pants I clenched my teeth again. Khaleq tucked the cuffs of the pants into the boots. If Khaleq hadn't been standing behind me I would have left. The headman's son was also there. I heard him weeping. The headman said, "Mostafa, what are you waiting for? First of all go and kiss Aqa's hand." Khaleq pushed me, he even took my left hand and pulled me towards you. My feet wouldn't move forward. I came in front of you. I was weeping. I know you saw it. You saw that I was weeping. You said, "Mostafa, you shouldn't cry, my dear. You are doing this for merit." Do you remember? Do you remember that you said, "For forty years I have been reminding people of the alienation of my ancestor but I still cannot make them weep like you are doing. See how Mash Taqi is weeping." Then you said, "Now let me see what you are doing on this noon of Ashura. I want you to do something that will shake up the heavenly throne!" So I gripped my sword firmly and stopped weeping. You said, "Now you have become a real Shemr. Be strong! The more merciless you show yourself to be the more you will make people recall the abjectness of my ancestor. Don't you know that anyone who produces one teardrop from a person earns the merit of one big *hajj*?"[17] I was no longer shaking. I wanted to kiss your hand, to kiss your feet, but I stood right there in the center of the room, in front of you. Mash Taqi was crying and beating his forehead. You said, "Do you see how you are making people cry right now? From now on, when people see you with your pointy mustache, even if it is not Ashura they will think of my ancestor and start weeping." Then you put the hookah pipe in your mouth and began to puff on it. Khaleq was standing next to me. Mash Taqi wanted to leave but Khaleq grabbed his hand. The headman's son wasn't there. No, he wasn't. You glanced at the headman, then at Khaleq, then at Mash Taqi, and said, "Good, let's stand up, in fact, let us earn some merit. Be strong, Mostafa. If you start crying you will lose your wages. Be strong." Khaleq came forward, as did the headman, and both gripped your arms. You said, "Come on, I haven't become so old that I can't walk these few steps." They had lifted you up. I was watching. Your feet were not on the ground. They were bringing you towards me. You said, "I can do it myself. I can walk. By God, don't trouble yourself." I went to the side as they carried you outside through the door. From the terrace they carried you downstairs. I too set off. You were saying, "By God, don't embarrass me." When I reached the edge of the terrace they had put you down on the edge of the garden. Your turban had become askew. Your back was to me when I reached there. The headman's son also came before you bowing and gripped your feet. I didn't see him doing that. You saw it, certainly. I came closer. The headman's son made a sign to me, he looked at me from behind your shoulder and made a sign. I lifted your turban. The cloak had fallen off your shoulders. Khaleq said, "Why are you waiting, Mostafa? It is exactly noon time." When you turned around I saw your eyes. You looked. You looked at me, at the headman. The headman and Khaleq had grasped your hands. Khaleq said kicking me, "Why are you waiting?" I heard Mash Taqi weeping. He was crying like a woman. The yard door was shut. I took hold of your beard and brought the sword forward. Khaleq yelled kicking me, "From the neck, stupid!" Your beard was in my hand. I could see your head was turned up. I saw your eyes. Your hennaed beard was pressed in my left hand. Your eyes were wide open, completely. You were gasping for breath. You shook your neck and your chin trembled in my hand. Your lips did not open. You couldn't open them. I placed the sword on your neck. The headman wept. The sound of his weeping was loud. I

---

17. Hajj is the pilgrimage to Mecca.

did not hear the sound of Mash Taqi weeping. I pressed the sword behind your neck. Khaleq had said, "It would be better if you can do it with one blow." But it didn't work. I pressed and pressed. I let go of your beard and pulled back so that I couldn't see your eyes. I heard you saying with my own ears, "Strange!" I pulled back and kept pressing and pressing. Then when Khaleq and the headman sat down on the side of the garden, your head was in my hand. Blood was dripping from it. I realized that Mash Taqi was pounding his fists in my back. He was pounding hard but I was only looking at you, until the headman's son said, "Do you want water, Father?" He kept hitting and then stopped. The headman was still crying, as was Khaleq. Khaleq said between his sobs, "Put that severed head on the ground, you Shemr-e Zeljawshan, go away, get lost." I saw that you were still sitting on the edge of the garden. Your legs were shaking. Your hands were still held by the headman and Khaleq. Then I again saw the head in my hand, in my left hand. The sword was in my right hand. The headman said, "Go away, get lost. Go and take off those accursed clothes so that we can wash them." The head fell from my hand. I stepped back, looking at you, at your headless body. The blood was still dripping from your severed neck. Mash Taqi had passed out on the ground. I sat on the bench of the terrace. The sword was still in my hand. It was bloody. I threw it away. Then I took off the helmet and threw it away. The boots wouldn't come off, however much I tried. I wept and applied force. Then my eyes fell on the sword, I picked it up and ripped off the boots. Then I took off the chain mail and ripped up its strap. I couldn't take the pants off, not in front of you, there by the edge of the garden where you were lying. I remember your thin frame. Your ribs were visible. They had placed your head next to the neck. The headman's son poured water and wept. Khaleq also poured water. He did not weep, only poured water. Someone knocked at the door and the headman's son went to open it. It was Hassan, the barber, with a coffin on his head. He shouted, "Be quick. The crowd is coming this way. I told them that the seyyed had died." The headman's son said, "Come in now so that I can close the door." I came next to you. I dragged myself next to you and kissed your hands. Khaleq said, "Step back so that we can finish our work." I kissed them again. I was afraid to look at your head, at your severed neck. I only kissed your hands. The headman said, "Hey, Mash Taqi, come and help us." Mash Taqi wrapped the shroud around your body. The headman said, "Khaleq, your washing wasn't correct." Khaleq said, "Nobody washed their ancestor's body." Then they placed you in the coffin. I wanted to hit myself, I lifted my hand to strike the sword on my head but the headman's son grabbed it.

He grabbed my hand. People rushed in and grabbed the sword and threw me to the ground. The headman's son was sitting on my chest. I wish he had killed me. Khaleq said, "We should wash these and put them away for the *ta'ziyeh*. See how he ripped the boots up. I told you that this Mostafa is a bit stupid, but who listened to that?" I can't say anything more. My mouth, my tongue is dry. My head—but I know that you know everything. You know how much I cried for you, following your coffin how much straw I threw on my head. I hit my head, how much I hit my head on the wall. At that time they threw me out of my native place. They threw me out of Afjeh. They threw me out of Deh-e Bala, from Khosrow Shirin. Now I am still in exile. You know what exile is like. I knew that whenever you perform a miracle they will come to me. I wish you would perform a miracle. Everyone who said that there has been no miracle, it is all lies." I stood up to him. It didn't work in Deh-e Bala. I was an alien. But right here I fought so many times for you. Even now, with a thirsty tongue, I am kneeling before you. I brought these candles to light up the six corners of your grave. I will light it all up. Let Mash Taqi see the shower of light upon the grave of my Aqa Hossein, let him say tomorrow that the grave of my Lord Hossein was shining, let people know tomorrow that my Lord Hossein has performed a miracle. Let all the people of Afjeh, of Khan-e Mirza, of Deh-e Bala, of Khosrow Shirin, even of Habibabad, say that Mostafa Shemr, no, Shemr himself came at night to the tomb of the Aqa Hossein in supplication and chained his neck to the bars of the shrine. But I swear to you by the blood of your throat, by the moment and the hour when Shemr severed your head from your neck, before God, on the day that lasts fifty thousand years, be my intercessor! The intercessor for this shameful one, me....

Portrait of an Innocent: III

TRANSLATED BY

FRANK LEWIS

The gamekeepers had seen him going up a goat path. At first they probably saw his motorcycle parked in the shade cast by a boulder. After that it would not have been much of a problem to find him, as they could follow his footprints and the marks left by his walking stick in the soft soil of the sharp incline. He wasn't aware that hunting had been forbidden on this mountain as well, he had said as he gestured toward the summit. The summit could be seen beyond the delicate veil of fog. In the knapsack slung over his shoulder he had an ax, a few rolled-up pieces of paper, some plaster and wax, even a tape measure. He also had a pot full of kabab-e shami and five or six pieces of bread, which would have been enough food for only about two days.

They had come to his house as well. His wife knew nothing about it. She thought he had gone to another town on a job. "He sold his motorcycle," she said, "picked up his tools and took off."

His wife had cooked the kabab for him, as we later learned. A couple of days afterwards, when the mourning cries of his children could be heard, the neighbors had come to visit her. She said, "They broke into his strongbox and made off with everything he kept in there." She showed the strongbox to the women. It was one of those old freezers with brass nails and galvanized iron washers. The lock was still in place, but the hasp was broken. She said, "He always kept the key with him. And he never opened it in front of me."

This story was first published in *Stories from Iran: A Chicago Anthology 1921-1991*, edited by Heshmat Moayyad (Mage Publishers, 1991).

They found his work tools, too. They were behind a bunch of little knickknacks and other junk in the cellar. My wife said, "He had the sketches for his plasterwork designs back there. Paisley shapes, flowers, bushes, that sort of stuff, and a thin man that seemed to be clad only in a loincloth. There were a few sketches of birds and deer, too." Then there was a bricklayer's plummet, a cord, and a trowel.

I had seen him. He was thin and tall, with a narrow chin, slightly prominent cheekbones and eyes that never looked straight at you. His clothes were always covered with globs of plaster. The saddlebags on the back of his motorcycle were made out of finely woven pieces of carpet. The design on it was a banquet scene of some kind that you couldn't quite make sense of. He would greet you with a nod of the head. The neighbor's wife had said, "When he worked in our house he was always reciting poetry."

He would recite loudly, she wasn't sure what. They had hired him to do plasterwork around their guestroom, the molding in the corners near the ceiling and the heater. He did good work. He did paisley shapes on the framing edges and filled the background with gazelle, deer, rabbits, birds, and flowers. In the foreground you can see the skinny man my wife was talking about, with his loincloth. He is sitting on the ground, using his left arm as a pillar for his chin.

He insisted on doing an entire banquet scene in plaster above the heater. He had even brought the sketch for it with him. They didn't like it. Later on they built a cabinet with some boards and added a glass door with a handle on it to cover up the plasterwork. They set out their bric-a-brac behind the goblet on top of the cupboard—colorful dolls with long eyelashes, some asleep and some awake; a few china deer and one or two rabbits; a couple of wooden horses, one black and one auburn—that sort of thing.

His apprentices heard the news. There were two of them, their clothes covered with globs of plaster. They had come on Friday morning and left their bicycle leaning against the wall. We came outside when we heard them ring the doorbell. No one opened the door for them. My wife said, "Maybe there's no one home."

"No, they're home all right. I can hear them." I couldn't tell which one of them had said it.

My wife knocked on the door as well, but no one opened it. First she rang the bell and then she banged on the door with her fist. His apprentices were the same height, both with big dark eyes. A wisp of hair hung out from under their caps onto their foreheads. You could only tell that the one was not the other by his left cheek. The one who had no plaster on his cheek said, "We've come to see if they need any help…money, or if there's anything we could do for them."

My wife said, "Their kids are crying, they're just sitting on the other side of the door, crying."

"What about his wife?" I asked.

"I don't believe she's home," she said.

The one with plaster on his chin said, "I saw her myself through the keyhole."

The other one said, "She's got something against us, that's why she won't open the door. She's told her kids it isn't their daddy, just Asghar and Akbar, don't you see?"

The man next door asked, "Where's the sculptor now?"

They started to answer at the same time, "We just heard about it...." One of them continued on his own: "We heard about it in the coffeehouse. We simply couldn't believe it." Then he took some money out of his pocket. It was a fistful of crumpled bank notes, damp with sweat. The other one said, "Give this to the sculptor's wife when she opens the door. We can't stay here forever." Then he wiped the two globs of plaster from the cheek of the first one. After one of them had mounted the bicycle and put his foot on the pedal so that the other could climb on the back, my wife asked, "What will you do now?"

The one sitting in back said, "We don't know."

The neighbor's wife asked, "Do you know why he went to the mountains with an ax and a tape measure and that other stuff?"

The other one said, "No, but I swear to God it's not our fault. Tell the boss's wife we told him over and over again not to go, but he wouldn't listen." He said this quite loudly so that the boss's wife would hear if she was listening at the door. Then he started to pedal. They hadn't reached the turn in the lane when the man next door yelled, "If you hear anything, don't forget to let us know."

The one in back waved his hand. My wife had the wad of money in her hand and I thought she was about to bang on the door again when all of a sudden, it opened. One eye was all you could see at first. It was black with lashes so long they cast a shadow on her cheek. As she stuck her hand out to take the money, we saw the oval of her face. Her mouth was small and red, so small, in fact, her lips looked like a tightly pursed rosebud. We saw the mole next to her lip later, of that I'm sure. But we heard her name that very day, from my wife, only I've forgotten it now. Maybe because I didn't think it was important.

"Why didn't you open the door?" my wife asked her.

She said, "You heard, didn't you? They knew about it. But would they tell me? I was their auntie, I raised them. It's not like I was a stranger, that they couldn't confide in me."

"Well, what was it he was going to do, anyway?" I asked.

"He went to the mountains, that's all," she said. She had her *chador*[1] on, and we could only see the one eye now.

"Don't you know where he is?" I asked.

"They didn't say. How should I know, anyway? But he must have gone a long way away. He went with his motorcycle and there aren't any high mountains hereabouts."

After she closed the door, the neighbor said, "Surely he can't have gone to that mountain there." He was pointing toward Mount Soffeh. You couldn't see it, behind the buildings, but it was certainly somewhere in the direction of his outstretched arm. "I've been there," he said. "Not recently, of course. It's not more than two hours to the summit—that is, if you go up the steps. You've seen the steps, haven't you? They've cut steps into the mountain face so you can go up all the way to the top on horseback. You can get there quicker by a shortcut. Of course, it's forbidden to go, now. I believe they've recently carved an inscription on the summit."

Then he pointed farther into the distance, toward the southwest. "The tallest peak in the Shahkuh range is over thereabouts. I've never been, but I think it would take about three hours by motorbike to reach the foot of it."

"Maybe that's where he went," I offered. "Hunting is forbidden there, too. To protect the game. Mountain climbing's forbidden, as well."

"Why would they forbid mountain climbing?" he mused.

"I've never been," I replied.

Just then, the woman opened the door again, the same chador still covering her head. One paisley-shaped wisp of black hair, only finer and somewhat longer than a paisley, had fallen across the white background of her forehead. When she closed and locked the door behind her, you could hear the cries of the children. Through the keyhole she said to them, "I'll be right back."

"They can stay at our house, if you like," my wife offered. "It's not their fault this has happened. They'll play with our kids."

"They won't be afraid," she said. "They're used to it." The woman was tall, even taller than her husband.

The old lady living on the other side of their house said, "We're good neighbors, you know. At least let us know if we can do something. Maybe my boys can help him out."

---

1. A chador is a sewn sheet of cloth, mostly black, worn by Iranian women in public. It covers them from head to toe to comply with Islamic prescriptions of modesty.

I had just noticed the old lady. She was sitting on her doorstep. It was like she was waiting for something, whatever it might be, to play itself out. The sculptor's wife said, "I don't know. I don't know anything about it. You heard for yourself everything they said."

The old lady said something which I didn't hear. I was staring at the sculptor's wife. I've never seen a gazelle walk, with its soft, spritely, prancing steps, gently hopping over a plant or brook or something, just as the old poets used to describe it, but I imagine this must have been just the way a gazelle walks, with her shoulders gently swaying like that and the chador now and then taking on the shape of her rump and the hidden curves of her waist as her legs moved.

The next afternoon I heard he had come back. Mr. Maqsudi gave us the news. "Do you think we should go over and see him?" he asked.

"I don't think he would appreciate it," I said.

"We'll find an excuse to go see him," he said. "If you want to, you could.... No, no, I will.... I'll tell him to come do a plasterwork design on the space above the heater in our family room, that banquet scene he wanted to do."

"Don't you think it would be better to send the women over first and let them know we want to come over?" I asked.

When my wife returned she said, "His wife says he's got a fever. He was delirious. He's just now dropped off to sleep. Asghar's gone to get the doctor."

"Did you see him?" I asked.

"No," she said, "I heard his voice, though. He was yelling. His wife said, 'Do you hear that? He's awake now. Maybe he's delirious. His whole body is black and blue, like he was hit by a falling rock or something.'"

Mr. Maqsudi asked, "What was he saying?"

"I couldn't hear him properly, but I thought he was saying, 'I can. You'll see that I can!'" My wife wasn't sure what in the world he meant. We couldn't figure it out either.

I saw him the next day. I pulled up in the lane next to him. He had a big watermelon under his arm and in the other hand, his right hand, he had some bread. His head was shaven. "Thank God you made it through all right," I said to him.

"It will grow back, it will soon grow back," he said.

"What?" I asked.

He gestured toward his head with the bread in his right hand. The nails on his hand were neither chipped nor broken. "If you've got time, I'd like you to do one of those designs for us," I said.

"You mean the kind that Mr. Maqsudi didn't like?"

"I don't know what you did for him," I said, "but I'd like to have that scene of Shirin bathing in the spring, where it says in the poem:

> *Her limbs with travel's toil were wearied,*
> *Her clothes were caked with dust from head to toe.*
> *She circled for a time about the spring,*
> *And, spying no sign of life for mile on mile,*
> *Dismounted, tied her charger to one side,*
> *And put aside her fear of prying eyes.*
> *At sight of her, that fount of light, approaching*
> *The spring to bathe, tears welled in heaven's eyes*
> *Her waist she tied around with sky-blue silk,*
> *Entered the water, and set the world afire.*

I couldn't remember the rest of the lines just then, or maybe it wouldn't come to mind because I thought he wasn't paying attention. He was staring dazed, not at me or at my eyes, just staring, and if I hadn't been there or if someone else had been there in my place, it would have made not the slightest bit of difference to him.

"Will you do it?" I asked.

"Do what?" He was blinking like someone who had just been awakened from a deep sleep.

"Didn't you hear what I said?" I asked.

"I never heard that poem before, but there is something or other like what you said. I don't have a sketch of it, but I can find one somewhere. I'll find it for you, if you like."

That night I told my wife about our conversation. She said, "Asghar came over. The sculptor had told him to ask us if he could borrow that book for one night."

"Was it Asghar or Akbar?" I asked.

"How do I know?" she said. "Don't go asking philosophical questions. Will you give it to him or not?"

"Why didn't you give it to him?" I asked.

"I didn't know which book he wanted," she said.

"Didn't he say?"

"No," she said. "He said, 'Your husband knows which book.'"

My copy of Nezami's five romances is very old. It's a leatherbound copy, lithographed, foolscap size, illustrated by artists of the Qajar period. I thought he must want it for the illustrations. I put a bookmark next to the black-and-white drawing of Shirin bathing in the spring with her round face, round as the full moon, just the way the old poets would compare and describe it, with a cute, full chin and full eyebrows that run together, like two hunting bows. The long tresses behind her ears curl together and fall like little lassos on her throat and shoulder and then twist down to cover her breasts, but not so much that you can't see anything, or maybe they drew it to make it look like Shirin deliberately left half of her left breast—shapely as the silhouette of the first-quarter moon—open to view. You can only see Khosrow's head, with its royal diadem, behind the branches of a tree.

I gave the book to my son to take over and then we forgot all about it. It just slipped my mind. Even though they had the book for over two weeks, I didn't remember it. I had to get up in the morning, shave my face, brush my teeth and go to the office. You can't go on foot, and even if you've got a car you still have to rush. No matter how much I plan to wake up a little earlier and get in a few Swedish exercises or at least bend over and touch my toes a half-dozen times, it never works out. Every two or three months I've got to let my belt out another notch, and there're only two more notches left before I reach the end. When I do manage to get up early and have the presence of mind to remember the exercises, I get tuckered out after two or three counts and lose my breath. And you'd think I could stop smoking—I'm not talking about quitting, but couldn't I just not smoke in the mornings? My teeth are all yellowed, too, and one of them's got a cavity, but where do I find the time to get it fixed? I've also got two matching holes on either side of my mouth between my front teeth and my molars. I have to chew with my front teeth and it's getting harder to sleep with each passing night. "For God's sake," says my wife, "cut it out. Didn't you promise you were only going to smoke just one?"

When I want to talk to her, she's asleep. She sleeps with her eyes open and talks in her sleep. She's cut her hair short and dyed it. She's been dyeing it for a few years, a different color every time, some color that you only know won't be black by saying it isn't black, black and long and wavy with a wisp or ringlet dangling over her forehead or over her ears. Her stomach has stretch marks, little white lines. With every child, she gets two or three more. You can see them even in the faint nightlight. And she always forgets to wash her hands with soap or something. She knows I don't like the smell of fried onions or whatever it is, but she still forgets. "I forgot," she says. She sleeps so lightly that you can't even tell whether she's been asleep or just staring at the ceiling. You can never be sure enough to strike a match and light up. And it's really annoying to have to read silently all the time. Sometimes you feel like reading out loud. There are some passages that you have to read out loud properly, as if you were a professional reciter of poetry and the author of the verses is sitting at the head of your gathering on a silver chair of honor, listening to your recitation of his work.

And if I get an opportunity to stay at home for an afternoon or evening and sit in my room sipping a bottle of arrack and reading something, do you think those kids will let me? Either they've got the TV turned way up or there's the clinking of the dishes being washed or the water dripping from the faucet, or there's my wife worrying about some man who's in love with this woman and he…oh, I don't know…he doesn't know that she's really his sister, and her hair…. Will they let me not worry about it, or not know what happens next?… Her hair is short and her big eyes are wide with surprise and her body is limp and flabby, as if she'd always driven everywhere and never walked. And her brother, the very lover who will surely later be revealed as her brother, is so ugly that…. Do they listen if I tell them to turn the TV down? And so you forget what you were reading in the previous chapter and the arrack doesn't hit the spot anymore and the cigarette tastes like smoky straw that just sets you to coughing. And then if you lend a book to somebody in hopes that he'll come tomorrow or, let's say, a week later, and talk about it with you or that maybe you'll be able to sit quietly sipping arrack and read a few pages of the book together, the person either keeps the book for so long that you forget all about it or he himself forgets to read it. And when he brings it back or you send someone to fetch it, there are these stains on the cover or, even worse, on the pages, where he has spilled gravy on it. Or maybe the first few pages are marked by his wet thumbprint and the rest of the pages are just as clean as they used to be.

Then my wife said, "The sculptor is at the door and he says he wants to see you." I thought…I don't remember when it was. Anyway, it doesn't matter. I only remember thinking that maybe he'd come to borrow some money or ask me to do him a favor or something the next morning, I don't know…. My wife said, "Didn't you hear me? The sculptor's at the door."

"Okay," I said, "tell him to come in." His hair had grown out, not too much, just about an inch or so. Not quite long enough to cover the front of his head, not just yet. That night I understood. He was standing at the threshold of the room with the book underneath his arm. It was the collected romances of Nezami.[2] "Please come on in," I said. "Why did you go to the trouble yourself? You could have sent the book over with one of your boys."

He stood in the middle of the room, holding the book in both hands the way you would hold a tray and offer tea or something to somebody. "Put it over there on the table," I said.

"I don't understand it. No matter how hard I try, I just don't understand it. There are a lot of parts of it that are really hard for me," he said.

Well, if my hand accidentally hit the liquor glass and knocked it over onto the floor where it broke, it wasn't anybody's fault, but the sculptor got very embarrassed. He had bent over to collect the broken glass, and I wanted him to stop looking for the little pieces, because it was delaying us from our purpose. I wanted him to sit down somewhere as soon as possible, on the chair at the table or even on the ground, next to me, leaning on a pillow. That's just what we did in the end. We sat next to each other on a pelt-covered seat, our backs resting on two pillows. We began on page one. Next to every line that he hadn't understood he had put a faint mark in pencil. We turned the pages, reading. I had to read the whole page or the whole section in order to understand or remind myself what was going on. There were some passages I didn't understand either, so I had to go get a couple of dictionaries.

When my wife said, "Why don't you drink your tea?" I had a notion. "Bring us two glasses and a plate of yogurt and cucumber salad. Put some pennyroyal and dried sweet basil in it, something to make it smell nice. Bring some ice, too."

The sculptor said, "Just bring one glass."

"Just one? Come on," said my wife.

He didn't respond. After my wife left, I said to him, "Don't you see how Khosrow used to drink glass after glass of wine?" I brought two turquoise wine cups with crystal bases out of the cabinet.

"Farhad didn't drink. I'm sure that Farhad didn't drink," he said.

Then we talked of love. I was drunk. I badly wanted to read the death scene of Shirin for him, the part where she goes to the funeral tower of Khosrow and pulls the dagger out of his heart and stabs it into her own heart, dying right there next to him. The sculptor said, "I've not gotten

---

2. Nezami of Ganjeh, a Persian poet (ca. 1141–1203), is the author of the famous *Khamseh* (Quintet or Five Poems). One of the five poems describes the romance of the Sasanian King Khosrow and the Armenian Princess Shirin (*shirin* means "sweet" in Persian). An episode within this poem tells how the stonecutter Farhad falls in love with Shirin and loses his life in loyalty to her.

to that part yet. Read this part first. You read it, and I'll listen. If I don't understand it, it doesn't matter."

He had separated the pages with a bookmark. I imagine it was in the place that he especially wanted to read over again or have somebody read and explain for him. We read where Farhad the stonecutter, in love with Shirin, has been challenged to tunnel through a mountain in order to win her hand. The sculptor said, "If Farhad hadn't listened to that false messenger and had opened a passage through the mountain, do you think he would have won Shirin's hand?"

"No," I said. "I'm sure that they would have come up with another plan to trick him. And anyway, Shirin is in love with Khosrow."

"But Khosrow was in love with Maryam at first and later on with Shakar, the courtesan from Isfahan. On top of that, every night he had a different dish, one virgin after another. That's not being in love! Besides, he swore an oath to Farhad that if Farhad could split the mountain in two, he'd win Shirin's hand."

I didn't remember whether Khosrow had sworn an oath or not. I read on. I believe that when we got to the death of Farhad, he began to cry. I cried too. I even kissed the sculptor, on his hand. He protested, "I should kiss your hand. You are my teacher."

In the morning I realized I had fallen asleep. I'd gotten so drunk that I just nodded off. My wife said, "The sculptor said he wasn't sure if he had your permission to borrow the book again."

"Why didn't you give it to him?," I asked.

"He wouldn't take it. He said he ought to get your permission directly."

I had a headache. It wasn't from the arrack or anything. Drinking was nothing new for me. We drank more of the stuff at our weekly get-together of co-workers. But this time, this morning, I was so tired that it seemed to me like I'd been walking for years carrying a heavy boulder on my head. I couldn't remember what else we had talked about. I seemed to remember he said something about his strongbox, the designs he kept in it. "They were my father's," he said. "Nowadays you can't find them anymore. They're like the designs you see on carpets."

He said that they'd even taken his sketches. He talked about some sketches of scenes he had had in which, instead of a man, an old woman brings the false news of the death of Shirin to Farhad.

I had heard this version of the story, too. But in Nezami's account, it is a man. I read it for him and told him why, for example, Nezami couldn't stick up for Farhad and place the blame for his death squarely on Khosrow's shoulders. As the poem says, it is fate:

Who can tell the age of our time-worn earth,
Can see the ancient past and how it was;
Once every hundred years an age begins,
One cycle ends another starts anew.
To no man's given life beyond his age
Lest he should fathom time's deep mystery
Each age deals us the cards, both fair and foul;
In this has God, the Knower, cloaked a mystery.
Unless you seek an increase of injustice,
Keep every age's secret from the next.

He didn't understand. I had to explain to him that there were tyrants in Nezami's days too, and Nezami himself was a Farhad trying to split the mountain with his hands and his pen instead of an ax. I told him about Afaq, Nezami's wife who had died, how Nezami had modeled the character Shirin on her, on how Nezami may have been buried next to Afaq. Now I remember that Nezami has a line describing the man who gave the false message to Farhad—this in spite of Nezami's fear of the tyrants of his day—and the line is later repeated about Shiruyeh, the murderer of King Khosrow:

One brutal, like a butcher, reeking blood,
One spitting sparks, like instruments of war.

After that, I think I must have fallen asleep, that is when the sculptor started talking about himself. All I remember is that he was talking about moonlit nights and the round disk of the full moon. He was saying he was afraid that one of these moonlit nights, with the full moon shining bright, he would do something to himself. Why, he didn't know.

My wife told me that he had invited us over that night, if we could make it. "All of us? The kids, too?" I asked.

"Yes, of course," she said. I wanted to see him, but without the wife and kids. I couldn't make it.

Actually, we had one of our weekly gatherings. All of us co-workers get together for an arrack-drinking session. Everybody tries to tell some new tidbit or joke and then we play a friendly round of poker. And now and then, it might come about that you see the beauty spot next to a pair of lips and you try to forget that this one's hair is blond because she dyed it and forget that her eyebrows are so thin that she looks like someone's accidentally made a mark between her hairline and her eyes, or her lips are so huge and red that you're afraid that if she kisses you with those big red lips their outline will forever remain upon your neck or cheek. So it's enough that you squeeze her hand beneath the table and accidentally pass her in the hallway or in another room and, in honor of those lips, kiss her beauty spot. It's because of moments like these that you try not to let your belt bulge out to its last notch and you shave your face with double strokes of the razor and stand before the mirror fiddling with the knot of your tie. It was about this time that I got to know one of those types. She's a secretary at the office. It didn't take a week before I said to her, "I love you." It's come to be real easy to say, almost no different from saying, "Hand me that glass," or something. The thing developed to the point that I pretended to be on a business trip so we could spend the night at a friend's house. She was a virgin. She said so herself. I don't like to fiddle around with boys; but I pretended that's what the girl was, so she was still a virgin in the morning. Her beauty spot was rubbed off, my head was throbbing, my mouth tasted bitter and I had a toothache. The girl had thrown her arms around my neck, with her short, shoulder-length hair and was saying to me, "Call me 'my sweet' again."

I couldn't remember why I'd called her 'my sweet,' but I did. Several times. I didn't even remember why as I kissed her beauty spot. When I returned home, I was so giddy that I didn't remember that I was supposed to have been on a trip for three days. When I remembered, it didn't matter anymore, for my wife, I mean.

"They brought him home last night," she said.

"Who?" I asked.

"The sculptor. He had gone to the mountains."

"With his ax?" I wondered.

"What would he be doing with an ax?" she said.

"Well, it's obvious. When that man who brings the false message—or let's say it's an old woman who tells him—of Shirin's death, he has to throw his ax to the top of the mountain. The blade of the ax goes into the soft earth up to the handle. After a while, the handle sprouts and grows into a miraculous tree. I don't remember it or I'd recite the story for you."

"You don't look too well," my wife said.

I had a fever and I dozed off after a little while. My wife said, "Did you have to come back in the middle of the night like this?"

"Did I say something in my sleep?"

"I don't know what you were saying," she said. "You were saying something about boys and girls and you kept going 'Shirin, Shirin.' Then you started sobbing."

"I must have been dreaming about the sculptor. Don't you remember that night?"

They had brought the sculptor's body. His face was all bruised to a pulp; you couldn't recognize him. They said he had fallen down the mountain.

By the time I got up, put my clothes on, and made it over to the cemetery, the local villagers were carrying him on their shoulders from the mortuary. They had been unable to wash his corpse, and had just wound the shroud around his blood-stained clothes. They were saying that the blood had seeped clear through to the shroud. The twins were taking turns as pallbearers, one in front of the coffin the whole way, holding the right-front handle on his shoulder, the other walking behind the coffin crying.

His wife sat at the side of his grave wailing. "I told him over and over not to go," she was saying. "'Don't go,' I kept saying, 'You can go tomorrow night.' You saw yourself how big the full moon was, how white it was."

My wife took hold of her by the arms to lift her up. "Please, Afaq, stand up. Think of the children."

"Please," said Afaq, "just bury me here next to him. He said himself it would end like this." Her chador had slipped off her head and fallen down around her shoulders. Her long black hair had fallen over her breasts. It was then that I saw her beauty spot. It was just under her left cheekbone. She had five or six bracelets on her left wrist. "It was my fault, I did it! He kept begging me to open the door, imploring and imploring, and I did!"

She told my wife about it. "He said I should lock the door. He made me swear not to open the door no matter what. For a week he had been working in the evenings on the design for our living room. Then, the night before last, he started begging me to look at the round face of the moon, how it had come right in front of his window. 'Open the door, for God's sake, I beg you to open the door,' he said. 'If you don't open the door, I'll split my skull right here with the ax.'"

"You hadn't locked the door on him, had you?" my wife asked.

"Yes, I told you. That's what he wanted me to do. He said, 'Tonight is the fourteenth of the month. I'm afraid the moon is going to make me do something crazy again. Put this lock on the door. Don't open it, no matter how much I beg you.'"

"Who?" I asked, "Who was going to make him do something crazy?"

"I don't know, he didn't say."

The twins didn't know either. They sat on the ground on opposite sides of the grave, drawing in the dust. I sat down next to one of them and said,

"A martyr goes to heaven." Either Asghar or Akbar said, "He knew himself it would end like this, but he couldn't do anything about it. It came to him in a dream, or maybe he was awake when it hit him. He thought that if he went to the mountains, if he—I don't know—if he exerted himself, he could break the spell. 'Every hundred years it happens like this,' he said. 'Somebody has to go.'"

"Where?" I asked.

The other one said, "To the mountains, of course."

"He went to Mount Soffeh," they both said together as one of them pointed to the peak, or maybe to the stone inscription that had recently been carved there.

"What in the world for?" I asked.

"His ax is missing," one of them said. "It wasn't with his other tools. We looked all over for it."

"He wasn't a stonecutter," I remarked. "He couldn't carve a scene in the rock of the mountain."

The other one said that he had sculpted a scene before he left. "He did a plaster cast of it. You should see it."

I did see it. It had nothing to do with the full moon or an old woman bearing a false message. After the customary week had gone by, we went to see his family to offer our condolences. It was then I saw it, when we came back to their house from the cemetery.

On his grave they had laid a stone with the outline of an ax surrounded by a few paisley designs. But as for the design in their living room on the piping above the heater, that was one of Khosrow's royal banquets. I believe it was still unfinished, not quite complete. I say this because there is just one layer of plaster in the place where Khosrow's face would be. He had finished Shirin, with her long, curly locks, the little lassos of her tresses twining about her neck and then falling over her bosom and coiling around her small, round breasts. She is sitting on the throne next to Khosrow. The minstrels are sitting in a half-circle around the throne. A harp player with hair hanging down to her shoulders and ringlets curling about her ears is sitting on the left-hand side at the front of the semicircle.

You can see her profile. Two other women are sitting facing the throne. A harvest of curly hair spills over their backs. Their shoulders, arms, and wrists are unfinished, maybe on purpose, so that they look as though they are covered with white sequins. Only the edges of the *tonbak* and *santur*[3]

---

3. The tonbak is an Iranian drum with one skin, also known as the chalice drum. The santur is a seventy-two string trapezoidal-shaped instrument struck by light wooden hammers (*mezrabs*), held by three fingers of each hand.

they are playing are visible. On the right side of the semicircle, in the front, a singer is standing in profile. The outline of her face appears to be the same as the outline for the face of the harp player, except that her lips are parted. The harp player's mouth is small and pert, but white. There is a dancer in the middle of the semicircle, half-naked, next to the throne. Her breasts look like two round, white lemons, and her hair is hanging in a lovelock over her left shoulder. Her knees are resting on the ground, her arms joined in a circle above her head. Her large thighs are bared. Her face has the same features as Shirin, almond-shaped eyes and eyebrows arched like a bow, with a black mole on her left cheek. The mountain is off in the background and you can see a thin blue line running down its side. Farhad, the same height as Khosrow, is in profile, but without crown or sequins, his ax in hand. He seems to be sitting closer to the banquet than to the mountain, which is off in the distance. The stream of milk he carved out for Shirin is hard to make out. A few boulders have fallen off the mountain and rolled down near the throne. Farhad's forearms and wrists, still grasping the ax, are drawn as though he is still digging up the mountain, as though with but one more blow, he will shift the whole mountain out of the way.

Portrait of an Innocent: IV

TRANSLATED BY

ALYSSA GABBAY & HESHMAT MOAYYAD

I don't feel well. I can't go to work. Last night I had another nosebleed, in my sleep. After that I couldn't get back to sleep. The truth is, I was afraid to fall asleep. After all, at least when you're awake, your fate is in your own hands. But when you're asleep, what then? Of course I'm not just talking about a nosebleed. How do you know that in your sleep you won't say things that you shouldn't? The old woman who owns this house was saying that I scream in my sleep—me, of all people. She's a good woman. She was saying, "You have to try to sleep." Well, I can't. It's out of my hands. Maybe if I moved to a different house, it would be possible. I have to move, so don't say, "Why do you move every two or three months?" Now you should understand why. For example, isn't this sleeplessness a good enough reason? Or the nosebleeds? My whole body aches as though a bunch of guys had beaten me up. Maybe also from too much walking, yesterday, or not that much, I mean I was forced to turn into alleys, and later from this alley into that alley. Then I saw that if I suddenly got to one of these same dark alleys, maybe even a dead end, then what? Then, I mean...you, you know that I'm afraid of men with glasses, especially dark glasses, I'm afraid of them, especially if their faces are very clean-shaven and their hair is combed, and of course if they're very polite. First I avoid them, I turn away from them. Then I see it won't work. Everywhere I go, they're there. I have to say hello to them and to be polite to them, to shake their hands, even to drink with them. It's then that I can't even feel comfortable in my own room anymore. I'm telling you, one of them was saying, "If your room had two keys, it would be much better." Now, let's say that you don't show yourself, you don't say hello to them, when one of them is coming from across the street you look into the store window, or you hold a cigarette under your lip so as not to kiss him. I think in this way I've made a lot of enemies. That's why I told you I'm afraid. Just yesterday afternoon the same things happened. I was walking on the sidewalk of Chahar Bagh when I saw one of them. We didn't know each other. But I said hello to him. It wasn't out of fear. After all, when someone stares at you like that and smiles and when even the lines on his face are so similar to all of the others', what can you do? And anyway, me, I don't owe anything to anyone. But while I was standing there and saying hello, how are you, I gave up on going to the bar. Maybe it was later that I gave up on it, later when I thought that of course he's following me. That's why I turned into the alley. I thought, what if. Then I went back by the street to the riverside. I thought, God bless crowded places. Well, if more of them were there, let them be there. I was dying to have a drink, especially when I saw the bridge orange-tinged from the light of the sun. That's how it always looks at sunset. After all, if you stand in one of these openings, facing the sun, and look at the grass that's deep green or at the narrow stream that when it reaches the trembling reflections of the bridge flows so slowly and the water becomes so clear that you can see big, moss-covered rocks and even pebbles that the small and constant waves can't roll, it's impossible not to drink. I'm telling you, it had been a week since my lips had touched alcohol. I wanted to go to a cozy corner, to sit and have a drink of arrack: a glass, and after it a spoonful of beans and maybe some kabab with *taftoon*.[1] After that, you yourself know better. You light a cigarette, and you gaze at the smoke, at the circles of smoke. These aren't great expectations. But do you think it's possible? When you're about to light your cigarette you see that one of them has turned up again. It's enough for them just to say, "May I?" In the second place, I believe in the obliging honor resulting from drinking with someone. That means I think if you clink your glass to somebody's glass and say, "To your health!" you shouldn't try all the time to lead the conversation to…I don't know what. So what, that I don't know who said what, where. As for me, when I've found a cozy corner, I don't want to think in a loud voice. I'm telling you, a week ago when I was sitting in a corner and I'd just gotten warm and the whole time I was thinking of a dream I'd had the night before….I think I wrote it down for you. Yes, I wrote it down. But I didn't send it. Of course it wasn't anything. I don't even remember all of it now. It seems there was a caravan, let's say a Syrian caravan, that was going between two long and high walls instead of passing

---

1. Taftoon is one of the many varieties of Persian flatbreads.

through a desert. Of course no walls were visible, or because there were no doors and no windows or the light of a lamp, I believed there was a wall, or for example that it was long. I was also among the captives. There was no sign of camel bells and chains and those things that are in the books of *Maqatel*[2] or *Shohada*.[3] But I was sure that I was among them, and even that I was sick. I think just my neck was tied to something so that I couldn't turn my head or avoid looking, I don't mean at the sun, I don't know.... It's really impossible to say how it was. Let's say in the horizon, at sunset, the sun being put on the tip of a spear, that same red and bloody sun, and on top of everything else the spear isn't visible. For example, if it were behind a wall. Eyes and eyebrows and sometimes his beard weren't visible. Maybe it was from being too bloody, or strongly red or luminous, that they weren't visible. But the sound of reciting the Koran was heard. OK, I was thinking of just these things; maybe I also wanted to figure out why I was so scared in my dream, so much so that you'd think the cut-off head was mine, when suddenly I saw one of them looking at me from behind a window. I don't know why you recognize them so quickly, or why I do, without having seen them before, just like I'd seen them in my dream, of course with a helmet and chain mail and even a twisted mustache and glaring eyes. Now don't say: How do you know he was looking at you? Of course other people were also there. But...I don't know. Really, he was looking at me, I'm telling you, even though it was late. I'm someone who—I can't help it—when I see someone looking at me I get scared. It's true that a cigarette is nice after a glass of arrack. But only if they let you smoke it at your leisure. I had also ordered a dish of yogurt and shallots. Arrack, you can't drink it in a haphazard way. Me, I like to play with my glass of arrack. If I just drink it in one gulp my throat burns. I even forgot to give the waiter a tip. Dressed in black from head to toe and wearing his wide tie with blue stripes, he came and stood near the counter. Me, I don't know how some people can drink arrack while standing, especially so quickly, and on top of that to look at other people at the same time, all the time at someone else and not at the circles of smoke from their own cigarettes or, I don't know, at the green color of the parsley next to their kababs. The day after that I talked about it to Mr. Zain al-Abidini, he said: "Those whose accounts are clear, what do they have to fear?" I said, "I know this, they don't know it though."

He said: "Wait a little while, they'll also figure it out."

---

2. Generic name for books describing the events of the martyrdom of Imam Hossein in Karbala.
3. Arabic for "martyrs" (plural of *shahid*).

Wait? How long? And anyway, let's say they realize that up until now, for example, I haven't been, I don't know, Mr. So-and-So. But what about tomorrow? Of course I didn't say that to Mr. Zain al-Abidini. God forbid…. Of course, he's a good man. He has a wife and two kids. I think you know. He's a joker. He says, people of the world are of two kinds. One of them consists of those who have joined a group, a community, a political party, a club, or even an organization, a company. These people, their minds are at ease, whether they're left or right, red or black, each one of them is every one, is a crowd. Even when they're all alone in their rooms, they know there are lots of others who think the way they do, or at least act that way. That's why whatever happens doesn't affect them as much as a fleabite. It doesn't disturb their peace of mind. But the ones of the second kind are lonely. In spite of the fact that there are many of them, each one of them is a single being, a single being against the rest of the people of the world, against the sky and God, and their sleeplessness or their dreams.

I think he was trying to say that I belong to that second category of people, and that's the reason why I'm like that. Maybe. He was saying, Go, young man, before it's too late, cling to one of these crowds, these groups, and put your mind at ease.

He always says, "You're dangerous, young man, for all of those groups, those crowds, with their idols and altars. That's why they have to pay attention to you, they'd like to have accounts of all of your actions, even the number of cigarettes you smoke every day."

He's calculated how many kilograms of meat and bread and, for example, how many kilos of sugar and tea he'll waste over the next ten years, and how many thousands of kilometers he'll travel, and even how many barrels of arrack he'll drink. He says, "Let's assume once a week with the wife, and if it also happens unlawfully once a month, it turns out to be 640 instances of sex." Finally, at the end of ten years, he's given installments to his bank and…. He says, "I couldn't care less. I've insured my life so that if, God forbid, from a ton and forty-four or forty-five kilos of meat—five hundred or two hundred kilos are left over, my children won't go hungry. Now if two guys are standing in the street or even in my room and are whispering to each other and if one of them is looking at me all the time, well, let him."

He also reads the newspaper every morning. He even argues with people, with anyone possible—though not with me—and on top of that he argues with them very loudly. He says, "You've seen these screens? As long as the world has existed they've been like that. On one side there are vicious people, each with a uniform shape, with a helmet and chain-mail and glaring eyes, and on that side friends with connected eyebrows and a mole on their foreheads and a halo around their heads. Well, now let's see which side wins. On one side there are cut-off heads and captivity, and on the other side the pot of boiling water and the saw, and even the signs of the Day of Resurrection, the snake of Hell and the fiery club."

And if someone says to him, "Well, so what?" he says, "Which side are you on, huh? You like the tip of the spear more or the inside of the pot?"

One day when I said there have also been some who didn't go to this side or to that side, he jabbered that…now I don't remember exactly what. It's also impossible to write down everything he says. Zain al-Abidini is a fearless man. Or it's that…I don't know. After all, he thinks, "War is essential to progress and is the sole means of the perpetuation of the human race. All of the inventions and discoveries of the last half-century are the result of war mongering." On top of that he says, "If for another ten years no war occurs and suddenly the population of the earth becomes seven billion or more, what will my children and I do?" He doesn't like rationing. Then again, he's tasted it once. He was twenty. Once—I don't remember when—he said, "Stolen things have a different flavor. You know, the really good sex was when…." I don't know where, of all people with a woman who was willing to do it for the sake of money. I think he said he enjoyed it more because the woman was crying and looking at the door. But sometimes he says things that, if it weren't for the sake of politeness, I definitely would cover my ears. Even when I get up and close the door or peer out of the windows, he screams and says things over and over again in a loud voice and pounds rhythmically on the table. Of course he doesn't mean to make fun of me. But sometimes…I mean, he himself says, "You have to enjoy." When I ask him, Why, if it's at the expense of other people's suffering? He says, "Boy, you're being a prig. OK, a simple joke isn't so…."

A simple joke? Really, it's ugly. A man returns from the bathroom, has just lit a cigarette, lifts the venetian blinds and looks into the alley to see, for example, when the blind beggar again throws his money, somewhere just close, throwing it when no one would be around him, then he looks for it, stretching out his hand on the ground, goes back and forth a few feet. When he finds it he laughs, loudly, in such a way that you'd think he's found some money…I was saying, or for example you're whistling very slowly when your colleague announces, "Some guy called. I think he wanted you." I think it was a month ago. At first I thought that maybe again…you do remember it, don't you? I'm talking about the same case of the old woman's son. I wrote you about it, I think. Well, it's true that

I told them I'd never seen him. But if I were in their shoes, I wouldn't have believed me. But I didn't lie to you, at least. More important than anything, the telephone—it's not that I'm afraid of it, I don't like it. When my eye falls on the telephone, on the receiver and its numbers, I start to shake. You don't know who might, at this very minute, call and ask for you. Apart from that, when the telephone rings, how can you know who it is? Zain al-Abidini knows this. How? I don't know. Maybe because too many times I've said, "Please, see who it is." Well, I ask you, "If someone calls and doesn't say who it is and from where, and on top of that knows your name and then I don't know what…." That is what happened that time. The time that I wrote you about. No, I think I forgot to mail it. I'm telling you. Maybe also because it was impossible, I couldn't, I forgot. So you don't have to keep writing, Why don't you write? Or, I don't know, for example, "It's six months that we haven't had any news from you." There is no news. Or, according to Zain al-Abidini, I'm also wasting my portion of meat and bread and sex. I asked Zain al-Abidini, "He didn't say who it was?" Or, I think, "He didn't say what it was about?" He said, "No, he didn't say anything. He was just looking for you. I said, I don't know, he just went out."

You see? He's just gone out? So what? Now whatever thoughts crossed that guy's mind is none of Mr. Zain al-Abidini's business. And when I ask, "Well, what did he say?" he says, "I don't know. But he did say, I'll call again." Neither of these are friends at all. That's why I'm not friends with anyone. But I have to be with this one. I'm his colleague. It's true that I'm a stranger in this city, but, still, in these ten years I could have made some friends. At least you know that I'm not so pathetic. But how can you be sure that…. Let's say for example you're sitting in your room, under the *korsi*,[4] you've closed your eyes and in that position you're thinking to yourself. You're trying very hard to think of a river, or a tree, or even of those sweaty windowpanes of our room, or for example of Mother—of her white hair, the brooch below her throat. Or if it's very late and no sound of steps can be heard in the alley, of our late Father, for example when…you don't remember. The last time I saw him he didn't look like his picture at all, he looked as if he had shrunk, as if they had pulled a layer of skin over the bones of the face of a man. In all of the family pictures his hair is thick, curly, like your hair. But I always, I mean, every time that I think of Father I remember his shaved head. His eyes were black and sparkling. He had grown a beard—it wasn't even as long as a

---

4. A korsi is layers of quilts spread over and around a wooden framework over a central brazier, under which people warm up, relax, and sleep during the winter.

fist—with a few white threads close to his ears and chin. Only from his eyes I knew that it was Father. You were in Mother's arms. First you looked at Father, then you cried and hid your head under Mother's chador. You remember? Well, I was thinking of Father. No matter how hard I tried, I couldn't remember where his hands were. They weren't in his pockets, or on the bars that, for example, he might have gripped. Now I think they were behind his head, logically they must have been there. I know that of course you'll pick this up and write, "Why are you thinking of Father, and on top of everything why just of this scene?" Me, I told you it was late at night. And apart from that, for me this scene has become like an old photograph that's ruined in two or three parts and its lower portion, from the neck down, is torn off. What would you do if you had a picture like that? Wouldn't you try to remember the rest of it, or at least to reconstruct it? Why now? It's not in our hands anymore. Maybe this is why his name's on our identity cards or when anyone hears our last name, he remembers Father right away, "How are you related to So-and-So?" There they also said it. One of them was saying, "Assuming that you're telling the truth, what about your father?"

Actually, I've decided to change my last name. To what? I don't know. Maybe I'll ask permission from Zain al-Abidini to use his last name. Tomorrow I'll ask him. You do what you want. But I'm forced into it. Look, when the armies of Ibn Ziad[5] or Hadjdjadj[6]—I don't remember which—are attacking Medina, according to a report they kill twelve thousand of the common people, they even kill seven hundred Immigrants and Helpers of the Prophet.[7] There's another story that for a number of years no one married off his daughter with the condition of virginity. Well, Ali ibn al-Hossein[8] was in Medina during one of those two attacks on the residents, and for the sake of preserving his life and protecting the Point of Truth[9], he took shelter in the gravesite of his grandfather. Some have written that God drew a curtain between him and the armies of the enemy. It is also plausible that they didn't bother him out of respect for

5. Ibn Ziad, Governor of Kufa who is responsible for the events in Karbala surrounding the martyrdom of Imam Hossein in 680.

6. Hadjdjadj, Omayyad governor of Irak before the Abassid Caliphate was established (d. 712 or 713).

7. The "immigrants" (*mohajer*) were the Meccans, who followed Mohammad to Medina in 621, and their descendants. The "Helpers" (*Ansar*) were residents of Medina and their descendants who supported the Prophet.

8. Known as Zaynu'l Abidin (658-712 or 713), the fourth Imam, and the only one of Imam Hossein's children to survive the battle at Karbala.

9. Ali, the first Imam.

the holy sanctuary. There's also a report that the armies of Syria didn't violate the home of the Prophet and that a lot of people and followers who had taken refuge in that home weren't attacked. But now, for example you're sitting in asylum, even in your own room under a korsi, when suddenly a guy throws a rock at your window. Now if your light should go out, so be it. He throws another rock. You just have time to put on your slippers and you forget to smooth your hair. And probably you forget to throw the book that you've just finished into a corner, for example to put it under the pillow. Anyway, do you think these guys sit in one place? Do you think you can say to them, "Please don't touch my books," or, "I don't lend my books." I'm telling you, one of them had come and was asking me for books, I don't know what books. It's true that I've read them (I found two of them in a used book store), but I didn't like them, they were junk. On top of that, how could I say to that guy that I've read them, that they're not novels, that it's better if he goes and I don't know, gets a few books of sociology. Then when I brought tea for him he said, "Hey, sneaky, you said you didn't have any of them?"

I said, "Of what?"

Then he reached under the korsi and brought out the book. He waved it just like he had a victory flag in his hand. Then he also read a few pages very loudly. When I turned on the gramophone he read louder. He was actually screaming. Now don't say, "Because you're so stupid." After all, I'd put the book behind a bookshelf. I'd also torn off the cover and had made a new cover for it with two pieces of cardboard. I'm telling you, I liked this one. Actually I wanted to read it again. Apart from that I thought maybe he was warming his hands under the korsi. That's why I said I don't have any friends or acquaintances. For example, this one had said that So-and-So—meaning me—his hands shake and, I don't know, he spilled the tea on the quilt of the korsi. You see? After all, no one turns up to say to them, "What is it to you?" Not only did I give him the book as a gift, I also went to the street and bought eggs and a small bottle of arrack. I also got yogurt. Well, I really am stupid. When he got drunk he said, "You're afraid, you're even afraid of your own shadow."

I told him about the events of Medina, and even the fleeing of the Prophet and the taking refuge in the cave and I talked about the spider and the web that made a dam of protection for the Prophet and his companions. I even showed him my books, the mark left by the thumb wet with saliva. He also saw the envelopes with the torn letters and the empty spot of the pictures in the album. I also told him about the single ones, according to Zain al-Abidini. He didn't understand. He had also told others. About the books, too, I'm sure. Because a week later one of those same ones had come to the office looking for me. My colleague was saying so. I'm sure this time he wasn't lying. Maybe he was. He said, It was a tall guy with broad shoulders. Even if he were short and, I don't know, skinny, it wouldn't have made a difference. Zain al-Abidini was asking, "You know karate?"

Himself, he understands certain things. He was saying, "There are people who can break the neck or back of a man with one blow of the hand." I think he's read a karate book. He advised me to read it, too. He was saying, "It can be of use to you, young man. If you want I can lend it to you."

I said, "Thank you."

Actually, I wanted to read it, but I thought he'd definitely ask for a book of mine in exchange, and what sort of books! And then, was it possible to say, "I don't loan books to anyone, even to someone who's a colleague, who, I don't know,—according to him—knew my father?" Anyway, why should I lend it to him? You, you know I've stamped all of my books with the date, the place, and the amount of purchase. Zain al-Abidini was saying, "Even women know how." I myself have seen it in one of these American films. I don't remember its name. Even if I remembered it I wouldn't write it to you. What's the point? A delicate-bodied woman with black hair who you think is only good to be lifted in your arms, or, for example, to be put on your knees like a child so that you can play with her long black hair and maybe caress the white skin of her throat, she knocked down a male monster—I'm telling you!—with just one blow. That guy even had a knife in his hand. When Zain al-Abidini said, "You can come to our house to read it," I wasn't ready to do it. I was afraid we'd get into those same discussions or, for example, that in drunkenness I'd make some kind of an agreement that I shouldn't. His young daughter brought tea. It was clear as to why. Her mother was there. Her brother was also there. Certainly she isn't bad. I liked her. She's a student. At the dinner she was seated next to me. She drank beer. I also drank beer. There was also arrack, bitter and sharp and with the smell of raisins. I didn't drink any of it. I was afraid of getting drunk and of talking. You remember that I promised you never to drink more than a small glass of arrack in a cafe or one of these kinds of places. Maybe like the girl you'd also say, "When you're at a party there's no problem." Outwardly there isn't, especially when a pretty girl with black hair and glowing cheeks pours for you. But look, for example, that same night when my colleague got drunk he started to talk. I think his daughter was also drunk...even with two glasses of beer. That's why it's wrong to drink too much arrack. As for Zain al-Abidini, he is none of my business. I must not drink too much, especially in company. Of course, sometimes it's possible, especially in my room, on top of everything else when the next day is a holiday and it's about eleven or twelve at night. I put on some classical music. I turn up the sound, not too much, I mean so much that if I become drunk and suddenly....You do understand? After all, I've seen how when you get drunk you start talking, loudly. Me, I'm like that. I don't know whether I wrote to you about what happened one night when I drank too much? It wasn't my fault. No, it was my fault that I listened to my colleague. He read something from the paper to me. He even stood next to my desk and showed me some pictures. I, stupidly, also bought a paper on the street and folded it into quarters and put it in my pocket, my breast pocket. I thought, I'll go home and read it. I didn't know that I didn't have any arrack left. It was ten o'clock when I had to go out. I went to one of those same bars. The price was high. I knew it beforehand. I drank lime vodka. Two glasses. I drank more. How many? I don't remember. Then when I left and saw that the street was empty and quiet, and worse than everything, that green arch over the street and here and there rings of light amid the green leaves and a breeze that played with my neck, that didn't let me go home. The moon was so big, so white, especially the way it was suspended and fixed above the branches, above the green arch, that it was impossible not to be completely intoxicated. On my way, I stopped in one place, gulped a glass, and then I walked on in the street, I don't know, and I turned in the alleys and I think finally I sat down in a place next to one of these same water-filled canals. I don't remember where. I just remember the dark, bright surface of the water and the trembling of the moonlight and the reflection of the branches in the water. I think I also cried. I might also have spoken. I told you that it's wrong to get too drunk. For example, if I'd been sober, at least I'd have heard the sounds of steps behind me. Or at least...I think it's impossible that I said those things, especially that I said them loudly. But, after all, the night watchman didn't have anything against me. He reported, "He was sitting next to the water canal and was reading very loudly." I think I read the newspaper for him and, I don't know, I said certain things. He reported that I insulted him and grabbed his collar. Of course I denied it. In the end they attributed to me things that it's impossible I'd say in my sleep, let alone in drunkenness. But in the morning I realized, from the spots on the front of my shirt and on the collar of my jacket that it's not so impossible. Of course my nosebleed had stopped. I didn't see him again. I confessed that I had drunk too much and I promised, in writing, that I wouldn't exceed my limits anymore, but they wanted me to sign a statement saying that I had played the drunk. I didn't sign it. That's why I pledged never to drink outside, not to drink too much. Of course my colleague can if he wants. It's his house. I said that he got drunk. Then he even argued with his daughter, in such a way that if the television hadn't been on and its sound—I'm telling you—hadn't been turned up by the mother, I think, things certainly would have been bad. My colleague is a polite man, but nevertheless, he made his daughter cry. In a very blunt way he was saying to his daughter, "So, you little nothing, what do you have to say?" He was right. The next day of course he apologized to his daughter. He himself said so. But that night he wasn't letting up. Even when they were playing chess he picked up one of the black pieces and said, "Now if you're a man, win." I think his daughter was playing with white. She turned red. She was saying, "First of all, Daddy, I'm not a man, secondly this is a game, there are rules."

My colleague laughed, he was saying loudly, "No, play, play and win from your old father. Hurry up already and play."

The girl was saying, "At least take off your rook."

He was saying, "No, I want to take this one off."

He was squeezing a piece in his fist. I didn't know which one it was. He was saying, "If you win, from now on you're always right."

Then he started to make fun of me, even in front of his daughter. Of course, he was drunk. He was saying, "In the end, Mr. So-and-So will be shot from behind. Maybe he's already been shot." It's a corny story. Have you heard it? An American soldier in this South Asian war says to his friend, "Hey, what color is blood?" His friend says, "Why do you ask?" The other one says, "If blood is yellow then I believe I've been shot from behind." Imagine, a man saying that who on the other hand was saying to his daughter, "When a nation can put a man on the moon, even a bunch of slant-eyed men shouldn't dare to say to them, 'Above your eyes are your eyebrows.'" He was saying, "You're an educated person, aren't you worth much more than a hundred people like the neighborhood grocer, or, for example, like that laborer who dug up our garden today? Well, it's obvious that you are. So it's you who has the right to survive. Are you willing to become the wife of some barefoot man, huh, are you ready?"

His daughter was saying, "Daddy, the value of a human being isn't in his diploma or status. You have to see what he does. Those same barefoot men want to build a new human being, a new world, a world in which...."

Zain al-Abidini was screaming, "Everyone equal, huh? And you for this reason expect a great nation, with that civilization and superior technology, to surrender to a bunch of barefoot men? If they surrender you know what will happen? The next day, two or three million people would want to live for themselves and, I don't know, have no one to rule over them. No, it's impossible. I'm just saying, Long live Hitler, long live Göebbels!"

I didn't get involved. That same night I also decided not to go to their house anymore. After all, I may happen to get drunk one night and things would turn out to be like that night. Believe me, if my colleague hadn't intervened, I mean if he hadn't humbled himself in front of a couple of friends and acquaintances, I would definitely be stuck now. Also that other night in front of his daughter he said to me, "I advise you to marry this girl. You two are like opposite poles—positive and negative. Well, you can neutralize each other. And on top of that when two or three children drop around you, your hands will be plunged into so much shit of this one and abominations of the other one that you'll forget a day you embraced."

I personally don't think his daughter would agree to this marriage. Because she was criticizing the things her father and I were saying. She was saying, "Let's say that we buy a car and, for example, go to the seaside once a year or instead of lima beans and rice, and chicken and beans, we have caviar and whiskey and this and that, or for example...." Then she also talked about incidents of that night. Zain al-Abidini had definitely told her. You see? It's impossible to trust anyone. She even asked, "You still have nosebleeds?" She was saying, "These days, a person has to choose for himself."

But the whole time I wanted to talk to her about stories, stories by Chekhov or Dostoevski. I even started to give her summaries of one or two stories. The one where a woman and a man are riding in a sleigh and the man—in such a way that the girl doesn't see or thinks it's the sound of the wind or the sound of the sleigh—says in her ear, "I love you." Or even the story of that guy who every few months walks many kilometers to have his hair cut for free by a hairdresser who's a relative, and who has promised his daughter to him. And the story starts from the place where the girl is betrothed to him, and the barber in the middle of his work, when he's shaved exactly half of that guy's head, realizes that.... But do you think she would let me go on? She was saying that literature is now in the category of the irrelevant.

Why? She didn't say, that is, her father didn't let her. He was drunk. He was shouting at the top of his lungs, "Long live Hitler!" He was marching like the SS soldiers and saluting like the Fascists. Then he said, "If they had been allowed the world would now have become solidified, unified, it would have become a bouquet of flowers, we would have one world government with one ideology. All of the junk of these minds would be in the trash cans of history."

His daughter was saying, "Excuse me, Daddy, but you're a Fascist."

Zain al-Abidini was saying, "That's right, I am. I'm proud of it. What does it mean if every few million draw a line around themselves, claiming that we carrots and potatoes are also part of the fruits? And anyway, is it bad if all of these people, all of these hungry nations, accept the superior technology, the superior civilization of superpowers?"

He was saying, "Is whiskey or, for example, champagne better, or this shit arrack of ours that Mr. So-and-So drinks every night?" He gestured at me. Then he screamed, "Certainly it's better that we read Hamlet instead of Sa'di's *Golestan*[10] and that instead of the poems of, I don't know, whichever *Pashm-al'din,* "wool of religion,"[11] the poems of This One and That One."

He didn't know their names. The whole time he was defending a single language, a single civilization. He was saying, "Anyone who doesn't want it, either doesn't have enough sense and it has to be injected into him by force, or he has to be done away with, to be dumped into the trash bucket."

His daughter was saying, "How do you know that American civilization, for example, is superior? Is building rockets a sign of a superior civilization, a superior culture? Well, the Japanese can do it, soon they'll also be making them. In the second place, to become one, to become one color, if for example everyone had one language, one belief and one kind of clothing—"

Mr. Zain al-Abidini was shouting, "Tell yourself, ask yourself." Then he began to cry. He cried bitterly, bitterly. I didn't understand why. Of course he had drunk too much. When his wife came in she said, "You young people, do you know what this man has endured?"

She was gesturing at me. Her daughter said, "Mom, they were arguing with me."

---

10. *Rose Garden,* the poet Sa'di's (d.1291) masterpiece written in verse and prose in 1254.
11. A sarcastic title.

The wife apologized to me. Then she grasped my colleague under his arms and took him away. Zain al-Abidini kept crying in that same way and all the while was saying, "Vile imposter, vile imposter!"

Imposter? Who was he calling that? I didn't get it. That's why when his daughter said, "Want to play chess?" I said, "I don't know how." You understand why. She said, "I'll teach you, look...." Then she explained. I apologized. It was late. I took a cab home. I thought if I walked, God forbid if I ended up next to one of those same water canals again. It's true, I hadn't drunk a lot. But those three bottles of beer had warmed me up. Of course, if I had walked again I would have passed by one of those same bars, and then who knows what kind of trouble I'd get into. Maybe it would be possible if I changed my last name. The night watchman reported that I argued with him. He wrote, "I showed him the newspaper and I pointed one by one to the pictures and I said, 'It's nothing to be afraid of, a cut-off head.'" I took a cab home; I had forgotten the key to the door of the house. The old landlady opened the door for me. They are good people. One of her sons is abroad. I haven't seen the other, either. She showed me his picture that night. She said, "There's tea if you want it." Then she showed me. The picture was six by four and there was a black mole between his two eyebrows. Then she said how it had happened. His face was familiar. I think I'd seen him. I might have seen his picture somewhere. She said she wants to throw a *rowzeh-khani*. I was very surprised. After all, this is an unusual activity for someone who has a television in her home and goes out with just a kerchief on her head, and one of her sons now most certainly has a foreign wife. She invited me, too. She said, "I'll let you know about it." It was yesterday. During the gathering, they served coffee instead of tea. Men and women were separated. The men were in the courtyard and the women in the room, four mullahs had been invited. Her husband was seated quietly next to the door. He was hitting himself on the forehead only when the reciters digressed. It was the second reciting when the old woman yelled from the room, "Sir, please read the *Rowzeh* of Ali Akbar."[12]

When the reciter read the Rowzeh of Ali Akbar, the sound of the old woman's crying grew louder. Why Ali Akbar? I didn't get it. The third reciter read the Rowzeh of His Holiness Qassem,[13] without introduction. He just commemorated the affliction. Someone sitting next to me asked, "The first reciter, which rowzeh did he read?"

---

12 The story of the martyrdom of Ali Akbar, a son of Imam Hossein, taken from *Rowzat al-Shohada*, a collection of stories of the early martyrs of Islam written during the Timurid period.

13. A son of the Prophet Mohammad and his first wife Khadijah, who died before the age of two.

I said, "At first he talked about the necessity of the Point of Truth, then about the dissimulation. He also interpreted the tradition of the Innocent."

He said, "What about the digression?"

I said, " He read the sermon of Her Holiness Zeynab.[14] And then he talked about the cut-off head and the bamboo stick."

He said, "What do you think the third one will do?"

I said, " I don't know him."

He said, "He'll definitely speak about His Holiness Qassem."

He was right. "I told you so." When the third one was commemorating the affliction, I asked, "How did you know?"

He said, "Aren't you their neighbor?"

I said, "Why do you ask?"

He didn't answer. The next reciter didn't come. I didn't understand why. The gathering automatically broke up, and in spite of knowing that I definitely shouldn't go out, I left. Then—I said I think—I walked home, without having drunk any arrack or, for example, going down to the river bank. It was eight o'clock when I got home. I took two pills so maybe I could sleep. I thought to take my mind off things I'd read something. I picked up *Crime and Punishment.* No matter how hard I tried, it didn't work. I would read a few lines, and then realized I'd forgotten the previous ones. Then I sat and just smoked cigarettes. I think it was ten o'clock when I heard the doorbell ring. I pulled the quilt over my head. My light was out. I even tried to sleep. In the end I thought, one of them has come again. He had come. He didn't have any business with me. The old woman said so. Then I think I slept. Of course now I don't remember what I dreamed. I just remember a picture. It was a picture of me. It was in my hand. It was six by four. But I think they had crumpled it. Or I had been crushing it in my fist. It had been covered with lines, red lines, red streaks. Just like the time that I saw my face in the bathroom, that same first time I had a nosebleed. That's why I wished the lines would turn white or at least that I would be able to close my fist again. It didn't work. I think the picture was stuck in my palm and my fingers remained stiff. In the picture my mouth was open, wide open. There wasn't even one tooth in my mouth. I think I was sitting next to a water canal, or a river. But I was only seeing the surface of the water, the tranquil, waveless surface and the moon that remained huge and red on the motionless surface of the water, just like a cut-off head from which blood trickled. Now what I said, or what happened later, I don't remember. But the old woman said, "You

---

14. Sister of Imam Hossein, also present at the events in Karbala.

were screaming." It's possible that when I heard the sound of footsteps I screamed or spoke. A sound, it was exactly the sound of my colleague's feet when he was marching in the room and saluting and screaming, I wanted to turn my head so that this time I wouldn't be caught unawares. It wasn't working. Or at least not to see the picture. It didn't work. I couldn't even close my hand. I told you so. Then I spoke. About what? I told you that I don't remember. I even screamed so much that the old woman came and knocked on the door. She said, "What's going on? Is someone in your room?"

I said, " No, no one."

I was sure. I had bolted the door. I do that every night. She said, "Then who did you tell, 'You did all of this to me for one ton of meat and three barrels of whiskey?'"

I said, "I was dreaming, Ma'am."

There was a black scarf on her head. She said, "Did you hear? They came to find out, 'Why did you read the Rowzeh of Ali Akbar?'"

I said, "What is it to them?"

She said, "Well, what can I say. Then he asked, 'Is your neighbor upstairs?' I said, 'I think he's sleeping. Do you want me to call him?' "

I said, "In my sleep, I didn't say anything else? Did I?"

She said, "I think you were screaming, 'Long live Sa'd ibn Ziad.'"

I said, "I already told you, I was dreaming."

Why Ibn Ziad? Well! If I had said, Long live Jefferson, or Franklin, or at least Hitler, it's one thing. I myself didn't get it. Maybe if it were possible to sit in sanctuary somewhere, I wouldn't have said it, or maybe I said it because I want to be part of a group, part of an army, for example, the Syrian army. Or I said it from fear lest I have another nosebleed, or I remembered that whenever His Holiness Zain al-Abidin[13] saw the cut-off head of a sheep, he thought of the cut-off head of Abu Abdallah[14] and began to cry, my nosebleed started and I said it, I screamed. When the old woman left, I got up and I washed my hands and face. Then I don't know how it happened that I performed my ablutions. I'm telling you, just like that. I didn't read the three prayers. I couldn't. It was during the prostration of the third prayer that I saw it wouldn't work, I couldn't. Right there bent over the *mohr*[15] I cried, soundlessly. And I thought that

---

13. Son of Imam Hossein, survived the battle at Karbala and became the fourth Imam.
14. Imam Hossein, the third Imam.
15. A stone Moslems rest their forehead on during prayers, traditionally made from earth of Karbala or Mashhad.

if I would perform an evening prayer, or repent in the middle of two prayers, I would never have another nosebleed. It didn't work. I told you so. Some people are like that. Even when I read "If ye help him not" several times, up to the part where it is said, "When they two were in the Cave and he said to his companion, 'Have no fear, God is certainly with us!' Then God made his tranquility descend on him," it didn't work. Then I realized that it would never work. I even became convinced that if I had another nosebleed, it wouldn't ever stop, like now that my nosebleed has once more begun.

What Has Happened to Us, Barbad

TRANSLATED BY

MAURICE A. POMERANTZ

They would come and go. It had become a hotel here, yet I was alone. Now only Barbad and I remain. Barbad and Ra'na. She goes to school. Barbad sits in a corner quietly and stares. I don't look at him. I can't. I turn around. I go. I come. I look out the window. They aren't coming. No one will come anymore. I said, "Don't you see?"

He smiled. His mustache was shaved off. He was like a lamb shorn. He shaved his mustache when they closed the newspapers down. That was when they attacked the bookshops and threw the "cocktails." I couldn't look at him. After he shaved it off, he hovered over me and said, "Look!" I was asleep. No, I hadn't fallen asleep yet. He said, "Look at what I have become!"

From the corner of my eye, I peered at him. He had become another man, a stranger who suddenly enters your bedroom. I closed my eyes. I said, "In the morning…can't you see that I'm sleeping?"

But in the morning, I couldn't look at him either. The patch above his lip had become even paler. He looked like one of the eunuchs—effeminate. When I saw the color of his face, I realized how pale it was, as if it were yogurt perhaps, or as if a piece of white muslin had been pulled over it. He'd come forward suddenly and stand before me and blow a puff of air into my face. I closed my eyes. When he kissed me, I thought that he was another man. He didn't understand. He rubbed the patch above his lip on my chin. I thought I ought not to cry. But do you think he understood me? He came close to me, again grabbing me by the ears and pulling my face up. He blew into my face. I laughed and shut my eyes. That patch over his lip was like the empty bookcases. I picked up two of my son's dolls and placed them in the bookcases, along with a couple of the wind-up cars and a woolly bear. I put the recorder on another shelf. But the dull, flat color of the wall was still visible, like the empty space where a tooth has fallen out.

Back then they were always coming and going. Night or day made no difference to them. Who is it? Is it Asghar? Who is it? Is it Roqiyyeh? Who is it? Who is it? Two rings and then one. Three rings. Or they would call on the telephone. First the telephone would ring. Then you'd pick it up, and not a word. Then a second time—no one there. Finally it would be Majid. My husband would say, "I'll get it myself."

His hair was also cut short. He took off his glasses when he went out. He was cross-eyed. Without his glasses, he looked strange.

I said, "You can't see and in the end a car will hit you."

He said, "Oh, I'll see the cars. Just pray that the cars do not see me!" After this he set out, throwing his weight first on one foot, then on the other, as if to say, "I am a partridge." Then he imitated the partridge's caw. He said, "Pray that the hunters do not see me, otherwise...." He then turned and slit his throat with his index finger, as if it were a sharp knife and laughed, "Pukh!" And then, one foot this way, one foot that way, strutting like a partridge, he left. One hour. Two hours. The entire time, I'd wait behind the window.

I go near to the window and watch, like Barbad, who now only stares. A car is parked in front of the house. It is a Dodge. It's the neighbors' car across the street, a married couple with two kids. The man still has some nerve left. He appears in front of his window with his collar open. With his wife he approaches, wearing a pink undervest.

I said, "Do you see that? People are still living their own lives. They just don't care." He said, "They will understand. In the end they'll get it." He didn't understand. He did not understand it at all.

The neighbor appears before the window. He stretches his head out into the alley. He looks out. He doesn't smoke a cigarette. He always looks down the alley, sticking his entire neck out. When I wipe the floor with a wet rag, he mimics my manner of washing the floor. He points to himself and imitates my manner. What nerve that man has! He is asking whether he can come and help me. Then he places a hand under a curl of his hair and tosses it backward on his head. Something is hanging from his neck. It moves back and forth over his woolly chest. It is an "Allah" or something. He winks at me. What can I say to him? I really want to throw something in his face. Perhaps I'll find a severed hand and I will throw it at their window. Perhaps I'll throw a clump of braided hair. I'll throw it! He'll see me throw it! A clump of jet-black hair taken out from the root, still covered with the bloody skin. I will make this into a ball, and with a piece of stone wrapped into a scarf I'll throw it at their window.

His wife comes in front of the window with a tray pretending to be cleaning rice or lentils. She looks one way and then the next. Their radio is on loud. I'll throw something. One day just as he is standing there, running his hands through the hair around his neck, I'll throw a clump twisted in a handkerchief into his face! Whatever will be will be! I said, "No matter who takes power, these people will follow the crowd. Don't you see that in a couple of days his collar will be buttoned up, he'll be wearing a collarless shirt and sporting a beard."

He said, "And what about us?"

He placed both of his hands around his head so as to form a headscarf, and imitated the way pregnant women walk. Like those women who wear uniforms. On their bodies they hang bag-like dresses with buttons and collars. He made his voice high-pitched and said, "Mrs. Baji, will you come? Let's go to Qabr-e Aqa[1] and cook halva." Again he would prance coquettishly moving his hips and buttocks as if the *chador* were on his head, and then as if it had fallen on his shoulders all of a sudden. He said, "Oh, woe is me, may God strike me down!" and winked. He said, "I'll see you in the hall of the Mosque of Zacharia."

I answered, "Don't be foolish." That bare face, without a mustache, and that womanly voice—I wanted to throw up. I want to throw up. And then I go out. I come back. I prepare something. I sweep. I don't smoke a cigarette. Barbad stares. He doesn't say a word.

Meanwhile, they all sat and talked, "The structure of our society is capitalist." Akbar said, "We are not questioning that, but the crisis has destroyed it. The earthquake of the revolution, or we should say the uprising, has weakened its foundations. The big shots fled. They took their money and escaped. Or, from the very beginning, they had their money over there in Swiss and American Banks, and now they keep doing their business there as well. The workers have slowly become aware of their own rights. Their councils were one of the Revolution's harbingers. Now all that happens, every act that is undertaken, is for the re-establishment of that very same capitalist structure."

Roqiyyeh said, "Even wearing the veil, or throwing cocktails into bookshops? Or cutting off the arm of a petty thief, or the hand and a foot of

---

1. Qabr-e Aqa, generally called Sar-e Qabr Aqa, is a neighborhood in the South of Tehran, known for the grave of Aqa, an important nineteenth-century Moslem cleric.

one of the 'opponents of God?' All these acts, what do they have to do with capitalism?"

I wanted to say something. I didn't say anything. I brought in the tea. Her headscarf had fallen around her neck. She was wearing a blouse and a skirt with long knee-length socks and shoes without heels. Isma'il or someone else said, "All this is just a cover-up, for the sake of distraction, it is just a pretext through which they justify their repression."

Roqiyyeh said, "Certainly, but…."

"Certainly…certainly…." I wanted to vomit. I said, "Hamed, dear, who are 'they'? Isn't it enough already?"

"Those cutely dressed ones, don't you see? Will they go around with a bomb and place it in some garbage can in a public square and flee, or will they just sit around and at night tune into Radio America to play "Who Have Nothing" for Asi or Nisi.[2]

And he sang,

> I, who have nothing;
> I, who have no one.

And with that loud bass voice he shouted into my ear,

> I love you.

I went over to the window and shut it. I said, "Enough of this damned capitalism that no longer has anything to do with your books, with Ishqi[3], with Iraj[4] with Farrokhzad[5] or even with Ferdowsi[6] or Khayyam.[7] Capitalism doesn't enter your closet or your brain."

He said, " I know, but in a different way it is linked…."

And all the time with the "But's" and "Of course's" with which they spoke! They sat and smoked cigarettes and they talked. Our society would be seen as connected to capitalism. The working class was ignorant, not organized, and thus deluded. The intellectuals, not to mention anyone else, were too concerned with themselves, petite bourgeoisie. The problem was only this middle class. They were set next to one another closely, like the layers of onion when it is pulled apart. This one layer of the petite

---

2. Asi and Nisi, two feminine names

3. Mohammad Reza Ishqi (1894–1924), a journalist and poet

4. Iraj Mirza (1874–1926), a poet

5. Forough Farrokhzad (1935–1967), Iran's most famous 20th century woman poet

6. Ferdowsi, 934–1020 or 1025, the most celebrated poet of Iran, author of the famous national epic *Shahnameh*

7. Omar Khayyam, (ca.1048–1131), mathematician, philosopher, author of the famous *Ruba'iyat* (quatrains)

bourgeoisie was radical. The other layer was traditional. The traditionalist layer had two folds....

I said, "Hamed dear, I saw it, I told you, just as he was riding by on a motorcycle a man cut off the arm of a woman with something sharp like a dagger. Do you understand? He hit the naked arm of a woman and ran. Um, who was he? Of which one of your 'layers' was he was a member? The arm of the woman hung on one piece of flesh and skin. And he left. And he didn't even look back!"

He said, "All right, this is proof of what I was talking about. He struck that woman so that you would wear long sleeves, and your friend in the house across the street would stay at home. Afterwards when they make the street off limits and they put roadblocks in the alleys, and they inspect the pockets of every one passing through, these same fellows with their daggers or their G-3's and machine guns will go face the workers who want...."

Every morning at the school entrance they searched side and breast pockets and even the inside of Ra'na's books. When Hamed went to work in the administration, he said that they searched him. Akbar had found work...I don't know where. Little by little his hands became worn and blistered. Then they became hard. A patch became tough. Each time he shook my hand; it was as if he had placed a piece of iron in my palm. He said, "Yours sincerely, please forgive me, Ma'am, for all the bother." He said, "You must go out among the people. When you are among them you will see what all of their pain is about."

At the time he thought only that their pain was that children were sick and they had no money to buy medicine, or to pay the doctor. We also have no money. The rent on the house is six months overdue. They cut off Hamed's salary. That was one year ago. Ra'na is fine. She goes to school. Barbad is all right as well; he just doesn't talk. He is silent. He sits in his room. I bring papers and his colored inks and I sit and draw for him. I draw a car. He looks. I draw a cat. He looks. I draw a tree, a stone, a bird. I try to draw everything that I can draw. In the same way that he used to draw when his father Hamed drew with him. He looks. He looks at me. Ra'na returns from school and sits at his side and draws for him. She lifts a hand and washes his face. He is clean, yet she washes him again. She combs his hair. She takes his hand and leads him outside. They sit in front of the door. Ra'na sits on one bench, Barbad on the other. They watch young boys playing soccer. Barbad doesn't even move his hand lest his eye stray from the ball. He only gazes in front of himself, at a place that I do not know. I do not know what he is looking at. Ra'na comes up from the stairs, breathing heavily. She places her head on my lap. She buries her face in my skirt and says, "Mama, Mama!"

Hamed doesn't understand. I said, "You have children. Those men are a lost cause. Our workers, are they like Akbar? Or are they peasants who came from their villages? There are still skilled workers in the oil refinery, or the steelworks. The Iraqis destroyed our Abadan. The refinery workers have now become peddlers on the street, or receive only half their salary, or have retired. Only a few of the factories have survived, but if raw materials don't arrive, the factories will sit idle. Under these circumstances, you wish to organize the people?"

He closed his book. He took off his glasses and he looked at me. With those squinty bloodshot eyes, he said, "Well?"

I said, "Akbar doesn't know. He doesn't understand. He didn't go to work so that he could live. He doesn't have a wife and a child. He realizes that at the most it is for one year, maybe two. He has a cause. He has a goal. Those men do not."

Akbar said, "One has to start somewhere. We actually believed that it would be sufficient to become armed and shoot. We would knock over one or two banks, terrorize two torturers, two Americans, until the people rise up."

Sadiq, or somebody said, "Excuse me, let's not bring up what has already happened. I don't agree. These things need a great amount of discussion."

Hamed said, "Why shouldn't we kill?"

"Well, why shouldn't we kill?" I said to Hamed, "Let's look at other events, not only those from the period of the Constitutional Revolution."[8]

I said, "Don't you remember when you came to ask for my hand in marriage? When they found out what you were and what your beliefs were, what a fuss they made! They said not even a 'wet hand' should be extended to you.

"My father said, 'Well, this gentleman is your ladyship's teacher, isn't he?' You have learned these ideas from him and that is why you have stopped praying.'"

Now he says, "Well, you wanted him, so suffer the consequences!" He never visits his grandchild. "If I knew myself exactly what he was up to, I would denounce him. You are all counter-revolutionaries."

He had just learned the slogan "counter-revolutionary"—me, Hamed and the nine-year old Ra'na? Father says, "She is no longer a child, she's reached the age of maturity."

---

8. The result of the 1906-1907 Constitutional Revolution was that Mozaffar al-Din Shah granted the constitution in 1906 and signed it one week before his death in 1907.

I say, "What maturity? Having a husband? Having a child? Cooking? Or, maybe having a fifty, sixty year-old male ghoul sleeping with her?"

He says, "Why fifty or sixty years old, why not fifteen years old?"

I say, "All right, fifteen years old. I suppose two more years and they will have children, how can they study then?"

He says, "And you, who have studied, what good has it ever done me?"

I say, "Fine, Ra'na and I. We are your 'counter revolutionaries.' So be it, we are. What about Barbad? Tell me. Um? Why Barbad? Why doesn't my son speak? Why must he always sit and stare?"

Barbad stares. He never comes over and places a hand on my head. He never sits at my side and pulls at the hem of my skirt. He said, "You are both at fault. It is your own fault! Why did you bring a child there?"

I answered, "They permitted him to enter. Do you understand? They only permitted a five year-old boy to see his father. Now tell me why he doesn't speak?"

I don't know myself. The doctors also don't know. Doctor Sadiqi, the psychiatrist, a friend of Hamed, came over one night. He said, "Does he suddenly wake up at night?"

I said, "No."

He said, "Does he make sounds, for example, does he grind his teeth, beat his hands or feet together, or wake up suddenly?"

I said, "No, he sleeps."

He said, "Before, were these symptoms not present?"

I said, "No, in the middle of the night he would come to us from his room. He'd stretch himself out between us and squirm around. With his elbow he hit my side. When I rolled over, and slept on my stomach, he tickled me. I said, 'Go to sleep Barbad! Now that you have come, would you at least go to sleep!' Hamed placed his hand over his eyes and said, 'Why are the lights still on?' Barbad then batted away his hand and let out a burst of laughter in Hamed's face in the same way that Hamed does. He said, 'Daddy doesn't have a mustache, Daddy doesn't have glasses.'"

The doctor went into the children's room. He had brought out a train for Barbad. He steered the train himself and made it go. But all in vain! Barbad was just sitting there. He stared. He did not even look at the train. The doctor said, "Do you know how to draw?"

The doctor sat at his side. He picked up Barbad's colored pens and began to draw. He drew a car. The doctor showed it to him and said, "Come, why don't you draw?"

But Barbad only stared. His hands were placed over his knees and he sat. The doctor drew a pigeon and said, "Now then, draw this one."

He continued to draw. Barbad did not look at him. He asked me, "Did he used to draw?"

I said, "Yes." I showed him. He said, "He is talented. What is the matter with him now?"

I brought out several folders. Lines were scrawled all over the pages. He flipped through the pages. Again he looked at them from top to bottom. He removed his glasses, rubbed his eyes and looked again. All the while Barbad was looking at him and listening. I knew that he had been listening. The doctor said, "I don't understand, if there is something the matter with him, there must be something in these same drawings. With your permission I will take these drawings with me."

What! I was the one who didn't understand. He had merely drawn some lines of different colors. For example, there was a sort of black and red cloud. Another was like black earth, or like the waves of the sea, but gray. I don't know what else.

Father still says, "You all are to blame. You must pay the penalty for your sin. You spoke in front of the child constantly. You conversed in front of the boy, just as you did with Ra'na. We have a *hadith*[9] that says that the inborn nature of every human being is pure, is divine. But you ruin it."

I say, "Has Barbad returned to the state in which he was created?"

Hamed would say, 'What inborn nature'? What self? A person is created according to the conditions of his environment. A person is created through his culture. One born in Africa is born according to the tribal conditions, one here…."

Father would say, "But all of them, all of them believe in one thing."

I say, "Father, well, these believers of yours, must they consume those who believe in another thing or nothing at all? Eat them alive? They say that there is a man who eats the ears of people for good fortune and blessing. In the lines of those waiting to visit, a young girl returned from meeting her mother and father and they asked her 'well what's new?' She said, 'Daddy has a beard and mommy has no arm.'"

Father says, "That is a lie. It is a rumor."

I say, "Then why do all of the prisons never open until the reporters come to inspect? At least they should deliver Majid's body to an international organization or to a medical team so that they could investigate what was done to him."

---

9. Traditions related to the Prophet Mohammad and valid for all Moslems while those attributed to the Imams (the descendants of the Prophet Mohammad) are valid only for Shiites.

He says, "But they are the enemies. Don't you understand? The enemies!"

I say, "Yes, but they shouldn't stretch us on a torture rack, and employ the *hadd*[10] penalty, or amputate a hand or a foot."

He says, "But if it is the law, then it is necessary to cut off the foot and the hand. What do we do with an infected limb? The doctor tells us that we must cut it off. They cut it off."

Yes, they have amputated hands. They cut off the hand of that child's mother so that she most certainly said, "Daddy has a beard, Mommy has no hand." If only Barbad would say as much!

They would sit in the salon then, smoking cigarettes, and they would talk. Majid would say, "Gentlemen, gentlemen, you are so noisy, interrupting one another's speech. I am the one in charge of this meeting, so to speak. Ask for permission. Please! Now it is the lady's turn, then Sadiq, and after him, myself."

The hairs on his forehead had fallen out. They raided his house. He wasn't at home. He came and stayed for a week. From morning until night he would sit in a corner. He made a pile of the delicate yellowing papers, put down carbon paper and began to copy. The pile was a mountain of press clippings. His cigarette was giving off smoke, and his tea became cold. I said, "Majid-Khan, your tea is getting cold."

He said, "I drink it cold."

He would leave in the afternoon and come back late. They arrested him on the street. When Hamed came, he was angry. He said, "He shouldn't have gone outside, he really shouldn't have gone out at all!"

Majid used to come in the evening, late, with a lot of news. He had brought with him Nima's[11] "Makh Oula,"[12] a leather volume, embossed with gold. He said, "I found it in the alley. They had placed a sack filled with books on the side of the alley and left it, as if it were a bag filled with trash. When I arrived, a child who had been fiddling with the books threw down this book and ran away."

Afterwards, they sat together and they read the poem "Streetwalker" out loud:

---

10. *Hadd* is the physical punishment stipulated by Islamic law for certain violations of religious prescriptions.

11. Nima Yushij (1895–1959), the founder of free verse in Persian poetry

12. Makh Oula, the title of a poem by Nima and the name of a valley in Iran's northern province of Mazanderan

Every night a streetwalker
Visits me.

They read to me as well:
On one of those nights,
One of those lonely nights
To which every bitterness was attached,
And that streetwalker
Had visited me.
Her long curls—like moss on the water—
Turned around my head,
And threw me
Into helpless and twisted torment.

He said, "We saw them with our own eyes and we didn't believe it. Do you know, one day two women had brought fresh, crisp bread for them into the prison. The 'gentlemen' were in the adjacent cell. They managed their affairs separate from us. I had just arrived. I figured, they are older than me, so I ought to show them some respect. I took the bread in front of their cell and I gave it to one of them. He squinted at me. He took the bread with two fingers as if dragging the tails of two dead young puppies. Then he tossed the bread into the trashcan. Afterwards he stuck his hand in the water basin three times. Poppy-seed bread that had just been taken from the ovens! One of their devotees had sent it. I didn't know who. We didn't understand that we were *najis*.[13] The SAVAK[14] agents were not unclean. The Shah was also not unclean. They didn't spread their clothes out on a line. They always took their long cloaks and hung their clothing on the only tree in the compound. In the spring we couldn't see the blossoms. One of them put his underwear on his head and dried his forehead. From morning until noon he would walk across the courtyard, his shorts on his head. Every day he would do the same thing. He walked with his shorts on his head!"

Majid laughed, and he hit his balding forehead. He kept saying, "What asses we were, we saw and we didn't understand!!"

He said, "Do you believe that two of them went around inside the courtyard with their shoes wrapped in plastic bags. 'Khash! Khash!'"

---

13. Ritually unclean.
14. The secret police during the regime of the Shah.

He laughed. "Yes, 'khash, khash,' in the morning. 'khash, khash' in the afternoon. They didn't talk with one another. Because everything was clear. It is clear. One only had to open the book and see the source. 'Khash, Khash.' Their arguments at night were generally about the stomach, and their nightly dessert consisted of dirty jokes about sex, homosexuals, intercourse and the like. Would you believe it?"

He whispered something in Hamed's ear and they both laughed. I went into the kitchen. They laughed again. Hamed found an excuse and came to me and said, "Really, wasn't it funny?"

I said, "You both are just like them! Two sides of the same coin, or else...."

He frowned. He said, "Don't start again! We did it ourselves! We ourselves ought to take it!

Then he bent over and picked up two plastic bags from the drawer and twisted them around his ankles and tied them with plastic strips into a knot. I said, "Hamed, don't do that, he is our guest, you'll make him uncomfortable."

He put his finger over his lip and strode out of the kitchen. "Khash! Khash! Khash! Khash!" Majid was laughing. He was doubled over in laughter. Hamed didn't laugh at all. With great seriousness, he slid across the tiles. I wanted to say, "Isn't it enough?" But I couldn't. Because the way he walked was funny. Stepping widely, as if he had a swollen prostate gland, or as if he didn't want the wet seat of his trousers to touch his legs. Majid also got up. He tore off a piece of the newspaper and put it on his head and walked beside him. They went back and forth. Majid with one hand held the piece of paper as if it was his wet shorts, and with his other hand he grasped his trousers so that they wouldn't fall. I laughed and then placed the tray with the tea on the floor and sat down. I said, "God, will you stop that!"

Hamed placed his finger on his lip and again they went, "Khash, Khash!" They killed Majid. They executed him. They knew him. He had always been the chairman of the meetings. He would say, "Now it is your turn, Madame, please, keep it short and to the point."

Roqiyyeh kept saying, "Look, gentlemen, I only have one piece of news that I wish to report to you. It is reliable. In the north of the city, yes, in the quarter of the Taghutis,[15] the very place where all the leaders have now taken up residence, a little girl, wearing pants, was riding her

---

15. *Taghuti,* adjective of '*taghut*' meaning idol (used in the Koran several times), since the Iranian Revolution of 1979 the current term for anything or anyone connected to the regime of the Shah.

bicycle around the outside of the house or in the alley. The officers in charge of public morality arrested her for indecent exposure and took her away. Her parents found out. They went everywhere, until at last the next morning they found her. They investigated the matter and realized, that for the crime of not wearing a veil or indecent exposure, the required penalty is the hadd, 100 lashes. Her father and mother began to cry and beg, saying that after all, the child was only nine years old. They said, "She has reached the age of maturity." They said, "We promised that…."

Akbar said, "Madame, please, make it shorter, we just don't have time to listen to this story."

Majid said, "If it is necessary, I will give reminders."

Roqiyyeh said, "I'm sorry, I'll sum it up. All right, in the end they lowered the penalty to fifty lashes. The father and mother both made affidavits stating that from now on she will wear a veil outside. When they brought out the girl and she understood that she was going to receive the hadd punishment, she began to cry. 'I cannot….' The judge said finally, 'She must receive thirty lashes since she has reached the age of maturity. It cannot be decreased.' The young girl stretched herself out on the couch and placed her head on the skirt of her mother, who said…."

Akbar said, "I object."

Roqiyyeh said, "Yes, I'll sum it up. They only gave her six lashes, the sixth blow hit her spinal column and she died. The end. Thank you."

Akbar again shouted, "I have an objection."

Majid said, "Don't shout, please, especially here, because…."

He himself was shouting. Afterwards everyone spoke softly. Akbar said, "First of all let us examine what percentage of our population has a problem wearing the veil. Among the peasants, the case is clear. The wives of the workers or the housewives cover their heads, or even wear the chador over their heads. That leaves the middle class…."

He was explaining that one section of the middle class and most of the upper classes and I don't know what…I wasn't listening. I said to Hamed, "This foolish talk, what is it for? In the end, who are they?"

He said, "Then what's really happened?"

I said, "If you do not support the rights of every individual…allowing for the most basic rights of man, like your religious beliefs and mine, then how can you stand up for such and such a person?"

He said, "You are going too fast, my dear. We have just started. We have only recently arrived in the history of the world. Allow them to learn their lessons. Afterwards they will understand."

He did not understand himself. I say we have been crushed. We have been consumed and crushed. When the members of the Komiteh[16] stormed the house and took the books! I said the same thing when they were ripping open the mattresses and the cushions. They even tore open the stomachs of Ra'na's old dolls. I said, "Please, I don't know if what you are doing is Islamic or not. But this is my room and my house. It is just like when the Mongols or the Arabs attacked. It is exactly the same!"

They said, "We should take you away too. But for their sake we won't."

I said, "OK, kill them, or take them as prisoners of war. Without a father and without an income, how can I raise them?"

I also said to Father, "They want to make it like Saudi Arabia here."

He said, "And is that bad? If something gets lost there, for example, if it has fallen on the ground, one month later, it is still there. Go to the police station and you can pick it up."

I said, "I have seen it, I know. In a Cadillac some women with a chador and a facemask are crammed inside, while the shaykh sits in the front seat. As if a woman were a chicken. For the task of laying eggs, one rooster is sufficient!"

Hamed said, "They can't do it here. We have had Hafez,[17] Rumi,[18] Ferdowsi, is it really possible here?"

He said, "In India among all of those Hindus, Brahmins and Buddhists, a man became the leader. Every morning he would drink a glass of milk and then a glass of his own urine. He wouldn't do it only in private, he even gave interviews about it. He would say, it follows the same cycle as man himself follows. Thus it gets purified, it purifies, and helps one to live longer. But the practice didn't catch on. Why? Because a little bit of democratic tradition has taken root there. For the urine of hungry people has no nutritional value, especially if they are seventy years old, and have no milk to drink."

I said, "But these people, these so-called friends of yours, all of them dividing up society layer by layer, how come they don't understand?"

He himself did not understand, either. I said, "Let's gather up these books and let's take them somewhere. I will place them in a sack, and every day I will take some ten to twenty books and will drop them somewhere. Look and see what people have done already. Go and see what has

---

16. Komitehs are committees formed at the beginning of the Islamic Revolution in neighborhoods and on a national level, with power and authority to quell any kind of resistance.

17. Hafez (ca.1325–1392), the greatest lyrical poet of the Persian language

18. Rumi, Jalal al-Din (d. 1273), the greatest mystical poet of the Persian language

been dumped along the edge of the canals or in the abandoned lots! They have piled book upon book and then left. Not to mention the newspapers! When water comes through, it carries only proclamations. And yet, you keep collecting them, stacking them next to each other and above each other."

He said, "Me and my books. If they are no longer here, I do not exist, either. I will not exist."

He was sensitive toward books, only books. In the end, the books were taken. They were all taken away. The empty bookshelves, with the faded color of the wall behind them! Barbad no longer touched anything. Hamed had taught him to sit down and draw something. When they had discussions he would sit next to him. "Daddy, Daddy, look!" Hamed said, "OK, afterwards I'll look, don't you see that I am busy?"

They were all so busy. They all had work to do. What about me? Father said, "And what of the *pasdaran*?[19] They also have wives and children like the rest of us."

I said, "Like Taqi?"

He was his errand boy. He always had an open pimple leaking puss somewhere on him, either on his chin, or on the tip of his nose. He would cast his eyes downward when he said hello. He was obedient, trustworthy and he said his prayers regularly. I said, "Hamed, don't you get it? You, who divide society into different 'strata,' find me a place for Taqi. All of these men, to what class do they belong? From which of your 'folds' are they? All of a sudden, this one has taken a G-3 into his hands and has put on a pasdar's uniform, and he is on the hunt for the likes of you. I know who he is. I have looked into his eyes—when I was a girl. The moment the hair on my head showed, he'd put his head down and leave. Yet at the same time, his eyes showed that if he could, he'd secretly snatch a clump of hair from my head."

No, I didn't know what it was. I thought it was only sexual repression. Now I don't know what it is. Like those dreams I have, last night and every night. To whom can I speak about them? They amputated a man's arm and leg. He was one of "God's opponents." They cut off his left leg and his right arm. I dreamt that he kept dancing on one foot. All the while, from his right shoulder and above his left thigh blood came spurting out as if from a fountain. But he kept dancing and dancing. He came to my side…. Last night I was in the middle of a forest. I had fallen asleep on my back on the ground. He came at me, dancing on one foot, hips

19. Pasdaran (plural of pasdar) are revolutionary guards with special police powers.

swaying. His hand was making circles in the air. He came and became bigger and bigger. It was almost as if his hand were in the sky, in the clouds that were not there. His foot was just a stump. It smashed and settled on the ground and then went up. It dragged across the stones and made the sound "khash...khash." His shadow fell upon me...upon me, Barbad and Ra'na.... Upon me, Ra'na, Barbad, Hamed and Majid...even Akbar, even Father, and Taqi. The sound of "khash...khash" of his feet covered in plastic like a thousand broken drums...I don't know. He would keep coming and coming. I didn't even tell the doctor about it. I thought that he would speak again about the subconscious, for he thinks that something was definitely wrong with me. I took Barbad to see him and I said, "Doctor, what is wrong with him? What should I do with this child?"

He said, "Please, I have a lot of work. These days so many people are nervous or even crazy that I don't even have time to scratch my head."

I said, "Something must be wrong. But I really want him to speak, I desperately want him to say what he has seen there."

I said that the visitation was for him. I said that because they wouldn't give me permission to see him. I went before dawn. I stood in the line with the two kids behind me. I had hoped that the children would cause them to have mercy upon me. At around noon I reached the door. They said, "He doesn't have visiting privileges. We will call." They didn't. I went there again, I went to the office of the state's attorney, to the Evin,[20] to the Majles, "Parliament." They said, "These games from the time of the shah when you could exchange information with the prisoners are now over. We are experienced. We have been in prison. These tricks of yours will no longer work."

Ra'na was wearing a headscarf with her school uniform. They didn't permit her to go in. I said, "At least allow this one? He really wants to see his Daddy."

If only I had kept my mouth shut and hadn't said it. My son went in. On those two little feet of his, he went. He went hand in hand with one of the guards. He went in. One hour. Two hours. Afterwards he came out. He came out hand in hand with the same guard he had gone in with. A piece of candy was in his other hand. He didn't eat it. The guard was laughing. Barbad wasn't. He wasn't laughing. He was only looking. I said, "How's your Daddy doing, darling?"

He didn't say a word. I said, "Did you see him?"

He didn't say a word. I said, "What did they do to him?"

I took the collar of the boy and began to shake him hard. I pulled at

---

20. Evin was a much feared prison in northern Tehran, before and after the revolution.

the top of his head, but even then he didn't cry. I said, "Doctor, what has he seen? What happened to my husband? I know he exists. He is alive. I went to a forensic specialist and I asked, and I went to Behesht-e Zahra.[21] They said, "They have not brought anyone with such a name here."

He went to get Barbad's drawings and spread them out over his table. He said, "Look. This child is an artist, this much is certain. He is talented. He has been able to take the things that he sees and represent them on paper directly. But I don't know what is going on now."

He then asked, "Have you ever told him stories about spirits, genies, and fairies?"

I said, "No."

He said, "What about his grandmother or his grandfather? Those who know these kinds of stories…like the story about the demon that rose in a column out of a bottle in a cave? Or, I don't know, a story about the sorceress Rayhaneh, or about the dragon with the seven heads and the snake of the Day of Resurrection?"

I said, "I don't know. But he owns some books that his father read to him that deal with men from outer space, for example."

He said, "A person's subconscious is very powerful. Our conscious thought, our reason, is only a covering that hides the subconscious. The depths of the subconscious contains much information, filled with these very same things, or at least appears in the forms of these things, like the very same horned demon which came forth from a bottle in a column of smoke."

I said, "Doctor, what do I care about the subconscious? I don't want the child to explore his soul. I want him to speak. I want him to tell me what he saw there."

He showed me the child's drawings. Amidst all of those multicolored crooked and squiggly lines there was something that was the shape of a dragon…or I don't know…a place where two eyes were. They were two large eyes with red pupils and black veins inside the whites. The doctor kept saying there is also a millipede somewhere else. A broken line and he calls it a millipede! The edge of the paper was torn. He would say, "Do you see? There are more."

I said, "He didn't go and see animals in there. He didn't go to a zoo. Inside there are prisoners and prison guards, where they torture, cut off limbs, and stretch people out on the gallows in front of all of the prisoners. Let's suppose that Barbad is like that little girl who saw that her father

---

21. Behesht-e Zahra is the main cemetery in Tehran.

has no arm. What connection do these things have with the horned demon or the dragon with seven heads?"

He said, "I don't know. It's just the way it is. These are just the things I understand. This boy does not speak. If he spoke you would understand. He doesn't even make signs."

Barbad does not speak, not a word. When I do the ironing, he passes the clothes one by one to me. When I sew, he comes and sits beside me. I say, "Barbad, are you listening? Shake your head. Did Daddy have a beard?"

He stares at me. I make a gesture with my hand and I say, "Did Daddy have no hand? Or was Daddy blind?"

I place my hand over one eye…or I place it over one ear…or I twist my ear and make a gnashing sound with my teeth as if to say that they ate his ear. He only looks. He doesn't even shake his head. He understands. I know he understands. From his eyes I understand. I am his mother. From the shaking of his fingers I understand. But he doesn't cry. Hamed said, "When Khosrow's[22] horse Shabdiz died, no one had the courage to tell him, for Khosrow had said, 'whoever brings me the news of Shabdiz' death, I will kill him.' Barbad went and sat and sang so sadly and so mournfully that Khosrow said, 'Did Shabdiz die?' He himself said that Shabdiz had died."

My father said, "Barbad? A singer? You named my grandson after a minstrel? Shame on you!"

I didn't want it, either. It always reminded me of how Barbad kneeled humbly before King Khosrow. He does not say anything, not a word. If he would speak, only two words…a couple of sentences, I would understand what happened…or what he saw there…or at least to find out what is going on here, what is happening to us.

22.Khosrow was a Sasanian king whose story, and that of his minstrel Barbad, is told in Ferdowsi's epic poem, the *Shahnameh*.

My Nirvana

TRANSLATED BY
JUDITH M. WILKS

If there were someone who would throw me towards you,
I would put myself in a sling.
                              -Rudaki[1]

Of course, sometimes a man feels depressed and, well, he goes outside into the street, he sits on the front steps, or perhaps beside the gutter in front of Hojjati the engineer's house, and if he has a cane, he grips the shaft of it with both hands and rests his chin on it, or at least rests his forehead on the back of his hands. My wife was saying, "How could you not see him?"

Well, I did see him but I wasn't in the mood to strike up a conversation. We were coming out of the notary's office. I had finally signed the permission form for Akhtar to travel abroad. But to tell the truth, deep in my heart I wasn't happy about it. There are some things that a man has a feeling about beforehand, even if, as in my case, his hand does not tremble when he's signing it.

I didn't think he of all people could be crying, Dr. Haqiqi, a high-ranking judge, albeit in past times, with his imposing stature and his way of nodding hello in those days. How much older than myself was he, anyway? Seven years, at the most. Of course, I had heard that he was ill. There was always something wrong with him, this time it was his blood pressure. But I was not at home. Banu had come to our door first. She never talks much. The engineer always says of her, "She's so discreet for a servant!"

She had only said to the engineer, "Help us take Aqa[2] to the hospital."

There she said to the doctor, "I believe Aqa is saying, 'I don't know why I'm so tired.'" It had happened one day before noon. And Banu had planned

---

1. Rudaki of Samarkand (d. 940) was the first renowned Persian poet.
2. Banu always refers to her employer as "*Aqa*," meaning "master, sir."

to go someplace. Perhaps to see some relatives. And in the evening she had not been able to return. When she comes back the next morning, she sees that Aqa is asleep. She thinks he's taking a nap again. When she takes him his food at noon, she has to wake him up. Then Aqa says, "Didn't I say I was tired? Why don't you let me sleep?" Then when he gets out of bed, he sits down and asks, "Haven't you gone yet?"

At my wife's insistence I went to see him. She said, "Have you forgotten how he helped us?"

It was about Behruz. He had been arrested in the demonstrations of 1356 (1977). I knew nothing about it. His mother had phoned Akhtar. It was nothing serious. He had denied any involvement. Moreover, things no longer were as they had been before. Not that I believed it. Behruz had told his mother they don't use torture any more. He had shown her his hands and even his legs. Saideh was trembling as she described it. How she had aged, it had been ten years since I had seen her. Then later, when I found out that the novels had reached her, I began to believe that something was really happening. I didn't want to know what, that's why I didn't write. She was always worried about Behruz, or rather, about all the Behruzes who had filled the streets. Dr. Haqiqi helped them find a lawyer. He really presented a good defense. After the revolution I saw him again a few times, once I gave him a lift in my car. He said he had been forbidden to practice law. He was now working in the law offices of one of his acquaintances. He said, "Who would have believed things could get this way?" He wouldn't accept any money from us. My wife said, "Now we should repay him for his legal advice."

I felt embarrassed doing it. Of course, now we're talking about how influential Dr. Haqiqi was in those days. He also helped the engineer out, I believe. He doesn't talk about it. That's why the engineer still likes him so much, or at least he used to. Sometimes he would invite him over. I also went to one of these gatherings, what a great party it was! The judge hadn't yet become the way he is now. The engineer was saying, "He doesn't talk any more, he just dozes off suddenly."

I really wasn't in the mood for it, although I was never in the mood for it before that, either, in the days when he used to keep his car in front of their house waiting for Banu's brother to come and put it in the garage. And then when the inevitable happened, he was always talking about his Laleh or Leyli, and how they had met, or where she was now. It was before the revolution, in '55 or '56 (1976 or 1977). I don't know how they had figured out that it was all over. At that time the woman had one foot here and one foot in the Gulf emirates. She used to say, "How many times does one come into this world? It's always been the way it is now, and after this, 'Oh, would there were the hope of springing forth again.'"[3]

My wife was saying, "She's smuggling jewels."

She was only guessing. But it was certainly true that the judge was selling his houses and properties in exchange for dollars or pounds or, let's say, jewels, and his wife would take the money out of the country. We later learned that she had deposited it in her own name in the Bank of England.

I rang the bell several times. And I heard the sound of Banu's wooden slippers. I knew she was looking at me through the peephole. I said, "Banu, it's me. I've come to see the judge."

Finally she opened the door. She is short and chubby. I think she is about forty. She is still good-looking, with her round red cheeks and large bluish-green eyes. She always looks as if she has a piece of candy or chocolate in her mouth. She puckers up her lips, makes a sucking sound though there is nothing there to suck, and then finally she says something. She said, "Aqa is asleep."

She spoke quietly. She opened the door only enough to show her round face, and I could see half of her body. Later I found out why she hadn't opened the door all the way. I heard the voice of the judge, as if moaning. I couldn't tell what he was asking for. Banu had seen the bouquet I had brought right away, of course. I had told her why I had come, but she went away again. She closed the door, of course. When I was describing this later to my wife, she only then realized why Banu usually talked with the neighbors through the kitchen window. Finally Banu came back and opened the door for me. She was wearing the same blouse with a dark blue background and tiny white flowers on it. She had put the judge's vest on over it. She had both sleeves rolled up. The hallway was entirely empty. There wasn't even a chair. There were several marks on the wall where paintings had hung, and in place of the chandelier there were only two bare wires hanging. The door of the parlor was closed. Banu walked ahead of me, one foot in front of the other, just as Lily or Leyla would have done, then again perhaps so I wouldn't hear the noise of her wooden shoes on the bare floor. Their bedrooms were on the upper floor. Dr. Haqiqi was in the room, which I believe had been Banu's own room when the lady of the house had still been there. Dr. Haqiqi used to always call her by a different name, for

---

3. Quoting a verse from Omar Khayyam. The full *bayt* would be: "Would that after one hundred thousand years, like the green grass, there were hope to spring from the heart of the dust again." From *The Ruba'iyat of 'Umar Khayyam*, translation by Parichehr Kasra, Persian Heritage Series no. 21, Scholars' Facsimiles and Reprints, Delmar, New York, 1975. Verse # 163.

example Leyli or Lily or Leyla. Banu would only call her "Khanum." Even my wife doesn't know what her name really was. But we really didn't socialize much, I mean, my wife didn't want to. When the case of Behruz came up, I was the one who had to go and see them. Laleh or Leyli, or whatever it was, had read my book, "Barbara and John," when she was a university student. Then later on, when she learned that I am, I mean, who I am, she came "to have the honor" of making my acquaintance. She also brought a bouquet of white daisies. I was completely taken aback. Afterwards my wife teased me, saying, "You're very happy."

At first we only exchanged a few words about the story. Like everyone else, she wanted to know whether these things had actually happened or not, for example, was John the sort of man that I had described, or was I myself, the narrator, personally involved in the triangle with Barbara and John? She put her hand in front of her mouth so I wouldn't see that she was giggling, or rather so that I would understand that she was giggling. I said that John was a real person, but of course not as I had described. Then we moved on to more general matters. This is the way it always happens. For example, they ask, what is literature, in your opinion? Then one is obliged to explain. Then comes another question, and one starts talking, and they think, what a marvelous, intelligent person. But I was already past this stage where in one interview I would unravel the clothes that I had once put on to cover my nakedness, or rather, that I should vacate these stalls that once had been my shelter, so that they could perhaps serve as shelters for those just arriving. For this reason I speak of irrelevant things, so that they can make an effort to find things out for themselves, even, for example, for Leyli, with her shiny black hair, short but tousled, with a few white hairs from the temples down to behind the ears. She fiddled with those hairs constantly. She would moisten her lips with the tip of her tongue, and my wife would come in and out. It was obvious that she was angry, particularly since Leyli had come into my study. She herself had become acquainted with me in this same way. I was seated behind my table, doing something, I don't know what. Leyli had said to my wife, "Oh, for goodness sake, just let me see him as he is."

I was wearing an old pair of Lee jeans, a short-sleeved shirt, and slippers. Thank goodness that my wife doesn't permit me to wear pajamas, even in my own room. But then again, Leyli wasn't wearing anything too alluring, I mean, for instance, sleeveless or with a low neckline, such that a man could not imagine looking somewhere else, even in the presence of his own wife, who had insisted that he receive her very cordially. At the first glance I noticed what a tiny waist she had. And her legs were really beautiful, although her skirt was long and she didn't cross her legs or anything. Her blouse was white, with long, puffed sleeves, and her long skirt was pleated. When my wife brought tea, we had already started talking about politics. She was saying, "I'm not staying."

She also talked about her interest in painting. She had bought many paintings. Of course, by then she herself didn't paint any more. I later saw her easels and paintings, the day the judge moved out. He didn't have much. Out of all those carpets and rugs and chairs and couches and, I don't know, cabinets and silver and china sets, only that one iron-framed bed was left, and a few trunks and a few boxes that must have contained their cooking utensils, and a small refrigerator. The judge had even sold quite a lot of their china sets. Or perhaps Leyli sold them. At about the time when she said that she was going to London. She had returned from Dubai. She was saying, "Why are you staying?"

I spoke about my hopes, all the hopes we all had in those years. Leyli thought that this was no longer a place one could live. They had thrown acid on the face of one of her friends from her university days. She herself had been through quite a lot. They had not let her participate in a demonstration until a woman gave her a headscarf. She was saying, "I can't take this."

They even put a picture of the Imam [Khomeini] in her hands; she was in the front row. Later, I don't know, she sees her own picture in the newspapers, even the foreign newspapers. But she didn't mention this to me. Akhtar was saying, "The women in chadors had pinched her so hard that there were bruises on her back here and there. And in the end she couldn't endure it, she ran away crying, and when she got home I don't know if she burned her headscarf or what." She was saying, "I hated my father, he was always giving me orders."

I said, "If the Shah leaves and this damned organization SAVAK is eliminated, I would not be opposed to my wife wearing a chador."

She said, "What about you yourself? Are you willing to grow a beard and wear a collarless shirt like they do?"

With bloodshot eyes, of course. He was sitting upon my chest, and with a voice that sounded like snoring and came forth from between empty teeth grinding something that didn't exist, he was saying, "I'll cut off your head."

My wife broke in, "Of course not, it's easy enough for him to say."

Then the conversation turned to the youths, those wearing Lee jeans and military pullovers and worn-out athletic shoes. She said, "Those guys from the university interrogated me, and all for the crime of wearing ordinary clothes like these. I don't want to wear Lee jeans." It was in those days that she decided to marry the judge. She was saying, "Those leftists are worse than the women in chadors or the bearded men." I even remember that she was saying, "If I could once get my hands on them." I didn't understand exactly whom she was talking about, perhaps she meant the guy who had thrown the acid, or else…I don't know. Maybe she was talking about me and others like me. She said, "For years I've wanted to get to know you."

I know what she meant. Perhaps she also thought that there was still in me some remnant of that person who used to write, so she could see whether or not he was still in love. Leyli wanted to know what I was writing now. Perhaps this was why she had come, so she could see what the papers on my table were, or what, for example, I was doing to support the wall of the house we were raising, that is, our common cause. I got really flustered. Not from the scent of her perfume, nor from her graceful hands or her long fingers that leafed through the papers on my table. There were so many pleats of fabric on her chest that one could not even discern the curves of her breasts that were surely quivering underneath. Later, when my wife was interrogating me, I understood how she had seen it, insofar as it's possible to see it as she had. At night I surely would kiss Akhtar's earlobe, but my fingers would all the while be groping for those few gray-colored hairs that Leyli had been curling around her fingertips. Then, too, maybe I didn't want to be one of the points in a triangle of which another point would be Dr. Haqiqi, who came to see me the next day. He said, "I don't want to leave, but since Lili wants to leave, I'll go." He asked if I would be kind enough to prepare for him a list of old works and even new works of literature, especially the editions that explain the meanings of difficult words. He didn't say anything, but I thought he surely would want to read the Khamseh of Nezami [Nezami's Quintet],[4] or for example, that he had already read "Leyli and Majnun," but as that was so difficult, he had concluded that he had to start from scratch. So he said, "I don't have much time. Actually, I don't even remember what I read yesterday."

I bought ten or fifteen selections for him, and along with them a couple of my own books of which I had extra copies, and of course also the long list that I wanted Leyli to read, and I gave them to Banu, telling her to be sure to give them to Aqa. The next day I learned that they had sent the money in payment for these things, along with a memo that said something like this, "Please oblige me by buying the rest of them yourself. Please be so kind

---

4. Persian poet Nezami of Ganjeh (ca.1141–1203). One of his five romances is 'Leyli [also Leyla] and Majnun' which has become the Eastern archetype of star-crossed lovers, the equivalent of Romeo and Juliet

as to accept this in payment." Leyli later learned about this and said to my wife, "These guys are so dull." And then we started with the demonstrations and the strikes and finally the clashes of the second half of 1357 (1978) that left no time for reading books. We were always reading newspapers and declarations, and if I wrote anything, it was about things I had known before I started writing, not as I am writing now, so that perhaps I might send it to Leyli. I saw her again. She brought me a bottle of whiskey as a gift when she came back from London. Banu brought it over. And once she invited us over to their house. At the last moment my wife decided not to go. I had seen the trees of their courtyard from on top of the roof. There were black poplars all around, and three weeping willows. I thought there must also be a pool in the middle. But there wasn't. They had set up a large wooden deck in the middle of the courtyard. And all around were gravel beds, and four triangular arrangements of vines. Hojjati the engineer and his wife came. Leyli was all dressed up. She was wearing a sleeveless blue blouse. Her chest was so well covered with pleats that if my wife had come she wouldn't have had any reason to snipe. She remembers everything. She even remembers where we were sitting when I was talking about the soft, downy space between her breasts. When Leyli turned around, if I remember correctly, in order to talk with the engineer's wife, her bare back dazzled me, my eyes remained fixed on it, just like most of the men who, according to Akhtar, these days see only a few strands of hair peeking out from the corner of a headscarf, or who cannot take their eyes off a bare ankle. Even before dinner, the men and women had separated. We sat on the deck around the brazier, and the women sat down around the table, sitting on large logs that had been placed there. I couldn't take my eyes off Leyli's back, especially because framed in that trapezoidal opening was what I desired, so much so that even if I covered the outlines of her vertebrae with little kisses a thousand times, I would still want to do it one more time. Dr. Haqiqi was stroking the curve of Leyli's right shoulder. He was saying, "Believe me, until this past month, my lips wouldn't touch the stuff."

Leyli said, "I'm afraid to touch it, because I know myself."

The judge said, "You're wrong, my dear. Moreover, you can't get it over there, and even if there is any, you, the loveliest of all misers, would not want to look at it from a mile away."

He smoked some opium and followed it with a glass of arrack. He said, "One must seize the moment. Moments like these are all we have in life."

How proudly he spoke about the weakness of his memory. He even considered his lack of imagination a good thing, but later on, when Leyla didn't even write a couple of lines any more to inform him that such and such a sum of money had arrived, he would write, for example:

"Leyla, do send me a few pictures. It doesn't cost anything. You know yourself how weak my memory is. Now it's even worse. Sometimes I even think I've dreamt all these things, that's why I always imagine that at last one afternoon you will appear at the end of the street, without any veil or shawl. I believe at the time you went away these things had not yet become compulsory. Please at least send me a picture of you, full-length of course. I'm ashamed to say it, but to tell you the truth sometimes I can't remember what your hands look like, Banu's hands come to mind instead."

But that evening he was saying: "One must live each day to the fullest, I mean, that's what life is all about. A person who always pines for things of the past is just killing himself."

I believe that later on, when he realized that he had forgotten the warmth of Leyli's hands, and when he could no longer recall the exact spot of the mole between her vertebrae, just as now there is no longer any thought of the soft down on Akhtar's breast, he substituted the rituals of that brazier for all of these things. Hojjati the engineer was saying, "It's poison to him, but do you think he will listen to advice?"

Lately he had started smoking opium every day, we knew this from the smell of it. Nevertheless, we didn't think, the engineer and I, that things had gone this far. When Banu opened the door and said, "Come in," I saw that he was busy emptying a hookah. He wanted to smoke the burnt opium. The engineer couldn't believe it. He said: "No wonder, you find it wherever you go. These days, when prayer is not for the sake of getting close to God, but rather for the purpose of being promoted, this is the only way one can reach God."

Recently he has come to believe in the divinity of an Indian baba, "guru." Every evening, precisely at an appointed time, he lights a candle, sits cross-legged, and tries to internalize the warmth of the candle, and then he recites invocations.

Dr. Haqiqi put on some burnt opium for me as well. I said, "It gives me a headache."

He took a matchbox from the pocket of his housecoat and put it in front of me. There were only five or six little pills in it. So that his silence would not drive me nuts, I smoked a couple of them. He moaned about how expensive things are. I said, "Why should that be a problem for you of all people?"

He said, "You know how expensive things are over there."

He pointed to the kilim under his feet, or rather, to where there used to be a carpet. His hands were trembling. And his charcoal was giving off sparks. He had not yet sold the samovar and the brazier, maybe he never did sell them, even later on. He said, "The cure turned out to be worse than the disease."

I thought he meant to say that now he had nothing left but his addiction. I mean, that instead of breaking those barriers of the mind that impede the imagination, we have broken our bodies. And sometimes he would suddenly fall asleep. His head would be bent down upon his chest, and once he bent so far down towards the brazier that I thought he was going to fall at any moment. A string of saliva hung from the corner of his mouth. I offered him a few pills of burnt opium. He washed down one pill with tea. Then he spoke of Leyli again. He said, "I could give her a hard time."

Perhaps. Maybe in England he could. The engineer knew more than I did. Two years after the revolution the judge went to, you know, be with his wife and child. Their daughter was six years old. When they lived here, she was usually at Leyli's mother's house. He retired and left. There was nothing left for him. Of course there was still this house, which was owned by Leyli, and a sauna bath. There was also a dilapidated house, an inheritance from the judge's father. He went to England so they could, you know, live together. Leyli wouldn't even let him in. This was what I wanted to know. It was incredible, the two of them had realized that things would turn out as they did. He said, "I was a judge. You know that. I had studied international law, I could have given her a hard time."

Then he said: "For example, they want to take this house away from me. Well, I am not without influence, I still know a lot of people. At least I could get some money from a profiteer and entrust the house to him. Who could ever kick him out? I know many such people."

Then he began reminiscing again about his younger days. He couldn't remember exactly. Apparently he was in Shahrkord. In the early days of the unrest he had taken a stand against a local *khan*, "landlord." He was the chief justice of the court. In order to intimidate him they took his clerk and pulled down his pants and hung him on a tree in front of the judge's house. He said, "I wasn't intimidated. I went with a few policemen and arrested him."

He wanted me to stay for supper. I excused myself, saying I had work to do. He didn't say anything. What surprises me is that, as soon as people find out that I write, they immediately start talking about their lives and think that only the events of their lives make good material for stories, even Leyla, even when nothing had happened yet, that is, she had not yet begun to make her life a story; but Dr. Haqiqi didn't care about such things. He said, "I have copies of all my letters. If only I could send myself there instead of just writing."

I saw the engineer the next day as he was watering his trees. He greeted me. I had to stay and talk a while. He wanted to know how we had managed to send Behruz away. Surely Akhtar had already told him. I went through hell to get 300,000 tomans together as a pay-off. I sold my car. It was in my wife's name, but she was willing to do it. Then he talked about his children. About our daughters, his and mine. Until I put this little brick house in her name, she won't leave me alone. Behruz, for example, has taken his share, and the rest of it must be left to her and her daughters. She doesn't say this openly, but it's clear that's what she means. Then again, what matters is not Akhtar and our daughters, who are gradually beginning to learn that one can leave a lock of hair outside the veil, as if it had just fallen out. Perhaps this is why I should write. In '56 and '57 (1977 and 1978), I had devoted all my time to the young people; we drafted declarations or I signed their declarations, I had to write about it so that I could understand it. Maybe I should write about all these things. The writings were fragmentary but, well, that's what they are. I gave a speech at the University of Ahvaz, well, it's true that I was talking about literature and the calamity of censorship, but right in the middle of the talk they put before me a memo saying that there's a riot going on outside the door of the literature division, and suspicious individuals are walking around. After the speech it was suggested that we wait a bit so they could go away. In the end we went out through another door. We were walking with a few professors and a number of students when all at once I saw them coming straight at us. A few of them were carrying sticks. They were saying, "Death to the Soviet Union!" That meant me, as I had spoken about the samizdat[5] of the Soviet Union and many of them didn't like it. They roughed me up quite a bit. One of them sat upon my chest. He raised his fist, saying, "I'll punch you in the mouth, you filthy Jew!" Not only that, he wanted to cut off my head, but he didn't have a knife, but he said that's what he wanted to do, and all I could see were his two red bloodshot eyes. In the end the policemen rescued me. I think he also had a beard, like all those guys who were always showing up at every discussion at the University of Tehran, with shaved heads and wearing collarless shirts, they would elbow people and disperse the gathering, yelling, "Talk about it after the Shah is dead!"

Now, of course, it's too late for such discussions, the fragments have joined forces, all those in the university or even in the streets who tore up the declarations, or who threw bottles and rocks from the bridge at the unveiled women who demonstrated just a few days after the revolution.

---

5. Samizdat: the underground literature of the Soviet era.

But now I can write about these things, for myself. As for Haqiqi, it was clear what calamity was about to befall him. One month later he came to see me. Banu came and let us know that her Aqa wanted to pay us a visit. I couldn't believe it. He came with his briefcase, the same briefcase that he had used for years. Banu supported him under his arm as he walked. He hadn't even sat down when he said, "I want to speak with you alone."

I told my wife, and she said, "I'm going to my mother's house." She took the girls along, too. Only Banu was left, and she went to the kitchen. The judge first opened up his briefcase. In it were the deeds to his houses and lands, I guess. Even some of Leyli's travel tickets. There were also copies of her letters. He arranged these things in separate piles on the table. He said, "You see, I could prove it. Now I can at least prove that this house belonged to me, but I don't want to, let it be hers. Besides, I myself gave it to her."

Then he started with his reminiscences again. He showed me their marriage documents. He was over forty when he had met Leyli. It was a legal case, concerning Leyli's inheritance from her uncle. Leyli was only eighteen years old; she had just finished high school. She had come with her father. Then they were in contact for two years. Leyli herself called him first. The judge had been living alone. They got married in '54 (1975). Leyli was already pregnant with their daughter. The judge smiled, "I didn't want her to have an abortion."

He was speaking in fragments. He kept leafing through the pages until he found what he wanted. It was Banu who reminded him of what he had been talking about. When she brought the tea, she came and sat down next to the door facing the hallway. He also talked about his last trip. Leyli had left London. Banu reminded him that she had rented out their house. He didn't recall how he found her. She was in a suburb of Leeds. He remembered the house. It had a sort of garden, and it had a swing and a slide. There was even a gazebo. There was an Englishman sitting in the gazebo, young and tall and blond, wearing shorts, reading a book. He recognized the judge. Perhaps from photos. The judge spoke to him in French. The man didn't understand, and finally he said in Persian, "The lady has gone to get Yassi."

The judge sat down to wait for his wife, and they conversed in Persian. The Englishman, let's call him John, had been working on his doctorate in Persian literature. He had even spent a few months in Iran. Banu said, "That was where they first met." John returned before the revolution. He said, "Whenever people saw me, they would shout, 'Yankee go home!'"

I didn't understand why he had come to see me, until he finally pulled that book of mine out of his briefcase and said, "She was reading this book at the time. I found it yesterday, I tried to read it, but I didn't understand it."

Then he started reminiscing about his time as a student, how he had tried very hard to read stories by Hedayat. He said, "I didn't understand them. You know, I don't understand. Of course, it's my own problem. For me, this room is this room, and each man is a particular man in a particular time in circumstances specific to him, such that those exact circumstances could not be found in any other place or time. But in literature, instead of talking about this place or this day, they mostly talk about something else, or someplace that I've never seen or that I would not be able to imagine at all. I used to debate this with Lili a lot. She would always say, 'You have to have imagination.' And she tried, as she used to put it, to give a blood transfusion to this faculty that I just do not possess at all, or perhaps that I possess only weakly. For example, once…I can't remember."

He looked at Banu. Banu was biting her nails. She drew back her hand. He said, "Leyli used to say, when a writer cannot write about his own time, he goes around looking for similar situations. But I say, is it even possible for him ever to find a similar situation? We even got into arguments about it. She always called the Islamic Revolution a revolt, by which she meant to compare it to the Afghan invasion.[6] OK, even if in some ways it is similar, but then, where is its Sultan Hossein? Or why is there no Ashraf? Or, in the end, a Nader? I used to say to her, you people think like these revolutionaries. Whenever anything happens, they find a comparison for it in the Early Age of Islam. The Basijis[7] are going forth to do battle with Yazid and Ibn Sa'd,[8] this time they want to prevent their Imam from having his throat cut ear to ear by Shemr."

---

6. The "Afghan Invasion" refers to events in the waning days of the Safavid Empire. Some eastern provinces of the empire had declared their independence from the weakened Safavids, and subsequently the Afghans invaded Iran and took over one city after another. In 1722 the Safavid ruler Sultan Hossein lost Isfahan after a six-month siege by the Afghan leader Mahmud. Mahmud went mad and died a few years later, and his cousin Ashraf succeeded him. Tahmasp II, a son of Sultan Hossein who had declared himself Shah at Qazvin in 1722, was helpless to do anything about the situation. But Nader Khan, an Afshar Turkmen chieftain, was able to expel the Afghans from Isfahan in 1729, and he continued to fight the Afghans and exert control over large areas of the former empire, sometimes with Safavid princes nominally in charge. (Summary based on Louis Dupree, *Afghanistan*, Princeton University Press, Princeton, New Jersey, 1980, pp. 324-330.)

7. Basiji: a member of the special Revolutionary Army in the Islamic Republic of Iran.

8. Ibn Sa'd: the military commander leading the Umayyad troops against Imam Hossein in the battle of Karbala.

He was panting, and sometimes he scratched some part of his body. He said, "I don't think that history repeats itself."

He pointed to my book, "You're the same way. Poets are even worse, of course. They make the lover address his terms of endearment to the deer or the antelope or the crow because they have something in common with the beloved."

What could I say? Perhaps I, too, didn't understand. But I thought he was trying to say, why should one call it "the doe's eye" instead of "Leyli's eye." Or perhaps, with his appearance, with his formal clothes and his briefcase next to his hand, and his shiny cufflinks and all, what resemblance did he bear to the events of Majnun's time? He was saying, "Leyli always wanted me to act like Majnun. She wanted someone to write poetry for her. She would extend her hand and say, 'What does my hand resemble?'"

He looked at the back of his own hand, bare skin, yellow, flaccid and trembling. He began leafing through his own letters. When he looked at Banu, I thought he was waiting for her to remind him of something. Banu hid her hands in her skirt. I said, "You were talking about Leyli's hands."

He said, "I remember. Well, I loved those hands, just the way they were at that moment, not because, I mean, three years ago when I came home I saw that she was covering her face with them..."

He looked at me and at Banu. He went on, "I loved those hands, those long fingers, that warm skin and those long nails. I can't kiss a hand made of ivory, or shower the tip of a branch with kisses."

Banu said, "Mention the letter, Aqa."

He said, "Be patient."

He again leafed through the copies of his letters. He said, "Leyli was always very fond of you. And she still is." Later on I read a few of Leyli's letters; Banu brought them to me. The letters Dr. Haqiqi had written were more about his day-to-day life, sometimes also about how it was going with the sale of their things, the items that were sold one by one after he came back. He had even told her, for example, to which shopkeeper he had sold the carpet. In a later letter he wrote about who had bought the carpet. He read them one by one; then he went on to the next letter. Leyli's dressing table had become part of a bride's dowry. The people who bought it thought it was brand new. Banu again said, "Aqa, you're tiring yourself."

He said, "There's only a little left."

Then he said, "Most of them are like this. This is the only way I know how to write. Leyli doesn't even answer me any more. She used to say, 'You are so dull.' Well, people are different. I'm trying very hard; it just doesn't work. I'm reading some things now and listening to some music."

Banu said, "We don't even have a tape player."

He said, "I know. But, well, the neighbors play tapes. But sometimes I wake up and find that I've fallen asleep unintentionally."

He went on speaking. What did he want from me? Did he want me to write on his behalf? If I can recollect his style correctly and reproduce it, he himself had written something like this:

"My dear Lili, I've been waiting for three weeks and two days. Suddenly my eyes have developed cataracts. They said I should be patient until it improves. I see somewhat dimly. It's not important. Recently, every afternoon I go to the door of the house, I sit on the steps, and sometimes I turn around and look at the end of the street. You know I'm not such a daydreamer that I would, for example, mistake any woman who appears for you, or whenever a car comes this way, that I would rejoice, imagining that you are sitting in the back seat of it. Even if I smoked twice as much, I would not have such hallucinations. For example, I know the mailman in this neighborhood comes twice a week, on Mondays and Thursdays, and he comes to this street between the hours of 8:30 and 10:00, but I still go and sit near the door. And now Banu, too, keeps asking me to write you what I told her this afternoon. Well, I'm writing this for Banu's sake. When I was getting dressed, she asked, 'Why do you always go and sit in front of the door lately?' I said, 'I go there to cry.' I wasn't lying. But after all, she knows that if I feel depressed, I will go upstairs and sit on our bed, on the edge of the bare bed. I close my eyes, I keep thinking of something that doesn't exist, so that perhaps I will start thinking of you. It doesn't work. The albums are there with you. You know that I'm not attached to material things, that's why I sold everything. But now, in an empty room, especially when I can't even remember one thing about you, not even one of your hairpins, I go to pieces. Then I gaze at a narrow mark on the floor or the wall, I can't even remember the color of your armoire...I don't know. What good is it anyhow? And now you aren't the one using these things anymore anyway. Then suddenly I start crying. But not in the street. Banu says it's not right, people will see."

He wasn't crying. He went on reading. The same sort of things. He had even sold Leyli's brushes, even her shoes. He hadn't sold them by public auction, as most people do these days, putting price tags on everything from children's clothing to an enamel bowl with a chipped rim, and then they leave. He said, "These things that I am writing are useless, but perhaps if you write to her about my condition, it would make a difference."

Then all at once he rolled up the cuff of his trousers. His leg was bandaged. Banu said, "Aqa!"

She had jumped up. Dr. Haqiqi said, "It doesn't matter, if he's going to write for us, then it's better that he should see it, you don't have to make such a big deal of it."

He unwrapped the bandages. It was a hideous sore. I couldn't look at it. He moved his leg in front of me so I could see it. It was a gaping wound in the skin, or, to write it in the style of Dr. Haqiqi, the skin and flesh of his leg was split in a small horizontal line seven centimeters long. The edges of the wound were red, and deep inside it was a yellow line, scattered here and there with blisters that oozed red and then burst open. He said, "There's more."

I guess he also had some sores on his stomach. Banu was busy rewrapping the bandages on his leg. She didn't even let him lift up his shirt. There must have been more, or perhaps the skin was splitting open in exactly those places where he kept scratching himself. He said, "I have diabetes, it's true. But I don't know why it should be like this? It suddenly splits open, then it heals, but then it starts up again somewhere else."

While he was putting his papers away in his briefcase one stack at a time, I said, "I'll give it a try."

He said, "Thanks, you're very kind, but it may not work."

When I saw the engineer, I asked him, "Don't you think the judge is playing the role of Majnun?"

He said, "Leyli and Majnun?"

He was sprinkling water in front of his house. Hojjati the engineer had not read it. My wife doesn't like Majnun; she thought Dr. Haqiqi was right about this at least. In any case, I don't think Dr. Haqiqi had read these things, or at least he had not remembered them at just the moment when they were needed:

> *An eye that with the smallest glance*
> *Pierced not one, but a thousand hearts,*
> *To look at, she was like an Arabian face,*
> *Yet when it came to stealing hearts, she was a Persian page.*
> *Unlike the dark shadows of her hair, her face was a lamp,*
> *Or rather a torch with ravens weaving their wings around it.*[9]

But judging from what he had said, Leyli had at least read him the story of Majnun rescuing the gazelles, or the story of his freeing the antelopes. In those days when I was thinking of telling Leyli about these circum-

---

9. Translated from the Persian by R. Gelpke, *Nizami: Layla and Majnun.* English version by Bruno Cassirer, London, 1966, pp. 16-17.

stances, I jotted down these verses, the part where Majnun gives his gazelle-
like horse to the hunter and in so doing ransoms the gazelle:

> *He was left there with a few small gazelles,*
> *The hunter left and took his horse away.*
> *He kissed the black eyes of the gazelle,*
> *Not from pity, but from love, singing:*
> *Dark as the night like hers, your eyes!*
> *What I have lost you can't return,*
> *They waken memories that burn,*
> *Sad happiness and joyful sighs.*[10]
> *He said many blessings over the gazelles,*
> *Then released them from the trap.*

And now I see that Nezami in his first description of Leyli talks about a
gazelle and a raven. Then later on in the life of Majnun these same animals
again play a role; after he sets the antelopes free, he talks to a raven:

> *He saw a raven squatted on a branch,*
> *Eyes glowing like lamps,*[11]
> *Black and ravishing like the locks of an idol,*
> *Going directly to the heart, like the liver.*

I didn't write it. To begin with, I myself was caught up in it. I fell ill. It
was not serious. And Akhtar was usually talking about her co-worker's husband, or about things she had heard about computers. She was saying,
"These days they have made robots who can perform the most minute
tasks. And they don't make mistakes."

As I would express it, just as Haqiqi used to say, when they see a raven,
they don't start thinking about a lover's lock. But then look at me, the only
thing I know how to do is to go around looking for a precedent or a connection in everything. No, I have to write, this time I have to do it, and I
have to finish it, not leave it unfinished like the notes that I have, these
things that I've written. Then things came up so that I couldn't continue,
to be honest it was several nights that I was thinking, it's enough, already.
Perhaps since I didn't want to get mixed up again in the spell of the triangle, and pursue it, and discover it, and then…then what could I do? It was
better that I wouldn't get out of bed at all, and in the morning when I see

---

10. This line and the preceding three lines are from Gelpke, p. 93.
11. These two lines are from Gelpke, p. 99.

that I'm still here, I'm still alive, and Akhtar's co-worker and her husband are coming again to pick up Akhtar and take her to work, I would close my eyes again. First once, then twice they beep the horn for her, so she goes, and then I don't see her until the afternoon, and then the girls set off for school, and I'm left alone with all that blank paper and notebooks of various colors. At exactly noon the girls come, and when they take off their overcoats and throw off the face veils that now must be long enough to cover the chest, I feel a little better, but most of the time they don't even ask me what I've been working on. Even at the table they just bend over their food and whisper into each other's ears and huddle over, giggling over their half-eaten lunch. I can deal with all these things, but the afternoons just drive me crazy, especially because Akhtar is so tired, or angry, just to buy a ration of meat takes at least several days of running around, not to mention the long line. The girls don't do so much as put a bowl back in its place. I help, but do you think that does any good? I have reserved the afternoons for helping with the family finances, whatever needs doing. Well, I get tired, too, and in the evening when I come home I believe Akhtar has now finally calmed down a bit. They've eaten their dinner, the kids are sitting in front of the television, and Akhtar has fallen asleep with a book in her hands. If she wakes up again, she'll start talking about her co-workers again, or about the mountain her co-worker's husband climbed, or their child who is sick. And she wants to invite them over. She says, "We've lived our lives, we have to think about them."

Lying in the corner of the bed, facing the wall, I hear the sound of the faucet, or the girls quarreling. Akhtar calls out from the bathroom: "Hurry up." She doesn't even come here to comb her hair. The problem is not that I can't see the line between her vertebrae, or the ever-increasing white hairs, or even that longing for one more kiss after a thousand kisses. What bothers me more is the other things missing in spite of her presence. She says, "Also, over there one will eventually put down roots and form some attachments."

She's only happy in a crowd, or in any case any place but here, in this house. No, I didn't want my skin to open up in a gaping wound or my hair to go white all at once just so that she would know what I'm talking about. I was more abject than that. Then suddenly one day it happened. I woke up in the middle of the night and I realized it was about to happen. I couldn't breathe. No, I didn't want it to happen this way. I've always been afraid of being suffocated, even when I was a child. I got up and went to the living room. I was tired, too, so tired that I couldn't sit up. But as soon as I would lie down, it would start up again. I couldn't inhale. Actually, the walls and ceiling were preventing me from breathing. I sat up and drew a breath. I even tried to lie down there on the sofa hoping that I would fall asleep and die in my sleep. It didn't work. I got up, I paced the room. I even went into the courtyard. It was still difficult to breathe. I was filled with anxiety, and the walls were the physical embodiment of that feeling. I then went out into the alley. The air was cool and filled with the scent of the approaching autumn. I went back home, back to my room. I thought I would stay awake until morning. I was becoming the laughingstock of the town, certainly these same things had happened to John. Then, contrary to the view of Dr. Haqiqi, does history repeat itself, does it even go in cycles, forever? God help us if we return to the world another time, just as the engineer says, in the form of an animal or another person, until the time when the attachments of the soul to all material things is broken off, and at that time, with the dissolution of the body, the soul goes to Nirvana? He used to say, "All these invocations and meditations are for this purpose, so that a man can, at the last moment, think about what he needs to."

I thought, I'll have to try to focus my thoughts at the last moment on an animal, even if it be a raven, but not a person, especially not a writer who holds within himself everything at every moment together at one time: and he can be the soul of Barbara and the soul of Leyli, and himself, and Dr. Haqiqi, and even that husband of Akhtar's co-worker about whom I even know that he had asthma when he was five years old, or that he bought shoes yesterday from such-and-such a store at such-and-such a price. I have really become ridiculous. I even tried not to breathe, that is, not to wait for the asthma to attack me again, to lie down, and just as they internalize the light of the candle in the abode of their hearts, I would internalize all the decay of all the limbs, or the sudden cessation, just as another leaf detaches its heart from all that remains and slowly falls off the stem. It didn't work. With all my walking around and sitting down and getting up, perhaps I even moaned, Akhtar woke up. She was terrified. I saw her two hands trembling. When she handed me tea and rock candy, and stretched out her hand to wipe away the sweat from my forehead, which she said was cold, it stopped. That's all there was to it. What happened afterwards is not important. Perhaps Leyli didn't want to read between the lines of Dr. Haqiqi's reports. There was nothing wrong with me. They thought I had developed asthma. But I hadn't. The doctor inquired as to whether I might not be afflicted with the depression that had become endemic here these days. I said, "No, Doctor, I write, and if that were the case, it would be good material for writing, you wouldn't have to cure me of it."

The engineer also came to see me. The doctors had said I have to rest. They had also given me some tablets. I still take them. The engineer said they had sent his son out of the country. They had heard from him in Pakistan. I learned that the cost of it was now five hundred and fifty tomans, of course with a visa for a European country, preferably Sweden or Denmark or even Belgium. He said, "I can't see my son sitting around wasting his time here."

Then he said, "I envy you."

He also has two little boys. Akhtar said, "What difference does it make, do the bombs know the difference between boys and girls?"

When the alarm sounds, she turns pale, then all at once her hands begin to tremble. No, not only that, she suddenly freezes, right in the midst of whatever she's doing, and turns pale, then we talk with her, or we try to, perhaps, bring her under the doorway of the entrance hall or finally under the steps, her hands begin trembling and I or the children must take her hands and sit her down somewhere. From the trembling of her lower lip, one realizes what a state she is in, from her two blue eyes gazing in astonishment, as if fixed on a predetermined place where she thought the bombs would fall. Well, later on, or the next day, she starts nagging me, saying, "Let's go, at least let's save the children's lives."

What can I say? Should I say, for example, this is my home? No, I don't have a home, there is no ceiling left. The walls and ceiling of my home are the very things that I write, this way of writing from right to left, in this curvature of the *nun* (letter n), and my shield against all calamities is the top strokes of the *kaf* (letter k) or the *gaf* (letter g). Must I not at least mold the bricks of my own Nirvana? Or to begin with, where could I even go so that once again, by stringing together these things, I could make sense of what is happening or what is going to happen, for example, why have things turned out for the judge the way they have? He had given up everything, he had even been defeated in the courts of England, all that was left to him was the child. Lili or Leyla had said, "If you want, you can take her to live with you."

Then he came back from the hospital. They had removed one of his kidneys. He himself used to say, "One can live with only one of them."

Dr. Haqiqi did not have cancer. They had done all sorts of tests. He started reminiscing again. Each time Banu interrupted to remind him of something, such as what he had been talking about, he would make a gesture with his hand as if to say that he knew. But then he couldn't remember. He was saying, "She was like my daughter, true, but you yourself know that women—I don't know why—but usually they are very perceptive for their age, they really catch on quickly. Before anything had happened, the whole of my life fell into Lili's hands. First she went to an accounting course, and she learned to type. She had become my secretary. For the child's sake, she had no choice but to stay at home, but after the child got a little older, she took her to her mother's house and left her there. Every night I used to go and bring her back. She was always fast asleep."

Banu said, "Aqa, you were talking about England."

He said, "Oh, yes, the court? That was not important. The whole time I was looking at my Leyla. What a beautiful woman she had become! What did it matter to me that her lawyer was stringing lies together. I saw that my Lili was happy to be getting away from me. In the lawyer's view, I had sucked away the beauty and freshness of a young girl, little by little. I had plundered the wealth of Lili's father, and I still wanted to take these things from her, I wanted to take the woman away, that is, bring her back here. He was right about that, it would be a pity. She was wearing her hair in a ponytail. My daughter was also with her. Sometimes she would turn around, and when I would wink at her or stick out my tongue at her, she would laugh. Well, I've allowed her to stay there. I have no money left to spend on her."

I asked, "Was she really willing to give the girl to you?"

"Believe me, she said, 'Take her away if you want, she's yours.' And if I brought her back here, then what? Aside from all of that, I couldn't bring her up. Well, I have my retirement, there's the dilapidated bathhouse, it brings in some income, that's true. But she would need a home. I said, 'No, let her stay with you, I'll send support money for her expenses...' Believe me, she couldn't believe it! I drew up an affidavit. When I signed it, she ran to me and hugged me and kissed me on both cheeks. That was it, I never saw her again."

Then he added, "Now I think how good it is that you only have to see once that it's gone forever."

Maybe what he meant was this, that it's not as it is written in the Upanishads, where it says that, those who have attained fulfillment in offering sacrifices and doing good deeds in the worlds, and have kept an eye on the results of their deeds, after the passing of the body, they reach the guardian of smoke, and the guardian of smoke brings them to the guardian of night, and the guardian of night brings them to the guardian of the days of the waning moon, and he brings them to the guardian of the six months during which the sun inclines to the southern direction, and he brings them to the guardian of the spirits of the forefathers, and he brings them to the moon, and there they serve the angels, and when the results of their good deeds are complete, they come to the Bhuta Akas[12] and from Bhuta Akas to the wind, and from the wind to the rain, and from the rain they come to the earth for the punishment of the deeds that occurred during their lifetimes, they enter a hell that is in this world, and there they will be turning into a worm and a moth and a dog and a snake and a scorpion, and they will keep going round and round from birth to Leyli, and from their Leylis to dust, and again from night to the day of the waning moon, and back to the second six months of the year, until they reach Bhuta Akas, and the wind and the rain and the earth, and they are born again to come back in another form. In spite of all this, I would see him every afternoon sitting on the steps in front of his house, holding onto his cane with both hands, resting his forehead on one hand, not caring even to look any more.

When he received a summons to appear in court, he didn't go. Banu now came only in the afternoons, she would do some shopping, she would cook something, perhaps she would also wash a few things, then in the evening at sunset, she would leave. Of course she would also stop in to see us or the engineer. She would say, "For God's sake, please keep an eye on him, would you?"

What could we do? I mean, myself, for example, if I wrote these things to Leyli, would anything change? It was last year in autumn when the order came to vacate the premises. Banu and her brother brought a van in the evening. Banu had said, "We mustn't let it turn into a scandal."

They left, but the judge came back. I didn't see him. The neighbors said he came in a car. Usually in the afternoons, riding in that same van, he would take one turn around the street and back again. Then when I no longer heard about him coming, I thought it was over. The engineer said that he had sold his bathhouse and sent her the money, and that now he had gone to live in that little dilapidated house. He didn't know where it was. And so it was until just this past week when Banu came at sunset. She had come in her brother's van, she had a large shopping bag in her hands, and she said, "I've come to pay a visit to the neighbors."

She stopped in to see everyone, one by one.

---

12. Bhuta Akas (or Akasha) in Hinduism is the ether, the finest of the five gross elements. The other four are air, fire, water, and earth. (*The Oxford Dictionary of World Religions*, ed. John Bowker, Oxford University Press, 1997; p. 37 "Akasha," and p. 146, "bhuta") This entire passage in the story is based on the account of what a soul experiences after death according to the Chandogya Upanishad 4.15.5. A transcription and translation can be found on pp. 371-373 of *Chandogya Upanishad*, ed. Swami Lokeswarananda, translated and with notes based on Shankara's commentary, published by the Ramakrishna Institute of Culture, Calcutta, February, 1998.

She was sitting with my wife in the hallway. I went in to say hello, too. I asked, "How is Aqa?"

She said, "He died."

Finally I understood why she had come. When she was leaving, she said, "Excuse me, if it's possible, would you write to my mistress? I can't do it myself, you know."

And she had brought along her address. Letters from the lady, and also copies of the judge's letters. In separate packets. What need did I have of them, when I myself had already seen them? And I had tried to write. I'm still trying. Where were those long, narrow, and mostly dark corridors that I saw? The revolving doors. It didn't have spots of light so that I would say it was a metro. It was just that corridor, but the sound of the rattling of a train was coming. I was going from one compartment to another. Akhtar and the girls were someplace, there up ahead of me, sometimes even just behind me, and I was always running into a door that was closed, or I reached a crowd of people who wouldn't let me pass through, they even intentionally reached out their hands in order to block my way. I knew I couldn't get there, but I went on, all night, all day.

Mehr, 1366 (September/October, 1987)

Nightmare

TRANSLATED BY

NAEEM NABILI

Mr. Sedaaqat, I said, all I'm saying is let's say something, anything, just let's say something. We can even all talk at the same time. About what? I don't know, but definitely no one should yell. I mean, we should talk as if we're talking to one another, or as if one of us is talking, and the others are all listening. We can even shout, I mean, if somebody wishes to shout, he can, but not so loud that the woman downstairs might hear us. Maybe we can close our eyes and talk, as if nobody is there, or as if it's okay if someone's listening. Let's just talk, or, at least, I want to talk, to the point that I won't have to think that I'm full of grief, that I'm going to cry for sure.

Even if my eyes tear up, or yours do, you can put your head on my shoulder. I don't mean that literally; you don't really have to do that. I just wanted to say that you should cry just like you would whisper, or like when you used to put your head on your mother's knees, without being embarrassed about someone seeing you. Anyway, at least that's how I feel.

"Farkhondeh khanum,"[1] I said, "believe me there is nothing wrong with me. I mean it's nothing that can be fixed by pills and injections or…I don't know…wandering the streets or smoking a couple of cigarettes. Believe me, at times it seems as if I can't breathe, and it's not because I have a lump in my throat or something like that. I just can't, like right now, see—I stretch my arm out like this; my fingers are trembling. Why? I don't know. Am I anxious? Is it because I don't sleep enough? No, that's not it. This large cake of Mr. Sedaaqat's, for instance, or this bunch of

---

1. Khanum, meaning madam, is used in Persian to show respect when referring to a woman.

flowers, is driving me nuts. Why? I don't know. You must forgive me for saying this. Or, for instance, Uncle's black tie that he's been wearing for the past fifteen years, as if he only has this one, or all his ties are the same color, or only that color goes well with his suits. You've been telling me, 'Drink some arrack, go to a cozy bar and drink a couple of shots at the counter.' What for? So that I don't get drunk? Impossible. I can't even get drunk anymore, not so quickly anyway. There's only giddiness. And if I drink a lot, it gets even worse. And what's the use anyway? What about the next morning, apart from the hangover and a bad taste in your mouth, you realize that you've been only asleep, such a deep sleep that it's like you haven't been alive for seven or eight hours; you're heavy, numb, not rested, with no dreams or anything.

"Uncle," I said, "remember my neighbor? I'm not sure; maybe you've never seen her. Well, it doesn't matter. She's tall, but from that balcony she doesn't look so tall. At sunset, she used to come out into the garden. Between the tips of her thumb and right index finger, she would hold the closed tip of the morning glory trumpets and would snap them off with her left hand. That's all she did. The two or three days that I saw her, that's all she did. In a small garden, especially when there are only a few morning glories, how many flowers can one find, especially unopened ones? At the sunset of the fourth or fifth day, she was still coming across more. She would poke around and eventually find some. Finally, by the sunset of the sixth day, I think, she didn't find any. She had to hold the tip of the flower, and crush the unopened trumpets with the tips of her thumb and left index finger. She did so several times, but there was no sound. I thought maybe I couldn't hear it, or perhaps because she was not holding the tips of the flowers tight enough, they wouldn't snap. I wanted her to find some. I knew that if she didn't find any, it would start. She tried too, definitely more than other days. She even went into the garden and checked under the leaves, too. I could only see her shoulders moving.

"Madame Ashraf al-Saadaat!" I asked, "is there something wrong?" I even wanted to say, "Ashraf al-Saadaat, Ashraf al-Saadaat! Didn't he turn up last time?" But I didn't. I just said, "Madame!"

She didn't hear me. I repeated louder, "Ashraf al-Saadaat! Please excuse me for bothering you."

She was sitting on the edge of the garden. She didn't look at me or up here. But I realized that the entire width of her face was wet with tears. She was smiling too. I mean, seeing the brightness of her teeth, I thought she was smiling.

"Is that you?" She asked,

"Isn't Mr. Nabavi home?" I asked.

"He's inside," she replied. "Would you like to talk to him? Do you want me to call him?"

"You should…," I said. I wanted to say, "You should search more. You might be able to find some, perhaps, on the wall or near the clothes line."

"I should do what?" she asked immediately.

"Well," I replied, "I thought your children had again…. By the way, how is Nasrin?"

"She has just finished her milk," she replied, "she won't wake up for at least two hours."

"Asghar, what about Asghar?" I asked.

"He's fine," she replied, "His dad is teaching him the times tables."

"So forgive me," I said, "for bothering you."

"Why?" she replied, "You haven't bothered me."

"Would you like me to read to you," I asked, "A poem or something? I can even play a record for you; surely you like music."

She was sitting there, right by the garden, on the cold and stony edge of the garden. She had her head cast down. She covered her eyes with her hands. I talked to her about the sunset, about the sunset blues. I even said, "Lots of people are like that. They have no control over it. Maybe because the sunset is not just this curious colorfulness of clouds at the edge of the horizon, or the orange color of the edge of that fluff of the white cloud or even the flocks of crows that fly…."

Then I said, I mean I wanted to say, "For instance, you can see for yourself, these flowers close their trumpets before sunset, and before dark, they go to sleep. And then you come and break the ones that might have opened tomorrow before sunrise comes. That's why, in the morning, you seldom find flowers on their stems or even beneath the leaves. And on the sunset of the sixth day, you can't find any unopened trumpets."

I just talked to her like that, gratuitously. You won't believe it, I even tried making faces for her! But she just sat there and maybe drew lines in the dirt with the tip of her big toe. She had bare feet; they were naked and fair. And then I guess I said—well, I confess I didn't say, I didn't say a word to her, but I wanted to say—even before the orange color of the ridge of the clouds disappeared—I even repeated these words to myself and even once or twice I grasped the handrail and leaned toward her to say something, whatever would come out of my mouth. I even rattled my chair so that when she looked up, I'd have to greet her and say, "Hi, how are you?" Well, it wasn't my fault she didn't look up and just sat there until it got dark, and I could only see her silhouette sitting by the garden. That's why I said you have to talk and say something so that you won't cry, and without noise at that, such that even if someone is sitting next to you, they won't hear you.

"Ali, my brother," I said, "at least you've got to understand what I'm saying. You say, even if he has been lost for an hour, how far can a little six-year-old kid walk? Even if exactly one hour ago he had put his head down and walked off."

Why then, if you make an effort, a step here, and a couple there, that's it, you'll have found him.

Ashraf al-Saadaat, too, had gone out, had dashed about, without her veil, barefoot, and had asked everyone she had seen at every corner of every two-way intersection or fork in the road. She had affectionately approached the kids in the neighborhood, but he wasn't there. The shop owners hadn't seen him. Nobody had seen the little six-year-old boy with straight hair, black eyes, rosy cheeks, wearing a blue striped sweater. No one had seen him. From the way people were looking at her, and all those kids were following her, and—I don't know—the shopkeepers who muttered their curses against anyone who might have harmed the child, if anyone else had been Ashraf al-Saadaat, they would have thought that they would never see their Asghar again, or maybe they would have thought that their Asghar had returned, he had gone to the end of the street, by the neighbor's house and had, by now, come back and sat down by the door of the house, and now, right now, was rubbing his tearful eyes with his knuckles.

Barefoot and bareheaded, she had run to the house. He wasn't there. He wasn't inside the house either. He was neither in the rooms, nor the closets, nor even under the table in the neighbor's house. They had checked; they had searched again and again. They had called. Nabavi, her husband, was at work. By the time he arrived and was able to do something, even if no one had gone near the kid, he would have reached the other side of the world, even with his small steps.

Ashraf al-Saadaat hadn't even thought of calling him. And when the neighbors called, Nabavi had said, "What? It's not possible. He is not a kid anymore."

The neighbors couldn't understand why he had said, "It's not possible; he isn't a kid." They didn't even realize what Nabavi had gone through to get home. I understand. How many times do you think he bumped into people? He had left his briefcase somewhere. He had run half the way like a madman. He had also hastily looked down a couple of streets. How many police stations, would you say, had he stopped by? They hadn't seen him. I mean, "Lady! How many hours are there in a day? How many legs does a human being have? How many places can he stop by in one day?"

That's why Ashraf al-Saadaat had come to the yard, next to the morning glories and was looking for a flower, just one flower.

What can one do? I said, "Ashraf al-Saadaat! Lady! My dear! He'll be found. This is not fifteen years ago. We have notified all the police stations, haven't we? Someone will definitely find him and will hand him over to a cop or someone else, and he'll take him to the station. And then, they will call us. We will rush to the station; we'll get a taxi. I will go myself. Such things happen; it has happened before."

It was dark. I could no longer see her. I couldn't even see her shadow, but I knew that she was sitting at the edge of the garden. She wasn't even crying. I couldn't hear her, but I was sure she was there, with her back to the door of the house, as if she was confident.

"Aunty!" I said. "I, myself, called. I told you to let Uncle know by any means you could, didn't I?" Then I thought to myself, I mean it crossed my mind, that if Uncle comes, with that tie…I thought, "No, it's not necessary." I was concerned on account of her age. It's true that Uncle is a capable man with many friends and acquaintances. All he has to do is to use his influence and ask around, but, then, by the time he arrives and they search for the boy…. He is just a kid, a fragile flower. Let's say he has fallen on the ground, or while crossing the street…well, we can't just expect people to help.

Maybe that's why Ashraf al-Saadaat had dashed about from this street to another. His eyes were black, his sweater dark blue. She had rushed and asked. It seemed as if she had gone through all the streets of the city and had checked every corner. How much energy do you think a woman has?

"Ashraf al-Saadaat!" I said. "Enough is enough! How long do you want to keep at this? How long do you want to keep asking? My dear! If worse comes to worst, we will have his picture printed in the paper, the 3 by 4 you had taken a month ago. We will provide them with his description too—black eyes, straight black hair, and a small mole between his eyebrows." But does she listen? Does she settle down?

She was out in the streets asking. She would lean against a wall or something when she was inquiring. Are there just a few black-eyed kids around? She had seen that herself. There were twenty or thirty sweaters, all the same style and color. This one was the very size of her Asghar, as if it had been knitted for him. "I put it on him this very morning."

She had, again, dashed about.

"Didn't you say you had found him?" I asked her. "Didn't you say that you yourself had seen him in the arms of that blue-eyed man?"

He was leaving, with long strides, as if he were running, or as if he were a giant and with the next step, he would reach the other side of the mountains. The kid had put his head on the man's shoulder; he was asleep, perhaps from too much crying. Ashraf al-Saadaat had run again. But could she have reached the man? She had even screamed and yelled. She thought she couldn't make a sound, just like she were asleep, and if she didn't wake up at once and put one foot after the other, the man would turn onto a side street, and she would never see him again.

"Sister!" I said, "you remember; you saw for yourself. It's not like you were asleep. The young guys had beaten him up. His nose was bloody. But didn't you say, 'Look at his eyes! They're glowing!'"

His face was pockmarked. He fell down on his knees before me saying, "I'm sorry; it was wrong of me."

"How could you?" I asked him.

They had given him a good beating. Then he grabbed the hem of Uncle's overcoat appealing for mercy. But Ashraf al-Saadaat wouldn't give up; she still hasn't. It's as if she is still asleep, as if she is still running and will never reach the man. She herself had said that she had reached him and grabbed him by the collar with one hand and had taken the kid with her right hand, and by the time people gathered around, she had thrashed him. And if Asghar hadn't burst into tears, she would definitely have done something to the man. But does she remember? Can anyone remind her of that?

"Ashraf al-Saadaat! Ashraf al-Saadaat! My dear lady!" I pleaded with her, "Didn't you find him yourself? Don't you remember you scratched his face? Didn't you say you wanted to gouge out his small blue eyes with your fingernails?"

After Asghar had cried and some young men had gotten there, she let go of him. They had really beaten him up. "I got my punishment." He said, "It's for my betters to forgive."

"What betters?" Uncle said, "We are not even your equals. But if they let you go, without doubt you will...."

"I swear to God!" he begged, "I won't do it again."

"Ashraf al-Saadaat!" I said, "Didn't you see the police officer slap him in the face? You were there yourself."

"He has a record here," the officer said, "this is his third time, but the previous two times, we didn't have any evidence. Ma'am, I ask you not to rescind your complaint."

"This kid was lost," he claimed, "he was crying. I was taking him to the station."

"Then what are all these sweets in your pocket for?" the officer asked. "And two kinds of candy and a chocolate bar at that?" They were on the desk wrapped in a silk handkerchief.

"I bought them for him at the street corner," he replied, "so that he would stop crying. I didn't do anything wrong, did I?"

The officer slapped him again. "You degenerate!" he said, "If you haven't done anything, then why did you want to get them to rescind their complaint?"

"Ashraf al-Saadaat!" I asked, "Didn't you say, 'It's not for myself; it's for the sake of the other mothers that I won't rescind my complaint even if they execute him'?"

She was sitting there; it's as if she's been sitting there for ten, fifteen years. And yet I wish she would cry. I wish her voice could be heard, that subdued, monotonous whimper.

Now you ask, what could I have done for her, play some music for her? Or recite a poem to her? Or, like Uncle, just put on my tie? Or, like Sedaaqat and his wife, Farkhondeh, just go downstairs and offer her their condolences?

"Woman!" I cried, "you are now getting on in years; you're no longer in your twenties to be able to dash about the streets. Settle down! Who knows, maybe there will be a knock on the door, and there he is."

It can happen. He is just a kid. He's gone to the neighbor's house, under a table, somewhere. He can't stay there all day, all week, or say, the entire fifteen years. But, does she understand? She just sits there, as if she can no longer run, or just like the other day, as if she's asleep, and sees the blue-eyed man turn onto another side street, and she can't take one step after the other, or say one word.

"Didn't you find his picture in the paper yourself?" I asked, "Didn't you see the number on his chest? Didn't you say, 'Nabavi! Look at his eyes, they look like Rumpelstiltskin's'?"

But will she remember? I even showed her the newspaper cutting; I read it to her. "Look, they've given him fifteen years; fifteen, that's no short sentence."

She wouldn't listen and still won't. "Nabavi!" she says, "I can't; I'm not in my twenties anymore. You go, go yourself to the corner of the street, go. Maybe you'll see him and find him. He's a kid; if they haven't abducted him, he couldn't have gone far.

"You're a man, go try the police stations, the sheriff's outposts. Take his picture along, too, the 3x4 you were talking about. Show it to everyone, from the guard at the door to the police officers all the way to the chief. Tell them he's six; tell them he's lost. Maybe they'll remember; maybe they've seen him."

"When will your senses come back to you?!" I exclaimed.

"I'm a woman, with gray hair under my scarf," she countered. "What is it possible for me to do? You go. You remember: he had blue eyes with a pockmarked face. Run! You might be able to catch up. Didn't you say he was given fifteen years? Go! What are you waiting for? You can see I can't run anymore. My feet are dead; I can't catch him."

That's why I said there was something, right here, caught in my throat, as if a spider or something had clutched onto my Adam's apple, and my arms were turned to stone at my sides, as if by a spell. So, what can anyone of you do for me? Didn't I tell you to go over to her, to Ashraf al-Saadaat, who's still sitting over there?

"Nasrin," I said, "at least you go and tell her Nabavi says, 'Enough of this! You've been sitting there for fifteen years, for what?' There is no kid any more."

But, for what? What can I do when she has been asleep for fifteen years, and thinks all the time that she has to dash about, go out, inquire, and not be able to put one foot after the other, and even unable to call for her Asghar? What can anyone do when she is sitting on the cold stone edge of the garden, her back to the door, as if he's never coming back? It seems that Ashraf al-Saadaat is doing the right thing, and I, too, should go there beside her, and sit on the edge of the garden, and not cry, not even make a sound.

Green as a Parrot, Black as a Crow

TRANSLATED BY HESHMAT MOAYYAD

Every time we see Hassan Aqa we ask, "Well? Did it work? Did you have any luck?"

And he answers, "No…didn't work. Again, he just cawed."

We say, "Good man, must you do it?"

He answers, "Oh, I only want a parrot, someone I can talk to and share my pain with. But…oh these parrots of Hossein Aqa—what can I say, every word is just one too many. Not even a simple dry 'Hassan Aqa' can he utter, as you and I would do. They manage to caw all right…ghar, ghar, ghar.

And there he goes again to see Hossein Aqa, buys another parrot and is disappointed again. We don't see him for a few weeks, maybe for two months or even for a whole year. Then suddenly he shows up…unshaven, his eyes all red like bowls of blood. He squats down, takes off his hat, places it on his knee, and pounds the ground with his fist and says, "Again it didn't work."

We ask, "Again? This time again?"

"I bought everything you can think of for him. I fed him sugar with my own hands. I talked to him for three or four hours every day. I put him in front of a mirror…but it didn't work, it did not work."

We ask, "But he did not caw, did he?…"

He replies, "Well…what do you think, he said 'Salaam' or 'Good morning, Hassan Aqa,' just the way you and I are used to say?"

We say, "For goodness sake, why did you let yourself be fooled again?"

He answers, "By God, I pulled my mind together. I looked at his wings, his claws, his beak. Nothing was wrong with him. Hossein Aqa swore that he was a parrot, indeed a truly original parrot, and that he was also speaking Persian. Only during the last two or three days had he become withdrawn. If someone would just spend some time with him, he would surely start talking again."

Then tears fill his eyes. Not to let us see them he takes a cigarette and puts it in a holder. We light a match for him, place a cup of tea in front of him, and talk about other things, relevant or irrelevant. We talk of sluggish earnings. We talk of Mohsen Aqa who has started to believe that His Holiness has appeared to him in a dream, placed his hand on his shoulder and said, "Enough of sitting back." We talk of China and Indochina, we talk of the Arabs....

Do you think it works? Hassan Aqa doesn't give a hoot. If you say wheat, it reminds him of the color green, the color of the parrot's wings. If you say jungle or mountain, it reminds him of a cage, the cage of the parrot he recently bought, and of the place where he bought it and the person he bought it from. And in the end he is not ready to admit that he is not altogether with it and has not properly understood the ins and outs of the matter. Being a parrot does not depend on its wings or its beak.

But we better say no more. We like Hassan Aqa. He is simple, he is pure, how should I say it....He has no deceitful pretense, but...he is forgetful. If you break his head today or cheat him out of money he will have forgotten by tomorrow.

I say, "After all, Hassan Aqa, don't you remember? Wasn't it just yesterday that he embarrassed you in front of all your neighbors?

He answers, "Who?...where?..."

We say, "We saw it ourselves, we witnessed it."

He answers, "You get what you deserve."

He took that green-black croaking critter with the crooked beak back to Hossein Aqa and protested that it doesn't talk, and is not capable of uttering one word.

He says, "Oh, people, you have ears, you have eyes. Is this a parrot?"

We say, "Didn't you say so, you dummy? Open your eyes, look underneath its wings. It's all turning black there. Have you ever seen a parrot with black wings?"

He answers, "Well...perhaps I was angry. Blood made me blind. Hossein Aqa did say it, though. The poor man even explained it."

And then he certainly will go to Hossein Aqa to make up to him. But even before he will have a cup of tea with him he will have bought something from him that looks like a parrot and he will take it home.

We say, "For heaven's sake, keep your wits about you this time."

He says, "Now I understand. I have become an expert. I will look at the wings, I will examine the beak."

He does look, he really does, even more than once. He touches below the wing and even looks at all the tiny feathers lest the down show a tinge of black. He even bargains for the price to make sure he is not charged double.

We say, "Can it be that a thief sneaks in, takes the parrot and leaves a crow or something instead?…"

He asks, "You think that's possible? The front door is locked, and even if he climbs over the wall, he won't find it. It's inside, in my bedroom next to my pillow. Unless he breaks the door, kills me, or kills all of us…." He shakes his fist, gazing at the thief who hasn't come and yells, "Only if you walk over my dead body."

Then he adds with a lower voice, "My children's mother sleeps ever so lightly, you can't imagine. She says all the time, this matter doesn't let me sleep."

We ask, "But why then?…"

He answers, "This is beyond my grasp. My children's mother says: 'Perhaps he has caught a crow this time and painted its wings a deep green.'"

We ask, "Well, what about its beak? A crow's beak isn't curved, is it?"

He answers, "That's just what I say. The children's mother says, perhaps he held the poor thing over the flame of a stove or a lamp and bent the beak as soon as it turned soft."

We say, "What? Are you saying that Hossein Aqa twists the beak of a crow? And that over the flame of a stove?"

He answers, "Well, you tell me. Is that possible? Hossein Aqa is not that evil? He is merciful. The poor hapless guy hasn't done any harm."

We say, "Um, well, let's assume: he does it once, he does it a second time…but after all, is it possible? After all, Hossein Aqa has so many parrots that you can't imagine that. And then how is it possible to bend the softened beak so it looks exactly like the parrot's?"

He answers, "That's precisely my argument. I have put that question before Hossein Aqa and he says: 'Well, if such a thing is possible why then don't you try it on your own? Why do you come to me? There are plenty of crows around. Just catch one, paint its wings, hold its beak over your stove….' I answer him: 'you mean, we should do that and simply for the sake of filthy gains in this world?' He answers: 'You tell me.'"

Hassan Aqa sighs, throws his cigarette down, tramples on it, takes his hat off his knee, tugs at it twice, indicating that he must go.

We say, "What's up, why so soon? Come on, sit down."

He says, "I must go and talk with Hossein Aqa and make it up to him. After all, you shouldn't have a falling-out with your neighbor for the sake of filthy gains."

We warn him, "Be careful this time. Open your eyes wide!"

He grins, meaning, "You thought...."

When we say, "You choose yourself. Don't allow Hossein Aqa to do it for you."

He answers, "Don't you worry. I am an expert now. Even if he recommends a bird to me, I'll check out the wings, examine the soft feathers one by one. And if only one of them is not deep green, I'll know that the bird is a crow. But what about its beak? Parrots, as you know, have curved beaks. It is a beautiful curve and if you look at it from afar you know it is a parrot."

We entreat him, "Hassan Aqa, by God...."

He puts on his hat, waves his hand, meaning "stay calm" or "trust me."

We say, "Then at least open your ears wide this time."

He stops and stares at us the same way Hossein Aqa will certainly stare at him.

Finally he says, "Why you? What if the bird says 'Hossein Aqa', what if it says 'Good morning' around sunset, what if addresses me as 'Bibi, Bibi'?"

We say, "Well, what's wrong with that?"

He answers, "Of course, it's wrong. I buy a parrot to greet me every morning by saying 'Good morning, Hassan Aqa.'"

Well, what more can anyone say. At this point Hassan Aqa is right. One buys a parrot to share one's pain with, to talk to, a parrot that understands and can differentiate between morning, noon and evening, not one that cannot tell the difference between Bibi, Hossein Aqa and Hassan Aqa or Seyyed Mohsen Razavi.

Even if that parrot were the prettiest parrot in the world it wouldn't do.

Big Bang

TRANSLATED BY
STEPHEN MEYER

I'm just saying, why doesn't anyone ever give me a call just to say, "Fazlullah Khan, this morning my son Kayumars got his first tooth"?

Are you listening, Amineh Agha?[1] They're nothing but prophets of doom and gloom, the lot of them; all they can do is moan and groan, "My beloved auntie has passed away."

My ribs hurt, my ribs there on the right side, but I don't talk about them. My right leg's been killing me for I don't know how many years (are you listening to me, woman?), but I don't talk about it. They're like a traveling companion to me in my old age, these pains. Not worth mentioning. To quote the Master: "You've got to moisten a morsel of grief with saliva, swish it around with your tongue and then swallow it." Not worth mentioning. Somebody came by, presumably to visit me. He sees that I'm lying here bedridden, he sees the two crutches that keep me company day and night, and he says, "You just can't imagine how expensive taxis have gotten. If you don't say 'a hundred tomans' or shout 'two hundred tomans to Vanak Square,' they don't give you a second glance."

Are you even listening to me, Amineh dear? My brother Mohammad's boy Asghar came by to visit his beloved uncle, namely me. "What's new, dear boy?" I asked.

"What do you want me to say?" he asked.

"Tell me something nice, my dear," I replied, "something that will cheer me up."

---

1. "Agha" spelt with the Persian letter "gheyn" (gh) is the feminine form of the word and was often used as an honorific for women, similar to "madam," in the nineteenth century, as opposed to the masculine form, "aqa" spelt with the letter "qaf" (q), which is an honorific for men, similar to "sir," and commonly used today.

He just sighed, which made me wonder what was really on his mind. Are you following? "The rent is going to be the ruin of us," he said. "Whatever I manage to get with one hand I give to the landlord with the other."

"What's with your wife, son?" I asked. "How does she manage to dress the way she does? Does she at least throw her arms around you sometimes when you come home, even with just a puny little bouquet of narcissuses?"

Did you hear what he answered? "You're in a good mood, uncle!"

They're liars, Amineh, believe you me! I know all about these people. When they're feeling good, when they're making preparations for a party, the first thing they do is pull all the curtains closed, tight as a drum. But God forbid an aunt or a cousin should die on them, or an esteemed acquaintance fracture a leg, not a real break but just a hairline fracture, then just watch them loudly broadcasting their woes, hey people! Last night when you were sleeping a noise woke me up. When I listened carefully, I realized that it was raining, raining very softly, and now and then a drop or two would strike the windowpane. I wanted to turn the light on so I could see, but I thought to myself that it might wake you. So, fine, I reached my hand over and carefully picked the phone up from the stool and rested it on my chest. I wanted to give someone a call and tell him to get up and, if he could, light a lamp and go out into the courtyard, out on the terrace and lift his head and hold his face up to the rain so that the small, cold drops would strike his forehead and trickle down onto his cheeks. Thus I wept bitterly as I thought and thought about whom I could call that wouldn't say, "Has he lost his mind?" And, truth to tell, I was still afraid that I might wake you and you wouldn't be able to fall asleep again. Then I said to myself, why don't I get up, first I'll just pull myself up, then I'll sit up and turn and reach my hand out and then one crutch under this armpit and one crutch under the other and then I'll stand up and then it's step by step until I get to the door, and then the elevator, and then I can ask Mash Rahmat or that Yussof or whoever's watching our door to help me out to the courtyard of our building. But it was no use. This body of mine has a mind of its own, Amineh Agha, these two legs have really let me down. Not that I'm complaining; they took me all over, even a bit astray at times. I didn't tell you about that. I was a bachelor, unattached and in love. I headed down the road, looking this way and that way, then I sprang up and grabbed the edge of the wall and was over it in a single bound. I didn't know the meaning of fear. She was awake, she heard me and asked: "Is it you, Fazli?"

"Were you expecting somebody else?" I replied.

"Don't shout so, you'll wake everyone up," she said.

All people can talk about these days is the exchange rate, that the dollar is up to over two hundred tomans. And the way they talk, they've got you believing that if only you'd bought ten thousand of them, you'd be sitting pretty, as rich as Croesus. To hell with these crazy times! People just don't have character anymore. I swear, not a single one of them ever came up just to say, "look at the shirt I bought." I still have a heart that beats. "Take off that veil, girl," I say, "turn around so I can see the pleats of your skirt."

"I don't wear skirts," she says.

Did you hear what I said? Safieh said, "I always wear blouses and trousers. They're more comfortable."

That's just my luck. Do you remember that red and white skirt? You must have stashed it away somewhere. I came across it a couple of years ago. I held it up in front of me and started to cry. From joy, believe me! It struck me again the way she used to whirl about so that the pleats of the red and white skirt flew around her pale plump legs. She says, "I wear blouses and trousers." Well, well, well. "They're warmer," she says. "And what about at home, in front of your husband?" I ask.

"Daddy, no one would even think of saying such things nowadays," is what she says.

Oh my, if only I'd been able to, if only you'd been here to help, the two of us could have grabbed her and set her down on the bed and spanked her a couple of times on her tender behind. It would have done me a world of good! She says, "The kids are hunkered down in front of the TV until the wee hours. And before you can say a word to Aqa Mahmud, he's nodded off."

She can't be serious. Surely the ice age is not yet upon us? Tell the truth, old woman! What's going on outside, what's happening in front of the window, on the other side of the wall? How can it be that every blessed night, Mahmud turns his back on our daughter and snores until morning, while poor Safieh sits staring out the window smoking one cigarette after the other until dawn comes and she's got to get up again. First she takes the kids to school and then she heads for the office. She's got to cover her hair, fasten her headscarf under her chin and be mindful until 3:00 or 3:30 that no stray hairs peek out. She told me so herself. My blood was boiling. Are you listening, woman? I asked her, which walls would collapse out there, where would the skies open if a bit of my lovely daughter's hair peeks out from under her headscarf, a strand the size of the egret design on that yellow handkerchief? "Who's afraid of my daughter?" I asked.

Anyway, yesterday I read in the newspaper that fifteen billion years have gone by since the origin of the heavens and the earth. They've even taken a picture of the beginning of the world. Apart from that—are you paying attention?—billions and billions of years have to pass before each atom has broken down and the atmosphere has cooled off. Hasn't the atmosphere cooled off, isn't it intensely cold outside? It must be even colder than in the ice age. It was just yesterday that the orange light of the sunset fell on that wall. And Safieh says, "There's no more cough syrup, Daddy. Aqa Mahmud went to more than ten pharmacies, they said that even the Foundation pharmacy didn't have any, but then he went to Naser Khosrow Avenue and found some."

I read a lot, you know that. Every day I read both of the popular official national newspapers. I also read books. But they don't say a word about any of this. I've always got the radio on as well. I listen to the "Good Morning" program every day. At two on the dot I turn on the news; today was no exception. The temperature must be about a hundred or a thousand degrees below zero. So Safieh wasn't lying after all. I tell you, this is an intellectual magazine as well. But not a word about any of this. They grumble a lot, but I don't see a single one of them writing about how splendid Damavand[2] is in the morning, when the sun first peeks out over the horizon. It's as if they're already dead. They do nothing but complain. You weren't there, you'd gone to get the bread or perhaps some vegetables, I don't know. Early in the morning, somebody phoned and said, "Two young people have made a date to dance in the middle of Vanak Square at five in the afternoon."

The first thing I did was ring up a few people, I kept dialing numbers and passing on the news. Someone even called me up to tell me about it. I rolled out of bed and crawled over beside the window and finally managed to pull myself up. God knows my heart was heavy. There wasn't a soul to be seen from any of the windows. Were they all dead? Then I stretched my hand out and, with a great deal of effort, managed to open the window and, using my elbows for support, pulled myself up. Just to give an example, I looked down at the bench in front of our building and I saw that it was empty. The one in front of the entrance to number three was also empty. Where are the young folk, why don't a couple of them come to sit on the bench under our window? The girl at one end, the boy at the other, and then he starts to dig at the wood with his fingernail and asks, "So, how's it going?" And she answers, "I'm okay."

---

2. Mount Damavand, about 18,580 feet high, an extinct volcano in the Alborz mountains about 40 miles east of Tehran. The cone shaped peak can be seen from the city.

And he looks around and rubs the cold wood of the bench, and says, "So, you're okay?" And the girl says, "Not bad."

I was shedding tears, no fooling; you saw them, didn't you? But I didn't say anything; I was afraid that you'd call up Safieh or maybe that good-for-nothing and tell them, "I just can't cope with that father of yours any more." I just said, "You're late, I was worried."

I do worry when you're not there. When you go out and I listen so intently and I can't hear a thing I get...goosebumps. Are you listening, Amineh Agha? I shiver and I worry. I worry about Safieh and even about Sediqeh. They can't even spare us one little line. And your precious son, who's doing quite well for himself, can't find the time to give me a call once a week to ask, "How's it going, Dad?"

When was it that he called up and asked, "How's it going, Dad?"

"I'm fine," I said, "I'm getting by. How are you doing? Still going fishing?"

"Sweet dreams, old timer," he replied.

I said, "After all, you coward, they haven't managed to take Fridays away. Take the wife and kids by the hand and head for the river. You can pick up some sandwiches on the way so Tal'at won't feel like she has to prepare any food. You've already got the fishhooks. Go and sit on a boulder by the riverbank—"

He cut me off, saying, "Are you awake, old man?"

"I've been awake for sixty-five years and three months," I said. "You're the one who's asleep, you idiot!"

At this point I hung up. As a result, he hasn't called back. He most likely sleeps until noon, even on Fridays. Safieh says, "Both of the kids are taking the university entrance exams. If he gets them a private tutor, that's going to cost at least three thousand tomans an hour."

Is this true, what Safieh is saying? How much does a semester of medical studies cost at the Free University? Why isn't there anything in the newspapers about this?

But listen to me, Amineh dear, let's assume that there is famine, prices are exorbitant, but there's something else too, something that I don't get. Something must have happened downstairs. Did someone die down there, because I don't hear the sound of the neighbor's *tar*[3] anymore? It's been a while since I've heard it. Do you remember me saying, "Go and take a look and see if the downstairs neighbor is dead?"

And you said, "No, we still hear their voices."

---

3. An Iranian musical instrument with a sound-box, a long neck and six paired strings, much appreciated for its sonorous and velvety sound.

"I still hear something, too," I said. There was that night when I was awakened by the screams of his wife or, who knows, maybe his daughter. But he doesn't play any more. Remember how he used to play for half an hour in the afternoons at quarter past three on the dot, always the *Bidad* melody?[4]

"You need to be in the right mood to play the tar," you replied.

In the right mood? You need to play when you're *not* in the mood, to get *in* the mood. No, there's something going on, something that even Safieh doesn't know about. You don't know about it either.

When you go out you've got to be careful every step of the way so that you don't fall and break a hip again like you did that one time. That's why you don't notice what's going on around you. Open your eyes, woman! Pay attention to what's happening. For the last fifteen billion years, since the Big Bang, stones and rocks have been swirling around and crashing into one another until we appeared, until two young people appeared sitting at opposite ends of a bench and one says, "How's it going?" and the other one says, "Fine," and they slowly slide closer together. But we now no longer bend down to kiss the ground.

We need to show more respect. These people are ingrates. Just to give an example, they don't dance like our Milky Way, which is forever revolving and turning about itself. Are you listening, Amineh Agha? Look at all these windows! There have got to be two hundred or four hundred families on every block in this Ecbatana neighborhood. They've all got their windows closed. And if one happens to be open, all you hear is the blare of the television.

Have I already told you this? One time we went to a spring above the village of Khosrow Abad, in the Chahar Mahal region. Myself and five friends of mine. Two of them are no longer with us. Or maybe they are and I just haven't heard from them. The spring was in the form of a pool with water bubbling up from below. We spread out a blanket, or perhaps a kilim, on a stone ledge under an ancient elm by the bank of the pool, and spent the day from morning until night either in the water or sprawled out willy-nilly.

The water was so cold that when we emerged from it, our teeth would chatter. But we just ran around and flapped our arms and stamped our feet and then leapt back into the water. Every day one of us would cook. We had determined that no one would bring books or a chessboard or

---

4. In addition to being the name of a melody in one of the twelve modal systems of traditional Persian music, *bidad* also means injustice. The pun serves Golshiri to express a political point.

even paper. You've seen the Master, haven't you? He was there too. We stayed six days. In the evenings we'd go to Khosrow Abad and sleep in the village schoolhouse, and the next morning we'd head back to the spring. We even gave them the names "summer quarters" and "winter quarters." Mornings we went off to the summer quarters and evenings it was back to the winter quarters. At nightfall it was someone's duty to keep us all entertained: he'd dance, perhaps, or, I don't know, sing or tell stories or think up some game to play. Afterwards we would give him a grade. The fourth night, it was the Master's turn. "I'm not good at anything," he said. "My voice is terrible, and I don't want to reveal any of my personal experiences. But I'd like to tell you something that I heard. Four or five months ago I'd gone to Darband, to visit a sick friend. On the way back as I was going downhill I noticed that the gears were not shifting properly, and also the tire pressure was not right. Further downhill, around a curve, I noticed that there was a mechanic's garage. I pulled over and backed up beside the shop. The mechanic was an old man, and he told me to bring the car into the garage. I did a lot of maneuvering back and forth until I finally got it over the pit. He was alone, and he said, 'Go take a walk for half an hour while I get this fixed up.'

"I went over by the stream. I noticed how beautiful the water was. The twilight was reflected in the water, as well as what appeared to be the shadow of a withered branch. I sat down at the very edge and sank into contemplation. The water was limpid and eddied up in rills before flowing on. Suddenly I noticed that the mechanic was standing beside me, wiping his hands on a cloth."

'Pretty, isn't it?' he remarked.

"Yes, I replied.

'Very pretty?' he continued

"Very, I said.

'Yes, I can see that,' he said. 'I've been seeing it for forty years. I've come across hundreds of places with a lot of traffic where I could have set up a shop, but whenever I come over here and sit by the edge of the water, I realize that I'd never have the heart to leave. This place, as you can see for yourself, is unsuitable for a mechanic's workshop, but....'

"Do you know what he finally said, Amineh Agha? That mechanic said, 'I'm a prisoner, sir, this bend in the lane and that stream have taken me prisoner.'

People are no longer prisoners. You've heard the saying, "Your bowels are pressing so that you've forgotten all about love"? These folks feel the pressure of their bowels and they can't find a restroom. They're always feeling the pressure. Someone comes by to visit me, he even brings me a book, but he hasn't finished sitting down before he starts to whine, "Kids just have no idea of the meaning of money."

"Neither do I, my esteemed colleague," I said. "Like you, I'm a retired bank employee. And these legs that you see here have left me in the lurch. But I'm still alive, and every morning, with the help of my wife over there, I stand up and go over by the window and I scatter a few grains of rice and some stale bread that I've crumbled up the night before so that later when I've lain down again, I can hear the sound of their cooing. I can't see them, but I can make out their cooing. When they fly off, if one of them happens to fly this way, towards the setting sun, I can see him."

"Good for you," he said, "it's nice that you're still in that sort of mood. I have no idea when sunset is, let alone in which direction the sun sets."

"Hoist me up and I'll show you," I said. He didn't do it. He kept changing the subject so that I'd forget about it. As he was leaving, he said, "You'll have to forgive me if I don't pop in to see you. Lord, am I swamped with work."

He does have problems, but he's not imprisoned by them, this former teller at the Saderat Bank. That old guy, though, he was imprisoned. "Since that time, I've never been back to Darband,"[5] said the Master. "And I've certainly never been arrested."

"No fair," cried Bahram. "You've got to tell us something else, something that happened to you."

"No, no, he's got to dance," insisted our esteemed Sedaghat.

"Then I'll dance," said the Master, "even though I've never danced in my life." And so he danced. His body was stiff as a board and his arms and legs seemed to be made of wood, but he danced. Are you listening, Amineh Agha? He danced, he moved his head and his arms around, he turned in circles and his hips swayed. Finally he sat down and all at once he began to weep. "I just can't," he was crying.

Whatever became of him? Are you paying attention? "I just can't," he said, "I've never danced before. I've always been afraid to dance or sing. I don't even allow myself to sing when I'm alone in the bathroom."

Maybe the folks down below are afraid, too. For example, our downstairs neighbor, who no longer plays the bidad melody. Maybe you know something you don't want to tell me. Has something happened, Amineh

---

5 Darband is the name of a popular summer resort north of Tehran. The word also means "in chains" or "imprisoned." The pun along with the word *gereftar* (meaning both "attached" and "arrested or imprisoned") has, of course, political connotations.

Agha? By all you hold dearest, tell me the truth. During the time I've been bedridden, has it gone out of fashion to dance, or for street kids to sing love songs of the village lanes?

I want to know, I have a right to know. If we can grasp the origin of creation, how come I have no idea what's going on thirty or forty meters away, behind the house? Come give me a hand so I can go and see what's going on, why my daughter, daddy's little girl, hasn't called in fifteen years or written one measly line, and why it's always just Safieh who comes and says, "Sediqeh says hello."

I don't give a damn about her hello! Did you hear what I said? "I don't give a damn about her hello!" If I can't see her, what use is her hello to me? I just hope that something bad hasn't happened to her. I'm talking to you, Amineh Agha! Captivity is bad, but if you're imprisoned by something, like that mechanic, it's not so bad. When he wakes up, he knows why he's awake. That's just what I'm trying to say. But no, I was about to say something else. Yes, that's right, I was just saying that somebody called an hour ago to say, "This afternoon at five o'clock, two young people are going to dance in Vanak Square."

He called while you were out. I'm not sure that he said Vanak Square, but I'm sure he said that they were going to dance. So I called up Asghar and said, "My dear boy, have you heard that two young people are planning to dance in Vanak Square this afternoon at five o'clock?"

"Why?" he asked.

"I don't know why, but I know that they're going to dance," I replied.

Then I came up with the reason myself and kept on calling. I told the Master, "They're dancing for joy at the image of the creation of the universe."

"That's quite something, count me in," he said.

He said that just as I heard the sound of the door when you came in. Come on, you call too and spread the word! Call up whomever your heart desires! Then help me get up and give me a pair of trousers to put on. The new ones! Then we'll go downstairs together, and I'll ask everyone, I'll ask the taxi driver, "Is it true what they're saying, that today a young man and a girl are going to dance in Vanak Square?"

If he asks, "When?" I'll say, "At five on the dot!"

Then we'll head over there and sit on a bench on the edge of the square. It'll be enough if we let two or three people know, then we'll go and sit on a bench in the middle of the square. If the two show up at five on the dot, fine, but if not, then give me those crutches, one under this arm and one under the other. Then you stand up and the two of us will dance. Did you hear what I said, Amineh Agha? Why don't you say something?

Banoo'i, Anne, and I

TRANSLATED BY
HESHMAT MOAYYAD

When it turned dark I went back in. As I opened the door I saw a woman sitting opposite him. I said hello and nodded. Banoo'i said in Persian, "This woman just walked in. She says she is a painter and has been taking a walk in the neighborhood and dropped in to have a look." I introduced myself and we shook hands. Banoo'i said her name was Anne Peters. "I didn't understand a word," said Anne in English. Banoo'i told her he had spoken Persian. They were having a cup of coffee. He turned on the electric kettle. For months we would prepare coffee and tea this way: we switched on the kettle and when it started whistling we simply poured water into a cup over a teabag or two spoons of coffee.

She was talking with Banoo'i. She wore earrings made of several hoops hooked into each other like a chain. Her hair was the color of smoke. Her neck was long and white. At the corner of her eyes and above her lips a few tiny wrinkles were visible. She was about forty-five, or perhaps fifty years old. She wore a black blouse and a white-hemmed shawl wrapped around her shoulders.

"Do you travel alone?" I asked.

"It has been months since I cut off connections with my friend," she answered and smiled.

I saw the two rows of her large white teeth. Her eyes were a light blue. Now, with her head down, she was playing with her coffee cup.

"Any children?"

"I have a grown-up daughter."

She laughed again with her entire shoulders and the shawl. Her profile was clean and firm.

"We are friends."

"Do you travel alone?" I asked again.

"I have a car and a few warm blankets," she answered.

Turning to Banoo'i, she said, "Last night I went into those areas."

And she motioned with her hand towards the meadows that we could see through the window, or even the trees further away. With her right hand she traced the round curve of a valley and with her finger she pointed to the bottom of this invisible valley.

"I pulled the blanket up to here," she pointed to her nose.

"The sky was clear. There were stars. The dawn was...how should I put it?"

"Splendid?" Banoo'i suggested.

"No, not splendid. Splendid is too much of a human quality, mixed with arrogance. Dawn is rather soft like...."

She touched the edge of her shawl with her hand and, turning her face towards Banoo'i, she said again, "Like...."

"Velvet?"

She smiled, "Yes, like velvet. It is like mist in the air, like a window covered with vapor." She looked down, "I can't speak English very well. Do you know French or Spanish?"

We shook our heads. She was German. She had long straight hair rolling over her shawl and her shoulders. She sipped her coffee.

"Would you like some more coffee?" Banoo'i asked.

"No," she replied.

"What about tea?"

"How come she appeared here? Who is she to begin with?" I asked in Persian.

Banoo'i said, "I don't know. She simply knocked on the door. I thought she was an employee of the Foundation, or perhaps a neighbor. She asked whether she could come in. Then she explained that she is a painter and has come to this area to look around and paint and at night sleep outside in the open."

Anne said, "What a beautiful language!"

"Aren't you afraid of being alone?" I asked her.

"Of course there is some fear, I am afraid."

"You are very courageous," I said.

"Not courageous. I am very...."

She looked at Banoo'i. But Banoo'i was fiddling with my cap. He put it on every time he went out. He would say, "My head feels cold." His hair was short. It had been black before, hanging straight down to his shoulders. He was bothered by dandruff, so he had it cut short.

"If it is not exposed to fresh air all day long, the skin gets itchy."

I said, "Didn't you hear what she asked?"

He turned to Anne and said, "Please, excuse me. I didn't hear you."

"What is the opposite of courageous in English?" she asked.

"Timid?"

"Yes, timid," she continued. "I am very timid. But the sky is so very beautiful at night, and then the fog at dawn, how should I describe it, like a curtain made of those small, cold and transparent drops that settle on leaves like crystals early in the morning...."

With her fingertips she outlined their tiny size.

Banoo'i said in Persian, "Do you see her hair?"

And turning to her he said in English, "Dewdrops."

"Oh, yes, dewdrops. At first it's dark everywhere. The air is frozen, it looks like glass...it looks as if nothing exists behind the expanse of the air. It is impossible to guess from where morning will first appear. And then, after the horizon has cleared on this and that side, only a wide strap appears like ice, the color of ice."

Banoo'i had made two cups of coffee. He poured milk into one of them for himself.

I asked Anne, "And no none bothers you?"

She answered, "I have nothing of value. My car is old and I have a few blankets, old but warm. I also have about ten to twenty palettes, some paint and some brushes."

"What about money or credit cards?"

"Not much, it's not worth the trouble."

"What about yourself," asked Banoo'i. "After all, you are a woman."

She laughed loudly, "I watch carefully. I stop in outlying places, far off from highways and villages. There are only hunters who occasionally make some noise—boom." She raised her hands as if she was holding a gun, "And disrupt my watching the dawn. The hunting season started a few days ago in this region."

"What about tonight?" I asked. "Would you like to stay here?"

She gazed at us and shook her head. Her earrings dangled.

Banoo'i said in Persian, "But we don't know her. And particularly the way she has shown up here and it is only our first evening here."

"But there is that other room with a bed in it." I turned to Anne and said in English, "We just arrived today. We are guests of the Foundation. But, nevertheless, you can spend the night here if you want to."

"I have my own house near Hanover. It's not a bad house. It's for the sake of watching dawn that I have come here. I paint."

She moved her hand as if she was holding a brush and drawing a line on a palette. Banoo'i explained in English that her works had been exhibited a few months before. Anne mentioned the name of the place and said laughing, "I didn't sell a thing. I am not famous. In this area people only buy the works of dead artists. Besides," and she pointed to herself, "I am very modern."

I asked, "Not even one painting?"

"None," she said.

"Then how do you live? Do you have a state grant?"

"No, no! That's bad. It would be humiliating. It kills one's personality."

Banoo'i rubbed his short hair with his hand. The only thing missing was his biting his fingernails. All the way from Tehran to Frankfurt he kept biting his nails till the tip of his middle finger started bleeding.

I held his hand up in the air and told Anne, "If we stay here, that is, if we have to...." I did not remember the word resident. Banoo'i looked at me. I asked him in Persian for the English word.

Banoo'i told Anne, "We won't stay here permanently. Our children are over there. I won't."

"How many children do you have?" Anne asked.

"Two. A boy and a girl. My daughter is fifteen years old."

I asked her, "How do you live without money?"

She shaped her hand to look like a paint brush and pointing to the wall moved it up and down, "I paint houses. I still can do it occasionally."

Banoo'i gently pulled his hand out of mine.

He asked Anne, "What about now? With no money, only a broken car and several blankets?"

"I also have a kerosene stove (she pointed to our kettle) for making coffee, three cups a day. As for food, I eat something when I am on the road. At sunset I look for a place, a place somewhere away from the road...." She looked at Banoo'i for the English word. Banoo'i, while chewing on the nail of his left forefinger, glanced at me, stroked his chin and said, "Cozy?"

Anne continued, "I find a cozy place and sleep until the next morning. Morning is a very beautiful time. Not really beautiful. A beautiful object remains unchanged. However, morning is different. It keeps changing. Each morning has its own colors. This morning, how shall I say—the air, the entire expanse of the air, was like a piece of ice, like polar ice before it begins to melt. No, that was a bad description. Morning is like nothing. Each morning is unique. You cannot paint it. No matter how fast I paint, I cannot catch up with it. This morning I cried."

Banoo'i said, "You described it very well in English."

"I am not even able to describe it in German," she said. "The air was one frozen piece. And there was a narrow white line like polar ice along the entire horizon...."

She shrugged her shoulders, wound her shawl around them and knotted it in front. She added, "I love the orange color of morning very much. I do not wear it."

Banoo'i asked, "What about eating? You can't live on hot dogs and cheese alone."

"Food is not important. My husband used to love warm home-cooked meals. I told him I couldn't do it. He left me. Now he lives with a girl younger than myself. I feel more comfortable now. I usually buy something somewhere and eat it on the road until I reach a new cozy place."

Looking at Banoo'i she added, "Thanks for the word cozy. Before lying down to sleep, I prepare everything for the next day. In the morning the air...(she moved her hand as if she was driving something into the air) you simply can't describe it. It changes. I wish I could paint all those changes everywhere."

I asked, "How many years have you been painting?"

She untied her shawl. She looked at me and raised her eyebrows, "How many years? Um, I have not counted them, but I have been painting since childhood. With the arrival of spring I set out and occasionally continue into summer since it is less cloudy. Right now I paint only in the morning. As I said before, I am not famous. But I do paint...several paintings in the morning. And afterwards I go wherever I want to. When it is cloudy I may stay on for a few days. But when there are no clouds I begin before sunrise with the green of a meadow, the shadow of some branches."

Her eyes closed and she was drawing in the air.

Banoo'i said in Persian, "Shall I invite her to stay? She could stay in that other room. It does have a bed."

"We are strangers here, you said it yourself. We do not know her."

Anne remarked, "This is a beautiful language."

"And the morning?" I asked.

Anne answered, "Morning is not only beautiful. It is somehow like glass, not unlike ice. Just white and cold like ice. It cannot be shown with colors. Even before I have finished pouring green paint on the palette and some mixture of green and brown for the trees on the other side, and prepare some dark color for the shadowy spot of the thicket a little further away, the colors have already changed. I look at the place, not at the palette, just like when you type on the typewriter. And still it won't work."

Banoo'i said, "We have an extra bed. You can sleep here if you want to."

She shook her hand, "No, I sleep under the open sky."

Banoo'i brought a box of ginger cookies, opened it and offered her some. Anne wanted to know what they were and what the ingredients were. Banoo'i explained. Anne took some. With her eyes closed, she certainly was contemplating their taste. "They are delicious."

She got up. "I have a sample of my work with me. It is a photo from my exhibition." She went outside.

"How strange," said Banoo'i.

"She appeared here just out of the blue. She knocked at the door and simply entered. She told us her whole story, about her husband and their fights, about her daughter, about her home near Hanover. She had heard, as she told us, that artists were living in this house. I explained that this was not the case. Rather, the Foundation invites some artists from around the world, once every few months. And so, we too had been invited and had just arrived this very morning."

Someone knocked on the door. It was Anne. She was holding a big poster and a postcard. She handed them to Banoo'i. Here and there sketches of a meadow, some trees and the shadow of a hill were visible. One could only guess whether they were actual representations or simply blotches of color, a shade of brown mixed with green, or perhaps they were the image of a branch hanging over the white surface of the horizon.

"Where's the morning then?" I said.

She was sitting there playing with the handle of her empty cup. She said, "When springtime arrives I shall set out again, but only on the days when there are no clouds."

I said, "And nobody buys any of them?"

She laughed loudly and said, "I am not famous."

Banoo'i asked, "Nobody's ever bothered you? A passer-by, a drunk?"

"I own nothing."

"How about yourself? You are beautiful and a woman."

"My husband used to say, 'You'll be killed.' I only answered, 'I'll die anyhow. Let it happen this way.' What's the use of getting old and no longer being able to paint houses?"

She got up, "I must leave and find a new place. Or perhaps I will go back to where I spent last night. It is a cozy place."

She looked at Banoo'i, "Thanks so much. Each time I use the word cozy I will remember you."

Banoo'i pinned her exhibition poster to the wall.

"I painted this one last year. Now I am painting a morning scene. Yesterday I painted a few. It looked so beautiful, so very soft…. From deep within the valley the horizon on the other side looked like…like…."

"Like velvet?" suggested Banoo'i.

"White velvet, but cold." She waved her hand, "*Aufwiedersehen.*"

Together we replied, "Aufwiedersehen."

Written at the Heinrich Böll Haus in Farvardin 1376, March/April 1997

A Storyteller's Story

TRANSLATED BY HESHMAT MOAYYAD

Whatever else Akhavan[1] was, he was not a hypocrite. He was no angel, either. What you saw was what he was. If others could not take it straight he would find a way around it. If he committed an immoral act, as the poet has put it,

> *Nobody's clothing is free of dank.*
> *Though before the public's eye*
> *Others hide their filth,*
> *Whereas we hang it out in the sun*

Akhavan would not hide it. He would rather hang it up in the sunshine to dry out, then wet it again, as his expression of gratitude for the gift of the sun.

Amongst all his talents I liked best his skill in telling stories, and most of all when he narrated them himself orally. I heard the following anecdote from Akhavan himself. Dr. Haqshenas, to whom I dedicate this writing, is my witness. Each time we meet he urges me to write it down. Here it is now, dear doctor, the story as Akhavan told it. I have polished it without changing a single detail. And yet, I am not certain as to whether the event as reported is real or not. It doesn't really matter. What is important is the story itself. And I am a storyteller who leaves the haggling about it to others, the hypocrites.

---

1 Mehdi Akhavan-Saless (1928-1990), also known under the penname Omid, "Hope," whose characteristic sense of humor is described in this more fictitious than factual story, was one of the greatest and most celebrated twentieth-century poets of Iran.

One evening—or maybe it was midnight or even early morning, I can't remember—Akhavan, as if he suddenly found us worthy listeners, began to narrate the following.

He said, "I was informed that I was selected to attend the 'Youth Festival.' I realized that my ID card was back in Mashhad, and, of course, I could not get a passport without the ID card. So, I had no choice but to travel to Mashhad and retrieve it."

Akhavan was laughing.

Together with a fellow nicknamed Bolbol, "Nightingale" he set out walking towards the highway to hitch a ride to Mashhad with a car or a bus and then to travel on directly to the Festival from Mashhad. By the time they reach the highway, the sun has already gone down.

Well, at sunset, it is not unusual for a person to feel depressed in his heart, let alone Akhavan's heart. I used to get depressed every morning and every evening with or without any good reason.

Near the road there was a coffee house and next to it a *kababi*, "grill shop." And a little further away a man from the stock of Moses practiced his trade. The owner of the kababi in all likelihood adhered to both traditions [Moslem and Jewish]. In those places you usually find a narrow stream as well as a wooden bench or a wooden bed under a shade tree.

Akhavan said, "I told Bolbol, 'Go get us something to eat. One can't undertake such a long trip with a dry mouth.'"

It seems that at times when he was surprised or perplexed or any such thing, Bolbol would whistle instead of uttering a word. It's possible that the air passing through his broken teeth and the gaps between them would automatically turn into a whistling sound. That's why he was called Bolbol. Akhavan couldn't remember his real name.

Probably Bolbol was among his devotees at the time. Or maybe he was one of the comrades charged with the task of taking the poet to the Festival. In any event, he had a taste for ecstasy.

So, Bolbol goes to the shop, buys some kababs, a bowl of yogurt, two tender cucumbers—or perhaps four, Akhavan couldn't remember exactly. He puts them on a tray and comes back with a small, slender-necked bottle. They sit down and enjoy eating a decently good meal, followed by a "mouth wash."

Akhavan said, "Hardly had I realized what it was and how it tasted when it was already finished."

Their mouths still felt dry and they had a long trip ahead of them, followed by a journey to the "West" to join the comrades who desired to see the poet "drenched in liquid." No, it wasn't feasible to set off that fast. You cannot breathe or speak of God or the truth when your throat is dry.

He used to say, "It's not acceptable until your big toe feels it!"

Turning to Bolbol, Akhavan says, "My dear Bolbol, you went and got it, but why this one?"

He holds the small empty bottle in front of Bolbol's eyes.

Bolbol had the body of a champion. As for Akhavan himself, it's true he was short. But he was square-shouldered, in fact he was an athlete. Well then, it is obvious that two heroes, one of the tongue and one of the body, both from the stock of Abu Moslem,[2] couldn't be expected to undertake such a dangerous trip after only two small thimblefuls of the bitter liquid.

Bolbol goes again and this time, instead of the small slender bottle, he brings back a tall, fat one with a thick neck.

He must have bought some more yogurt and two more tender cucumbers—or maybe not. By now they were both in their element, enjoying the conversation like sweets, toasting and toasting to each other's health.

Still, it didn't work. Can you imagine for two Khorasanian heroes, two valiant men, to succumb to that small one and this tall one? Besides, they still have time until midnight. They might get on an International [bus] and move on slowly. Who knows God's ways? The driver may linger, halt, stop in some place and give them a chance to pay their due respects to one of those tall, square-shouldered bottles again.

So Bolbol walks over to the liquor store and returns, goes again and returns.

I kept filling up, he drank.
He kept filling up, I drank.
I surrendered to that happy, empty moment.[3]

When the bus finally arrives they agree between themselves to dally instead of departing because one of them still had a few drops left at the bottom of his well.

And the narration had just reached the point of "As I was saying...."

Akhavan continued, "I said, 'Dear Bolbol, does he still have some?'

'Um, of course, he does.'

'Well, my dear, we are two men of Khorasan and we only drink this

---

2. Abu Moslem, an Iranian military commander, killed by the second Abbasid caliph in 755, after he had overthrown the Omayyad caliphate and helped the Abbasid dynasty to come to power.

3. *Az in Avesta (From this Avesta)*, one of the collections of Akhavan's poems, Tehran, 1344 (1965), p. 102.

much? We are no less than Beihaqi,[4] who used to gulp down several gallon-goblets at a time. Besides, Rostam[5] himself hails from somewhere in this vicinity. Sistan[6] isn't far. Rostam was a hero, both in fighting and in feasting. For us this is fighting as well. We have got to empty this fellow's cellar. Imagine the gossip behind our backs if we leave even one bottle untouched!'"

Bolbol goes again and brings all that was still to be had in the store and sets down the bottles. After they finish, they look up and realize that no one is around. There is no traffic. No dust clouds raised by the bus are suspended in the air any longer. They call out "*Yahoo*" and get up when they hear someone say, "O God." Indeed, some "Rose of the Lord"[7] had just become visible on the dusty road. He was leaning against a tree trunk. He had fixed his pipe and was about to spread the smell of his grass. Leaning on one another, the two approach him and say, "Dear Mowla, you saw us but didn't offer us to partake?"

The dervish offers his pipe to Bolbol and Bolbol in turn to dear Mehdi Akhavan, and dear Akhavan passes it back to the dervish. And so they puff away, feel green, feel the sensation of spring, recite lines of poetry and top it off with a *ghazal*[8] until near morning, a morning of the sort Akhavan himself has described in a poem called "Sunrise."[9]

Well, they exhaust the dervish's bag. Noticing that no one is on the road, coming or going in either direction, they ask themselves, "Weren't we supposed to move on?" Perhaps this was the moment when the seed of his poem "Chavushi" (Caravan Leadership) was conceived:

---

4. There is no heavy drinking Beihaqi known to me. Golshiri's statement rather reminds us of the poet Qa'ani (1807-1853 A.D.) who in one of his famous poems has the following lines: "If I drink / to a drum's beat I drink. / Ten gallon goblets publicly I drink. / Pure wine, Magian's wine I drink. / I am not a yogi to be happy with poppy leaves." *Divan-e Qa'ani*, ed. Mohammad Ja'far Mahjub. Tehran, 1336/1957, p.810.

5. The world champion in *The Shahnameh*, the Iranian national epic, composed by Ferdowsi in the tenth century A.D.

6. One of Iran's eastern provinces, south of Khorasan and bordering on Afghanistan. Sistan was the homeland of the clan of the legendary Rostam.

7. *Yahoo* is called out by dervishes in their search for God. *Gol-e Mowla* is a Persian appellation for a dervish.

8 The most common form of a lyrical poem in Persian. It consists of seven to twelve mono-rhymed distiches. In modernistic poetry ghazal is applied to any form of lyrical composition disregarding its length.

9 *Tolu', Akher-e Shahnameh* (The End of Shahnameh), 1st ed., Tehran, 1345/1966, pp. 44-49.

In the fashion of wayfarers of old legends,
carrying their haversacks on the shoulder,
clutching a bamboo stick in their hands...[10]

The road ahead looked like a serpent resting on the high and low stretches of the plain. The weather was pleasant. The sun had not yet turned into that red-hot August copper basin—Mordad 1332 (August 1953).[11] The dervish was lying flat on the ground like a design, or, oh my God, like a corpse being cast down by two Khorasanians.

Our champions looked at the kabab shop. It was closed now. They glanced at that other fellow's shop that had nothing left to sell and so didn't need to open its doors.

Perhaps the dervish's snoring brought them to their senses.

They try to force their feet forward and realize they are unable to become each other's shadow, as described in his poem "The Sudden Setting of Which Star."[12] Bolbol sees with one glance that dear Mehdi is even more unstable than an undulating shadow. And Mehdi realizes that whistling Bolbol is no safe support to lean on, either.

Akhavan said, "I bent down and picked up the dervish's stick to borrow it, and started on my way. Bolbol followed me and we moved forward."

Indeed, they walk and walk, uphill and downhill, ascending and descending, following the curves of the road, they keep going. Maybe they told each other stories to shorten the long way.

By now the sun had risen above the horizon to at least the height of a lance or more; it was impudently hot.

They sweat profusely. The pores are not reliable either! However much liquid you have in your veins is wasted away in one sweating moment.

There was no coffeehouse as far as one could see, not even a tree. They walk on. No, it looks hopeless. Nader,[13] the savior, will not appear.

But meanwhile comrades at the Festival talk of Omid, "Hope" all the time. The traditionalists have given him the penname Omid.

---

10. *Zemestan* (Winter), another collection of Akhavan's poems, 2nd edition, Tehran, 1346/1967, pp. 151-159.

11. Mordad, the sixth month of the Iranian calendar (July 23–August 22). On Mordad 28, 1332/ August 19, 1953 a CIA-orchestrated revolt overthrew Iranian Prime Minister Mohammad Mosaddeq.

12. *"Nagah Ghorub-e Kodamin Setareh* "Which Star's Sudden Setting," *Az in Avesta*, pp. 97-106.

13. Nader Shah (1688-1747), founder of the Afshar dynasty, ended the political turmoil of Iran and restored unity and power to the kingdom.

Suddenly they hear the noise of a hearse, carrying the denizens of this contorted century. It comes roaring like a demon, leaving behind a column of smoke. It was an International, howling and raising a wave of dust.

The two friends hold up their hands and the stick in supplication. The intense expression of pleading written all over their faces fills the driver's heart with mercy. He halts the bus to let them board.

They try to get on. Oh dear, inside it looks like "the farmer's hut" in the poem entitled "The Man and [his] Horse." There is not even space to drop a needle. It is filled to capacity and more, with women and children, old and young.

> *The narrator said: "Thanks to God.*
> *Blessed be his will.*
> *Blind be the enemy.*
> *The hut was filled to capacity*
> *With all sorts of kids,*
> *Male, female, each one likable,*
> *This one attractive, that one charming."*[14]

They were all Arabs, only two old men among them. They were on the way of no return.

Akhavan and Bolbol emit one "*Yallah*" and "*Ahlan wa Sahlan*," "hello and welcome" and sit somewhere among other people's women folk, only to find out that it wasn't a real seat. They are sleepy, their bodies rocking with each clatter of the bus, their heads bobbing on their shoulders, falling now on the shoulder of a toothless hag, and now on the lap of a fairy-born creature who gently pushes the poet's heavy head on her soft palm back on his own shaky shoulder, and this keeps going on and on and repeats itself.

We know how bad the roads were in those years, full of potholes and puddles.

And occasionally his body falls on purpose.

Actually, when one is sitting face to face with a beauty that looks like she could have served as the model for the face, mole, and body of the cupbearers described in all ghazals, one automatically loses oneself, bends over and falls asleep.

---

14. "*Mard-o Markab*" "The Man and His Horse." *Az in Avesta*, pp. 25-26.

Akhavan said, "I kept falling asleep, waking up, falling asleep and on and on and again and again. Seeing we were moving, until all at once I realized that my head was resting on a lap. Whether my eyes were open or not, I saw, you might say through a ghazal of Abu Nuwas,[15] two black eyes gazing at me."

She seemed to smooth out his hair, which in those days was still lush and luxuriant. He also spoke of her smile and coquettish frowning. He would always remember "that coquettish frowning" when he alluded to the "first-rate quality of *dom-siah* rice of Gilan"[16] in another poem.

> *Happy, oh happy those lovely nights*
> *We strutted in Gilan's green woods.*[17]

until one of his later poems which begins and ends very harmoniously:

> *I am none*
> *I am none and less than none*
> *I am not of the world's people you see...*

A little further down in the poem we find him on the roof speaking of her:

> *And then I saw through a crack in the roof,*
> *A girl, more beautiful than dew drops in dreams*
> *Alone,*
> *As if being the spirit of water and water herself,*
> *As if being awake and yet asleep,*
> *As if being grief, clad in joy,*
> *As if being God's image in the loveliest frame."*

And then without any link the poem ends by returning to "I am none and less than none."[18]

---

15. A famous Arab poet at the Abbasid court, he died in 814 A.D.
16. See the collection *Arghanun*, "Organ," 2nd ed. Tehran 1348 (1969), p. 196. It contains an allusion to a woman called Turan from Rasht, the capital city of Gilan, with whom Akhavan had an affair. The episode is remembered several times with her name as well as simply alluded to. *Dom-siah* is a high quality rice cultivated in the Caspian shoreland of Gilan.
17. From the fifth ghazal in *Payiz dar Zendan* (Autumn in Prison), 1st ed. Tehran, 1348/1969, p. 16.
18. From a poem called "*Ma, Man, Ma*" "We, I, We," composed, according to Golshiri, in April 1990, only a few months before the poet's death, perhaps not yet printed anywhere. See Golshiri, *Bagh dar Bagh* "Gardens Within Gardens," Tehran 1378 (1999), vol. 2, p 578.

This fairy girl is certainly none other but Nima's "Afsaneh,"[19] or perhaps the "ethereal" woman of Hedayat's "The Blind Owl,"[20] or perhaps even more distant, the same one who "at midnight bent her head to Hafez's ear and tenderly asked whether he could sleep."[21]

Akhavan said, "She was a doll, one of those tawny faces, like a fresh twig that bends but does not break."

Akhavan and Bolbol were exhausted and had no control over themselves.

They fall asleep again. Opening his eyes at one point, Akhavan realizes the bus has stopped but no one is around. Another time, between sleep and awakening, he hears a whistling sound but drifts off again. The sound wakes him up once more and he sees people who seem to be getting off the bus. When he opens his eyes again, he finds his head cradled in the same lap or perhaps in a different one. He remembers her pierced nose and its ring. And once he sees the face, the same one described in his poem "Then After the Thunder," during the last moments of the chess game...

> Suddenly the woman,
> My partner in a dreadful game of chess,
> The game of no end and no winner,
> Broke into laughter that shook my back,
> And made me laugh a bit as well,
> Or so I think.[22]

It was twilight. Dawn or sunset? Omid could not remember. The Arab woman was busy lowering her face, with her long nose and its ring, cupping his lips with her mouth where only one tooth was left. He used to say, "She was sucking, my dear." And then she lifted her head, laughed and cupped again. She had a wart on the tip of her nose. She let her salt and pepper hair hang around Akhavan's face and bent down again. He would talk of her smell too, the foul smell of an oozing marsh, pretty much like our times. She would then draw in her cheeks and thrust her

---

19. Nima Yushij (1895-1960) was the founding father of modern Persian poetry. "Afsaneh" (Legend), published 1921, was his first major poem that displayed, in the form of a conversation between "Lover and Legend," his departure from the form and meaning common to classical Persian poetry.

20. A woman in Sadegh Hedayat's novel *Buf-e Kur* (The Blind Owl). See Michael Hillmann's *Hedayat's The Blind Owl, Forty Years After*, University of Texas at Austin, 1978.

21. *Divan-e Hafez*, ed. Qazwini-Ghani, ghazal 26.

22. *Az in Avesta*, p. 44.

only tooth into his cheek or chin, and suck, not unlike the very same *afreet*, "witch" whom Nezami thus describes:

> *When on that eye's light, that sugared fount*
> *His own approving eyes he bent,*
> *He saw a foul afreet, from mouth*
> *To foot created from God's wrath.*
> *A buffalo with boarish tusks—*
> *No one had ever dreamt of such a dragon.*
> *Her back a bow, her face a crab,*
> *A stench that reached a thousand leagues,*
> *Her nose a kiln for baking bricks,*
> *Her mouth like a cloth-dyer's vat.*[23]

Akhavan faints. When he wakes up again there is nobody left in the bus. He only hears Bolbol whistling. He gets up, looks around, sees no one, and gets off the bus. In the dim light of the coffeehouse he makes out Bolbol sitting there. A little further away are two old Arabs jabbering away in Arabic, in front of them two girls washing something in the gutter.

Bolbol asks, "Do you see?"

"What happened, my dear? Why did we stop here?"

Bolbol whistles and shows him the driver's boy who has lifted the hood and is fiddling with something down beneath it.

"Where is the driver?" asks Akhavan.

From his gestures Akhavan understands that the driver is somewhere in back of the coffeehouse, in one of those muggy rooms with one door, one single window, and bedding for one spread out on the floor. There is obviously something wrong with the bus and the driver has gone to sleep. The two of them eat a bite, or maybe they don't. In any case, hungry or not, they lie down until the bus starts up again. Once more Akhavan's head rests on a lap, his eyes open to a garden, a fresh branch bearing two lemons, or two moons, both new. A few hours later the bus comes again to a halt. The crankshaft is broken, or a tire punctured. Akhavan did not remember. And again more of the same at the next coffeehouse! And each time one of the two, either the driver or the assistant, stretches out under the bus or bends over the engine while the other is busy on some stairway or behind some half-fallen wall in the plain. The next time when the bus

---

23. From *Haft Paykar*, a medieval Persian romance. Composed by Nezami in 1197 A. D., translated with an introduction and notes by Julie Scott Meisami. *The World Classics*, 1995, p.193, verses 362-368.

stops Bolbol says, "We won't make it, dear Mehdi. They say that the crank-shaft is broken."

"What?"

Well, still one of them is there, the driver or his assistant. The two old men are sitting there, yelling, and jabbering away in Arabic. Some women, old and young alike, are just hanging around.

Akhavan said, "Bolbol said, 'I have counted the women. Each time one of them is missing.'"

This time Akhavan whistled, or perhaps the whistling was in his mind, thinking to himself, "These are real men, unlike us who are forever fan-cying and keeping busy with other poets' imaginations, or just walking in pleasure-grounds without ever having a real living beloved present."

He then cleared his throat and indicated that the following words in the poem are his own:

> *Tell me, woman, tell me why did I dream of you yesternight?*
> *Where were we?*
> *Where were we coming from that time of night*
> *the two of us alone?"*[24]

Perhaps these thoughts were the real reason for what he later did and was imprisoned for in the *Zendan-e Qasr,* "palace prison," the result of his adventure with the generous Butcher, swinging between PP [palace prison) and BP [butcher's wife] which he remembers in the following line:

> *I suffer this prison for the crime of being a man, o love,*
> *I am a bastard, if I committed any other wrong.*[25]

Well, the driver and his assistant were taking their paradise with them, well provided for with all the *Huris*[26] of all ages. Were they traveling to Mashhad or Herat? Akhavan didn't know. Perhaps they were going as far as China or perhaps they wanted to cross the few remaining miles in so many days, or even months and years, stopping briefly at every coffeehouse.

---

24. "Ghazal Eight," *Payiz dar Zendan,* p.28.
25. Ibid. p. 9. Referring to Akhavan's affair with a butcher's wife that cost him some months spent in Qasr Prison in Tehran. Allusions to this experience are found a few times in his poems, e.g. "*Arghanun*," p 204. See also Ebrahim Golestan's superb article "*Si Sal va bishtar ba Mehdi Akhavan*" (Thirty and more years with Mehdi Akhavan), *Iranshenasi,* vol. 2 no. 4, 1991, pp. 755-773.
26. Huris: Black-eyed beauties promised in paradise.

Akhavan realizes that in this fashion they will never reach the Comrades' Festival. Bolbol understands this as well. Yet, they have committed themselves to be there. The Party comrades will certainly get offended and publish evil accusations in their party paper, or tell the butcher, also a comrade, to sell Akhavan old meat and skin in the future.

They leave the bus and start walking until they reach the outskirts of the city. But they can't possibly go and simply fetch their ID cards and return with their dirty clothes and with faces unshaven for several days and hot with all the marks of cupping left by the afreet. They decide to go wash and clean themselves up first, and then return to the bus station at a certain hour. Most of all, Akhavan must remember to bring his ID card with him.

Akhavan said, "I had hardly arrived at Mashhad when I heard the news that dear Emad, Ahmad Shahna, dear Mohammad,[27] and X, Y, and Z had organized a party in a suburb close to this end of the city. They had even sent an Ekhvanieh[28] poem that included the following lines:

> Golden wine in a silver cup,
> The cupbearer a moonlike beauty,
> Companions with bodies bright as stars.
> We have lavished silver coins
> To prepare for golden pleasure.
> But how can we enjoy the pleasure without you?
> Without you I am void of myself.[29]

Akhavan thought he would start the return trip to Tehran sometime in the afternoon. But, aren't you supposed to say goodbye to friends? Their place is only a few steps away. One can walk to the station and in the blink of an eye you will be there at noon, simply say hello and return. Late in the afternoon you will be back here to join Bolbol. You know the rest.

He picks up his ID card, crams several notebooks in his bag and starts walking fast and vigorously like a panther until he reaches the garden and his friends, who already had a "ring of fire" going in the center and were busy taking turns reciting poems. Akhavan sits down. He hardly has time to catch his breath and exchange a few words of formality when it is already

---

27. Emad Khorasani, Ahmad Shahna, and Mohammad Qahraman, close friends of Akhavan, all poets and literary scholars from Mashhad.
28. Personal letters written in verse.
29. *Arghanun*, p. 201.

his turn to recite, [in the words of Ferdowsi] "Come on, show us how much of a man you are."

Akhavan had a repertoire of old poems, that is to say: ghazal, *qasideh*, *qit'a*,[30] rhythmic and rhymed quartets of equal meter as well as fully new ones in rhythmic and rhymed quartets in changing meters, though only in mildly new styles, of course! He recited and recited, interrupted only by "please, more, more," by catching his breath and offerings of tea, and on and on he recited. All friends present were young and yet were commanders in the realm of poetry.

"Twirl, spin, revolve, and we will twirl, spin, and revolve!"

All of them were equipped with powerful memories and each one had come prepared with pockets full of notebooks and poetry collections. And after they had exhausted their memories and their notebooks they turned to the creative fountain of their talents, extemporaneously reciting poems throughout the day, and on through the night, day and night, day and night. And every morning and every evening another hero joined the gathering, claiming the arena, keeping up the vigor! And then they would start over again, each one saying, "This is what I have composed...."

Akhavan said, "For a whole week we recited and recited. And when one or two fell off from our 'Pleiades'—oh God, no— and left the arena to us to keep it going, we realized that we were either '*Banat an'Na'sh,*' "Great Bear" or just *Na'shs*, "corpses." What was worse, there was nothing left of the smoking stuff. Besides, our sin-center was aching. And then I said I must get up and leave for the Youth Festival."

They do leave and return [to Tehran] and there learn about the events of Mordad 28th (August 19,1954).[31] It was already August 22nd and

> *the waves had rescinded. It was quiet and calm.*
> *The tempest's drum sounded no more.*
> *Flaming fountains were dry.*
> *No water was running the mill.*[32]

Akhavan stayed put and the trip abroad was off.

---

30 Different forms of traditional poetry used for any one subject of panegyrics, didactics, wisdom, description, elegy, etc. Hemistiches of different lengths are permissible only in modern verse.

31. See note 11 above.

32. "*Nader ya Iskandar*" "Nader or Alexander," from *Akher-e Shahnameh*, pp. 13, 15.

Again I was left with the city of no heartbeat,
With hyenas, wolves, and foxes
Sometimes thinking I should raise a cry
But knowing that my voice is low.[33]

He was laughing: "Those who had gone [to the Festival] were arrested at the border upon their return."

This time, he had escaped. When he was caught a little later, he feigned hallucinations. He bowed to avoid being broken. He had turned into a *malamati*,[34] thus provoking the blame of others, and into a *zendiq*, "heretic," and had talked inarticulately to avoid being understood.

Yet he continued to speak, compose, and move on. He wrote some qasidehs, expressing both praise and disdain, and modernistic poems of the highest heavenly quality, poems not like "limpid water," but like the roaring coming out of our wounded and bleeding throats; poems like "The Man and His Horse," "Then After the Thunder," "The Eighth Adventure," and whatever else their titles may be.

May he be showered with the mercy, not of Gods and *Amshaspands*,[35] but rather of the Pure and the Good. May it be thus, and be more, and more.

---

33. Ibid., p.15.
34 The name of a sect of Sufis who pretended to commit immoral acts only to provoke degrading blame by others.
35. Seven archangels in the pre-Zoroastrian religious system of Iran. In later times one of them is replaced by Ahura Mazda, the supreme god of Zoroastrianism.

Three Poems

TRANSLATED BY
FRANKLIN LEWIS

Let the Butterfly Go [1]

He came toward me, and fluttering,
the butterfly, in the cocoon of his hands,
was like a hundred-winged rose
I said:
   "Let the butterfly go, so that it can...."
He laughed
I said:
   "The butterfly is not a leaf that grows back,
   the butterfly is not a blossom that...."
                  I wept.
He laughed:
   "The butterfly is not a blossom, I know
   but—a pity!—in this garden
   the rose petals are on stalks of wind,
   the rosebushes in shadows of the night."
He laughed, and again:
   Colorful, lively and fluttering
   in the marbled frame of his two hands
   the butterfly was:
   gardens and twilight

I said:
"Let the butterfly go!"
Such a shame!
From the cocoon of his hands
onto the dust
the butterfly fell like a stone
He laughed and again....
Again I wept.

---

1. *"Parvane-ra raha kon"* from *Jong-e Isfahan,* 2, winter 1344/1965.

Laleh ²

1

With the troupe of gypsies
We came to the city
We called out:
O slaves to borders and measures,
We have fastened
on the backs of our horses
a waterskin filled from the spring of summer pastures,
a saddlebag filled with the luster of pennyroyals
The women fortunetellers
told the city girls:
May your future prove bright!
In the lines of your fate, sister,
are the hands of a child who will become a soldier.

2

On barebacked horses we sat.
We charged forward
with provisions and a shout of exultation.
We went right up to the abode of palaces,
We said:
O slaves to borders and measures!
The strange soul of the sea
the vast green of the willow
can not be contained within the proscenium arch.
From the petrifaction of stone roofs and pillars
clear a path to the colors.

3

When the spent black chargers
grazed the dark green of the meadow,
When lovers

---

2 "Laleh" ("Tulip") from *Jong-e Isfahan*, 3, summer 1345/1966

with stalks of jasmine
went to the city houses,
When the tambourine of Laleh, the gypsy,
made anemones grow from the stones
(and the men of the city
scattered coins on the ground
to watch),
When a cloud rained down
and the streets drank up the luster of the rain and wind
On barebacked horses we sat
with city girls,
we charged forward:
    O city girls!
    In gypsy tents
    make do with warm, fresh milk.
    Stay here, girls!

4

And the city girls saw:
the shepherd dogs, who were going along on the river's waves
the captive man, who they were bringing to the square for the firing squad
and Laleh, who was crying
on the boots of the soldiers
    O fortunetellers of the tribe!
    In the lines of which soldier's hand
    did you see these scorched tents?

The Palace of Samanbar [3]

There was springtime and the rains, and we were in the stone trench.
We heard the moments
ebbing down the mountain,
the vague anthem of a troop a thousand drops strong
          on the stones and rocks and earth
and we saw
the valley wash its body with the fingertips of a thousand drops
and the crystal beads of the rain garden grew on the rim of our trench.
And further down
through the vague strands of rain
was the abandoned palace of Samanbar
and I, on the canvas of rain, saw her on her ornamented throne
with the thousand thronged strands of her hair, more than there were
branches in the rain garden.
And there was the crimson outline of Haydar Bayk in the earth
"Come Samanbar,
Samanbar, come!"

"Did you hear the spring cloud saying 'Samanbar?'"
My buddy asked.
— Me, I heard it
but more beautiful than this, I have seen them
          with skin of alabaster and jasmine...
and I saw a group of girls among the vague strands of rain
singing:
     "Two tall cypresses we were, of even height
       now we are parted, both of us left to drink tears
     My hand cannot reach to pluck the rose
       and that tall cypress does not bend down"
A thousand more strands of rain and...
I saw the girls' blood splash in the strands

---

3. "Takht-e Samanbar" from *Jong-e Isfahan*, 1, Summer 1344/1965. Golshiri dedi-
cates this poem to his mother. The title alludes to a versified fairytale called
"Haydar Bayk and Samanbar," which local legend around Isfahan holds to have
taken place at the foot of the mountain called Kolah-e Qazi, to the southeast of
the city, where there are some ruins known as "the Palace of Samanbar." Etymo-
logically, Samanbar means one whose embrace smells of jasmine, suggesting one
whose embrace is as redolent and supple as jasmine.

The wefted veins overflowing with blood
and the blood churned and the carpet became a garden of rose.
"Come, Samanbar,
Samanbar, come!"
There was the roar of thunder and I spoke again:
— Did you hear it?
My buddy went off toward his intimate seclusion
And between our two persons, the curtains of his tears came down
Now the whiteness of the rain garden again and...
I saw the figure of a woman behind the pattern of the bars
who was telling her troubles to a patient stone:[4]

"Long ago, in a time
before God made the world,
there was a poor woodsman, and I was the very apple of his eyes
a precious, pure pearl of a girl in his eyes,
who for forty of God's days,
with forty almonds and forty droplets of water,
was companion of the man
in that large garden of which it is said:
The daughters of the king of fairies are in the nectarines and citrons
and dusk till dawn, their eyes are fixed upon the door,
or night and day the blood drips down
on the girl of stories in the water,
and the crimson rose glows like a lamp.
I am that daughter of the fairies, captive,
whose hands and feet were in chains,
whose eyes were in tears:
So where, then, the rider who storms in on his horse,
his face bright as the full moon
—his heart, though, the heart of a lion?
He opens the gate of the fortress
He caresses the girl of stories
He lifts her onto the back of his saddle
He carries her away to the lands of Cathay."

---

4. "patient stone" is a reference to a fairy tale in which a gypsy girl saves a prince
from a spell that has been cast upon him by eating only one almond a day and
drinking one drop of water a day. The story, in the version by Sadeq Hedayat, has
been translated as an illustrated children's book by M. and N. Batmanglij as *The
Patient Stone* (Mage Publishers, 1987).

I am that poor, weeping mother
Who has no companion in the night, cold and dark
So where, then, those three ladies, who come, candles in hand
to sit about the room,
who swaddle her naked and unsuckled daughter?
So why, then, does my daughter weep
and why do we have no pearly rolling tears?
    we have no laughing rose,
Our house is of adobe,
    and we have no bread?

There was springtime and there was rain and in the drizzle[5]
    we would go to the valley
which echoed with the anthem of the stream and the melody of rain
and from the crevices in the rocks and stones of the mountain
grew a thousand thickets of streams
and farther down, between the shadows, the bright patches of open plain
we saw the thick branch of the Zâyende River
    and the green rain-quenched leaves
    and the green unripe fruit of mother's city—of Isfahan
"Come Samanbar,
Samanbar come!"
My buddy said:
— Me, I heard it
but I have seen the troops of colored dolls in the streets
who flirt and sing:
    "If that Shirazi Turk...."[6]
And I likewise know
the sorrows of daughters and mothers in thousands of dark towers of
death[7]

---

5. For "drizzle" I read *nam nam-e baran* in place of *nam nam-ban*, a word not
attested in dictionaries (though perhaps it could be a rain parka).
6. "If That Shirazi Turk..." is the opening phrase of a famous poem by Hafez, in
which the poet promises to give the wealth of entire cities in exchange for the
favors of the distant Turkish beloved of Shiraz. This particular poem includes a
line about the overpowering charms of the gypsy girls who ravish the heart of the
city like Turkish warriors plunder food off the table.
7. "Dark Towers of Death" (*dakhme*) alludes to the Zoroastrian "towers of death"
which are used to expose the corpses of the dead to the elements and to birds, so
that the rotting flesh will not defile the pure earth. The ruins of one such temple
stand in the plain outside Isfahan.

feverishly working
rotting away in the vast heart of the plain
"Come Samanbar,
Samanbar, come!"
The white saplings of the rain garden and the tall wall of the mountain
    and us, going through the stream of the valley
which wends alongside the abandoned fortress
and upon the palace of Samanbar, the mountain girl
the vague arch of a rainbow
    rested upon the pedestal of our shoulders

About the Author

FICTION WRITER, critic, and editor, Houshang Golshiri was born in Isfahan in 1937. He was one of the first Iranian writers to use modern literary techniques, and is recognized as one of the most influential writers of Persian prose of the twentieth century. In 1965 Golshiri helped to found Iran's chief literary journal, and in 1968 he established, along with other writers protesting government censorship, the Iranian Writers Association. Golshiri's stories and efforts to establish basic rights for writers landed him in trouble—including imprisonment and a ban on his books—with both the Pahlavi regime and the Islamic Republic. In 1999 he was awarded the Erich-Maria Remarque Peace Prize for his struggle to promote democracy and human rights in Iran. Golshiri died, allegedly of meningitis, on June 5, 2000, in Tehran.

HESHMAT MOAYYAD, Professor of Persian literature at the University of Chicago since 1966, studied at the University of Tehran and received his doctorate in Middle Eastern studies from the University of Frankfurt. Professor Moayyad has written, translated, and edited several books in English, German, and Persian, including *Stories from Iran: A Chicago Anthology 1921-1991.*

Other Titles from Mage Publishers

King of the Benighted
Houshang Golshiri [Irani]/ Translated by Abbas Milani

Stories from Iran: A Chicago Anthology 1921-1991
Edited by Heshmat Moayyad

Stories from Iran: A Chicago Anthology 1921-1991
Edited by Heshmat Moayyad

Garden of the Brave in War
Recollections of Iran
Terence O'Donnell

Seven Shades of Memory
Terence O'Donnell

The Lion and the Throne:
Stories from the Shahnameh of Ferdowsi, Volume I
Translated by Dick Davis

Fathers and Sons:
Stories from the Shahnameh of Ferdowsi, Volume II
Translated by Dick Davis

Sunset of Empire:
Stories from the Shahnameh of Ferdowsi, Volume III
Translated by Dick Davis

My Uncle Napoleon
Iraj Pezeshkzad / Translated by Dick Davis

The Persian Sphinx:
Amir Abbas Hoveyda and the Iranian Revolution
Abbas Milani

Tales of Two Cities: A Persian Memoir
Abbas Milani

New Food of Life: Ancient Persian and
Modern Iranian Cooking and Ceremonies
Najmieh Batmanglij

Persian Cooking For A Healthy Kitchen
Najmieh Batmanglij

A Taste of Persia: An Introduction to Persian Cooking
Najmieh Batmanglij

Silk Road Cooking: A Vegetarian Journey
Najmieh Batmanglij

Inside Iran: Women's Lives
Jane Howard

*In the Dragon's Claws: The Story of Rostam
and Esfandiyar from the Persian Book of Kings*
Translated by Jerome Clinton

Borrowed Ware: Medieval Persian Epigrams
Translated by Dick Davis

*Crowning Anguish: Taj Al-Saltana
Memoirs of a Persian Princess*
Introduction by Abbas Amanat / Translated by Anna Vanzan

The Art of Persian Music
Jean During / Zia Mirabdolbaghi / Dariush Safvat

The Persian Garden: Echoes of Paradise
Mehdi Khansari / M. R. Moghtader / Minouch Yavari

Agriculture in Qajar Iran
Willem Floor

Savushun: A Novel about Modern Iran
Simin Daneshvar / Introduction by Brian Spooner
Translated by M.R. Ghanoonparvar

Sutra and Other Stories
Simin Daneshvar / Translated by Amin Neshati & Hasan Javadi

AVAILABLE AT BOOKSTORES OR DIRECTLY FROM THE PUBLISHER
VISIT MAGE ON THE WEB AT WWW.MAGE.COM OR CALL
1 800 962 0922 ❖ OR E-MAIL ❖ INFO@MAGE.COM

Printed in the United States
1204600005B/223-252